JASON ANSPACH   BLAINE PARDOE   NICK COLE

ORDER OF THE CENTURION

THE LOST LEGION

GALAXY'S EDGE

Edited by David Gatewood

Published by WarGate Books

Cover Art: Marc Lee

Cover Design: M.S. Corely

Website: Galxysedge.us

Newsletter (get a free short story): www.InTheLegion.com

Acknowledgments:

Jason Anspach's words to me were, "We were hoping at some point you might be willing to write a mech book for us for the *Galaxy's Edge* line."

Write a book about mech combat? Hell yes!

I love writing about mechs and from my reading of *Galaxy's Edge* noticed there wasn't much out there about them. That was both a blessing and a burden. Despite being in the middle of crafting three other books, I started making notes. Walt Robillard helped me refine the ideas into something palatable for the fans of that series. He planted the seeds in my brain that blossomed into some fun ideas. Walt was an enormous help and has my eternal thanks.

One element I wanted to explore was that of the lost legions. I have been fascinated by the lost Roman legion, Legio IX Hispana. I wanted to use this concept in some way.

Writing for *Galaxy's Edge* was a stretch for me. Not so much regarding the mech combat, but for the deeply embedded military mindset. I knew I needed to up my game. So I reached out to the US Army to go to Fort Benning and get a better understanding of the Army Ranger program, up close and personal. The Army's solution was for me to attend the Best Ranger Competition. It took some paperwork, including help from WarGate, but I finally got my media credentials set up.

For three days, I attended the Best Ranger Competition—not only following the competitors but interviewing many Rangers. I immersed myself as much as possible in Ranger culture, training, and gear. Just keeping up with the competitors was a challenge at times. Being the oldest member of the press pool was a distinction I savored. I learned a great deal, got some hands-on experience with equipment and gear, and made new friends along the way. As far as research trips go, it beat the hell out of a day sifting through the National Archives.

I tried to bring some of that experience to this novel. Also, three of the names used here are tributes to old friends/acquaintances from high school—Stephen Teuber, Jerry Tramel, and Bruce Nelson. I thought they might enjoy some time in the literary limelight.

Finally thanks to Lauren Moore, my editor. She makes me look better than I am.

Dedication:

To Alan Andrews, 101st Airborne Division, Vietnam vet and inspiration. Alan introduced me to wargaming, starting with PanzerBlitz when I had him as a customer on my paper route in my youth. We spent countless hours talking about military history and his time in the Army. We played some outstanding wargames during the heyday of the industry. He took a punk kid with an interest in history and ignited a lifelong passion for the subject. The impact of his time with me feeds my readers to this day. He died in February of 2023, but I cherish my memories of him and the battles we fought with cardboard counters and geomorphic maps.

The Order of the Centurion is the highest award that can be bestowed upon an individual serving in, or with, the Legion. When such an individual displays exceptional valor in action against an enemy force, and uncommon loyalty and devotion to the Legion and its legionnaires, refusing to abandon post, mission, or brothers, even unto death, the Legion dutifully recognizes such courage with this award.

98.4% of all citations are awarded posthumously.

QUICK REFERENCE:

Hunter-Killer Planet Pounder (HK-PP)—The core of the mech forces that the Republic deploys. There are several variants of this HK-PP, but it serves as the base platform for mech warfare. Armed with a pair of heavy blasters and two shoulder-mounted missile racks, it is well-suited for a variety of combat missions.

Hunter-Killer Scout Walker (HK-SW)—The fast, unarmored scout of the Republic's mech forces. Armed with only a pair of small blasters, it is used for reconnaissance and ECM warfare operations.

Hunter-Killer Mortar Platform (HK-MP)—This class of mech is a modification of the HK-PP built with a heavy mortar artillery system. The back-mounted mortar system can deploy in seconds, bringing deadly indirect fire wherever needed. HARD troopers refer to them as RTCMs—Roaring Thunder Crater Makers.

Hunter-Killer Sniper Platform (HK-SP)—Known as Shadow-Stalking Ass Busters (SSAB) by fellow pilots, this modified HK-PP frame is a sniper mech armed with a single shoulder-mounted precision blaster. The power-hungry weapons provides HARD forces with extra long-range direct-fire capability lethal to infantry and dangerous to unarmored transport vehicles.

Republic Armorworks "Cavalier" Main Battle Tank—The standard main repulsor tank of the Republic. Though usually mounted with a heavy blaster cannon, variants will sometimes mount a large-caliber rail gun as its primary weapon.

Republic Armorworks "Anaconda" Light Grav Tank—This platform is a smaller, faster, more lightly armed version of the Republic's MBT repulsor tank. Equipped with a pair of medium blasters on its turret, it is an excellent infantry support vehicle.

PART ONE :

Shattered Hopes and Lost Legions

1

Sergeant Carson Metzger fell flat a moment before the incoming artillery round went off. His Republic body armor was good, not great. There were plenty of gaps where hot shrapnel could penetrate and make his life miserable. Before he had joined the Republic military, he had assumed that artillery rounds killed with their spray of deadly shrapnel. That was true, but the concussion from the blast killed just as many warriors.

That knowledge couldn't help him now; it was a momentary flicker in his mind that he wished he hadn't remembered.

Ever since their drop on Frixon, things had been... chaotic. Combat was always a blender set on high and mixing mayhem and madness with death and destruction. This landing was a little more tumultuous than usual. Most of the members of his unit, the Republic Army's 444th Infantry Division, summed it up with a short phrase: "The frellin' Frix."

Republic infantry divisions were numerous and often seen as expendable. Ask any R-A grunt if even the Legion saw them as anything except fodder, and you'd get one, universal answer: Hell no. But if there was an exception, the 444th—"Three-Fours"—was different. They were fighters. Survivors. On Durral II, Okem, Ramstein, and half a dozen other worlds, they had fought with precision that garnered respect.

And they had lived to tell the tale.

The reputation afforded to a Three-Fours trooper was one of the things that Metzger loved about being in it. He had tried to join the Legion, but had failed the murderous selection process. He strove to be the best where he landed. Partly for himself, because that's the kind of man he was, and partly to maybe one day prove the Legion wrong for telling him he couldn't hack it.

To rub their noses in it.

Metzger was aware of that particular weakness of his. He *enjoyed* rubbing it in, more than he did proving people wrong. His father had constantly chided him for it, as had his sergeants and superior officers. But a man can't change who he is, and Metzger saw the frellin' Frix as an opportunity to show that he was, indeed, one of the best of the best. Frixon would be added to the litany of worlds stitched on the 444th's battle flag, and Metzger would be part of that story.

All that remained was the business of finishing the job, which proved easier planned than accomplished.

The dominant species on the planet, the Frix, had been chafing at Republic oversight of their manufacturing operations for a decade. During that time, reports had come back that they had been arming themselves, purchasing munitions and weapons—preparing for war. The House of Reason saw these efforts as a sort of bargaining chip to be expected. Lots of Republic protectorate worlds talked tough—it was part and parcel of being a planet on galaxy's edge. But when the consequence of an open rebellion against the Republic was a visit from the Legion... talk was usually all it was.

This time, though, the politicians guessed wrong. Frixon was one of those disgruntled worlds ripe for manipulation by outside agitators looking to spread their own rebellion beyond the mid-core and throughout the galaxy at large. "Outside agitators" of course meant the MCR—the Mid-Core Rebellion. And that in turn meant... a fight.

Good. That's why Metzger was there. He didn't care about politics—he was a sergeant who knew what his responsibility was. He had just one job to do: stack 'em high and stack 'em deep.

But ever since he'd arrived on planet, he couldn't help but wonder why anyone would fight for this place. Rock-sown deserts with massive buttes and stony plateaus rose up against a cloudless purple sky.

You fight for what's familiar, he supposed.

When he talked to his LT about what a wasteland Frixon was, he was told they were actually landing on the planet's garden spot.

If this is the lush garden spot, I'd hate to see what the rest of the world looks like.

Metzger's unit had been held back as a reserve until this most recent clash, so he'd gotten plenty of time to take in the scenery and the locals. All the Frix he'd seen prior to this point, though, had been dead. They pretty much looked like the mission briefs said they would—thick-headed aliens capable of living in a wasteland like Frixon. They had gray hide—a sort of natural armor that could resist light-to-medium blaster fire. Thick, stubby fingers. Small, curved horns and a bony ridge that protruded up their thick skulls. Big eyes, each with two lids, one for normal wetting, the other for protection from the random straight-line wind gusts that were a hallmark of Frixon. Their bulk didn't slow them down much; a Frix warrior could easily outpace even a leej on open ground.

Their native tactics were crude. If the MCR had done any training prior to helping arm the Frix, it didn't stick. Where most enemies equipped with modern weapons attempted to do their killing at a distance, the Frix liked getting up close and personal, even when it wasn't necessary. The armored Frix delighted in the charge, letting their thick hides and armor soak up blaster shots as they rushed in to stomp and shoot their foes at point-blank range. For the fire teams of the 444th, that was perfect—it meant their targets were coming to them, making them easier to eliminate.

The Frix attacked as though their hides were invulnerable, but something heavy like an N-18 or concentrated fire from a Miif-7 would take them down before they thought to fire a shot. The only problem was numbers. If enough charged so that some *did* get up close... from what Metzger had seen, they were brutal in-fighters. Best to kill them first—as it always is.

A Repub regiment had been garrisoned on Frixon with the idea that a military presence might somehow calm the situation. Maybe that was the belief of an R-A general, maybe the order of a politician—sometimes it was hard to tell the difference. For Metzger, this was a typical civilian political response—putting troops in danger to make a point. A regiment wasn't enough to be intimidating. All the assignment had done was give the Frix a target, one they gleefully lined up in their scopes.

A minor policing incident was used as the impetus for the Frix to go after the garrison.

To the credit of the garrison commander, an appointed officer, the location of his base had proved defendable, but the siege that was laid on it was long and arduous.

Surrounded in the rugged Blitzen Pass of the Pikes Mountain Range, they were being whittled down, bit by bit, each day. Someone had to come in, rescue and resupply them, and send a clear message to the Frix that further rebellion would not be tolerated. So the 444th were hot-dropped into the foothills. Their mission was simple: take out the Frix leadership, cripple the natives' supply lines, and relieve the Repub garrison.

On datapads, it sounded easy. The problem was, the Frix refused to cooperate.

Metzger raised his head, looking out at the newly formed crater, smoke still rising from its blasted and scorched center. "Anyone have eyes on where that artillery is coming from?"

"This is Ringo 517," a voice responded. "I just scouted the ridge to the northwest and have tagged all the enemy gun emplacements there. My data upload link to the battlenet is out, but I have what you need."

Dropping down his HUD, a small holoscreen lowered from his helmet to feed data directly into his eye, he spied Ringo 517's location on the battlefield map.

Five-One-Seven was an HK-SW—a Hunter-Killer Scout Walker, a mech that consisted of an elevated seat, a motivator unit, a power plant, and two bird-like legs. It was armed with only a pair of small blasters, hardly enough to make mounting them worthwhile but still something. The Republic military used them for scouting missions, and the pilots were considered a bit crazy—you had to be. Unlike the larger Hunter-Killer Planet Pounders (HK-PPs), the scout walkers didn't have the firepower needed in a hot combat zone; they didn't even have an enclosed cockpit to protect the pilot. Sitting up a few meters over the ground, running, they were often targeted. They might as well have been painted fluorescent orange with a big bull's-eye on the side. But they were designed to move, and move fast. "Speed is our armor" was the oft-repeated tagline of mech jockeys and light repulsor tankers.

Metzger had heard a few combat sled drivers take the motto up as well. In all cases, it was the truth.

Ringo 517 was moving about three kilometers away, using a twisting and turning gully for cover. He was way out there, no doubt on a forward reconnaissance mission. Then the HK-SW stopped. And not the good kind of stopped. A flicker of crimson on Metzger's tiny HUD feed indicated that either the mech was damaged or the pilot was injured. Maybe both. *Usually* both, because even when those things just tipped over, the pilots got their asses broken up.

Another explosion went off some eighty meters away, throwing dust and dirt into the stiff wind, turning it into an impromptu sandblaster. Metzger's combat armor showed signs of the stiff winds and dust, with much of his camouflage pattern having been air-blasted off. In the back of his mind, he knew what was coming, but he didn't dare speak it out loud. *Maybe they won't pick us for this.*

It wasn't fear talking—not fear of danger, anyway. Metzger was worried that he'd be called on to perform a recovery mission, which most likely meant missing the fight that was brewing.

The LT, an appointed officer named Dickerson, came on in Metzger's right earbud, speaking through a micro-comm. "Sergeant Metzger, I need you to take three fire teams and execute a recovery and exfiltration. Get to Ringo Five-One-Seven's position, pull his data core, and get him out of there. Pulling the core is going to take some time, but we need his targeting data for counterbattery fire on the enemy's tubes."

Dickerson was relatively new to the 444th but had done well so far. Replacement LTs could be walking disasters. Dickerson was not *that* officer. As Metzger's buddy Welch put it, "It's cute that he cares." There was something to be said about that. Dickerson was meticulous and careful.

"Copy that." It was hard to escape the feeling they had drawn a crappy assignment.

"Be advised, sat feeds show enemy grav armor operating in the grids just beyond your objective," Lieutenant Dickerson added. "We're painting two to three tanks—one of which engaged and took out Ringo Five-One-Seven."

Oh. Well, sket. This might be interesting after all.

The excitement at getting in the fight was dampened as Metzger thought about the potential vulnerabilities such a small team would face. Surely the Frix knew that they'd downed a scout walker and that Repub procedures were to move in and try to recover.

Things could get ugly in a hurry.

Using his forearm control, Metzger switched comm channels to the tactical platoon—TAC-P—frequency. "Listen up, we just got our orders. We are moving to grid coordinates Golf-Sixteen-Eighteen. There's a downed HK-SW there—Ringo Five-One-Seven." He glanced at his HUD feed. "Our job is to get the pilot and recover his targeting data."

"We can't just remote transmit?" asked PFC Hoehn, one of the younger team members.

"Assume that if we could, we would, Johnny," Metzger said, not truly believing it. "Either way, we gotta go in there for the pilot. Same as we'd want done for us. Now I want Charlie fire team to move fast and secure the hilltop to the south at the waypoint. You will provide overwatch for us.

Bravo fire team, you will move to the east and take the high ground."

Through a series of retinal focusing and defocusing, he highlighted the grid coordinates he wanted Bravo at and sent it to them, then continued. "I'll take Alpha with me. We drop into the gully and move up on our target from the south. Be advised, enemy grav armor is operating in our battlespace. It's old tech, but not so old it can't kill you. Make sure each team has at least one anti-vic weapon."

All three fire teams confirmed, and Metzger moved out from his position as Alpha formed up on him, moving fast and reducing their target profiles. He skirted around a thicket of brush-like trees, their sharp thorns scraping against his armor, managing to find his synthetic body suit and stabbing through it as he moved. On his tiny display, he saw Bravo moving quickly toward their objective.

Another artillery round went off near where he had been hunkered down just minutes before, throwing bits of blasted rock and sand everywhere. It was a good thing the Frix didn't have enough cannons to deliver a proper barrage.

The squads continued to shift to the west, finally arriving at the gully. The creek cut into the sandstone rocks and was easily three meters down. It meandered through tight twists and turns, with a small sandy shore on either side. Metzger dropped down onto the sandbank and sank deep, up to his shins. *Sket!* He had learned his lesson with the local mud during the first few hours of deployment. Attempting to pull one foot out would only sink the other deeper. Instead he spread out his weight, dropped to his knees, and crawled through the khaki-colored sand until he got to a firmer bank. Glancing back, he saw the rest of Alpha working their way to firmer ground as well.

It was smoother traveling after that, with no hostiles to be seen until they'd crept deep into enemy-controlled territory, near the downed HK-SW.

Flashes of blaster fire abruptly darted both directions over the coulee, mostly from the direction where Bravo had taken position. Things had kicked off.

"Talk to me, Bravo," he transmitted.

"Two squads coming from the north, converging on Ringo Five-One-Seven's position. We are laying down suppression fire," came back Corporal Shaneal's crisp voice.

A crack and hiss, followed by a dull blast, this time hitting some forty meters off, showered down bits of stone even in the depths of the creek bed. The sound of it was different though. Experience told him it wasn't artillery, but blaster cannon fire. "Where did that come from?"

Charlie's squad leader, Delannon, came on. "Enemy grav armor, two vehicles, moving in from the north. We're pushin' forward of our position to get a shot at 'em."

A check of Metzger's HUD showed that Charlie was moving in quick short bursts, from cover to cover, to where they could be closer to Ringo 517's position and possibly get a better angle. "All right, Alpha, tighten up on me, come on." He moved quickly, priming his Miif-7—the R-A just called them "Miffies," "Miffs," or "sevens"—as he moved out, keeping low, rounding every sharp twist and turn of the gully with his blaster ready to fire. A gust of wind above, one of Frixon's famous straight-line blasts of hot air, sent dust down on him and made an almost mist-like fog in the narrow confines of the creek bed.

As he rounded one twist, he saw that the coulee had opened up, the banks spread wide. It was almost open enough to be some sort of ford, except the east bank rose up several meters. And lying there, some thirty meters in front of his position, were the toppled remnants of the HK-SW. One blackened and charred bird-like leg was extended, twitching slightly; the other limb was blown out at the knee, the actuator still kicking out a thin wisp of white smoke. The lower part of the damaged leg was several meters away on the embankment, standing upright where the last footfall had come before its destruction.

Metzger focused his view on the cockpit. The pilot was bent in half at the waist where the walker had fallen and hit the sandstone embankment. Blood oozed through the gaps in his body armor, and the blown dust clung to the gore, highlighting the pinkish hue. His lips were blue and his skin pale. He hadn't survived.

"Alpha, you have incoming grav tanks—two of them, moving from the west in echelon," came Delannon's voice. As Metzger and his team went low in the coulee bank for cover, Delannon's voice rang out, "Missile loose."

A high-pitched whooshing sounded as the shoulder-launched aero-precision missile streaked out overhead. There was a distant explosion, but Metzger's HUD showed that the vehicle was still moving. The Frix tanks were built like their race—thick hides, dull brains. At least now the beast was on fire, though.

"No joy," Delannon called. "I swear this whole damn batch is defective. Missile loose," he called again as Metzger eyed his objective. Another missile whooshed over their position, followed by another blast. "Splash one," came Delannon's voice. "Second tank is going evasive. You have your shot now, Alpha."

"Copy," Metzger said. "Lobo and Preger—with me. The rest of you, provide cover." He and his team dashed over to the fallen HK-SW, taking cover behind the extended leg.

Metzger skirted around to the back of the mech, to where the data core module was. It wasn't big, but it was in a shielded box. A few hard jerks couldn't pry it open, so he unsheathed his tactical knife, which he'd nicknamed Prick, from his right shin and used it for leverage. He longed for an audience he could crack a joke with about having issues taking his Prick out, but that kind of thing would get you mandatory sensitivity training in the R-A. At least if a point overheard you.

The module was a small cube, just under four centimeters in size. As he reached for it, Corporal Shaneal's voice came over his micro-comm. "Alpha, you have an incoming grav tank, moving fast, coming from the west."

Bastard doubled back on us.

"Target confirmed," Delannon said.

Bursts of blaster fire filled the air over Metzger. He tuned it out. What mattered was the mission, and he trusted his brothers and sisters to do their jobs and protect him. Reaching down, he grabbed the module and pulled, but the small ceramic cube held fast.

Lobo and Preger shifted position, moving to flank the low portion of the ford, should the grav tank make that approach while the rest of Alpha held back near the canyon-like portion of the gully. Metzger hoped the tank would do its fighting at distance, but he also knew the Frix loved it up close and personal.

"What's goin' on, Sar'nt?" Lobo asked.

"Stuck," was Metzger's one-word answer. The cores were supposed to slide right out, provided you had the proper clearance code. Metzger had that, but something about the crash or attack had locked the damn thing in place.

A massive roar of the grav tank's cannon confirmed that the fight was getting close. A flash of yellow light from the tank tore out toward Bravo.

"Redeploying," called out Corporal Shaneal.

Another AP missile streaked overhead.

"Last round, downrange," Delannon called out.

Metzger repositioned his grip and threw his entire body back, and the core finally yanked free. He fell against the embankment, and for just a moment he was staring at the bent and shattered body of the pilot.

"No joy!" Delannon called out. "Alpha, you need to haul ass."

Cannon fire from the tank sent a large yellowish burst of energy-tinged death over Metzger's position to where Charlie was firing from. He couldn't see the results of the shot, but the explosion on the high embankment told him all he needed to know.

Pushing off the sandstone, he got to his feet and clipped the core to his shoulder armor. Suddenly Alpha opened fire, and he saw it—the Frix grav tank, roaring straight down the shallow slope from the west. It was a hulking thing, a gray monstrosity, boxy, with no sense of streamlining at all. Its turret was wide but not tall, mounting a massive blaster cannon that was slowly traversing as the tank headed right at him. Smoke rolled from the top right side, probably from one of the aero-missile hits that had failed to take it out. It made a throbbing sound, low and deep, as the grav units and inertial compensators were still in operation.

Typical Frix—charging at us like herd animals.

Metzger's mind instantly crunched the math of his predicament. Climbing up the embankment was no good, nor was trying to duck behind the fallen walker for cover, given its lack of armor and the firepower of the grav tank coming at them. Lying flat risked being crushed under the tank; a cruising grav tank exerted enough downward pressure to crumple even the best leej armor, and he wasn't in leej armor. The low-tech crap the Republic gave the infantry regiments would break apart at the seams.

That left a dash upstream as his best option. His legs were already in motion by the time his brain arrived at that conclusion. He had to get out of the path of the approaching behemoth. Alpha's blasters were ineffective against the tank, and Metzger hoped they knew that. He hoped they were just valiantly attempting to draw the tank's attention away from him for the sake of the mission.

He splashed in the shallow creek as he ran. The mud and the knee-deep water slowed him.

Metzger caught a glimpse of the tank starting to bank, slowing as much as it could. Was it trying to chase him down, or did the driver realize he was about to slam into the embankment and was trying to avoid it? The laws of physics were the wicked mistresses of grav tanks. As it turned, the inertia still carried it toward the embankment, arcing toward Metzger and his team. Preger dove for cover off to the side. Lobo hesitated, only for a moment, but it was enough for the tank to clip him mid-arc-turn. Lobo's body was thrown over a dozen meters into the embankment, and his body armor made a sickening crunch.

Metzger was running as Lobo flew; there was no option left. A part of him believed he would get clear of the tank before it slammed into the embankment. What he felt wasn't quite glee, but the euphoric exultation that he had acted fast enough. In his mind, he was going to beat the fast-moving tank. He was pure self-confidence.

He was wrong.

Metzger could feel its presence the moment before it collided with him. There was just enough time for him to turn and face the hulking enemy vehicle as the tank's armored front stabilizer slammed into his right leg, pushing him into the sandstone embankment.

The impact knocked the wind out of him, and he panic-gasped for air. Pain, excruciating, crimson-flared, engulfed his body. There was an instant crunch, crack, the distinctive sound of bones shattering. Metzger didn't fall—instead he was standing, his right leg pinned by the grav tank into the wall right at his hip.

His eyes couldn't avoid looking at the injury; the leg was nearly severed. The pressure of the tank pinning him to the wall was probably the only thing preventing him from bleeding out. He knew from experience that between the stone and the tank, his leg was pulverized into a meaty paste. It could be no other way.

A strange sense of déjà vu washed over him. Memories of Durral II returned, riding the pain he felt. He started to hyperventilate and pulled up his visor to get more air to fight the agony.

His vision tunneled; he struggled to form words. His gloved hands trembled in his sight—no doubt from the adrenaline surging in his blood and the realization of his predicament. He needed medical evac, and someone needed to blow this tank.

Alpha broke out from their position, swarming on top of the grav tank. Richards set up a hatch cutter, waited for it to slice open a small hole in the tank, then tossed a grenade in, screaming, "Frag out!"

Metzger heard the muffled blast from within the tank, and felt a bit of satisfaction knowing that the crew that had crushed his leg would meet their gods before he met Oba.

Smoke rolled out of the hatch, rolling over him and up the embankment. The tank was still hovering, still throbbing. The crew might be dead, but the repulsors were still powered. Their throbbing reverberated throughout his body. It was agony near the pulverized leg and up to the groin, but the pain was a reminder that he was still alive.

How the bulky vehicle had missed his left leg was a mystery. The grizzled sergeant wondered if he should consider himself lucky. A fresh wave of pain radiating from his lower body told him the answer: *No! Hell no!*

He saw Corporal Richards and waved the man over, growing agitated that the man wasn't immediately in front of him—the pain making him irritable and ornery. "Richards—Richards! Take the kelhorned core and get it to the LT." He fumbled to open the pouch as Richards got close. "Link up with Bravo and whatever's left of Charlie."

"Kark, Sar'nt," Richards said, taking the core but never removing his eyes from his sergeant's pulverized leg. "You gonna be okay?"

"*You're* not if you don't haul ass, kelhorn," Metzger said as a cold sweat washed over his body. The pain radiating from the pinned leg made him feel as if he were on fire. Every muscle flexed as if to suppress the pain, a battle they lost. He felt light-headed. A part of him wanted to rip his helmet off, but he drove those thoughts down deep.

Richards took off, and Preger came up next to Metzger. "This is beyond what I can fix, Sar'nt. I called in for some help to get you unstuck and stabilized."

Metzger shook his head. "Don't worry about me, Preger. I'm not going anywhere. Check on Lobo."

It was getting hard to form words through the pain.

"On it."

Preger moved, and Metzger struggled to get air, despite attempts to slow his breathing. He looked down at the leg he knew to be a total loss.

What was it with that damned leg?

The sounds of battle bounced and roared around him as he slid into unconsciousness. The fight was still on. Somewhere out there, his buddies were mixing it up.

Gordon. Tang. O'Keefe.

I hope they're doing better than me.

That was his final thought before the darkness overtook him.

2

Corporal Sheryl O'Keefe and her company were the far-left flank of the **444**th Division's line, tucked away in Tykaree Valley. The rumble of fighting off in the distance was ominous, a sign that the Frix were hitting her comrades hard. Delta Company had been spared most of the hard fighting thus far, but deep down, she knew that would change before long. If they weren't hit soon, they'd be sent to where it was going down.

And to think that a single destroyer and a company of legionnaires would be all it took to put an end to all this. But even the Republic's resources weren't limitless. Sometimes it fell to the army.

Somewhere out there were her friends. There was little doubt that Gordon had gotten some sort of wound in the first exchange of gunfire with the Frix. He had the unofficial division record for wounds. On Ramstein alone he had been hit four times. She liked to joke that they should station a pair of medics behind him when the shooting started, just to save time.

Tang was Gordon's opposite. A sergeant in Boomer Company, that man could dodge blaster bolts. Fate always seemed to ride on his side in combat. Doubtless he was in the thick of things right now, being charismatic and dynamic at the same time. One day he would probably make the jump to officer. If the points left any spots open for him.

And then there was Metzger. Just thinking of him made O'Keefe grin. Metzger had a knack for letting his mouth get in front of his thinking. He had risen to the rank of staff sergeant, but had stalled there, and everyone knew why—because the dude ran his mouth, even when it wasn't asked for. Not that O'Keefe was one to talk. She had been a sergeant and was now busted back down to corporal.

But Metzger... the man had a coarseness about him that O'Keefe both loved and hated. One thing everyone agreed upon was that Metzger had no fear. When the fighting started, he was the kind of person who took risks that others wouldn't dare—and willingly paid the price for it. His recklessness frustrated her even as it endeared him to her, and so she called him friend.

After all, *someone* had to look after him.

They had all enlisted at the same time, all from Huladoll. They'd gone through boot together, and when they got assigned, they had done what they could to be posted to the same division, which was very little. But things turned out all right, and theirs was a bond that was impossible to shake. O'Keefe cherished it. In a galaxy embroiled in war, death, and destruction, it was a constant she could rely on. The four of them were like siblings, three brothers and one little sister. Sort of. Tang liked to flirt, and more than once she'd considered a relationship with him, but she'd never followed through on it. She didn't need romance in her life, and if she did have it, she didn't want it with someone who might end up dead. Besides, her life was a string of long stretches of doing nothing, then trips to sket-holes like Frix. Hardly pleasant conversation topics on a date.

Corporal Vex moved up beside her, hugging cover behind the same boulder. "Sounds like the party is three klicks to the west."

O'Keefe glared at him through her lowered visor. "Don't get too excited. Parties like that have a way of finding us."

"We've got good ground," Vex said, gesturing to the hills sloping down to the twisting waters of the Tykaree River. Their bank was littered with large boulders like the one they were behind. The lush green grasses were short, but they caught the wind just enough to show the approach of the all-too-common blasts of wind. "I doubt they'll be coming this way. The rest of the division has them fighting in the flats."

"This is good ground, but I wonder if we're too far out," O'Keefe countered.

The thunder of distant artillery came louder... closer. Vex looked around, trying to mask his nervousness. "The captain knows his job, O'Keefe. You need to be more trusting. You've always had trust issues."

O'Keefe frowned. If there was one thing she hated about the R-A, it was the constant touchy-feely mentality drilled into its soldiers and popping up even at times like this—a far cry from the Legion. The R-A was very much the sort of place where people would high-five one another when a new sensitivity training seminar was announced. It was a reflection of the House of Reason, even the combat units.

And while O'Keefe was on the fighting edge of that bureaucratic behemoth of an army, she sometimes understood why the Legion showed such disdain for her and the other "basics."

"What does that mean?" she asked.

"Don't play sly with me. You keep everything bottled up. Aside from your boot-buddies, you don't talk much about how you feel."

"I just told you I'm nervous about being out here, extended like this."

Vex flicked a smile. "That isn't what I'm talking about, and you know it. You don't tell anyone what you're feeling or thinking outside of the current battlefield. I've known you for three years, and only last year did you slip and tell me what planet you're from."

His words hit her like a perfectly targeted artillery salvo. She was glad she had her visor down to hide the red rising in her cheeks. "Look, I'm plenty open."

"Not with us."

He's right, and damn it.

But she had good reason. Delta Company had had over a twenty-five percent casualty rate since she'd joined—one in four were either dead or wounded. O'Keefe didn't want to keep buddying up with people who might die. It was hard enough with Tang, Gordon, and Metzger.

"Point taken," she said.

Another explosion went off, this time along the top of the valley. Her head whipped around, and she saw smoke curling. "We're about to get hammered."

"Yeah," Vex said, checking the charge level on his blaster. "I think you might be right." Another explosion, this one even closer, made the ground throb under them.

"Find yourself some cover," O'Keefe said, forgetting in the moment that she was no longer a sergeant.

Vex scurried to a boulder some ten meters away and hunkered down snug to it. "You should be thankful that I'm checking up on your emotional well-being, O'Keefe. The Legion would never do something like that."

As O'Keefe carefully peered around her own cover, she saw a blur on the other side of the valley, several kilometers distant. It was the Frix, maneuvering to better hit Delta. Her stomach knotted and she felt her heart rate increase. The turns in the valley and the sharp rising banks littered with boulders prevented them from getting a good flanking move on the 444th, at least not easily.

That means they're coming here, right at us.

O'Keefe had seen battle on a half-dozen worlds; she respected what combat was and what it could do. People she knew were going to die, which was a good reason to not have a deep personal relationship with the members of your platoon. Emotional distance was her best defense in dealing with loss.

Her micro-comm hissed, then Captain Dorsey's voice came on. "We have enemy off to the south, a reinforced company. We are to hold this position at all costs. If the Frix drive us out of here or get around us, they will flank the rest of the division. I will not let that happen, nor will you. There is no retreat, no falling back. We have to stop them when they come. I'm counting on all of you to serve the Republic and honor your vows."

His words were solemn and rehearsed. The telltale communications style favored by a class of officers whose commissions were almost exclusively via political appointment. The captain only increased the tension O'Keefe felt. *Okay, Sheryl, you've got this. You trained for this. They're huge and will run into blaster fire just to get up close. You can't miss them.*

Her NCO, the burly Sergeant Fazzoli, moved up beside her, crouching low. "O'Keefe, I've got extra charge packs tucked in behind the boulder at your six. You need to keep a steady stream of fire. Make sure you move around behind this rock. Don't let them get a bead on you."

"Yes, Sergeant."

"You're going to be fine, O'Keefe. I'm in a position just to your left and a few meters further back. You heard the captain—we aren't going anywhere."

"Not my first rodeo, Sergeant. I'm good."

Fazzoli grinned. "No heroics today, just good old-fashioned killing the enemy. Don't wait for an order. Once they get in range, let them have it. They're tough bastards. A single shot isn't going to kill them. Those charge packs of yours need to be depleted when this is all done."

O'Keefe gave a fractional nod. "Stack 'em high."

"Stack 'em deep," Fazzoli said, moving over to where Vex was, no doubt to give a similar pep talk. O'Keefe respected the sergeant for that. He took care of his people.

An explosion went off behind her, sending bits of sod and fragments of rocks raining down, and she felt the concussion of the artillery blast in her chest. She had hoped the Frix wouldn't get a good bead on their position.

Is a Republic destroyer in orbit really too much to ask for?

Then another sound reached her, a low rumble, growing in tempo. Peering around the boulder, she saw the long line of Frix infantry surging forward to the Tykaree River. They were humongous, pounding forward on thick, tree-like legs. Their stubby arms and hands held blasters that looked both crude and deadly. A few of them fired, but the shots weren't aimed—there was no way they could be.

O'Keefe held her own fire; there was no point just yet. Once they came out of that river, *then* she'd start firing.

The Frix hit the river as if it wasn't even there, splashing and sinking into it, churning the clear water into a muddy soup. Blaster shots flashed at them, most missing, some finding targets but not seeming to do much damage.

O'Keefe raised her seven and took aim at one Frix that had reached her side of the river. Training and discipline kicked in as she controlled her exhale and squeezed the trigger. Her blaster rifle whined as it discharged, and the bolt hit the hulking Frix's armored torso. The Frix didn't even seem to notice. Once more she fired, hitting the alien's short arm, scorching a black burn mark on its hide. Howling, it recoiled from the hit.

Good. They can feel pain.

The Frix infantry fired back, their blasters unleashing bright green bolts of energy that rose from the river's edge to where the 444th was dug in. O'Keefe aimed at the Frix she had hit twice already as he lumbered up the hill toward her position, then fired a burst of three shots. One blaster shot missed, lost in the river. The other two hit the head of the Frix, finally dropping it.

An emerald blast struck the boulder near her head, cracking the rock and exploding bits of it all over her. Dust whipped in the breeze as she recoiled and picked a new firing position, this one over the top of the boulder. Finding another target, she hit it with two bolts in the leg and lower torso. The Frix fired back at her, forcing her to duck for cover again.

Looking over at Vex, she saw him ducking down too. "These bastards are hard to kill," he called over to her.

She nodded, then shifted back to her original position. The Frix she had been firing at was now farther up the side of the valley, but hard to get a bead on. She targeted a different one and fired a pair of shots that hit its massive chest, leaving smoking black holes. One return blaster shot hit the boulder, pelting bits of rock right in her face as she darted back to cover.

Something stung her left cheek. She touched her face with her glove and it came back with blood. She gently wiped her cheek, finding something sticking out. She pulled, extracting a small sliver of stone. The moment it came out, she felt a ripple of pain.

O'Keefe ignored it. She moved to the far side of the boulder, poking out and targeting another Frix. Along the far embankment, she saw another wave rushing toward where Delta Company was dug in. She fired again at the Frix, downing him, then turned to another of the aliens coming up behind him. An explosion went off, this time blasting the ground some fifteen meters in front of her, pelting her with more debris and forcing her to pull back. Checking her charge pack, she knew she had one more shot before she had to swap out for a fresh one.

She rose, targeting the closest Frix, and fired, but the shot missed. Dropping down, she ejected the spent pack and pulled a new one from her belt, slapping it into place. When she poked her head up, a trio of blasters hit her boulder, forcing her to drop back down.

"They keep coming!" Vex called over.

"So keep shooting!" she said, and both of them rose and fired at the same time, their bolts joining the crimson and emerald light show that filled Tykaree Valley.

3

Sergeant Metzger came to slowly, the memories of pain driving him to full alertness. His eyes were crusted with gunk, fighting his efforts to open them. His last memory was of the medics prying him out of the coulee bed as the rest of Alpha managed to get the repulsor tank back.

That was when the agony of the present defeated him and the memories stopped.

He couldn't sit up. He felt restraints on him, but they weren't needed; he didn't have the strength anyway. Finally prying his eyes open, he saw the dull gray of the ceiling, dotted with tiny lights. The sterile air tinged with disinfectants was another confirming bit of evidence. He was in a med bay, aboard a ship—probably being evac'd. He'd been in this scenario before. Too many times.

He had a knack for getting hit.

Metzger lifted his head just enough to look down his body. His lower torso and legs were in a cycler—a genetic regeneration chamber. That explained the restraints.

There was one thing he was thankful for: the lack of pain. He'd gone through the regen process several times. Instead of pain, it generated a tingling sensation, currently emanating from his right leg, as if the leg had been asleep and the blood flow was just starting up again. A prickling feeling—yes, that was the right word. Like thousands of ants were crawling through his skin. It was reassuring to feel it, because that meant the process was underway.

By now he knew the routine well. This was the second time he'd had his right leg replaced. Two to three months of regen, another year for conditioning, his leg would be back to normal. He could return to the division faster by using a powered leg brace, which would make up for his lack of leg strength while his muscles were redeveloped. But he would never be the same—not without some level of augmentation. That was the little secret of regen—each time it happened, you would end up weaker than you had been before. Didn't matter how much you worked the muscles out. There was a permanent atrophy.

Cybernetics were easier. But those came with their own issues.

The fact that this was the *same* leg, for the second time... he could be sure the rest of his unit would never let that go. He had lost his birthright leg in an RPG attack as a private during an assault in the jungles of Durral II. The explosion had thrown him in the air, and when he landed, his leg was next to his helmet. Never a good sign. The sight of that foot pointing skyward had been energizing, though.

His mouth was dry and his lips were cracked; he wet them with his tongue. While he knew they had been dosing him with micro-nutrients, his stomach grumbled for something solid. Fumbling around, he found the control stud for summoning his med tech, and pressed it.

It took a few minutes for someone to enter. She was a dark-skinned woman with brilliant emerald eyes. She moved to the side of the unit he was strapped down on, checked his stats, and seemed satisfied with what she saw.

"Finally woke up," she said. "How do you feel, Sergeant?"

"Fine." His voice cracked from lack of use.

She nodded. "What do you remember?"

This was fairly standard questioning. "I was on Frixon. A tank slammed into me. You know, the usual." He wanted to chuckle, but lacked the energy.

She was unfazed by his attempt at humor. "What are the last four digits of your service number?"

"Two-zero-five-five."

"Very good," she replied, looking at a pad. "Are you experiencing any unusual pain or sensations?"

"My leg is tingling, but I assume that's from the regen. Tingled the last time, too."

She moved down the table, checked the cycler, then looked at her pad again. "Yes, I see that you've been through this process before. Second right leg. That explains a lot."

Her comment caught him off guard. "What does that mean?"

She put the pad in its holder at his bedside, not making eye contact. "The doctor will be in shortly to discuss the details of your procedures."

There was something in her tone that made Metzger nervous. "Everything's okay, right?"

"The doctor will answer all of your questions," she said. It was clear he wasn't going to get anything more from her.

"Fine—can I at least get some real food?" He patted his stomach.

"I'll arrange for some *soft* food."

"Thank you. Can you also find out what happened with my unit?"

Metzger had no problem losing a leg; that was practically a habit by now. What he really wanted was confirmation that it was worth it. Lobo had taken a hell of a blow before Metzger was knocked out of the game; was he okay? And did his team take out those guns?

The woman pulled a datapad from the side of the bed and handed it to him. "You can access the ship's net and pull up whatever's available," she replied, using a control to elevate his head and shoulders.

Just the slight change of position set off a series of aches in his body. Metzger was only twenty-nine, but his body had been pushed to its limits—and sometimes beyond—for years. His joints had earned the right to complain every now and then.

As the woman departed, Metzger logged on with his bioscan and pulled up the after-action report of the engagement on Frixon. As he read through it, pride swelled in him. They had successfully recovered that data module, and the enemy artillery had been blasted. Lives had been saved, and he had played his part.

The Frix had hit the flank where Delta Company had dug in. It was a bloody affair, but Delta had held their ground. What was left of the 444th had pushed out and shattered the Frix's lines, forcing them into a retreat, which eventually cascaded into a full-out rout. Metzger smiled at that. It had taken another three days, but the Frix finally bent the knee.

Rebellions are all fun and games until the R-A drops on your ass.

His mind shifted from the fight to his friends. He flicked through the casualty lists. O'Keefe had been positioned right where the Frix had hit, so he checked for her first. She was listed as wounded, which filled him with relief; that meant she was alive. He then checked his own platoon... and was staggered by what he saw.

Over half of them were dead or wounded. They'd never before suffered losses like that.

Next he checked to see how Gordon and Tang were.

The same three letters appeared next to each name.

KIA.

He felt the breath flow out of his lungs. It was impossible to think of them as dead. Gordon got shot, a lot, but always lived. And Tang... Tang never even got a paper cut. How could they be dead? There were no details available. Just those three letters.

That leaves only O'Keefe and me.

There was no further information on the nature of O'Keefe's injury. But she was stubborn as hell. She'd live. Once Metzger had his new leg, the first thing he would do was track her down.

Then he noticed the current date, and his brow furrowed. *They've had me in a coma for three weeks?* Nervousness gripped him, a feeling of dread. He'd lost his leg before, and they hadn't kept him knocked out for anything close to three weeks. This was the first sign that something was really wrong.

No, it was the second. What had the woman said? *"Second right leg. That explains a lot..."*

He sat up slightly, looking down at the cycler, but he couldn't get a good enough angle through the curved glass to see his leg.

The doctor entered, a young man who, despite regulations, had what looked like a day's worth of black beard stubble on his face. He had the rank of captain. He was accompanied by an admin bot, who shuffled on two legs and immediately plugged into Metzger's bedside sensors to begin running predictive health algorithms.

"Sergeant Metzger," the doctor said calmly. "How are you feeling?"

"What's going on with my leg?" There was no salutation or small talk. Metzger wanted answers.

The doctor leaned over the cycler and looked down, then returned to Metzger's side. "To be blunt, we've had some challenges with the regen."

"What kind of challenges?"

"Regenning can be tricky, as I'm sure you know from your previous experience. There's always the chance that the body will refuse the process—attack the growth like a form of cancer."

"Okay… but I went through my first regen just fine."

The doctor nodded at the bot, who went into a clinical explanation. "Sergeant Metzger, the regenerative process relies on working with the biological and genetic material that's already there, in order to grow a precise copy. After your first injury, the available material was ample. But you have the distinction of losing the same limb twice, and now we have only the previously regenerated material to work with. Unfortunately, that material has proven insufficient for a successful regen process."

The doctor nodded along, a frown on his face. "I'm afraid what's left just isn't enough to regrow it this time around."

"Can I see it?" Metzger asked, deeply and slowly.

"Trust me, you don't want to."

Metzger struggled to sit up, ignoring the doctor's warning. The doctor gave in, and motioned for his bot to loosen the restraints. Metzger's lower torso was locked into place with the cycler, but he still managed to rise up enough to look through the protective transparent housing.

The right leg, *his* right leg, was there. But it was a gruesome patchwork of raw flesh and protruding, gnarled bone. There was no muscle to speak of beyond an odd bulge where his Achilles tendon ought to have been. The more Metzger stared at it, the more problems he saw. Two of the toes were grown together. The kneecap was sideways and weeping a bloody fluid.

At first, the realization that the deformed limb was actually part of his body revolted him. Then it made him angry.

"You've got to be able to do something," he demanded as he lowered himself back down onto the bed.

"I wish there was. What you're seeing isn't our first attempt; we've tried several times. The regen tech isn't going to give you a new leg this time. I am sorry."

"I appreciate that, Doctor, but I don't need your pity. I need a functional leg."

The doctor nodded, taking no offense. "You'll be transferred to the military hospital. They will be able to provide cybernetics there. That is beyond the scope of what we can do aboard this medical corvette, or we would have already started the process."

The words of reassurance didn't play well with Metzger. "No—that won't work. The Legion doesn't allow cybernetics."

The doctor and admin bot shared a look, as if wondering what that had to do with anything.

Cybernetic implants—bionics—were commonplace in the civilian sectors, but less so in the military, unless it was one of the non-combat roles. The Repub Army technically allowed them, but depending on how extensive the replacement was, it could affect where you got posted. And the Legion didn't allow bionics at all. Period. It dated back to the Savage Wars, when bionics could be hacked by the enemy. A bionic leg was an assurance that he would never get to serve as a legionnaire. He had always hoped that he'd be able to try out for the Legion again. What the doctor was proposing would make that impossible.

"As I said, there will be options," the doctor said calmly. "Your military life is not over."

"Well, I don't want bionics. What else can they do?"

The doctor shrugged. "You'll get better details once you've been transferred, but it's also possible for us to graft a donor leg onto your new hip joint. The process takes some time, mostly for your nervous system to fully adapt to the new leg. Recovery time to reach combat effectiveness can be anywhere up to two years."

Metzger shook his head slowly. "Doctor, this isn't your fault, and I appreciate your efforts, but I don't want to end up in a general replacement pool. If this thing drags out too long, I might lose a chance to remain in the 444th. I don't want to be slotted into another division."

"Perhaps you can transfer back?"

"And trust the R-A to approve it? I don't think so."

The doctor shrugged. "I wish I had better news for you. We've done all we can for you here. When you land, you'll get a medical team to address your issues. Repub marines have a reputation for being more accepting of cybernetics for front-line combat. Part of their history, after all."

"I'm infantry, not some knuckleheaded hullbuster."

"Trust me," the doctor said in a voice clearly meant to reassure his patient, "you will still have a useful life of service." He stood erect. "In the meantime, you need to relax."

"Apparently I *have* been relaxing. For three weeks. What I need is to be on my feet. Both feet."

The doctor didn't offer a rebuttal. He simply nodded and left the room, yielding the verbal battlefield to his patient.

"Good day, Sergeant," the admin bot said, and then trundled off after the doctor.

Metzger was left alone with the realization that the sensations he was feeling came from a deformed leg that would never be of use. Why they hadn't removed it entirely was something he couldn't understand. Maybe they'd realized he would need to see it before he could accept just how bad it was—how hopeless. There was no arguing with a reality *that* ugly.

They'd probably amputate it when he reached whatever hospital he was destined for.

Crossing his arms, he stared at the ceiling and fumed over his situation. He'd lost Gordon, Tang, and half of his people. He'd lost his right leg. And now he might lose the 444th. They were his home. Where he belonged. Where he was comfortable.

Growing up, his home life had never been great. His father had bounced from job to job, the family always strapped for money. Metzger didn't have the test scores to qualify for university and he hadn't wanted to end up like his dad, working in some dingy factory. That meant military. Which was the best decision he ever made. He never realized that he wanted a stable family, until he had one. The R-A was his home.

Now, thanks to the Frix, he had lost his brothers—but his home, the 444th, was still there. He had to get back to it. And if he was laid up in a hospital for any length of time, he might get reassigned somewhere else.

Metzger wanted answers. He wanted resolution. But most importantly, he wanted his life back.

4

O'Keefe lay in a hospital room at Camp Zuma on Reacher II. With every movement, she felt a dull pain on the left side of her head—a pain she'd grown accustomed to over the last few weeks. Her doctors had assured her that her regrown skull cap would be completed in another week or so, at which point she would finally be able to remove the irritating brace that held her head and neck in place. They proudly told her she would even have her natural hair growing there. As if she gave a damn about her hair. She'd kept her head shaved close. The helmet felt better that way.

The medical team had told her she'd suffered an open head injury. But she'd done well on a number of tests, notably moving her arms and legs with little difficulty, which gave both her and her physicians some relief. It meant a full recovery was possible... although still not likely.

When she first heard the words "open head injury," she worried about what she might have lost. O'Keefe had always had an eidetic memory, or what some people called a holographic memory... was that going to be impeded? It had been such an integral part of her life. At her insistence, the doctors included that in one of their tests, and she passed. So maybe, she thought, she would be just fine.

But then a doctor asked her what she remembered of her injury, and things fell apart. There were fragments, starting with the trip to Frixon, tiny little memories that didn't seem to make much sense. O'Keefe knew she had been in a battle, but her mind seemed to feed her only glimpses, disconnected puzzle pieces. Images of rocks, green Frixon grass, random explosions.

Her doctor assured her that wasn't uncommon in traumatic situations.

Maybe. But it was sure as sket uncommon for O'Keefe.

Things changed when she was weaned off her painkillers. Memories came to her then, a trickle at first, followed by a tidal wave. They weren't like normal recollections, either; they were true *experiences*. She could smell them, taste them. Scenes of the battle seemed to reach out, grab her, and jerk her back to Frixon. They came so fast and so jumbled, her stomach pitched. At first O'Keefe threw up on herself as she struggled to cope with them. When the doctors asked her what was wrong, she couldn't explain it. Her own words were as mixed up as the all-too-real memories.

The hardest part was that despite their detail, these memories were incomplete. No matter how vibrant they were, they were still disconnected puzzle pieces. It was like having a violent flashback reach out and grab her, without context. Some came with the voices of her squad; others were simply the jumbled carnage of battle. And they were absolutely overwhelming. On more than one occasion, the hospital staff had been forced to restrain her, and ultimately she'd had to be sedated. The sedation pushed the violent experiences back to whatever recesses of her mind they'd emerged from.

The medical staff was perplexed. More testing was done, each test requiring them to allow her to experience the relentless barrage of life-like memories once more. There were assurances that a solution was going to be found for her, but aside from keeping her medicated, none were presented. She trusted the medical team—she had little choice in the matter—but they were army doctors and nurses, not miracle workers.

Yet despite the seriousness of her condition, it wasn't even the thing that weighed heaviest on her mind. As soon as she'd been able, she'd looked up what had happened to her squad and the rest of the 444th Division. She'd wept at what she saw. Her entire platoon was dead, except for her. Delta Company had only a handful of survivors, and none that she knew. When she tried to pull up the after-action report, to learn what had happened, it was listed as classified.

How could it be classified? They hadn't been doing anything other than holding the flank. What was the army covering up?

Those thoughts were disturbing, but not nearly as disturbing as the realization that she was the sole survivor of her squad. Vex, Fazzoli, Slither, Geroux, and the others... they were all dead.

How is it I survived and they didn't?

It was a question she grappled with for hours as she lay in her bed, starting at the off-white walls.

Fate was cruel. And adding to that cruelty, she knew the answer to her question was somewhere inside her head— but unavailable to her.

Of course she'd immediately checked the casualty lists for her friends. The deaths of Tang and Gordon were like a kick to her stomach. Her memories of the last time they were together were still intact. They had been in a bar, having fun, drinking far too many shots. Those good times would exist now only in memories. Somehow that made them all the more precious.

Carson, at least, was alive. If he had been gone, all of her connections to her military past would have died on the same day. Wounded, but alive. Apparently he was somewhere on Camp Zuma, too. Lying there in that hospital bed, her memories thrown into a mixer and blended into confusion, she found that her friendship with him was the one thing she could cling to.

The nurse came in, and O'Keefe hit her with the same question she asked every time she had awakened. "What day is it?"

The nurse grinned as she checked the apparatus on O'Keefe's head. "Relax, Corporal. You were only asleep for seven hours."

O'Keefe closed her eyes and nestled into her bedding. "If you had a brain injury, you'd be nervous too."

"I understand. Speaking of which, have you had any more of your visions?"

She opened one eye. "No, thankfully."

It had been three days of stability since her last random memory event. That one had involved Geroux looking over at her from behind a boulder, just as if he were in the room with her, accompanied by incoming blaster fire. He called to her, or so she assumed—an explosion obscured the sound of his voice. Then, as suddenly as he had appeared, Geroux vanished, and all that O'Keefe was left with was a sweaty bedsheet and stark fear—due both to the bit of memory and the knowledge that she didn't have control over her own mind.

"That's good news," the nurse said, pulling a datapad from the end of the bed and making a notation.

"I get this thing off soon, don't I?" O'Keefe tapped the device on her head.

"That's up to your doctor. But from what I see on your holos, it could come off any day now."

"Good. I'm looking forward to being able to roll over at night."

"I bet." The nurse returned the pad to its holder. "You feel strong enough for a visitor?"

"Depends on the visitor. Who is it?"

The nurse's smile deepened. "Says he's a friend of yours. Metzger ring a bell?"

O'Keefe felt a thrill of excitement that morphed immediately to worry. Carson would be dealing with the loss of Gordon and Tang, same as her; he would know what she was going through. But did she want him to see her as she now was?

Her desire to see him overrode her shame.

"Yes. I'd like that."

The nurse nodded and left the room.

Three minutes later, the door opened. O'Keefe strained her eyes to look to her left as Carson Metzger entered, his usual imposing figure gone. He limped over to her on crutches, with one leg missing from the hip down.

"Geez, O'Keefe. If you wanted to lay around for a few weeks, there are better ways to go about it."

O'Keefe returned his jab. "You lost your right leg *again*?"

That brought a grin to his chiseled face. "What can I say? I think this is Oba's way of saying I don't need that leg."

"They have repulsor chairs for people like you, you know."

Metzger smiled. "Had to bribe a nurse to fix these up for me. Repulsor chairs don't work out your arms."

O'Keefe rolled her eyes. "You and your arms."

"Nice hat you're wearing. What's it there for?"

"Rebuilding my skullcap and skin."

"The nurse said you had an open head wound. Are you doing all right?"

O'Keefe was honest. "No. I'm having some memory issues. Pretty nasty stuff." She left it at that.

"Trade ya," Metzger chuckled.

"No way. I wouldn't wish this on anyone." She reached for a cup of water and sipped at the straw for a moment. As she set the cup back down, she asked, "Why aren't you in regen?"

She could see that her question made him uneasy. His cheeks picked up a hint of crimson. "Doc's telling me there's some complication. Apparently it can be difficult to do multiple regens on the same limb, especially when the injuries are as severe as mine were."

"I'm sorry. So what's the prognosis?"

"I'm meeting with the docs. They're talking grafts or bionics."

"Bionics? That'd limit your duties."

"About as much as a brain injury," he fired back.

If anyone else had baited her like that, O'Keefe would have been pissed. But this was Metzger. He'd earned the right. And yes, she'd already contemplated how her injury could restrict her choice of assignments, though she'd deliberately not yet raised the topic with her care staff. Until someone told her otherwise, she could continue to believe that she was returning to active duty. She wasn't ready to be told otherwise.

"You never know," she said.

Metzger shifted on his crutches. "I was sorry to hear about your unit. The rest of us got hit bad, but you guys got the worst of it."

O'Keefe closed her eyes. "Maybe I should be glad I don't remember."

"Maybe so."

She looked at Metzger again, eyes growing moist. "With those kinds of losses, the division is probably a good year before being combat-ready."

Metzger nodded, eager to encourage her fighting spirit. "Yeah. If we're lucky, both of us will be ready to start stacking baddies again by then."

"It's hard to picture us as the grizzled veterans."

He crooked an eyebrow. "I'm *experienced*, not *grizzled*."

"You *are* staying in the service, right?" she asked.

"Of course. Someone has to finish all the bar fights you start. Especially now that you're some sort of Savage marine with that weird helmet you have on."

"I *never* started the fights. That was Gordon and you."

The mention of Gordon made Metzger's face sag. "It's hard to believe he and Tang are gone. I still feel like they'll walk through that door at any moment, giving us both sket for getting wounded."

O'Keefe nodded, unable to form words. Metzger was the one person she could have cried in front of. He was also one person she never wanted to see her weep. "You get any details of what exactly happened to them?"

He shook his head. "Everything's classified. I did see a news holo that the rebellion on Frixon was suppressed. Another 'glorious' victory in the history of the Republic Armed Forces."

"I couldn't get info on what happened to my squad either."

"You really don't remember any of it?" Metzger asked.

O'Keefe shrugged. "Just bits and pieces. When they come, it's like I'm there."

"Is it PTSD?"

"No. The bots already did tonal therapy and I'm good. I'm good. The doctors theorize that it's somehow tied to my head injury. When the memories come, it's not pretty. I'm back there, Carson, really back there, on Frix, but in a montage of sight and sounds that I can't control. I know they're memories, but it's just like being there."

"Is there anything I can do to help?"

Those words might have been meaningless if they hadn't come from a true friend.

"Thanks. I wish there was. They're trying to figure out the proper medication to keep the memories suppressed without doping me up beyond recognition. Your just visiting helps."

Metzger shook his head. "Look at us. Me unable to walk, you having memory issues. It occurs to me I might actually be able to win an argument against you some day if you lose that perfect recall of yours."

"I don't need a perfect memory to know I'm right."

"Maybe not. It also occurs to me that we aren't exactly recruiting poster candidates for the R-A."

That was Metzger, using humor to deal with harsh realities.

"Well, the Frix made one mistake," O'Keefe said. "They didn't kill us. We'll bounce back. Once we get back in the division, things will return to normal."

But even as she said the words, she wondered if she actually believed them.

5

Rexnar Koff considered the report he had been handed, studying the holoimages of the wreckage. To the untrained eye, the shattered starship was nothing more than debris—old and worthless, a relic of the Savage Wars era. His mining company on Vargas had discovered the crash site during one of the surveys and had contacted corporate for instructions on what do to.

A lesser man would have ignored the report, or simply forwarded it to the Republic. Rexnar Koff was not a lesser man. He saw value in the crash site; it was merely a question of how to leverage it.

His eyes drifted from the report to a holo of his son, Tamar. The boy—truly a young man, but Koff could never quite see him as such—was resplendent in his Legion dress uniform, a broad smile on his face. The boy was his only son, his eldest child, a young man destined to take the reins of the vast Koff family holdings. From birth, Rexnar had groomed his son for greatness, all the way up to getting him a choice appointment to the 14th Legion as a lieutenant. The elder Koff had made it clear that this was only to be a short-term assignment, a career stop-over to put on his resume when he ran for Rexnar's seat in the House of Reason. The family seat. A brief stint in the Legion meant Tamar could run for office as a war hero, one of the best of the best.

And then... Tamar was killed.

His commanding officer had been less than forthcoming with details when Rexnar inquired. But Koff's own, private sources covertly investigated, and they came back with information Koff did not want to hear: Tamar had somehow failed in his duties during the battle, and that failure had cost him his life.

Koff didn't believe it. Not for a second. No—his son was made a scapegoat for someone *else's* failure. That was the only explanation Koff could accept.

He wrote the commander of the 14th Legion, demanding his son be put in for the Order of the Centurion. He was politely rebuffed. *That* was an insult that Koff would never shake. The 14th Legion was now on a short list of people and entities to whom he had sworn to deliver *justice*.

His eyes darted to the report again. He could use this; it was merely a matter of thinking it through. It was a game to him, a mental puzzle. One that he knew he could beat. The Legion would want what he now possessed in the form of this report. Republic law mandated that he hand over such information.

But where was the fun in that?

More importantly, where was the profit?

Koff smiled. A plan was taking shape.

The Mid-Core Rebellion had been a boon for Koff Holdings; Rexnar had masterfully played both sides of the conflict. He secretly funneled money to the rebels through a myriad of shell companies, and in turn they supplied their armies by buying from corporations he owned controlling shares in. In reality, he didn't care if they won or lost—all that mattered was that the rebellion continued on, ensuring more sales and bigger profits.

An even bigger payday came after the fighting. The Republic felt obligated to rebuild what they destroyed in the war, and that led to contracts that were rife with opportunities for graft. Companies that Koff controlled subcontracted to other companies he held, and they bought their material from still other companies that were, directly or indirectly, some distant part of Koff Holdings. At each level his people siphoned off cash, further lining his pockets.

To Rexnar Koff, war and reconstruction were profit centers.

He had always been masterful at playing by his own rules. Back at Hallgate, he had competed on the debate team, and during his sophomore year, when he was taking the affirmative side of one such debate, he planted false stories in the school library that he knew the negative team would use. He even dated one of the negative team members and dropped subtle hints about the articles, ensuring she would look them up. When they tried to use those articles in their finals, he exposed them as fakes, discrediting them—and crushed them in the final round. No one ever even suspected that he had been the one who had covertly seeded those stories to begin with; they merely saw someone who was at the top of his game. He had savored that victory, and still did.

That deviousness was something he'd learned from a young age; maybe it was hereditary. Tamar had been that way, too. Rexnar had modeled himself after his grandfather, a man who might have been labeled a robber baron in another era. It was his grandfather who started Koff Holdings and built it into the covert behemoth it had become—a spiderweb of companies that owned control of other companies that owned even more companies. Rexnar's father had further expanded operations, ruthlessly taking effective control of over a half dozen star systems. The size and scope of Koff Holdings was by now so large that when Rexnar ran for a House of Reason seat, his election was seen as all but guaranteed. He owned much of the media and countless other politicians; he even had the courts on his secret payroll. No one had stood a chance at preventing his rise to power.

His office reflected his subsequent success as a career politician. Plaques and awards were crammed onto shelves, along with holoimages of him with other leaders, all designed to give visitors the full impression of the breadth of his sway. He was both a power player and a "man of the people." He carefully kept his politics near the middle, maximizing his power as a "swing vote," and this was especially true when it came to the MCR. He encouraged diplomatic efforts to deal with the rebels, knowing it would only extend the conflict, while behind the scenes he funded both sides.

There had been probes into his activities, of course. The government investigations were easy to manage—he simply buried and bribed at the right levels of government to make sure they didn't go anywhere. As for any rogue reporters who foolishly delved into his machinations... well, most had simply disappeared, along with their research. His private security team assured him that their bodies would never be found.

There was only one organization that Koff felt might upset the money train that was the Republic's forever battle with the MCR. That organization was the Legion. When facing the rebels, the Legion's elite combat units racked up victory upon crushing victory. If Koff didn't do something, they might actually *win* this conflict—and end it. If not on the battlefield, then through simple demoralization. The Legion's string of successes had been devastating to MCR recruiting efforts.

Yes, the Legion was a problem. A nagging and constant problem.

A problem Rexnar Koff now had the means to deal with.

Especially the 14th.

His father had once told him, "Revenge is only meaningful if you can profit from it." And as Rexnar Koff sat at his desk, the throne in the heart of his kingdom, he knew he had the keys to not only get back at the 14th Legion, but expand his vast fortune doing so.

The idea came to him then, fully realized. He cracked a thin grin, savoring it.

Yes, it would work.

The key to any good con was letting the mark believe they were in complete control of the situation. You didn't tell them what to do—you maneuvered them into doing it of their own free will. A report of this discovery had the potential to elicit just such a response. The Legion loved its history and traditions, to the point of obsession. *There* was the string he could pull.

Pressing the control panel on his sleek black desktop, he summoned Major Hunter Sarn.

The major entered from his adjoining office, his dull green dress uniform bristling with the campaign ribbons of his service. Sarn had been assigned to him as a Republic military liaison, and Koff couldn't have chosen better. His team's digging had indicated that Sarn had grown disillusioned with the Republic and its lofty ideals. Like so many in the military, he saw credits being spent on defense, but nothing on the average soldier.

Sarn had tried to join the Legion and failed. Most did. But Sarn was one of those who held it against that regressive—albeit elite—organization. Koff would use that to his advantage as well.

Sarn no doubt suspected at least a little of Koff's double-dealing, but he said nothing—which spoke volumes. The major simply didn't *want* to know what was going on. His loyalty was complete, bought and paid for. Koff had long made sure that Sarn's family was looked after, sending them on posh vacations, flying in experts for the man's mother when she became ill. By now he *owned* Sarn, and the major knew it.

"You wanted to see me, sir?"

"I take it you saw this report." Koff gestured to the images on his desk.

Sarn nodded. "It's all preliminary, of course, but it looks like it could be the 552nd Legion. At least, that seems to be a ship from their task force. There's no local archeologists on Vargas, so nothing has been confirmed. The miners haven't even bothered to send salvage teams out there, that's how little it means to them. If you read the footnotes, you'll see that the locals there have been aware of it for years. They just didn't bother to inform the Republic."

Koff nodded. "It's fascinating, isn't it? A lost legion now found."

"If you say so, sir," Sarn replied, crossing his arms. "I'm sure that Legion command will be all in a tizzy over it once we pass the information on to them."

For a few moments, Koff said nothing. He simply looked at the enhanced images.

"This has been kept secret so far, I trust?" he asked.

"Absolutely," Sarn replied. "Your mining company on Vargas sent the information through corporate channels only—nothing to the government. Given both worlds' prickly relations with the Republic, the last thing anyone wants is for the House of Reason to make a big show over it and send in a lot of personnel to dig up old graves and solve old mysteries. No offense intended, sir."

Koff nodded. "The good beings of Vargas have been edging for revolt for some time, as I understand it."

"The humans have, yes, sir. Vargas has two populations. The human-led faction that mines the craters, and the K'llik, an insectoid species that's focused on the mountain regions. The humans' deep-core mining operation is heavily unionized, thanks to the local mining guild, and recent policy changes in the Republic regarding unions have, dare I say, not been well received."

"What would I do without you, Sarn?" Koff asked. "Your reports are invaluable."

In truth, Koff already knew what was being told to him, but there was value in making a man feel indispensable.

There was some irony in what Sarn said about the unions. Koff had been one of the silent sponsors of the legislation that had angered them. But of course, good markets didn't emerge on their own. They were created by men of vision, as Rexnar's grandfather used to say.

"There are reports that they've been purchasing heavy arms—mechs, tanks, and some other fun stuff," Sarn continued. "And that they've come up with a way of turning their old mobile heavy mining mechs into combat-ready machines. They want less Republic interference, and they're almost ready to push the issue."

Koff nodded. A Legion unit deployed to their planet could spark outrage, even rebellion. He suppressed a smile.

"And the other indigenous species," Koff said. "The K'llik?"

"They're no friends to the humans," Sarn said. "During the Savage Wars, they were all enslaved, and although they were eventually released, they've never forgotten that it was an offshoot of humanity that was so cruel to them. Translation with insectoid races is challenging, but they call their submission during the wars 'The Great Indignation.' Fortunately for the human miners, the K'llik keep their distance, but they remain humanphobic to this day."

Koff leaned back in his chair, templing his manicured fingertips. "So, we have potential evidence of a lost legion on Vargas, along with two factions that have great disdain for Republic meddling."

"That would be the short version, yes, sir."

"Tell me, Sarn: what will the response be from the Legion when they learn of this discovery?"

Koff already knew the answer, but he wanted to hear it from the major.

"The Legion takes their lost legions seriously, almost religiously. Only five have the status, all stemming from the Savage Wars. They will send a unit there to recover their dead and attempt to learn the truth of what happened."

"There's little chance it would be a Repub Army unit sent in, is that correct?"

"I can't imagine they would permit that. The Legion will recover their own."

"And their showing up might cause a military response by the locals, wouldn't it?"

"Vargas is already looking for a reason to rebel. For that reason they might send a Legion REC-Team. Something small."

Koff stroked his chin in thought. "You know what the problem is with the Legion? That's rhetorical. I'll tell you. Their air of arrogant invincibility. Even when they're mauled, they somehow manage to market that defeat as a 'glorious last stand.' No matter how badly they're damaged, they're able to recruit replacements and come back strong. As such, they are an inspiration to the Republic."

And their arrogance cost me my son, he did not add.

"Their reputation is almost as big as their egos," Sarn replied, and Koff didn't miss the bitterness in his voice.

"I have some pull with the Armed Services Committee," Koff said. That was putting it modestly. He had a *lot* of pull. "As such, I could influence *which* Legion unit would be sent to Vargas. I could, for example, tie up resources in another fight unless my late son's unit was given the honor."

The edges of Sarn's lips rose slightly. "I imagined you insisting on the 14th Legion, yes, sir."

"That would be fitting, wouldn't it? Of course, things do have a way of getting out of hand. A Republic military presence would infuriate both factions on the planet. A conflict is almost inevitable, especially if we prod things along. Could get very bloody."

"The Legion might crush the resistance," Sarn cautioned. "Another Legion victory."

Koff thought it through. "Yes. There are two possible outcomes. First, as you say, the Legion and whatever forces go with it to Vargas are victorious, crushing local resistance, destroying settlements and hardware in their usual brutal manner. If that happens, there will be a need to rebuild. The Republic will insist on it, as will I in the House of Reason. Those contracts will be lucrative, and my subsidiaries will have the inside track on securing them. In fact, we will go so far as to pre-position some of the material needed for the rebuild. But the second possible outcome..."

Koff allowed himself a small smile.

"What if a Legion unit were to be destroyed? Not defeated, mind you—I'm talking *completely wiped out*. From what I remember of the K'llik, that is a possibility. If the Legion were defeated by some minor backwater mining world—one that isn't even a part of the MCR—what would the consequence be?"

Sarn considered. "Well, the MCR would get a hell of a boost, morale-wise. It would also tarnish the Legion's reputation. Greatly."

"*Doubt,*" said Koff. "It would seed *doubt*. I learned long ago that doubt is a powerful weapon. The MCR needs a major victory against the Legion somewhere if it has any hopes of continuing."

Sarn seemed to understand what Koff was suggesting. "Although it seems likely, there is no guarantee that the locals on Vargas would engage the Legion, or that the engagement would be of sufficient force to cause one of the two outcomes you propose. They would need time to prepare, for one thing."

Sarn was thinking this through. That was encouraging.

"Someone would need to tip them off in advance," suggested Koff. "Warn them that this visit could be a prelude to an invasion. You know, fire them up."

"That would be risking these worlds joining the MCR."

"True. Far be it from me to promote treasonous thoughts," Koff said with a smirk. "This is all hypothetical. Simply brainstorming."

"Understood. It is not your intent to lead the Legion into a trap."

"Of course not. I am a loyal delegate in the House of Reason. Nevertheless... the Legion are not fools. They are cautious. And this... may appear to *them* to be a trap. Especially if they were simply handed this report. The only way the Legion knowingly walks into such a trap... is to kill the trapper."

"In my youth," Sarn weighed in, "I used to fish with my uncle. I found it boring, but I learned a lot about it. You can know where the fish are, but how you cast and what bait you use determines whether the fish will bite. It is all about dangling the bait just right."

Yes, the major was following the thread. *Good.*

"Go on," Koff said.

"Well, if one wanted to lure the 14th to Vargas, without giving them any reason to be wary... the best approach might be to let them discover the information about this crash site on their own. We dangle the right bait in front of them, just a little nugget, an innocent tip, one that forces them to do the legwork themselves. If they believe they've found this site all on their own, they have no reason to be suspicious."

There was a reason Koff kept the major around. His thinking was identical to Koff's own. But on this occasion, Koff would allow the major to take the credit.

"That is a fascinating idea, Sarn."

"Thank you. I aim to serve."

"And you do so to my satisfaction."

6

Metzger's deformed attempt at a regrown leg was amputated shortly after he arrived on Camp Zuma. While he'd never thought he would be so casual about a limb being lopped off, it was easy once he saw how ugly and useless it was. That wasn't his leg; that was a genetic mistake. He was glad it was gone.

He hoped the doctors here were going to give him some good news—news of some cutting-edge treatment that could get him back into the fight in just a few days.

They didn't.

Dr. Shrank stood at his bedside, rehashing the same limited options he'd heard back on the medical corvette. "Sergeant Metzger, I don't know what else to tell you. We can replace the appendage with a graft, or with a bionic replacement. That's it unless you wish to be a permanent amputee."

Metzger shook his head. "The R-A is my life. I belong on the front lines, fighting."

"I understand. I wish I had a better solution," the gray-haired doctor replied.

Metzger balled his fists. He knew he shouldn't be mad at the doctor. The man was trying, from the sound of it. At the same time, he was furious at what he heard.

"Damn it, Doc, every day I'm here reduces my chances of getting a prime slot back in my division. There has to be another way."

"Medically, I'm telling you: there isn't." Dr. Shrank's tone was firmer. "If you want to get back into combat, you're going to need to find out what you can do with the body you have now—or rather, the body you will have once you undergo treatment. For what it's worth, I understand your frustration."

"I don't think you do. Being in the 444th is who I *am*, Doc. It's my identity. It's everything I've worked for in my life. The people there, they're family. A cybernetic limb makes it far less likely I return to combat duty, which means it's far less likely I'll return to my unit. You're telling me I need to walk away—no, *limp* away—from everything that's important to me."

The older doctor looked at him, the wrinkles on his face deepening. "Sergeant, that is bullshit."

The words caught Metzger off-guard. He had expected the doctor to try to convince him he was wrong, not to shut him down.

"Your whining is grating on my nerves," the doctor continued. "The marines I treat here, when facing your situation, would simply say that they need to improvise and overcome. You... you just bitch. If you want a pity party, you've come to the wrong place."

This was no act. The doctor's words came through with a clear undercurrent of anger.

"I just—"

"Don't start again. I can't stand it. My patience is worn out. You want pity? Boo-damned-hoo! I have patients with *real* injuries, Sergeant, the kind that can't be fixed with bionics because they can't be fixed, period. I can't think of one who is nearly as self-pitying as you. You'll get a replacement for your leg. You'll walk and run again. You're in the R-A. Whatever duty you get, it's in the service of the Republic. If you were a legionnaire, you'd be out. No appeal. End of story. If you get married, you will bounce your grandkids on that leg. Other people in this hospital won't get that luxury. I've got an infantryman on three who has an irreparable spinal injury. Regen didn't take. He's paralyzed permanently. And I have two brain injury cases who will be lucky to hold a soup spoon in the next year unless we install a partial AI in their brain case. Either way, life as they knew it is over."

Metzger's thoughts went to O'Keefe, and he felt embarrassment wash over him. "Look, I'm just saying—"

"I don't care what you're saying. The army doesn't pay me to care; it pays me to patch up warriors like you. Most are thankful. I will give you some words of wisdom, though, from someone who's seen a lot of people mangled a lot worse than you. You are *not* defined by the unit you serve in. It's *not* your fault, it's just how wars work. Your injuries aren't bad enough to merit mustering you out, and you'll walk away from your years of service with experience and skills. But first you need to get your sket together, adapt to the new reality, and above all, stop complaining."

Metzger had always been led to believe that doctors were supportive and understanding. But as the man's words sank in, he realized the physician was correct on every point—and that hurt.

"You're right," he muttered.

"Of course I am. Big tough warriors, best of the best. You're all damned idiots in a hospital setting. Well, welcome to the reality of a combat injury. Now—I will arrange whatever model replacement limb you want...

assuming you're ready to quit bellyaching and move forward, Sergeant. Are you?"

"Yeah. I guess so. Yes."

"Good."

Three weeks later Metzger walked down the rehabilitation wing of the hospital without his hand hovering over the guide rail along the wall for the first time. His shirt was wet with perspiration and his gait was unsteady as he fought to keep control of the new leg and address the change in his center of balance.

He had opted for cybernetics.

The surgery had gone well, but his body had initially rejected the regenerative skin graft around the limb, requiring several different medications before the issue was resolved. Metzger's job now was to learn to walk all over again. It wasn't easy, but he knew he was up to the challenge. Each step was slightly less wobbly, a tiny bit more natural. The doctors expected it would take him another two weeks to master it, and he was determined to do it faster.

He heard footsteps coming up behind him, and when he turned, he saw O'Keefe. She had visited him almost daily, and seeing her was always a welcome sight.

"Look at you, moving like a toddler," she quipped.

"I'll be kicking your ass with this thing pretty soon."

"I doubt it. I remember hand-to-hand training in boot. It's going to take a lot more than a tin leg for you to kick my ass."

"How are you doing?"

O'Keefe sighed. "Still trying to get my meds balanced. How do you like it long?" She ran her hand through her short, regrown hair. There was a weariness in her voice. "At least *one* of us is fully healed."

"It suits you. I'm not there yet. This is only my first walk without holding the guide rail."

"You'll get there. This," she pointed to her temple, "is something I'm going to be struggling with for the rest of my life. Or so the experts say."

"What do they know? You'll beat it."

O'Keefe's face told him she didn't believe him. "We all have our burdens. Mine is between my ears." She hesitated, then added, "I got word this morning about reassignment."

"Really? You heading back to our division?" He was hopeful. With the grievous losses that the 444th had suffered, it would be great having O'Keefe nearby.

O'Keefe's frown was telling. "You haven't heard yet."

"Heard what?"

"They're standing down the 444th."

The statement hit him like a breaching charge. For several seconds, he could form no words. Despite the bionic leg, he'd still been determined to return to active duty in the 444th, in any capacity he could.

"Please tell me you're kidding."

"I would never. I got word from Lieutenant Meeks. The personnel still in the unit are all being dumped into the reserve pool for reassignment."

Another blow. That meant they would all be ahead of Metzger. Not that it mattered; given the choice between a soldier with bionics and one without, Metzger knew where he fell in the pecking order.

"You okay, Carson?"

Metzger looked up. He had no idea how long he'd been standing there, buried in his own thoughts. "No. I'm not okay. Not by a long shot."

"I know being in the division was important to you," she said, resting her hand on his shoulder. "You're an outstanding soldier, with a colony-ship-load of experience. Someone will scoop you up. It's just a matter of time."

"From your lips to Oba's ears. It's just that—I had assumed it would always continue. Now that Gordon and Tang are gone, only you and I are left from boot. I just figured we would always be together, in the same division. Now there *is* no division."

"It's not the end of the world. We all get assignments. Some we love more than others."

Something in her tone sounded off. "You got reassigned, didn't you?"

O'Keefe nodded. "They said I can return to light duty. I wanted to get back to a combat unit, but with this," she tapped her head again, "that's not going to happen."

"So where are you going?"

"R-A Historical Archives and Research."

It was the first thing she'd said that made Metzger feel like chuckling. He did, and immediately regretted it.

O'Keefe scowled.

"I'm sorry," he said.

"Your mouth is always five steps in front of the rest of you."

"Historical Archives. What made you choose that?"

"It was that or the Finance Corps. I mean seriously, when was the last time you heard someone say, 'Let's drop on this planet, but send in the accountants first'? That job is just supervising bots, anyway."

"It's not like they throw the historians into the fight, either."

"True. But I've always liked history. I hate math. And bots. Besides, having an eidetic memory will make the move a lot easier."

Metzger detected a hint of enthusiasm in her voice. He understood. With her injuries, working in the Archives might be the best she could hope to get and still stay in the service.

"Congratulations," he said.

"You don't mean that."

"I do. I really do."

"We can still see each other when on leave. I'm not abandoning you."

"You're moving on. I'm still trying to work through walking upright."

This time it was O'Keefe who chuckled. "You're going to be all right, Carson. You and I, we're survivors. We've fought and bled on Oba knows how many worlds, and somehow we got through alive. You'll land on your feet." She glanced down at his replacement limb and smirked.

Metzger laughed. "How long have you been waiting to use that line?"

7

Three months later

Corporal Sheryl O'Keefe sat at the Nuts to Butts bar as Wade the bartender—a bot, but it was a cheap bar—poured her usual drink. Bourbon—not the good stuff, the watered-down crap—mixed with the local equivalent of ginger ale. Mixing two bad-tasting drinks made for one barely tolerable one. She took her glass and cradled it, letting the ice do its job—which in this case was chilling the drink to where it wouldn't taste as smoky.

She looked once more around the bar, but Metzger still wasn't there. She wasn't surprised; he had been a mess as of late. When he'd sent her a message that he was on leave and coming to visit, she'd been glad... but also dreaded it. His drinking had evolved into a problem. The last time they'd met, he got unattractively drunk and spent the entire time wallowing in self-pity. She'd suggested meeting somewhere other than a bar, but he was insistent.

Nuts to Butts was an off-base bar much like every other off-base bar throughout the Republic. It was practically built right up against base perimeter, and smelled of spilled beer, spoiled dreams, and grossly exaggerated tales of battles fought and victories won. The tables and booths bore the scars of fights, carved names, and despair. The local R-A garrison kept the place alive, for better or worse. The owner was himself former R-A, with the tattoos and scars to prove it, and even the air in the bar was fermented history. To O'Keefe, the place was a connection to her past, and a grim reminder of what was now denied her.

She looked up at the wall that was covered with bits of armor of varying sizes—mementos of the dead. Each item had been nailed up there by comrades of the fallen, something for them to toast and remember. O'Keefe had put up one of her patches for the 444th to honor her former unit, and as she now eyed the patch, she remembered better times, when the division still existed.

She usually came to drink on Wednesday nights, not to mingle or swap war stories with the patrons, but out of tradition. Her squad had made a habit of going for drinks on Wednesdays, and she had no desire to break with that. Because that was all she had left, she told herself—traditions and memories.

This was a Monday night, though, and Metzger was late, leaving O'Keefe little reason to linger.

She checked her chronometer and swirled her drink with her straw. When she heard the door open, she looked, and there he was. Two days' growth of beard stubble on his face. He'd put on some weight, not a lot, but his face seemed fuller. Dark bags hugged his emerald eyes. But it was still Metzger.

She waved to him, and he gave her a smile.

"O'Keefe!" he said, walking up to her and swinging his arm out.

She grabbed his hand and squeezed it, catching a hint of body odor and the stink of alcohol on his breath.

"You started early," she commented as he took the stool next to her.

"Just a few," Metzger replied, almost—but not quite—hiding the slight slur in his words. He ordered a scotch from Wade. "You look great."

"You look like you've been ridden hard and put to bed wet."

"What do you mean?"

"You know exactly what I mean," she replied, taking a sip of her own drink to brace herself.

Metzger stared at her intently before speaking. "This hasn't been easy for me."

"What part?"

"Learning to walk all over again. The loss of our division, our home. Not being able to get a combat assignment. All of it."

She knew the right thing to do was to be supportive. At the same time, this was Carson Metzger. "So you turned to drinking. How has that worked for you?"

He pasted on a smile. "It hasn't hurt."

"It's not a good look."

"Cut me some slack, O'Keefe. Taking a few drinks helps get me through the day."

"Knock it off, Carson. A few drinks? You're sloppy-ass drunk every time I contact you. You're not going to get a combat assignment with your brain in a bottle. It's a wonder you're still in the R-A."

"You have no idea what I've been going through."

"Really? It must be horrible, all that pressure you're dealing with. Have you had to deal with random memories intruding into the real world lately? You lost a leg. Hell, in your case, it wasn't even the first time. You're hiding in bars, you're sulking around with booze. You have to deal with your injury. Move on."

"Oh, like you have? And what has it gotten you? You can't get a combat posting either."

The two looked in opposite directions. This wasn't what either of them wanted. But it couldn't be avoided.

His words stung, but she had been prepared for them. "I'm still serving the R-A. It's not a glamorous job, but like I said, I've *moved on*. You're still stuck back in the division." She felt a dull pressure in her temple, if only for a moment.

Metzger stared at his drink, and O'Keefe was sure he was going to slam it back. Instead he moved it a few centimeters away from him. "You think I'm hiding?"

"I do. I wish I didn't, but I do. I never thought I'd say this, but... you're afraid."

Metzger's jaw set. "If it was anyone else, I'd deck them for saying that."

"It's true, though, and you know it. You don't like change. Both of us getting wounded the way we did, the division being dissolved, it frightens you."

He looked down at his drink again. "Why?"

It was an honest question, not a challenge. An introspective question. It was also a *good* question, and it deserved a few moments of reflection before O'Keefe responded.

"We all thought we were invincible when we enlisted. Especially Tang. We went into nasty-ass fights, but we all survived, every time. Even Gordon, though he got punched into Swiss cheese a few times. The last time we were all together, all four of us, we joked about that— especially you. And then came the Frix... and our luck got trampled. We lost Gordon and Tang both, along with a lot of other damn fine warriors. I lost everyone in my platoon."

Metzger nodded mutely, the look in his eyes reflecting sorrow, anger, and maybe guilt. Then he turned his gaze to his drink, and his eyes reflected desire. That only served to make her deliver the hard message, the one he had to hear.

"For the first time ever, we have to deal with change and mortality. You hate change, Carson. That's probably one of the reasons why every time you're up for promotion, you do something to mess it up. But after what happened with the Frix, you haven't had a choice. What's more, things happened that we can't control. I can just *barely* control what's going on inside my own head." She paused as another throb of pain rose in her temple. "So you look for a bottle and try not to face it."

Metzger's eyes narrowed. "You know, you suck as a friend," he said, cocking a half grin.

"A bad friend would have told you what you wanted to hear... told you it's all right for you to be a drunk. A *real* friend tells you what you don't want to hear, but what you *need* to hear."

He studied his scotch glass. He looked like he was going to say something, then changed the subject. "You seem happy enough with your new assignment."

"I am."

The response was automatic, but not entirely satisfactory. *Was* she happy? Being a historical researcher allowed her to leverage her love for the military and her love of reading. But at the same time, she still saw herself as a soldier first, a researcher second. Unlike many who served in R-A Historical Archives and Research, she worked hard to keep her skills up and her body in shape.

She rubbed her brow as another ache washed over her. "I mean... it wouldn't be my first choice. I want to be a combat soldier. You and I aren't that different in that way. But I know they won't let me, ever again, not after having my brains jumbled up like this. So I'm doing what I can to serve. I've found a duty to fulfill, and that's the main thing.

You'll find one too. You just need to get off the sauce. Call off the pity party."

"You're the second person to tell me that."

"Then maybe you should listen." Now the pulse of pain came with a wash of heat. O'Keefe felt beads of sweat starting to ooze out of her.

Oh God, it's happening again. Not here, not in front of Carson!

She threw a credit chit on the bar for Wade. "I—I have to go."

"I just got here," Metzger said.

Then it happened: she saw a bright light at the end of the bar, and emerging from the light was Vex. To her it wasn't a vision, it was as if Vex was really there. It overpowered the real world around her, pushing Metzger's voice into a muffled background noise. As much as she tried to resist it, she couldn't. The flash of memory materialized before her.

Vex leaned against the bar in his fatigues. The white light beyond him was almost angelic. O'Keefe struggled to remember the context of the memory. Was this right before leaving for Frixon?

She slowly slid her drink toward Vex. "I got your drink for you." The words came automatically, by rote. The same words she'd said back on that day. She didn't want Metzger to see her like this. She felt deep embarrassment at what he would view as a lack of control. But she couldn't help herself. She couldn't stop it.

"Thanks, O'Keefe." Vex took a sip and set the drink back down on the bar. "We can't dawdle too long here. Shuttle lift is in two hours, and we've got to pack and prep. You know the drill. I don't think we're going to be back here for a while."

Her words from the past came involuntarily once more. "I'd prefer not to go this time."

Then she rallied, mustering her thoughts. She knew that Vex was an apparition, no matter how real he appeared, but he was also a memory. One of the memories that so far had been denied her. And only by interacting with these memories was she ever going to remember something more of what had happened.

She'd seen the flimsy after-action report, but it lacked detail. Just "The 3rd Platoon was overrun by enemy forces and all killed but one member, Corporal Sheryl O'Keefe, RA122-56-206." There was no clue as to why she had survived. Why she was spared. What had happened before she was wounded. And if the R-A wouldn't tell her, then the only way to get answers was to search for them in the myriad of memories imprisoned somewhere in her mind.

But to do that, she had to *not* just relive the moment.

"Vex," she said, asserting control, "I'd rather ask you a few questions." *Come on, Vex, tell me something. Don't just act like a holorecording.*

It didn't work. It never worked. The memory simply skipped right past her inquiry. "You don't get a choice. We're R-A—we go where they send us, we stomp the earth. You know the routine: *stack 'em high and stack 'em deep.*"

Vex's voice was firm, energized as always. It was one of the things she'd liked about him. When he first joined her company two years ago, he'd been a wet-behind-the-ears replacement. In the memory fragment, he was as he was that day, full of vim and vigor.

Experience had taught her that fighting the resurgent memories usually made matters worse. It was like getting aboard a rollercoaster: you were on for the ride whether you liked it or not, even if you puked your guts out. O'Keefe hated it. They were worse than nightmares, worse than bad memories. She would have much preferred nightmares—although she had none. In fact, she slept quite well. Instead, the jumbled bits of nightmare fuel came to her during the daytime—so realistically that they overcame her reality.

Maybe it was PTSD, but none of the treatments had done a thing to remove it. And if there was one thing the Repub military knew how to do, it was strip its soldiers of the emotional trauma that came with war. Hell, look at the Legion.

She felt a pressure on her shoulder and turned to see Metzger, his hand on her. "Sheryl, what's happening? Who are you talking to?"

"Vex."

He looked around. "Sheryl... it's just you and me here."

"He's right there," she said, pointing to where Vex stood, the man grinning as he had on the day of their last departure.

"Come on, O'Keefe," Vex said. "We need to get to the shuttle."

O'Keefe saw that Vex was now standing, angled toward the door. "Hold your horses, Vex," she said. "They won't leave without us."

She turned to Metzger. "We're taking off for Frixon."

Metzger's expression filled with concern. "Sheryl, what are you talking about? We're on Starkhold."

"O'Keefe, the first sergeant is calling us—we gotta roll," Vex demanded.

She rubbed her forehead and tried to ignore him. It took a lot for her to focus on Metzger.

"He wants me to go with him," she said softly.

"I'm leaving," Vex called from behind her.

"Go ahead, go," she said to the memory fragment, closing her eyes and trying to control her rising frustration. "I'll catch up with you."

"O'Keefe," Metzger said urgently. "You're weirding me out here. We need to get you over to the base hospital."

The pain came rushing forward in her mind again, this time sharper, as if it were slicing through her brain. Her hands started to tremble. The white light seemed to grow around Vex until she could no longer see him.

No...Vex... you have to help me remember what happened. Don't go.

Her vision tunneled and she threw up, then fell off her stool onto the floor. The last memory she had before she slid into darkness was Vex calling her name.

O'Keefe awoke feeling like her head was in a vise and being squeezed to the breaking point. She was in a hospital room, which she took as both good and bad. Good, in that she was receiving treatment; bad, in that it was a hospital room, which she hated. She shifted position, and every joint protested her actions, no matter how small.

I'm alive still, which is a start.

Her physician, Dr. Astin, entered and took a seat opposite her. Dr. Astin was a bot, a slender humanoid machine painted a comforting blue, with soft glowing eye receptors. The Republic Army preferred bots for such roles; their programming ensured that matters would be handled how the House of Reason wanted them to be, with maximum correctness and sensitivity. But from her first interaction with Astin, O'Keefe had seen this bot was different. It had a unique, almost human personality.

"Your friend brought you in here unconscious," Astin said. "He did not wait for an ambulance. He picked you up and carried you on base and then eight blocks to get you here. He said you were carrying on a conversation with a figment of your imagination."

There was no point in denying it, not with Astin. The doctor knew more about O'Keefe's condition than anyone.

"It's true," O'Keefe said. "It was Vex this time."

Astin nodded. "I checked your toxicity report. It looks like you adjusted your dosage on your own? And then you decided to mix in a little alcohol. We've talked about this, Corporal. You need to stick to your dosage."

"I hate being on these meds," O'Keefe answered, sliding up in the bed to more of a sitting position, her head pounding with the movement. "The side effects are irritating." Mostly constipation and knots in her lower torso. She'd discussed all of this with Astin before, on multiple occasions.

"The drugs are the only thing keeping that mixed-up head of yours in balance," the bot said. "You alter that in any way, and you invite a relapse. You do understand that, right? You're lucky your friend got you in when he did."

"I just really want to get off of these drugs, Doc. You know, eventually."

Astin shook its head. "I know you do. But I don't see that happening, not anytime soon anyway. You remember how it was before the meds—a crippling jumble of sights and sounds. To be honest, most people would have mustered out. But you fought through it, you've stuck with your program, and you still serve. That speaks to your commitment and character. There's nothing wrong with being on a drug treatment program. You don't have a thing to prove, Corporal."

"I'm not trying to prove anything."

"Then what are you doing? Why did you adjust your dosage? Is it really just the side effects, or is it something more?"

They'd talked about this too. About O'Keefe's desire to leverage her condition, to interact with these visions, in order to find out what happened.

"I'm not doing it on purpose, if that's what you're suggesting."

"I do hope not. Deliberately triggering your condition by altering your dosage isn't the answer."

"I'm not *deliberately—*" O'Keefe took a deep breath. "I just need to know. If it wasn't for my work, I might be in a padded cell."

"Tell me about that," Dr. Astin said. "The last time we spoke, a few weeks ago, you loved what you were doing."

O'Keefe sighed. "I *do* love it. I would love combat more, of course, but this is good work. In fact, recently I've started working on research into the lost legions. They've allowed me to dust off the old case files and give them a fresh look."

The lost legions were the stuff of legionnaire myth. There were five of them, all disappearing at different times and under different circumstances. The presumption was that they had been wiped out, and there was no evidence to the contrary, but still, learning their final fates was a commitment that the Legion had made to its people. And that was a commitment that O'Keefe respected.

Yet despite years of search efforts, nothing useful had been found. Every so often a research assistant, fresh to the job, would be assigned to try to find something that the algos, bots, and prior researchers had missed. O'Keefe was the latest in a long string of such assistants. There was no real expectation that anything would come of it, but as a light duty enlisted, all she could do was what she was told. And in time, there was an avenue for her to take remote university classes, then OCS. And then she could guide her own research.

That would be her future now that combat was out of the question. Surprisingly, she was actually looking forward to it.

For now, though, O'Keefe was determined to break that stalemate with history.

"It's given you a purpose, hasn't it?" the bot said. The thing was very perceptive. "That's something a lot of people wish they had."

"I'd prefer combat. I can fight the enemy." She pointed at her head. "I can't fight this."

"Perhaps. But you can control it... if you follow the proper dosage instructions. You know, one thing I've learned in my role in the auxiliary service is that we each have our own reality we live in. Yours may be more complicated than most, but you are what you accept and believe you are. You fought in the R-A, you spilled blood in battle, you helped us win some victories. You can be proud of that... or you can be ashamed that you aren't still out there jumping off combat sleds and firing your blaster. That's a choice that you and you alone can make."

O'Keefe had heard this lecture before, and she knew that Dr. Astin was right. But knowing it and accepting it were different propositions.

"It's not easy for me," she said. "I trained to be a warrior. I'm more comfortable deploying forward in a front-line unit and stacking bodies."

Astin nodded perceptively. "We all have hurdles to overcome. Even me. My programming is optimized for medical and psychological treatment, however my status as a machine automatically precludes some biologics from listening. You among them."

O'Keefe frowned. That was true enough. It had taken her a while to even be able to call the bot "doctor."

"Did you know that I served in an R-A unit as a med-bot? It was quite an ordeal to avoid having my programming and memory core wiped prior to this transfer. It took the intervention of some wise biologics to allow me to keep my medical knowledge, which I am now applying to your situation."

O'Keefe had never suspected the thing was a med bot. She'd seen the armored machines in battle before, had even been treated by one. This must be what they looked like underneath all that armor—and with a fresh coat of paint.

"But it is not just my programming that has me doing this work," Astin went on. "I genuinely care about my patients, unbelievable as that may sound to your human ears. Biologics think a machine cannot comprehend what you are going though. But Sheryl, I understand as well as any biologic doctor can, I assure you."

O'Keefe said nothing for a few moments, drinking in the words and burying herself in thought. There was a nickname for people like her, one spoken with a hint of scorn. *The Invalid Corps.* It didn't exist on any TO&E, but it was joked about by those who hadn't had to endure being transferred from active duty.

Maybe the bot felt something similar. It was... a crazy thought. But maybe it was possible.

"So where do we go from here?" she asked.

"You get back to your job, and I get back to mine. You promise me you won't play around with your dosage. You move on, and figure out how to cope with these ghost memories of yours if they happen again."

O'Keefe got up, the chair legs scraping on the tile floor with a low screech. "Agreed."

"Oh, and your friend told me that he'd left a message on your datapad."

O'Keefe winced. The visit had been a last chance before Metzger shipped out. And she'd gone and made a mess of it.

"Thanks, Doc." As Dr. Astin left the room, O'Keefe powered on her datapad and found the message.

O'Keefe,

They tell me you'll make a full recovery. You had me worried there for a few. I was afraid I'd lose you like Gordon and Tang. But I shouldn't have questioned how tough you were. The docs all say you're a remarkable person. I knew that all along.

I heard what you said. Seeing what you're going up against, it's sobering—on a few levels. You were right, about a lot of it. Dragging your unconscious ass to the hospital helped me see things in a different light.

Forgive me for not being the friend you need. For what it's worth, I'm going to change.

Contact me and let me know you're doing well.

Carson

8

Metzger ran on the treadmill as the med techs monitored his process. This was a standard six-month checkup, a boring procedure but one that was required. For him, it was a waste of time. He didn't need these docs to tell him what his new leg, not to mention the rest of his body, was capable of.

O'Keefe had already reminded him that he had fallen short.

Since his brief but disastrous visit with her, he had started to undertake a serious routine to get himself back into shape both physically and mentally. He ran daily, he spent time on the range, he tackled the obstacle courses along with the other personnel awaiting reassignment. It felt good to be active again, to be improving himself again, and he had started to drop some of the extra weight, too.

It helped that he stayed away from the base bars. He hadn't touched a drop since seeing O'Keefe.

According to the technicians, his cybernetic limb was functioning well. The sync circuits with his nervous system were working as expected. He was finally off of the rejection drugs and the nervous system enhancers, which had allowed them to make some aesthetic adjustments. The synthskin covering was now toned to match his own skin color, and the addition of artificial hairs made it look even more real.

It wasn't entirely identical in appearance to his old leg. It lacked that perfect imperfection of true humanity. Among other things, he no longer had a birthmark on his inner thigh. When he'd regenned his leg previously, the old birthmark had regenned along with it. He wondered if the techs could add it on. Probably. But it wasn't worth asking. It didn't matter.

The feelings were still weird, though. The bio-feedback responses from the leg weren't quite the same as he'd felt from his real leg. It was like wearing a pair of thermal leggings. Sensations were muffled, some to the point that they didn't trigger a feeling at all. Everyone told him it would get better with time, and so far that had been true. Each day lessened the sensation that the leg was somehow different. But the change was very slow, very gradual.

When the checkup was done—the techs reported that everything was fine, as Metzger already knew—he headed back to his quarters. The afternoon batch update to the replacement system would have dumped by now, and he wanted to peruse any new postings. He had applied for a lot of combat positions, and a few officers had met with him—probably mostly out of courtesy—but no transfer orders ever came down.

Before his meeting with O'Keefe, he would have gone straight from his doctor appointment to the bar. His old friend calling him out on his drinking had stung deeply, more than he'd ever admit. And then seeing what she was struggling with, how devastating it was... it made his own injury pale in comparison. If she could press forward with that kind of crap going on in her head, then he could handle a bionic leg.

During his walk, he started to think about his family. It was unusual for him to think about home, and such thoughts only came when he was calm. He lacked the fond longing for home of his fellow soldiers. Most of them were still close with their parents and siblings. Not so for Metzger. The moment he'd announced that he had enlisted in the R-A, his parents had played the doom-and-gloom card with him. His mother was convinced he was going to be killed. She was like that, only capable of seeing the worst possible scenario unfold. His father said he should have joined the Marines, that the army was for idiots. Not that *he'd* ever served. Metzger thought the real issue was his father's realization that he would no longer have control over him—and that he might return from service capable of kicking the old man's ass. Metzger's father was the sort of man who couldn't abide being anything but the lead dog.

There was an argument; harsh words were exchanged. After Metzger left, he invited them to his graduation from boot camp ceremony; neither showed. Not long after that, the messages to and from home slowed to a trickle, and soon they stopped altogether.

He didn't feel bad about it.

A few weeks ago, at the advice of his medical counselor, Metzger had sent a message to his mother—his first in three years. The hospital had even provided a template to make it easier. He'd received no response, which was no surprise.

That was fine. He didn't need them. He hadn't needed them since the age of thirteen. Clearly they didn't need him either. Everyone was better off.

Back at his sparse quarters, he found a message waiting on his personal pad. It was from a Colonel Gaetano

Inglima—a request for a meeting to discuss an available combat position.

Metzger felt a sudden rush. *Combat?* But the name wasn't familiar to him; he was certain Inglima wasn't one of the officers he'd reached out to about open slots. Who was this guy, and how had he found out about Metzger?

A search of the active-duty roster listed Colonel Inglima as the acting CO of the 72nd HARD. The HARD units were tanks, mechs, and support—real heavy hitters. Even the Legion wasn't above having the HARD units show up for support. Nobody turned down a tank or HK-PP when they could get one.

An assignment to HARD would be more than Metzger could have hoped for. But he tried to keep his expectations in check. He wasn't a tanker or a mech pilot. There was no reason for Inglima to be reaching out. Perhaps this was a mistake.

Mistake or not, he was going to make the most of it.

The next day at 0800 Metzger arrived at the recruitment building. The receptionist was cordial, but he could tell by the look in her eyes that she wondered why he still hadn't been assigned to a unit. He'd been in there a lot. She directed him to his assigned conference room, a tiny windowless room with two chairs and a small table. Metzger went to the far side and remained standing.

With a single knock on the door, a colonel in a dull green jumpsuit entered. The man looked to be in his mid-forties, with short reddish hair, thick eyebrows, and a square chin that made him look all the more rugged. The left eyebrow had a small gap in it, the result of a tiny scar that ran diagonally onto his forehead.

The patch on the officer's shoulder was one that Metzger didn't recognize. It featured the leg of a mech, an HK-PP, coming down on a small tank, crushing it. The bright red-and-black logo was topped with a single banner across the top that read simply: *72nd.*

"Sergeant Metzger," the colonel said, closing the door behind him.

"Colonel," Metzger replied.

"Thank you for making the time to meet with me."

"Of course, sir."

"You're not on duty, Sergeant. You can shelve the formality and the 'yes sirs.' I'm Colonel Gaetano Inglima." He extended his hand for a shake, which Metzger gave. The man's hands were calloused; this was a fighting officer.

Inglima eyed him carefully. "You have no idea why I'm here, do you?"

"No, sir. Other than I'm looking for placement in a combat unit."

"You know," Inglima said, taking a seat, "it's not every day that I get an unsolicited message telling me about a man who would be an asset to my unit."

Metzger was confused, and he was sure his face showed it. "I'm sorry? I'm not tracking that."

"I received a message from the Archives Division a few days ago. I assumed it was about our last operation and our after-action reports about Tralon. As it turns out, it was from one of your former comrades from the 444th Division."

"O'Keefe," Metzger said, barely hiding his grin.

"Yes. She went on about what a damn fine soldier you were. Talked about your experience. Said you were unable to get a combat posting because of a leg replacement. She had heard that the HARD units didn't have restrictions about cybernetics. Call it curiosity, but I pulled your records, mostly because I'm unaccustomed to some corporal in the Archives Branch randomly reaching out to me. A lot of what I saw impressed me. I thought I'd drop in on you, see if your files matched the man."

"I—thank you." Metzger barely caught himself from saying "sir."

"I command the 72nd Heavy Assault Regimental Detachment," the colonel said. "I'm always on the lookout for people with unique skills and backgrounds. People with a certain amount of audacity and a firm grasp of small-unit tactics. The kind of people who move *toward* the sounds of battle. In other words, I'm looking for experienced soldiers who have faced enemy action."

"I've had my share of that."

"I saw that. I also saw that you were an OCS candidate... and then you weren't."

Metzger felt a wave of warmth as the colonel's words summoned those memories. "I like to do what's right, Colonel, even if that contradicts a superior's orders. I should have handled it differently. I've also got a tendency to speak before I think, and sometimes that gets the better of me."

The colonel grunted. "You recognize a flaw, that's important. I prefer to have people under my command who know what the right thing is and take action. From what I read, that's exactly what you did."

"It didn't help my career."

"It's not going to, with most commands. But I think that if you were an actual moron, your CO would have done more than rescind his recommendation. He would have transferred you out of a combat assignment altogether. He didn't. That says a lot."

"He was a good man." *And now he's dead.*

"I did see one flaw in your file, though. A drunk and disorderly. The charges were dropped, but the incident, and the comments from your doctor, leave me concerned."

The mention of the incident brought shame and embarrassment. "I'll be honest with you, Colonel. I was in a bad place. I was drinking a lot, feeling sorry for myself. I couldn't get recruiters to even meet with me. Then a friend of mine knocked some sense into me. I haven't had a drink since."

"Good. You aren't the first person I've interviewed who's suffered from some sort of challenge. You also aren't the first to turn to booze to solve the problem. That said, I have a responsibility to those under my command to make sure this *won't* be a problem."

"That part of my life is behind me. The only thing I drink now is triple kaff, black and thick as syrup."

Inglima chuckled. "I understand that you've been on the bench for some time."

"Yes, s—yes. Most commands don't want someone with a tin leg."

"I'm not most commands."

Metzger tried not to let his eagerness show—not too much, anyway. "I'm all ears."

Inglima gave him a nod. "The 72nd is in the process of rebuilding. We took some pretty huge losses supporting a Legion unit in some damn hard fighting on Tralon. You'll learn pretty damned quick that what we are, as much as anything else, is a kelhorned magnet for enemy fire. Tralon was mech against mech, tank against tank. Our losses would have put us on the back burner for a few years, but we prevailed and in the process distinguished ourselves. Repub command has greenlit us to rebuild."

"I hadn't heard about the fighting on Tralon."

"Most haven't, and there's some reasons for that." The older man winced as if he were in combat with his own thoughts. "It was the kind of nasty sket that comes back at you in the middle of the night in a cold sweat, if you catch my meaning."

"I think I do." Nightmares happened, and with combat troops, they could be intense. Oba knew he'd had his own share of sweat-soaked sheets.

"Our pressing need necessitates a unique recruitment strategy, and that's where I hope you'll fit in. We're not recruiting fresh-faced new pilots; instead we're re-staffing our unit with veterans, and *teaching* them to be pilots. The young guys, fresh out of boot, they drive fast and fine—that's for sure. But it's an entirely different thing to do that and be combat-effective. Putting your missiles on target—that takes finesse and instinct. Truth is, I can teach a moktaar to pilot a mech. It's a whole different thing to teach someone to do it effectively. I need people in those cockpits who are innovative, can improvise tactical situations under fire, and can work together as a tight-knit unit. You've spent a big portion of your life learning new ways to stack bodies. That's what I need. I'm looking for some Oba-damned Spartans with killer instincts and soldiering skills who are trainable on the hardware we use."

Metzger drank in his words. He didn't know what a Spartan was, but he'd seen fighting from the ground level. That gave a person perspective. Perhaps doing that from a mech cockpit wasn't really that much different. Just with a sket-load more armor and speed at your fingertips.

"I'm trainable, sir. I'm confident I can master any piece of military hardware. But I've never piloted a heavy before."

"You'll like it. The HK-PP is a toy you'll never get bored with. You know what it's like in an urban combat environment. You have to clear rooms, check corners, make calculated decisions knowing that any shot at you is going to be at point-blank range. That tension can break lesser warriors." Inglima grinned. "With a mech, we don't go into buildings; we go *through* them. Working with your support troops on the ground, you can often save lives simply by blasting a building to rubble. And when you get a mech outside of a city, you can move faster, with a hell of a lot less effort, than rucking it on foot. Out in the open, a mech is the epitome of speed and firepower."

Metzger glanced down at his bionic leg, then back into the steel-gray eyes of the colonel. "Sir, what about my... injury?"

"In the 72nd, you're going to find that we have an abnormally high number of troops that have suffered a loss similar to yours. They were able to make the hop into the cockpit—and if they can, there's no reason you shouldn't be able to. You see, son, if the enemy has the capability to shut down that leg all buttoned up inside your cockpit, it means they have the capability to shut down your mech as well. In that case, you're karked either way."

Metzger nodded. "Yes, sir."

"To be clear, if it turns out your leg impairs your ability to fight, you're out. But I pulled your medical file, and according to your doctors, you're performing fine. As long as you can do your duty, we don't care what part is yours and what part came from a factory.

"Of course, I won't lie and tell you this is a cakewalk. Piloting a mech takes skill. Not everyone has it. What I *can* tell you is that you'll have the chance to fight. All I can do right now is offer you that chance. Where you go with that is up to you."

Metzger saw the appeal in working with people who had been through what he was experiencing. They'd understand where he was coming from. On top of that, they were battle veterans, so they'd share a bond that few would understand. Combat does that to you. For the first time since he had learned of his lost leg, he felt a twinge of real hope.

He wanted to jump all over the opportunity, but couldn't seem to form the right words to accept it.

That hesitation must have lasted too long, for Colonel Inglima spoke again.

"From what I read, you're a smart person. You want more information before making a decision; I respect that. Tell you what: why don't you come to our base? I'll set you up for a week or so to get your feet wet with a mech, give you a chance to talk to the folks in the 72nd. That'll also give us a chance to get to know you better. At the end of that time, we can sit down and make sure this is the right fit for both parties."

Rising to his feet, he extended his hand for a shake, which Metzger took.

"Sir, I simply can't find the words to express my gratitude and eagerness."

Metzger had lost his leg, his home, his friends. For too long after that, he'd lost *himself*. Now he had an opportunity to get back into combat. To form a new family. To have a purpose.

Not in a way he'd ever have imagined. But... maybe even better.

Inglima gave a slight smile. "I take it you will be dropping in for a visit?"

Metzger would have to think up some way to thank O'Keefe for this. He owed her, big time.

"Yes, sir, Colonel," he said. "I'd be grateful to come and try your hardware. Thank you."

9

O'Keefe looked at the holoboard that filled the space on one side of her tiny office. There she had posted everything she had ever confirmed or tracked as rumors about the 552nd Legion, the Howling Banshees. A lost legion. Holographic lines, like string, connected the bits and pieces of intel she had gathered, a bizarre spiderweb of connections. O'Keefe stood before it, looking at the snippets of old video feed, the fragmentary orders, the hypotheses of past researchers.

The young lieutenant who had initially given her this assignment had moved on to other things; she was now free to do the same. But O'Keefe had made the continued research her purpose. No one minded, so long as she performed her other duties.

Anyone who came into her office was overwhelmed—and often amused—by the data she had assembled, but the board was there mostly to help her think. She didn't need it, not with her eidetic memory; she could bring to mind these images, facts, data streams, any time she wanted. Her memory was a fantastic asset working in the Historical Branch.

It was ironic that it was also her greatest weakness. Memories from Frixon were always waiting like ticking time bombs ready to go off.

There was a knock at her door, and her immediate CO, Warrant Officer Dranes, entered. He was holding a large thermal cup of kaff and eyed her board from the doorway. "I take it you haven't cracked the case yet?" There was a hint of sarcasm in his tone. People had been working to find the lost legions for decades now. Danes had tried three times to talk her out of her obsession.

"Got a new tip yesterday, matter of fact." She pointed to a spot on the holoboard.

Dranes looked it over carefully while taking in a burst of caffeine from his mug. "A salvage crew in the Veimar system has located an old log buoy. Why is this important?"

"On its own, it's not. A message got routed to me that showed that the buoy may be from the *Sheffield*."

"O'Keefe, it's been a *long* time since I was an idealistic youngster hoping I'd be the one to find a lost legion. You're going to have to give me a little more than that."

"The 552nd was part of Task Force Equii. They were transported on the Republic frigate *Derfflinger* and arrived on Khara III, per the established records. We know from other units that while fighting there, Equii broke their enemy, the Shiktonga— allies of the Savage Nations. It was a full rout, chasing them into the Volkglas Mountains. One task force ship, the *Nightingale*, broke off to take back wounded. From the survivors on that ship, we have multiple reports that the Legion disengaged their pursuit— for reasons unknown. Task Force Equii was never heard from again.

"Searches of Khara III and interviews with the locals have been inconclusive. The Shiktonga call their alliance with the Savages the Great Shame, and don't like talking about it. A few of them claimed they drove the 552nd off-world, which seemed doubtful given the sorry shape the

Shiktonga were in. So the vast majority of our search efforts have been on Khara III."

"That's where the trail goes cold," Dranes replied.

"Yes. We've compiled thousands of tips over the years as to what happened to the 552nd. Most are just the pet theories of armchair historians. Obviously none have ever turned anything up. At this point I think it's safe to say that, whether by force or by choice, the 552nd departed Khara III. After that..."

O'Keefe shrugged.

The galaxy was a very big place.

Dranes gestured to the holoboard. "So where does this log buoy you mentioned come in?"

He was interested. O'Keefe hoped that meant he might assign her some additional research hours or at least some bots to use as resources. She tried not to let her excitement come out wavering in her voice as she answered, but she was sure her eagerness showed on her face, and she noticed her hands getting more animated as she spoke.

"As I said, a salvage company found it and reported it, though they never said what ship it was from. The Repub Navy asked for it to be returned, but the salvage company has so far held on to it, demanding compensation. The navy doesn't really care—it's an old buoy, Savage Wars–era. As far as they're concerned, it's of no real value other than being an antique, and the spacers have enough museums as it is. Only—get this—I received an anonymous tip two days ago." She paused to look around conspiratorially, as if now sharing a big secret for the first time. "It said that the buoy in question is from the *Sheffield* —one of the ships with Task Force Equii."

Dranes rocked back on his heels. O'Keefe could tell right away that he wasn't moved by this.

"You do realize the anonymous tip could be from the salvage company," he said, pausing for a sip of kaff before he continued, "trying to generate that 'compensation' they're after."

She nodded in agreement—but she didn't agree. Not totally. "That's what the navy thinks. And maybe it's nothing more than that. But if there's even a chance it's from the *Sheffield,* I have to investigate."

The warrant officer said nothing for a few moments. "Just to set expectations—you know this could all be a wild grunch chase. First, you don't know if the tip is accurate. Second, it's a pig in a poke; after all this time, the log could be blank, or a jumble of meaningless data. I'd lean toward the latter because the first thing salvagers do when they find old relics is scour it for Savage tech—illegal as it is—to see if there are any credits to be had on the black market. Them telling us about it at all more than likely means there's nothing there."

O'Keefe knew Dranes wasn't trying to discourage her; he was just thinking things through. He was always cold and logical—for him, things needed to add up. And in this case, she wasn't. She was playing a hunch. What he was saying to her was that it was a *wild* hunch.

"I've considered all of that," she said. "And still, I'd like to take a shot at getting my hands on it."

Dranes sighed. "Well, so long as you do it on your time, O'Keefe... good luck. How're you going to convince them to hand it over?"

Usually the department had a budget, albeit a small one, for acquisitions. But this wasn't an official project. This was her, a research assistant, a corporal, working on her own. "I guess asking for the department to pay for it is out of the question?"

Dranes's laugh answered that.

"Think about it," O'Keefe said, not ready to quit. "If we actually found a lost legion, the attention would be unreal. The Legion would be lobbying on our behalf for us to get additional funding in the hopes we can discover the other four, too."

Dranes shrugged. "If we plop down some hard-earned credits for this, every con artist out there will be trying to peddle something to us in hopes of a big payday."

That was something O'Keefe hadn't considered. There were a lot of enterprising scumsacks who would see the purchase of such an artifact as a means to cash in.

"This will have to be done discreetly, then," she said, trying to project the confidence of a full researcher and not just an assistant. "And we'll have to make sure we don't pay a lot for it."

"Agreed."

"Chief, I—" O'Keefe began, assuming he would reject her out of hand and would still require more salesmanship. But he had said yes. "Wait... really?"

"Yes, O'Keefe. Really."

She brightened. "Thank you, Chief. Thank you."

He gestured his near-empty cup of kaff at her. "No, thank you. There's not a research assistant I'd do something like this for... except you. I know what brought you to our ranks, O'Keefe, and I appreciate it."

She told herself not to let the chief see her cry. That was easiest done by focusing on the job. Same as always. "So how do we go about that? Do we use local resources to strike the deal?"

Dranes shook his head. "I'm not letting some stranger barter with our department's money. Not when I'm sticking my neck out for you. If anyone's going to go, it should be you and me... that is, if you're up to it."

He meant her medical condition.

They had spoken several times about the "incident" at the Nuts to Butts. Dranes checked up on her, and while she appreciated the concern, she felt it was unnecessary—and embarrassing. Her loss of control was not something she was proud of.

She had stayed on her meds since then. The memories did try to surface, especially ones of her being in combat, but the drugs made them less real, less vivid, little more than flashback moments—a snapshot of a few seconds of time.

"Everything is under control," she assured him.

"Glad to hear it. I know you've been through a lot. The injury you received would have broken a lesser person. We're all struggling with a few demons in the backs of our minds; yours are just a little more active, that's all. But I don't want to push you if it's going to cause a problem."

Dranes made it sound simple. That was one of his gifts, taking complicated things and finding a way of expressing them in simple terms. He could have chewed her ass for the incident; instead he had listened and done what he could to understand. Everyone else tap-danced around her on this subject. Only Dranes and Dr. Astin were willing to dive into the deep end of her pool of mangled memories.

And she *was* controlling her condition. She couldn't control the memories themselves, but she *could* control how she responded to them. And of course, she could take the drugs. She hated being dependent on drugs, but she had grown to accept that as a part of her life now. A part of staying in control.

Everyone pays a price for their decisions in life. This was hers. She had chosen the life of a Republic soldier, and this was part of it.

She shook her head. "I've got this. Wouldn't miss it, Chief."

"All right then. I'll let the navy know we're going to take point on this. I'm sure they'll protest, if only because we're now interested, but I'll assure them we'll turn the buoy over to them after we get a moment alone with it. In the meantime, I want you to assemble the means for us to validate its authenticity. You can do that during your daytime hours." He held up a hand to stop her before she could start. "Yes, that means we're doing an official piece of research on this. You've convinced me, O'Keefe. Though I doubt it'll stop you from coming in here at night to keep working."

She smiled sheepishly. "I'll work on figuring out how we can forensically extract whatever might still be in those logs. We should also let the scrapper know we're coming and to hold on to it."

Dranes nodded. "Agreed. I'll talk to the colonel and get approval for our transport there. What planet are we going to?"

"Veimar Prime."

"Never heard of that one. I swear, at times the Republic seems too big. It's no wonder there's people out there stirring up trouble. Managing all these worlds is a damn job."

O'Keefe nodded slightly, only half taking in his words. In her mind she was thinking through her next steps. This was all too good to be true. She'd need to get the specs on log buoys from that class of ship from that time period. She'd need serial numbers too. As for data extraction, Weaver was a top-notch cyber guy, and he specialized in old software. Quasi-retired from Repub Intel, he worked in the archives to give himself a sense of purpose after leaving the intel community. She would comm him next.

"O'Keefe," Dranes said, watching her distracted state with amusement. "You with me?"

"Yes. Sorry, Chief. I was just thinking through all the things we need to line up."

He eyed her carefully. Maybe it wasn't amusement. Maybe he'd thought she was having one of her memory attacks. She hated that, but she understood.

"Well," he said, "you get to work, and I'll start getting us the clearance to go." He left her office and closed the door.

As O'Keefe stared at the holoboard showing all her gathered evidence on the 552nd, she tried to hold back her excitement. This was all a long shot... she knew that. But if she was lucky...

I might get a chance to bring these legionnaires home.

As she allowed herself a smile, she heard the sound of blaster fire. It was muffled, almost as if it were in the distance. She knew that noise—knew it well—and a gentle throb in her forehead told her what was happening.

To her left, she saw a brightly lit outline of Wilks in full body armor. The woman looked almost angelic, a term that could never have been applied to her when she was alive.

"You can't go to the right, O'Keefe, they have us pinned! You need a different way around!" Wilks called out.

Many of O'Keefe's memory flashes were recurring; this one was new. Yet somehow she was certain it was from the day she was injured. She wanted to watch it play out— see if this fragment would explain what had happened to her team and to her. It was a seductive memory, playing a siren's song to lure her in.

Yet she also knew that if she went there, she would fall off her mental wagon. She couldn't risk taking that path. The same path that had led her to the incident at the Nuts and Butts. She was a Republic soldier, and had been schooled and equipped to fight and kill almost every species out there—yet she was slowly coming to realize that the biggest enemy she now faced was the one in her own mind.

Drawing a long breath through her nose, she emptied her head of thoughts. It was a technique that Dr. Astin had taught her.

The sounds of battle disappeared as suddenly as they'd come. When she opened her eyes, Wilks was gone.

10

There was nothing *prime* about Veimar Prime, at least not from what Corporal Sheryl O'Keefe could tell. She'd been on asteroids less barren than this planet. She was reminded of the time when she and Geroux were sent to the depot on Gurath for a supply run. That dustball was about as run-down and dumpy as Veimar Prime, but it also came with a pungent and pervasive odor of rotten eggs and burning garbage. Veimar Prime, by contrast, had more of a raw sewage smell in the moist air. Somehow that was an improvement over Gurath.

Usually spaceports had some amenities—bars, restaurants, the kinds of establishments that lured in crews and at least created an illusion of civilization. Not Veimar Prime. The buildings here were dilapidated adobe-printed structures, dull orange or boring tan, seemingly holding on to every stain that had ever splattered up against their surfaces. Rusty sheet-metal awnings cast dubious shadows where unsavory characters loitered.

Chief Dranes and Warrant Officer Weaver flanked her as she walked down the rough paving-stone street. The skies were cloudy, with twists of purple, gray, and dark blue. Lightning flickered in the distance. She wore her sidearm and was glad she had brought it along. Some of the grungy people looked like the type to have few qualms about rolling a few Repub troops for whatever they had in their pockets.

Dranes was packing as well, though he downplayed wearing his weapon. That was just how he was, always calm and in control. Even Weaver was armed, though it had taken some prodding on O'Keefe's part to get him to visit the armory. He was a techie, and not much for weapons. Being a warrant suited him; he was older than all of them, and calling him "Mister"—the respectful title until someone reached the status of chief—seemed fitting. He was also excited about the challenge the buoy presented. Much of the staff in the Historical Branch were there only because they had few other options, but Weaver had chosen the job. O'Keefe could now see why; it made him interesting to her.

Dranes had the address of the salvage company that possessed the buoy, and after consulting one of the less-shady locals, they found the street and made their way to the offices. The place was nothing but a tiny two-story structure, but the fenced scrapyard beyond it was sizeable. Stacks of old armored plates and ship parts were shoved into haphazardly stacked piles, leaving only narrow passages between.

As they entered the office, O'Keefe caught a whiff of some sort of smoked leaf. There were a lot of plants that got smoked on the worlds of the Republic; this was one of the less offensive-smelling ones. It had a cherry-like scent that she was sure was going to cling to her clothing. Two people sat behind the counter—a young woman, focused on her holodisplay, and a man with enough girth to be two people. The man had three rolls of fat under his chin, layered on top of one another, greasy hair slicked back, and a face that hadn't seen a shave in days. His gray unbuttoned work shirt and light undershirt bore stains of grease and possibly lunch from Oba knew how many days earlier.

"Welcome!" the man said.

"Are you Mr. Trennith?" Dranes asked.

"I am. Just Trennith, though—I have no family name. You must be those researchers who contacted me. I see you are as prompt as your correspondence indicated. The buoy is here on site, waiting for you, as intact as you would expect from a battle survivor of the Savage Wars. How will you be paying for it?"

If this was how the man looked when he was expecting visitors, O'Keefe didn't want to know how he presented himself the rest of the time.

"Sir," she said, "I'm Sheryl O'Keefe, the researcher who reached out to you. As per my message, before we negotiate price, we need to validate that the buoy is authentic."

Trennith took a step back. "I am insulted by the implication that I am anything other than an honest businessperson. Do you doubt my integrity?"

"No." It was a lie, so she kept it short. "It is merely policy that we confirm that this is indeed the buoy we seek."

Her words seemed to dissipate his obviously false taking of offense. "Very well. No data extractions, though. You can check the log, but no data dumping. Understood?"

O'Keefe glanced at Dranes, who gave her a nod.

"Agreed," she said.

Trennith motioned them through a set of doors at the rear of the office, and they stepped into the yard, the air pungent with old lubricants and chemicals. After a short walk, they stopped before a pallet. Strapped to it was an emergency log buoy.

It looked like a satellite, albeit an old-school one, about a half-meter tall, with a single thruster designed to get it clear of a ship. This one had some flash burns on its outer shell. Its broadcast antenna was missing entirely, with signs that it had been violently broken from its mounting point. One section of its shell was dented in, severely. O'Keefe wondered if that was from the recovery effort or if it was damaged upon release. Buoys were jettisoned only if a ship was in imminent danger.

She moved one of the orange straps that held the buoy loosely to the pallet, revealing the hull number that she knew belonged to the *Sheffield*—though it was only faintly visible. As she rested her hand on the dented plate, she wished the buoy could talk—could tell part of its story.

"Did the salvage crew find any evidence of the ship that this is from?" Danes asked.

"Nope. Not a bit. Frankly it was a miracle that they stumbled onto this. It was in an asteroid field. With all that metal floating nearby, it was practically invisible. Somehow their sensor sweep triggered a pinging device. The thing barely had enough power; as you can see, the solar array is almost entirely missing. It was enough for them to look and find it."

O'Keefe turned to Weaver. "See if this has anything that it can share."

Nodding, Weaver kneeled on the pallet and broke out some tools. Groping along the base of the buoy, he found a small, blackened plate. It took some physical coercion to convince the bolts to turn. "I've got a pry bar if you want it," Trennith offered, but Weaver shook his head.

After a few minutes of struggling, the small plate finally was freed. Using an ultrabeam, Weaver stared intently into the buoy, coming at it from different angles. "There's a data port here," he said, reaching up with his hand to feel it. "I'm not sure if the thing works or not. It's a bit crispy. Not to mention the interface is centuries old."

He linked his datapad to the port using a flex cable, and a moment later a deep, low hum rose from the buoy as he channeled power to it. It was hard for O'Keefe to not be excited, but she did what she could to mask it. She leaned forward to see what popped up on Weaver's screen as the warrant stabbed at the pad, opening multiple windows and scrolling through what looked like a sea of numbers.

"Anything?" she asked after what felt like an eternity of his fingers stabbing at the screen.

"There's data here, for what it's worth. The challenge is that this stuff is old code. It's literally written in a dead language—it's like finding something written in hieroglyphics. Fortunately for you, I did my thesis on these old programming scripts. I've tackled this kind of thing before." There was a hint of pride in his voice.

"Can you figure it out?" she asked, attempting to mask her impatience.

"I can write an interpreter for the data. I think it's a variant of the old CrossX10. But it's also a mess. Looks like it got hit with a magnetic field at some point, one strong enough to scramble the opburn data cards. I'm running a routine to try to unscrew it, but—"

He stopped.

"What?"

"Hang on... I think... Hot damn! I got a log file tag. It matches the one from the navy's archives." He looked up at O'Keefe and beamed. "It's from the *Sheffield.*"

Trennith matched Weaver's grin, rocking back on his feet. "I told you it was authentic!"

"Any sign of this being tampered with?" Dranes asked, still suspicious.

Warrant Officer Weaver's fingers fluttered over the datapad. "It's hard to be sure, but this looks consistent with other buoys that have been recovered from the same era. I can confirm with better equipment. Although even then, it's going to take some serious crunching to convert this data into something legible. And I'm sure it'll be fragmentary. There will be gaps aplenty."

Trennith smiled broadly, which did nothing for his looks. The teeth that he had left were yellowish with a tint of brown. "Something is better than nothing!"

That was true. Historical Archives and Research had been working with a lot of *nothing* for a long time. But O'Keefe knew she needed to control her excitement. This was at best a tip that might lead to a tip. Or it could all be a bust.

"You can unplug, Mr. Weaver," she said, then turned to the salvage operator. "So now it comes down to price."

"Well, now that you've confirmed there is data there..." Trennith smiled greedily. "I'm sure there will be a lot of interested parties who will want to pay big credits for this."

"Who?" O'Keefe asked.

"Excuse me?"

"Who, Trennith? To everyone but us, this is a piece of space junk. The only other entity that might even remotely have an interest in this would be the Repub Navy, and we've both agreed not to get into a bidding war. In fact, they made us the sole military entity to try to secure this."

"There are bound to be others," Trennith insisted, but he didn't name any.

"Doubtful," Dranes replied. "Your best bet might be a museum. But let's face it, the demand for something like this isn't strong. Nobody cares about satellites unless they made significant discoveries. That, and most museums don't pay for their artifacts, they expect them to be donated. You don't strike me as the philanthropic type. Then again, I'm sure you could sell the buoy for scrap metal."

Trennith frowned. "This is a *priceless* bit of Savage Wars history." But his conviction didn't sound nearly as bold as it had a few moments earlier. Dranes and O'Keefe had taken the wind out of his sails.

"Maybe you're right," O'Keefe said. "Maybe, with time and effort—probably a lot of both—you might find a buyer interested in owning... well, a minor historical curiosity."

Trennith looked defeated.

Dranes jumped in. "Or, we're ready to buy right now, and we can transfer the money to you today. It's your choice, of course. Credits in your account now versus the hope of something better in the future."

Despite his lack of leverage, Trennith threw out a number higher than what he had quoted in the messages O'Keefe had had with him. Dranes was in his element, though—he threw out a dramatically lower number. The two went at it for a full five minutes, firing salvo and counterbattery offers at each other in rapid succession. By the end of the negotiations, Trennith looked exhausted, but Dranes appeared to be more than willing to go a few more rounds. O'Keefe got the nod from her superior and transferred the funds.

The buoy was hers. It was the best lead on the 552nd to have come up in two decades.

She reached out and caressed the satellite's side. *You have secrets in you, jumbled all to hell, but they're there.*

In that, she and the buoy were a lot alike.

Rexnar Koff's chrono chirped, and he looked down at the message. It was from Sarn. *Package delivered.* He cleared the message and purged it. There could be nothing, digitally or otherwise, that could tie him to the events he was setting in motion. That was one of the hallmarks of survival in Republic politics.

Sarn had used an intermediary to send the anonymous tip to the R-A Historical Archives about the buoy. The buoy had indeed been a relic of a Rapier-class ship from the Savage Wars era, the same as the *Sheffield*. An expensive team of people had given it a makeover to make it appear as if it had been part of the 552nd's task force. They had spent three weeks crafting orders, some that could be cross-referenced with documented events, for an air of authenticity. Another team garbled the data—just enough so that it could be cracked—while making it appear that the garbling was due to magnetic damage. Even the best stellar archeologist would be hard-pressed to see the buoy as anything other than the real thing. For Koff, it was not a relic, it was bait.

Satisfaction with a tinge of narcissism came over him as he thought about what he was putting in motion. It would take the Republic's investigators some time to make sense of the data; that would leave plenty of time for Sarn to get the necessary materials shipped in. And when the recovery team arrived, they would do so eagerly, without suspicion—which would make them hasty. All of which would play into Koff's hands. Their arrival would light the fuse for resistance.

Then they would go to Vargas—he would make that happen as well.

And there, my son will be avenged.

11

Camp Archie on Tibul was at the base of a range of tall mountains. On the mag-lev ride in, Metzger was impressed with the variety of terrain he saw near the camp. Forests, lakes, swamplands, and hills were all demarcated by perimeter fences that stretched on for over two hundred kilometers on his approach. He was less impressed with the little swarms of insects weaving around him when he got off the train. He was met by an escort—a private who offered little in the way of conversation—who led him through a security checkpoint, then to a waiting military repulsor transport. Metzger had been on a lot of military bases in his career, and Camp Archie didn't strike him as any different.

But what he'd be doing here... was very different.

He knew how to be a soldier, but he was unsure if he could handle piloting a mech. While the opportunity was tantalizing, there was a part of him that wondered if he could retool his brain and body to being something other than a ground-pounding infantryman. It was a change of specialty; it would require a different way of fighting and thinking. He knew his limitations as a soldier, but what limits would he face from the cockpit of an HK-PP? Would it be like learning to shoot a new weapon, or would it be more complicated? There were a lot of unknowns in play.

At least the leg was no longer one of those unknowns. He had moved past the stage where he didn't trust that his bionic limb would perform. It was truly a part of him now, just like his original limb, and just like the Repub doctors had said. The sensations it "felt" were familiar to the point where he rarely thought about the fact that it was artificial. And to Metzger, that was a triumph—not a physical one, but mental.

They arrived at a dull administrative office, where he was ushered inside and greeted by a tall, dark-skinned man with short, curly black hair. A major by rank, the man had a rigid bearing, more than most officers. The only thing that betrayed a hint of his age was a light graying of his hair at his temples and around the tops of his ears. He wore a jumpsuit with a nametag reading *Meece*.

"Sergeant Metzger," Meece said as Metzger saluted, a gesture he quickly returned. "I'm Major Meece. Have a seat." He indicated the single chair opposite his desk, then sat down in his own chair. "I take it you had no issues with your trip in."

Metzger sat down. "No sir, none at all."

"Good. You want anything to drink? I can have my orderly scrounge up some kaff."

"No. I had plenty on the mag-lev."

"Very well. Colonel Inglima filled me in and sent me a copy of your records. He was duly impressed with your interview. There was some concern, though, that you might lose the leg again before arriving—that seems to be a pattern."

It was a light joke, one clearly designed to measure Metzger's reaction. Metzger wasn't going to take the bait.

"I hope it's a pattern no one tries to follow," he said.

Meece chuckled lightly. "Well, that's a pretty safe bet. Makes you wonder if the Almighty had an issue with that leg."

"I wouldn't know, sir."

"The colonel told me you aren't sure about piloting a mech. I'd like to get your perspective on that."

"Of course, sir. It's just that, I have skills that have taken me most of my life to develop, and I can contribute best in a situation where I can apply them."

It wasn't enough just to be back in combat; it was important to Metzger that he be *useful.* He was a weapon of war, and serving in some second-line infantry unit would be a waste of his talents.

"I understand," Meece said. "I was in the 20th Division. Like you, I lost my slot—though mine came courtesy of a blaster cannon that took out a chunk of my spine. The experience shook my world. I had only been a soldier for five years when they told me that medically, I could no longer handle the stresses of infantry combat. Joining a HARD unit was my best shot—my only shot. Understand: Same injury, same level of combat stress, different medical clearances. Since the Repub doesn't think about that big contradiction, neither do I. So I learned to pilot the HK-PP, and found I had a knack for it. The colonel convinced me to transfer to the 72nd right before Tralon."

"Tralon? I'm not familiar, sir."

Meece nodded and momentarily looked introspective. "Real damned meat grinder situation. Mechs and armor have a mix of speed and firepower. If you go up against another unit that has a similar mix, it can turn into a real firestorm. We suffered some significant losses, and we're now in rebuilding mode. If you're here long enough, you'll learn that the folks who came through it don't like to discuss it much. But that's why we have a few open slots."

It was clear as the major spoke that he was struggling with the memories. Whatever happened on Tralon must have been pretty nasty.

"I've been through rebuilding myself, on a personal level," Metzger replied. "It can be a painful process."

"It can also open new opportunities. Like this one. If you're a good fit."

"So how do we go about this, sir?"

Meece shifted in his seat. "We have a sim that will test your aptitude. What I'd like to do is give you the mech overview, then slide you into the simulator and see how you respond to it. If that goes well, we'll put you in a real cockpit and let you take a mech on what we call a test drive. Will that work for you?"

That seemed fast, but Metzger imagined that HARD had it down to a science.

"I came here to see what I could see and learn what I could learn. Yes, sir."

The major rose to his feet and gestured to the door. "Let me give you the walk-through, then."

He led Metzger across the base to a large structure adorned with the 72nd logo. He opened a personnel door and ushered Metzger into a hangar-sized space. Closed bay doors lined the back wall, each a good ten meters in height, with flanking walkways to give the techs access to their upper portion. Gantry hoists with chains hung from the ceiling. The air stung of lubricants, but Metzger was impressed at how clean, almost pristine, the place was.

But his attention was mostly on the one bay that stood open... and the mech that stood inside it.

During his time in the 444th, Metzger had not only been fully briefed on mechs—he had gotten up close and personal with them. Still, this was different. Back then, he was being trained on how to operate in conjunction with mechs and tanks; now he was looking at them from a very different perspective—that of a potential pilot.

The HK-PP was nine meters high, almost as tall as the bay, with two boxy, shoulder-mounted missile racks. Its arms were blasters, not quite as big as those on repulsor tanks, but big enough to be devastatingly powerful. Its legs reminded him of a bird's, with big claw-like feet. The cockpit was sleek, sloping downward, with a carbon weave that gave it a light crimson color, but the rest of the HK-PP was painted in a forest camouflage pattern, all green and brown lightning-like stripes jutting at strange angles. It was impressive, but it also made him chuckle.

"Something strike you as humorous, Sergeant?"

"Sorry, Major. No. It's just the camouflage. I mean, I've seen these in action before. How do you expect to hide something this tall, that stomps the earth the way they do, with camouflage schemes?"

His words brought a smile to the major's face. "I hear you. Welcome to the military. Repub specs demand that all combat vehicles have a planet-appropriate paint scheme, no matter how ridiculous that might seem."

Meece led Metzger almost to the foot of the mech, then stopped and gazed up at it with a look of reverence on his chiseled face. "This is the Hunter-Killer Planet Pounder, the mainstay of our mech forces. There are variants of it—the B- and C-class mount different weapons, and we have others we employ, though they're usually mission-specific, like the SSAB, the Shadow-Stalking Ass Buster, or the RTCM, the Roaring Thunder Crater Maker."

"Ass buster, Major?" Metzger raised an eyebrow.

The major winked. "Called so only by those who know it best, Sergeant. Repub military has them listed as HK-SS."

Metzger had seen those models but didn't know much about them other than the fact that "SSABs" were sniper-mechs—light on armor, slow, but with a big blaster cannon —and RTCMs—Metzger didn't know what those were truly designated as, but he knew no one in the Republic Army would authorize a name like *Roaring Thunder Crater Maker*—were mobile heavy mortar platforms.

Meece continued. "The HK-PP is armed with two five-rack aero-precision missile launchers, with one reload each. Generally we carry a mix of warhead loadouts—anti-personnel, anti-vehicle, and even bunker-buster." He gestured to the arms. "Two Mark 14 heavy blasters top off the standard offensive capabilities. As for defensive capability, this model features prismatic anti-laser glazing, kinetic dispersion, and nano-honeycombed, F-17-class carbon-weave armored plating. It can take a beating, but its best defense is speed. It clocks in at eighty-three kilometers per hour at a full run. We're fond of saying that speed is our armor, our best defense."

"Impressive," was all that Metzger offered. *And deadly.*

He reached out to touch the leg. It was cold, lifeless, much like his own bionic leg. Meece waited quietly, as if he understood the human desire to make tactile contact with the subject matter. Metzger appreciated that. Some officers didn't know when to shut up, as if they savored hearing the sound of their own words.

"I bet these are hard to keep operating." Metzger looked around for a maintenance team.

"Like any piece of hardware, for every eight hours these things are out in the field, it requires over an hour of maintenance, and that's just for routine stuff. If they've taken damage, it obviously takes longer. Thankfully, they rely mostly on standardized parts, so that at least isn't an issue. And there's a dedicated team of techs assigned to each pilot—techs are the backbone of any HARD unit. Without them, death can come at the hand of equipment failures. The last thing anyone wants is to have gaps in your armor or a weapon that won't fire."

"That makes a lot of sense," Metzger said.

Meece moved up beside him. "I can tell you, having piloted both mechs and MBTs, nothing tops the feeling of piloting a mech. It becomes a part of you when you do it right, like a second skin. I swear, there are times I've piloted one of these and I could feel the feet hitting the ground as if they were my own, and every chip, ping, and ding on the armor plates caused actual pain."

"How complicated is it to pilot one of these?" Metzger asked. "I had the basic orientation on mechs when I was in boot—mainly learning how not to get trampled and how to pull out a pilot. Controls must be intuitive if a sim and a test drive are all it takes to get an idea of aptitude."

Meece grinned. "Aptitude is all it will tell us. Let me walk you over to the sim center so you can see for yourself."

It didn't take long to reach the windowless building. Meece led Metzger to a room where ten large lozenge-shaped pods awaited—the sims. At the rear of the room was an elevated windowed control bay where a pair of operators looked down on the space.

"Welcome to *the whetstone*," Meece said. Seeing the confused look on Metzger's face, he explained. "Before precision sharpeners, warriors used stones called whetstones to put an edge on their weapons. Sharpening your blade was a mix of skill and ritual. Warriors relied on the sharpness of their blades to kill their enemies and survive. That's what this room does."

Meece hit a control stud on the side of one of the pods, and the front of the pod opened with a low hum. Inside, Metzger saw the reproduction of the cockpit. It stood at a steep angle, no doubt simulating the position of the cockpit in a mech.

"We've got ten of these sims, but two are backups. Usually a few of our pilots would be in here, but we have our folks on a nice little fifteen-klick hike this morning."

"A hike? I wouldn't think that piloting a mech would take a lot of physical effort. The featherheads in the navy don't hike as far as I know."

Meece grinned. "We aren't featherheads. Now, the controls have been dumbed down over time to make a mech easier to drive, but still, piloting, *real* piloting, Is as physically challenging as running in your full combat armor."

Metzger nodded once in acknowledgment, then poked his head in the simulator. "So where do I start?"

"The best way to learn is to get in and try it out. Go ahead, mount up." Meece gestured to the pilot's seat. "We've configured this as a standard HK-PP, though we can make it spin up variants as we see fit."

As he climbed in, Metzger had to bend his knees slightly, then adjusted the seat position.

"You put on the waist control strap first—that guides the orientation for the upper part of the mech's torso," Meece told him. "The five-point harness is self-tightening. It will feel pretty snug, but you'll come to appreciate that—trust me."

Metzger pulled on the waist belt and safety harness and snapped it secure in the center of his chest. The straps whirred, pulling him tight into the bucket seat. It was more than snug; it was *tight.*

"Let's start you off on basic movement," Meece said. "Look down, and you'll see two footpads. Pushing the one on the right drives the right leg, left drives the left. Push both down, you go straight. To turn right, you push the left pedal harder than the right."

"And reverse?"

"Just tilt your foot up and push down with your heels. The heel pressure drives the mech the same way as going forward, but in reverse. The older mechs had a lot of complicated control surfaces, lights, buttons, little levers—you name it—but it was too much to train on. Took too long to get new pilots spun up, so we went back to basics with this generation. We want the pilot to be able to easily focus on only two things: movement and shooting."

Metzger tried the pedals, both forward and backward, just to get a feel for them. He found it was a little harder with his bionic leg. While in ordinary usage the leg's feedback pulses were sufficient to make it feel like his own flesh and blood, judging fine differences in pedal pressure —especially the heel pressure—was something new. He had to judge the pressure based mostly on experience, which was limited.

"Your engine engagement knob is on the right side," Meece continued. "Push it in and turn it right to engage the engine. When the sim loads, you'll see a light green path on the ground. Follow that as fast as you can. Don't worry about making mistakes; this is just to give you the feel for a mech."

Meece must have pushed a button, because the simulator's big, curved lid closed, leaving Metzger alone in total darkness. Then a dim backlight flickered on and a voice came over a speaker in front of him.

"Hello there, Sergeant Metzger. This is SPC Eilenberger in sim control. I'm here to guide you. Power up when ready."

Metzger pushed and twisted the power control knob, and a throbbing sensation arose under his seat—no doubt simulating the feel of a mech's power plant. The lights flickered, and on the interior of the sim's lid he saw an image of a forest, with a narrow opening in the trees and a pulsating green line—the one he was apparently supposed to follow.

He relaxed into the armrests, which ended with control sticks. The right one was a true joystick and had three fingers and one thumb trigger. Those probably controlled the weapons systems. The left one was more like a horizontal handgrip, featuring still more controls. If this was the "simplified" control scheme, he was grateful not to be operating the previous generation.

He gripped his fingers around both sets of controls, careful to not rest his fingers on the studs—what he assumed was the mech equivalent of good trigger discipline.

"Before we have you run the course, take a few minutes to get a feel for the response," Eilenberger said.

"Copy," Metzger acknowledged, then slowly depressed both foot pedals. The mech pod rocked back as he moved, with a slight list to the side as each simulated footstep fell. It was highly responsive. He relaxed his right foot slightly, and the sim-mech moved to the right. He tightened the turn by pressing down harder with his left foot. The sim-mech lurched and turned sharply.

Using his heels, he then practiced backing up. Then he tried an outright run, punching both pedals down hard. He felt himself pressing back against the seat as the pod simulated the run. It even simulated the sound of the mech's footfalls. And it was fast—far faster than he had expected.

Movement was not intuitive, however. There was an initial feeling of disconnect between what he was doing and what the mech was doing in response. It wasn't at all like running in combat armor; this was learning to move in an entirely different way. But after several minutes, he felt his comfort, and confidence, increasing. With enough practice and experience, maybe this would even feel natural. After a few minutes, he'd at least mastered the basics.

Eilenberger must have sensed his confidence as well. "Sergeant Metzger, I think you're ready for the course. Move yourself to the start of the green line, and on my mark, run that line to the end as fast as you can."

Metzger did as he was told, and he began the run. His speed was good—or at least it felt good to him—but then a sharp turn came up, and he overshot the pace-line. The simulator was unforgiving; it tossed him hard, and he struggled to regain control and get back on the course. The second time a hairpin curve appeared, he used the reverse step on one leg and found that the momentary change of direction helped, though the simulator still threw him to the side given the speed. On the next turn, he found that if he twisted slightly at his waist, his view oriented to his motion, rather than the direction he was running, much like a tank turret turning in a different direction than it was driving.

By the time he finished the course, he was wet with sweat—both from exertion and concentration. The cockpit felt much smaller than when he'd initially gotten into it, too.

The pod opened, and Major Meece stood before him. "How was that run for you?"

"Some of those curves were tight," Metzger said. "I'm sure I didn't set the course record."

"This wasn't about competition, not yet. This is about getting a feel for it. And from what I saw, you adapted all right to the controls. How about some target practice?"

That was a silly question. Metzger never passed up a chance to fire weapons, even in simulation. "Sure."

"Good. Take a look at your hand controls. We've set up your arm-mounted blasters on the primary trigger. The weapons systems are fully customizable, but for simulation purposes, we've configured the thumb trigger for tandem missile launches alternating between your pods. It's mostly a matter of using your right joystick to aim the reticle and fire."

"The cockpit can't track my line of sight?"

That technology had been around for a long time. Legionnaires employed it in their expensive helmets, featherheads in their starfighters. It seemed that HK-PPs would have similar.

"Yeah, but your eyes have a lot to keep track of. Learnin' the stick is critical."

Metzger nodded. "Is it possible to custom configure the displays?" Several times during the run, Metzger had given a verbal command for the sim to adjust the view, with no results. Whatever onboard AI was there, it wasn't as intuitive as the sort found on a basic combat sled. Or maybe it was just user error.

Meece leaned in and showed him how to use the left-hand control to activate the voice commands for adjusting his display, then ran him through the basics. It took only a few minutes for Metzger to get his display to look similar to the dash of his personal repulsor sled, organized the way he liked it. When he was satisfied, the domed lid came down and secured in place once more, and the artificial terrain flickered into reality. Another green line to follow—but now with enemy targets.

Firing came much easier to him than moving had, and each time he fired, he felt an actual tug of recoil and heard the roar of missiles or the whine of blaster capacitors discharging their deadly bolts. He quickly found that he could respond faster to the flashing targets when he twisted at the waist or moved the mech in the target's direction. Now he was having fun.

Until he overshot the pathway and slammed into a boulder. The mech toppled over and threw him hard. No one had told him how to stand the thing back up, and though he knew he could ask Eilenberger, Metzger wanted to figure it out for himself. He shifted the arms, and the movement pitched the simulator pod, making the safety harness dig into him. That's when he saw the damage display flickering amber on the inside of the canopy. The fall had crumpled the armor in addition to tossing him around.

"Hang on," came Eilenberger's voice. There was a momentary flicker, then he was suddenly upright. The damage indicator had also vanished. "You should be good to go."

Things were a lot easier in a simulator. Metzger hated to think how much damage he would have caused a real mech—and how much trouble he'd have just gotten himself into if that had happened during battle.

He completed the run without further mishap. Now that the displays were configured, things felt comfortable... familiar. Sort of.

As the pod opened, Metzger wondered if he had done well enough to be considered for the unit. This thing was a lot like a holovid game, and while his reflexes might not be as quick as someone younger, *he* wasn't fresh out of basic training. He had valuable experience. But one doubt that he'd had upon arriving at Camp Archie had now been erased: he knew he could do this. He wasn't a master, not yet, but he could get there.

Meece stepped over to check on him. "Quite a ride, aren't they?"

Metzger undid the harness and thick waist control belt, then stood in the open pod. His left ankle ached a little from the footpad work. "Yes, sir. They look fast on the battlefield, but they feel a hell of a lot faster when you're piloting them. I think I could greatly improve my performance with a little more experience." He paused. "Should I ask how my performance was?" He wasn't sure he really wanted to know.

"This isn't about passing selection in one day," Meece replied. "You did fine, though. Better on shooting than piloting, but given your background, that doesn't surprise me. You adapted well enough for a first-timer to the controls, and you have good instincts. Most green kids who are in the cockpit for the first time go forward only. You pushed the machine and yourself by backing up from a full trot and using the reverse on one pedal to adjust your turning. That's the kind of thinking we like to see in recruits. The best pilots push the hardware."

Meece gave a solid evaluation, which Metzger appreciated.

"Thank you, sir."

"You *did* topple the mech once, but that's not unheard of. The sim path is designed to drop you unless you're moving at a snail's pace. And you tried to right yourself, which again demonstrates the instincts we're looking for. I'll get to it. I like what I saw enough to feel good about asking you to join us. We need pilots with your level of combat experience, Sergeant, and we need them now."

The statement was direct and to the point. For a few moments, Metzger wasn't entirely sure how to respond. Piloting a mech in simulation was more enjoyable than he had expected. More importantly, this was a path forward in the Repub military. "To be honest, sir, the HK-PP has a lot of appeal. I think it's a skill set I could master."

Major Meece considered Metzger as though he were looking into the man's soul. "You see yourself as an infantryman, not a mech pilot."

"Yes, sir."

"Sergeant, if infantry was an option, we wouldn't be wasting one another's time. But I'll tell you this, one former R-A grunt to another—being an HK-PP pilot means you're the biggest, baddest, most armored-up infantryman on the whole damn battlefield. Ask me if I miss being infantry now that I pilot a mech."

Metzger eyed the man. "Do you?"

Meece's face was stone-cold sober. "Hell no."

The words caused a thrill in Metzger. "In that case, Major, I'd be honored."

Meece grinned. "Outstanding. Let's get you over to the office and file your T30 request for transfer. Then we can get you into a training class."

"Thank you, sir."

Meece extended his hand. "Welcome to the 72nd."

12

House of Reason Delegate Rexnar Koff felt his breather unit snug against his face as he walked down the gangway and onto the spaceport. Glancing around, he saw he was in the depths of a deep crater. Even with the aid of the breather, the air was too thin and came with a coppery taste to it, coating the back of his throat.

Vargas was a starkly divided world. The humans worked the mining operations in the hundreds of deep impact craters that constituted half of the world. The K'llik worked the old volcanic flows on the surface, known as the uplands, and just below it, with their own mining operations. The insectoids wanted little to do with the human operations, and the humans had come to fear and respect the viciousness of the K'llik.

It had been tempting to send an envoy in his place, layering in a level of deniability if any of the details of his visit were made public. Koff wasn't worried enough for that. Vargas was not the kind of planet that attracted much media attention. It was an R-7 industrial backwater world. If it weren't for the abundance of heavy metals relatively close to the surface, no one at all would be in this Oba-forsaken wasteland.

His advance team had landed several days before, and from their reports they had reached their objective. They were working quickly to help craft the wreck site, to properly prep it for when the R-A would come. Koff was sure that they *would* come to Vargas; it would be far too irresistible for them to not show up. When they did, he would pull the necessary strings to make sure his son's Legion was present as well. It was simply a matter of time and patience, and he had an abundance of both.

A human moved toward him, stopped, and bowed deeply. "We are honored to have you visit us, Representative Koff." The man did not wear a breather unit. No doubt he was used to the thin air.

Koff returned the bow; best to create the illusion of respect. "Guildmaster Rune, please—no names. My visit here is, shall I say, unofficial." There was a small voice amplifier in the breather that took his muffled words and broadcast them in a more conversational tone, if a little tinny for his taste.

"Of course," Rune replied. "Per your courier's request, I have arranged for a discreet place for us to meet." Gesturing with a sweep of his arm, he led Koff and his small entourage off the landing pad and to a waiting repulsor vehicle.

Their trip to the hotel was brief. The ironically named "Grand" was carved out of the side of the crater. They entered and traveled down an escalator to meeting rooms. A large one bore a sign that read, *Reserved.* Rune led him inside.

"You should be able to remove your breather unit in here. Most of our structures are pressurized."

Koff removed the mask, and the cool air hit his sweaty skin where the breather had been attached. Moving slowly toward the oval obsidian table, he lowered himself into one of the seats along a narrow end.

The delegate had come to Vargas in person to avoid any chance of his communications being intercepted or monitored. The two shuttles that had accompanied him were loaded with hardware and munitions, on the assumption that Rune and the people he represented were agreeable. Additional ships were coming with rebuilding supplies in anticipation of a conflict. His reports suggested that the mining guild harbored little love for the Republic. Chances were good they would loathe a military force landing on their world, regardless of the reason.

"May I get you something to drink?" Rune offered.

"No thank you. I am pleased that you would take the time to meet with me," Koff replied, knowing the man had little choice in the matter. There were few people in the galaxy who could turn down a meeting with a House of Reason delegate without consequence.

"It is rare that we have visitors other than merchant traders. Members of the House of Reason, exceptionally so. Even our own representative does not come to Vargas."

"That is unfortunate. Despite your population being few in number, Vargas is important to the Republic."

Rune shrugged. "It doesn't seem that way. The new levies that the House has imposed on us have been... troubling." It was clear that Rune's feelings were far bitterer than he was willing to admit out loud. The new set of taxes had been aimed at diminishing some of the clout of the guilds and unions. The legislation had had the opposite effect.

Koff had taken a public stance against the new taxes, even dropping a few soundbites about the damage that they would do to the guilds specifically. Not that he cared about the aggravating economic damage raising taxes caused; all that mattered was that the guilds and unions saw him as a trusted ally. That was a critical step in his plan.

"I can imagine your people have some feelings of ill will toward the Republic," he said. "I am hoping that my visit shows you how much we value this world and its contributions."

"Oh, it does. But while the gesture is appreciated, what we need on Vargas is less government oversight and regulation out of Utopion. Our part of this planet is self-governing—independent. The guild ensures that the people are taken care of, that our welfare is looked after. We have parity with the K'llik, a mutual respect."

"So I have come to understand. I would hate to see that change."

"It pleases me to hear that. Yet the laws coming at us... they cost the mining companies a great deal. They have three ways of dealing with those costs: cutting back on miner pay, raising prices, or both. Utopion would benefit to learn that strife comes on the coattails of every new law aimed at making life better."

"That is the nature of legislation. Unintended consequences," Koff replied in a sympathetic tone.

"It *has* to be minimized." Rune's voice dropped an octave as he spoke. Clearly he was feeling the pinch.

"While I agree with you, there are elements in the House of Reason that don't have the same care that I possess when it comes to planets such as yours. That can lead to fits of overreaction, sometimes brutal in nature."

His words made Rune blush. That was purposeful. Koff knew about the incident four months ago.

"I think I know what you're referring to," Rune said. "The media made that out to be much more than it was. It was a protest, not the 'battle' that it has been called."

"Your guild members attacked Republic inspectors," Koff clarified.

Rune got defensive fast. "That isn't at all what happened. Those inspectors came unannounced. They walked into the largest mining operation on the planet and after being there for three hours, demanded that it be shut down under a false claim that we weren't following safety mandates—mandates we'd never even heard of. Then they brought in security teams to serve as muscle to prevent us from protesting the closing. All those miners—no pay. We had to take action."

"Violent action."

"Yes," Rune conceded. "But we didn't fire first."

"That's not with the official reports say. And the media showed the galaxy those up-armored mining mechs of yours looking like an army, waiting for the fight. A well-equipped army."

"The media—liars, all of them—they distorted the truth. Those are working mechs. But yes, we will use them to protect ourselves. We lack the security that the core worlds get, and have to provide for our own. We were *not* provocateurs. Another case of those who are skilled at taking a minor incident and making it into something salacious."

"They will do that," Koff said with an understanding nod. "But the incident did send a message to the House of Reason. And not a good one."

"And that message is?"

"Vargas is on the cusp of outright rebellion."

Rune shook his head firmly. "We have no interest in the Mid-Core Rebellion. The politics of the Republic mean nothing to us. Our people simply want to do what we have done for years: mine heavy metal and sell it. And the guild members want their freedom. They don't like these strong-arm tactics of the Republic. They don't want outside interference. You'll note that the Bronze Guild never has such Republic interference."

Koff gave a slight nod, conceding the point. The bounty hunters' guild was an army that would require the entire Legion to put down, if it ever came to it.

"Yes, exactly," Rune said, pleased that his point had been made. "As a guild, we deserve the same respect. We've been providing the Republic our output for generations now. We can govern ourselves."

"What of the K'llik? Do they share your sentiments?"

Rune sighed. "Who can say? I meet with my counterpart regularly, but our interactions are always abrupt and... unilluminating. You can't read them the way you can most humanoids."

Koff recognized this as useful information. He leaned back in his seat, steepling his fingers in deep thought. "I would like for operations here to have a good working relationship with the Republic in the future as well. I am a working man, much like you. I have come up through the ranks to get to my position. I come at this from your perspective." It was a lie, a boldfaced one, but he uttered it with such polish that he doubted Rune would think twice about it. "Sadly, I don't represent Vargas in the House," he continued. "But I could offer you advice," he said coyly. "If it is something you would desire."

Rune nodded. "I welcome your insight."

"People do not respect the weak. History is full of examples of this. You mention the Bronze Guild, and I say you are right."

"So we are to become bounty hunters?" Rune said dismissively. He was getting bold now, but Koff was far from insulted. This was exactly where he wanted the man to be.

"The galaxy doesn't need any more bounty hunters," the delegate said. "But the Republic *does* need its miners—miners who can show their *strength*. The timid, the overly cautious—they do not garner respect from their foes, political or otherwise."

"We are not *timid*," Rune said, straightening. "We are proud. We know the value of the work we do in the Republic."

"I have no doubt. But how do you demonstrate it?"

Thinking that over, Rune said, "We armed some of our mining mechs and crawlers. All that invited was violence."

"Perhaps because you were not armed *enough*. The Bronze Guild hasn't engaged in open warfare with the Republic... because it doesn't *need* to."

There. The seed was planted.

Rune pondered that for a few moments—or at least that was what Koff hoped. The man was crude, rough around the edges. Searching for the right words.

Eventually Rune said, "What could we do?"

Koff smiled. "It seems you have already taken the first steps in the right direction, arming your mining mechs. Your drilling and blasting rigs are practically tanks as it is. With the right implements and equipment, you could expand that program. Perhaps a few military advisors could offer training and suggestions on how to best deploy such forces, should the need arise."

That brought more silent thought from the guildmaster. "No one could fault us for arming ourselves," he said finally. "It should be clear we're not raising an army to fight the Republic. We're not the MCR. All my people want is to enjoy the freedoms that we've had for generations. The guilds have always had a place in the Republic Constitution."

"I agree," said Koff. "Having the means to protect yourself—a formidable force—is simply a way to deter anyone from taking advantage. It doesn't mean you invite conflict. Quite the opposite."

"Exactly. We don't want conflict."

"No sane leader does, Guildmaster. You are a wise man to seek protection for your people. We live in dangerous times. Of course, discretion is important. If word were to get out that you were looking to purchase arms, the intelligence community might interpret that as an indicator that Vargas is preparing to join the MCR."

"I don't understand. You encourage us to defend ourselves, but warn against purchasing the arms necessary to do so?"

Koff raised a calming hand. "It is the nature of our present reality. Both things can be true. Understanding that, I brought with me some items that might be of interest. It is listed as "mining equipment" on the transport bills of lading, but it is military gear and munitions... enough to get you started. We could arrange an equitable trade, something that has little paper trail... perhaps an exchange of some of your metals for the gear? I'm sure you will agree, neither of us wants to have our name tied to such an arming effort."

Rune gave Koff a speculative look. "You would be willing to do such a trade?"

He knows my position. He's wondering if I am traitor to the Republic.

"I would. My heart belongs to the Republic, which means protecting it from itself. The assault on the guilds cannot be allowed to succeed; if this government uses brute force to get its way, well, I don't need Article Nineteen to be declared before I know where I stand. Vargas is not in my galactic district, but as a member of the Republic government, the safety of *all* its citizens is ultimately my responsibility."

Rune nodded. "I thank you. The House of Reason could use more men like you."

Koff bowed his head humbly. "I merely wish to support the initiative you already show for your people, Guildmaster. We both hope you will never need to take up arms. But as a wise leader, you are taking precautions. The only tricky part is knowing when to respond with force."

"Yes." Rune mulled over his words. From what Koff could see, the guildmaster was eating out of his hand. To outside observers, everything that happened next would look as though Rune were the sole guiding force behind it.

"I was born on this planet," Rune said. "I've never left it. My knowledge of the depth of the Republic is limited. Let me ask you: how does one know when one is about to be oppressed? At what point should I see the warning signs of trouble?"

"Oh, many things could be an indication. For instance, the Republic has never had more than a company of troops stationed here, yes?"

Rune nodded. "Enough to help fight off pirates or other raiders, yes."

"Well... if you see a sudden influx of forces arrive, that would be your first clue. It could come under many auspices—likely something that looks benign on the surface. But you will know what is truly happening." Koff hesitated, then added, "Another sign would be the arrival of any Legion or armored units. Should *those* kinds of forces arrive... well, you can consider that as clear an indicator of impending violence as you are ever likely to find."

"The Legion?" Rune said. "What business would *they* have here?"

Koff leaned back in his seat, suppressing the urge to smile. "What business indeed?"

13

Sheryl O'Keefe had set up a temporary desk in the lab where Warrant Officer Weaver had been working on the battered log buoy. It had been weeks since they had secured it, and the process of getting at the data was proving painfully slow. The issue was not so much being able to get to the data, but extracting it. Weaver had wisely called for help, and a corporal with experience in navy protocols had come in to provide a consult. Even with the help, they hadn't been able to extract everything at once, but were only able to pull the encrypted pieces bit by bit— all while stabilizing the power feeds to the buoy to make sure the data didn't degrade any further.

As each bit of data came through, Weaver ran algorithms that unencrypted the data and reassembled it. He then passed on a completed file—a small one—to O'Keefe for analysis. Each day, another record or two was pulled from the device. Each one was both exciting and disappointing. Exciting because it was the log of the *Sheffield*, that much was clear. Disappointing because most of what O'Keefe read was either too fragmentary to be of use, or was complete but worthless. Bits and pieces of crew evaluations. A maintenance report on the ship's starboard laser battery. An older flight plan, not one related to the period of time when the ship went missing.

As Weaver dropped off the pad with his latest extracts, O'Keefe surveyed the contents. There was a partial ship's status, with fragments of sentences indicating that the ship was well—dated just shy of a month before the *Sheffield* disappeared. O'Keefe filed it and logged it on the timeline she was maintaining.

The next file that came up seized her attention:

SECU#@|TY LEVE[CRIMS@?
TO: TF: TRU^^*[
COL. *&$$ CASON, C*, 552nd BATT. LEG**+#
S-&&&*GE BASE L*C^TED ON VARGA! @ 371.*^=78.49
DEPLOY AND ELIMINA)(# ENE*Y FO#CES THERE
GOOD LU][K AND G??DSPE///
GEN~'\\L UTHERSO,*/, COMMAND#}}[

O'Keefe's heart pounded in her chest. The timestamp was incomplete, but it appeared to be in the window she was looking for. More importantly, this was the first message she'd seen that referenced the 552nd.

A voice came to her, loud and crisp in her ears. "Do you see the Frix a-comin'?"

She closed her eyes at the sound. It was Murdaugh from her former unit. The twang in his accent was crystal clear. She didn't see him, but his voice called out as if he were only a short distance away.

Had she forgotten to take her meds? No... she *had* taken them.

Right?

"Not now, damn it," she growled at the memory that was trying to surge to the forefront of her mind. She held her eyes closed, hoping that when she opened them, she would not see her former comrade.

"What was that, Corporal?" Weaver said.

O'Keefe pried her eyes open and felt relief upon finding that this time the memory surge was no more than a voice. Still, her hand drifted down to her pants pocket, where she kept her medication—just in case she needed it.

"Nothing, Mr. Weaver. This last file—are you able to clean it up anymore?" she asked.

"What you have is my best effort. And it's looking like that may be the last recoverable record. I'll keep trying, but the rest of what's in the log files appears to be pure garbage. I'm running some last-ditch routines I wrote to see if anything more can be salvaged."

"This could already be valuable," she replied.

Weaver walked over and looked at her datapad. "You serious? It's a hot mess."

"Varga..." she said, her fingers shifting to her keyboard control's gel pods. "Vargas, perhaps?" she asked as her query came up.

Weaver leaned over. "I've never heard of it. Put it up on the map."

She complied.

"Now add in where the buoy was found and the last known position of Task Force Equii."

Her fingers in the keyboard gel pods shifted, and the map put the other data points up.

"A straight line."

"It sure looks like it."

She pulled up summary data for Vargas. A mining world. Heavily cratered, ugly lava flows, rich in heavy metals, diamonds, and more. Much of the planet had not been re-mapped in centuries. The locals seemed focused on mining only in places where the heavy minerals were close to the surface. The population was abysmally small—it was basically vacant—just a few mining camps and ore-processing facilities.

Which means they could be down there. Undiscovered after all this time.

The log file said an enemy base had been located there. Why would the Savages set up a base on Vargas? The planet had no strategic significance, and it wasn't a world where they could sustain a large force for an extended period of time. There was mining, but when the Savages stopped for resources, they tended to deplete a place entirely and move on. It didn't make sense, unless the Legion found them mid-operation.

A chirping sounded from Weaver's workstation near the buoy. He went over to attend it while O'Keefe studied the scant few maps of Vargas, looking for any clue as to where the 552nd might be.

But there were no clues. It was a needle in a haystack.

She couldn't even be sure they'd made it to Vargas in the first place.

"You need to see this," Weaver said.

Shifting in her chair, O'Keefe realized she'd been staring at the maps much longer than she'd thought. She crossed the lab to where Weaver was sitting in front of his own holodisplay.

"What do you have? Did you salvage something more?"

"No. I'm afraid that came up empty. It's something else. Now that I've extracted what I can, I ran a few routines to map out the useful data. And... it's strange."

"Define strange."

"Look here," he said, pointing to a holographic cube of data. There were holes in it, gaps, squares missing out of a large tapestry of numbers and letters. "We've got the right amount of data we'd expect to find in a buoy; I checked with the navy on that. The types of data we're finding also are consistent with what we'd expect. But the gaps..." He made the cube rotate with a flick of his wrist. "You see?"

"See what? All I see is there's a lot of them."

"They're too... spaced apart. Not quite regular, but not quite... *not* regular, either."

O'Keefe sighed. "You need to translate that for me."

Weaver nodded. "Drive corruption after all this time is to be expected. It's flexware, that's going to happen. But typically that corruption starts at one part of the drive, maybe two, and spreads out from there. This, however... this corruption is all over the place, like insects burrowing through a tree. There's almost, but not quite, a pattern to it."

She stared at the rotating cube. "So this doesn't look like most recovered buoys."

"Not just buoys. This doesn't look like *any* data recovered from that era."

O'Keefe contemplated his words carefully. She wished he'd just say what he was thinking, rather than make her do it.

"So... this has been manufactured?"

Weaver shrugged. "I can't say that with certainty. What I *can* say is that this isn't consistent with anything we've seen before. That makes it suspect. Either someone crafted this information, or this drive corruption was unlike any other the navy's ever seen."

The joy O'Keefe had felt over finally getting a lead on the 552nd drained from her. "We need to go meet with Dranes," she said. "He needs to hear the full story."

Chief Dranes eyed the visual representation of the data cube that hovered over the holoprojector on his desk. At O'Keefe's urging, Weaver had kept their presentation simple and to the point. In response, Dranes said nothing for a full minute. The silence tore at O'Keefe, who wanted to say something, anything, that might break it. But experience had taught her to keep such temptations in check, especially with Dranes.

In due time, the chief finally spoke, summing up O'Keefe and Weaver's report. "So we have a lead, which we believe points us to Vargas. That lead may be from a less-than-reliable source."

"That's the short version," O'Keefe replied.

"Why falsify this?" Dranes asked.

O'Keefe shared a look with Weaver, who looked equally lost. "I'm not sure I understand," she said.

"If the data is false, and we go to Vargas, what would anyone have to gain from that?"

She appreciated that he was viewing the situation from a perspective that she hadn't considered. "I'm... not sure."

Dranes stroked his chin in thought. "I'm not questioning your work—either of you. It's just that if someone went to all this trouble, there must be a reason for it."

O'Keefe made a compact frown. "I'm unaware of anything out of the ordinary on Vargas."

"Nor am I. But given what you two have presented, I need to do some inquiries before committing to send a team in there."

"It wouldn't just be a team," O'Keefe said quickly. "The Legion will want to be there as well. You know how they are about recovering any fallen legionnaires, let alone finding a lost legion. To them, this will be a matter of honor."

"I'm well aware of that. And if we know that, maybe someone else does too. Perhaps they're even counting on it."

"To what end?"

"That's the open question. What I can do in the meantime is detail some satellite coverage on Vargas. There's a lot of that planet that hasn't been surveyed since the original colony was established there. Maybe we can spot something that will help us."

"Good idea."

"I'm glad you approve," Dranes said with a wry twist of sarcasm. "While I poke and prod at this, I want you to put together what you'll need if we decide to drop on Vargas. I want a full list of equipment, personnel, et cetera. Preplanning is going to be critical. You think you can handle that, Corporal?"

"Yes, sir."

"Good. For now, we keep this under wraps. If word of this were to get out—especially to a holonews network—it would put a lot of pressure on us to move. I prefer to tread carefully as we move forward—especially after what you two have presented here."

O'Keefe and Weaver were dismissed with a single nod. As they stepped out of Dranes's office, Weaver headed back toward his workstation, but O'Keefe paused and leaned against the wall. She closed her eyes and drew a deep breath. Dranes's question was bothering her.

Why would *someone try to lure us to Vargas?*

She couldn't come up with a single reason.

14

Sergeant Carson Metzger had always secretly believed that mech pilots had it easier than troops on the ground. After all, they didn't have to carry all their gear into battle; they rode in. They were protected by layers of armor, while infantry ran around in ablative body armor that covered vital organs and not much else. But the aches in his joints and the exhaustion he now felt every day as he left his simulator pod proved his prior beliefs wrong. Piloting a mech took a lot of energy and effort, especially to do it right.

As he stood outside of Major Meece's office, he thought back on the last few weeks. Coming into the pilot program as an experienced warrior had fast-tracked him somewhat, and many things were refreshers for him, such as combat communication protocols, but there were still plenty of times he felt like a complete rookie fresh out of boot. Piloting a mech so that you could move and shoot took a level of physical coordination that had to be wired directly into your mind and body. He was retraining muscle groups with a greater degree of precision and control than he'd ever had to before. He found himself stretched to his limits.

And despite his exhaustion, he loved it.

The simulations were far more complicated than the simple run-and-shoot he had gone on to first test if piloting a mech was for him. Urban environments were complex, and the pavement could be like skating on ice if you sprinted too fast. Metzger learned you needed to develop a sense of how big the HK-PP was in proportion to the streets and alleyways he navigated.

One instructor had told him that piloting a mech was more like flying in a starfighter squadron than he might think. Much of their nomenclature was the same. Mech fire teams were organized in squadrons, as opposed to squads. Piloting was not about solo hotdogging, it was about coordinating with the members of your squadron—working in unison.

And after weeks, he was finally becoming comfortable with his simulator cockpit—though still not as comfortable as some of the other pilots. Many spoke of an almost religious experience, the feeling that their mechs were part of their bodies. The same thing Meece had said. Metzger hadn't yet achieved that emotional connection, though he was gradually moving closer.

One thing he knew for sure about the military, though: once you felt a degree of comfort, they would up the ante. And being summoned to Major Meece's office was a pretty big hint that that was happening now.

Metzger didn't dread it; in fact, he thrived on new challenges. That was one reason he had succeeded in combat. He'd found that he craved a sense of personal one-upmanship, and training to be a mech pilot had fed that craving. But now he had to push himself further, harder.

"Enter," Meece called, and Metzger stepped inside. The major added, "Grab a seat."

Metzger complied quickly.

"I was going over your sim runs. You've scored high, in the top quadrille of your class. It has been concluded that you are ready for the next phase of your training."

"Yes, sir."

"The time has come to see how you handle a real mech, not a simulator pod. You'll be assigned to Captain Peltier starting tomorrow. He will run you through training in a real HK-PP."

"I look forward to it."

"Good. Sims are no substitute for the real thing—they provide a false sense of security. This next phase of your training will strip you of that. If you fall in a real mech, you *will* injure yourself—or worse. We're going to push you hard. The goal isn't to break you; the goal is to make you the best pilot you can be."

"I won't let you down, sir."

"I'm counting on that," Meece replied.

There was nothing new or shiny about the HK-PP he had been assigned. Its armor showed signs of past trauma, dents, buckles, and puckering—not from battle but from interacting with terrain at speed. And try as the simulator pods might, they didn't quite get the sound correct. There was a throbbing as the power plant came on, a subtle vibration that surrounded him in the cockpit—a thing you could *feel.* The sim's surround speakers didn't do it justice.

The HK-PP responded much like the pods, but with a heightened sense of resistance. Running at full speed, Metzger could feel the wind on the mech's body.

Then there were the weapons. Firing them unleashed a cacophony of noise that enveloped him in his seat. Launching missiles from the shoulder mounts made a rushing and roaring that was both exciting and dangerous. They were a reminder of the raw firepower at his fingertips. The blasters, when they discharged, seemed to resonate inside the cockpit—another thing he hadn't heard in the simulator pods.

On one of his first runs on a city street, his HK-PP lost its footing while rounding a corner too fast. It fell, sprawling on the street, furrowing up the blacktop on impact and throwing him hard in his safety harness. The straps dug into his flight suit; his ribs ached to where he wondered if he had broken them. He hit the button for auto-standing, and the computer that controlled balance and movement took over, running one of the routines to stand the mech, which proved almost as painful as the fall itself as his body weight dug into the straps.

Over time Metzger got to know not only his mech, but the other candidates. He was one of the oldest pilot candidates in his class, and at first they had kidded him about that, some calling him Gramps, thinking he was out of earshot. It was mostly the small group of kids recruited out of boot that made such comments. When they saw him in the showers after class, his 444th Division tattoo and the scars on his body worn like battle ribbons on a uniform, the kidding ended, or at least was done behind his back. No one dared ask him about his bionic leg, though he wasn't entirely sure they could see the seam as he washed up.

Two of the class, Tramel and Krock, were fresh lieutenants, young, still wet behind their ears as far as Metzger was concerned. He doubted that either had ever been in battle before, but there had to be some reason the colonel had recruited them. But the vast majority of the class was combat veterans. Captain Stan, call sign Razorwire, had even been a legionnaire, though not for long. On his first combat mission, his spine had been shattered in three places, and like Metzger, he'd lost his place in his unit. Stan hadn't even attempted to achieve the grueling Legion standards after that.

"I knew I didn't have it anymore," he told Metzger one evening after the showers. "My body was telling me, 'That's it, Leej. That's all you've got to give.'"

Rothchild was a warrant officer with a rare genetic disorder that had prohibited his use of the regen process. His loss of a hand from enemy fire required a bionic replacement too. Lieutenant Stamper didn't talk about why he was no longer in his original infantry division. He just used the line, "I came here so I can stay on the battlefield."

There was also a short, stocky marine transfer named Lieutenant Buck Nelson, who wore a perpetual scowl on his face. Metzger was one of the few people who seemed to be able to connect with Buck, though he had no idea why. He was an angry little man and did nothing to hide it.

There was an unspoken sense of competition between the pilots. It was something that the officers in the 72nd did not acknowledge or discourage, which meant they approved of it. Competing against each other was something the pilots got drawn into; it was unavoidable. When the weekly pilot rankings were posted, it brought about curses and grins. Metzger started in the middle of the pack, but slowly, methodically, crept his way into the top tier. When he topped Captain Stan, the officer stomped away from the ranking screen, his face crimson with anger.

Training was twelve hours a day, between classwork and piloting, and Metzger got approval from Captain Peltier to take an HK-PP out after classes, just to increase his skills and comfort. The work was grueling, but he loved being in a real cockpit, piloting a real HK-PP. The blasters were powered to nonlethal levels, but they could still do damage, and though the missile warheads were dummy rounds, they exploded all the same.

Teamwork was the core of being an excellent pilot. Mechs could take ground fast, but infantry support was critical to success; infantry kept mechs upright and pilots alive. They harassed enemy armor, engaged embedded troops, and brought plenty of smoke and other electronic counter-measures to keep the battlefield targets that were HK-PPs and tanks in the fight. It was a dangerous assignment for the grunts, though: one misstep and an errant footpad could grind infantry into paste.

Having been on the ground himself for most of his career, Metzger understood those risks. He emerged as a leader among the students, not because of his scores, but his ability to work with the other pilot candidates. Good lieutenants learn to trust a capable sergeant like Metzger, and this class was full of good lieutenants. Their movements became almost an orchestrated dance on the battlefield, a lightning-fast ballet of death and destruction that was also an ever-changing mathematical calculation of fields of fire, weapons ranges, speed, and firepower. Metzger understood the complex calculus of combat and threw himself into the equations with every bit of his experience and skill.

There were failures in the training cadre. One pilot, Cassie Rau, struggled with the transition to a real mech. In a simulator, she had been outstanding. In a mech, she was reckless to the point of being a danger. She collided with buildings and even fell over onto a tank. It was to no one's surprise that she washed out after that incident. Another pilot, Rin Eckhard, proved far too timid in piloting his RTCM. Try as he might, he couldn't get the feel for it. He kept treating the mech as if were no different from the simulator, not understanding the energy that a mech built up when moving, how the center of gravity shifted, and how that could impact firing solutions. One day Rin simply didn't show up for class. No one asked about his fate; they didn't have to. There was no room for those who didn't make the cut. Rin and Cassie served as a reminder of how dangerous their training could be and how high the standards were.

The last few weeks of training were about learning to fight as a unit. Mechs were deployed in companies called squadrons on the TO&E charts, each comprising three heavy platoons. The HK-PP variety was four mechs to a platoon, organized into two sections of two mechs each, with a pair of combat sleds to carry supporting infantry. Same setup for tanks, except their command section rode in combat sleds. A scout platoon would consist of a mix of repulsor tanks and HK-SW mechs. Then there was your typical headquarters platoon, maintenance section, and two-mech mortar platoon. It was all orchestrated with fine precision, with little room for individual heroics. Metzger understood this thinking. It was akin to what he had learned in the R-A. No one individual was an army; the unit worked together, as a whole.

One day after weeks of hard training, Peltier walked in and stood before the students. "I would like to congratulate you all for reaching this point. We have trained you in all the techniques that are in the books, and those of you who remain have the skills to be pilots.

"What now remains is something of a graduation exercise. You'll be going up against seasoned pilots from the 72nd, some of the best of the best. This will be a culmination of everything you have learned up to this point. Other officers of the unit will evaluate you, acting as referees. I will be on hand and at your assistance, but I won't be leading you men. That wouldn't be fair to the other vets."

He paused for the chuckles to pass through the nearly graduated class.

"You will need to select a commander for your student squadron. Beyond that, you will be augmented by a squad of infantry and a fire team of MBTs. After that, you'll be assigned to your individual roles inside the 72nd."

Metzger had been in such tests before. He knew the chances of success against skilled and experienced opposition were not great. Tests like these weren't about achieving victory as much as demonstrating that he was worthy of being included in their ranks.

Studying them all, Peltier said, "The evaluation will be tomorrow afternoon. For now, you need to select who will lead your squadron."

Metzger could feel the eyes on him. Then Buck's crisp voice rang out.

"I say Sergeant Metzger. I'm fairly certain he has more combat experience than most of us."

Metzger was tempted to decline the nomination, but he never got the chance. Turning to face his fellow students, he saw them all lock their gazes with his and give a nod. All except for Tramel, who was clearly not pleased with the decision; the crimson on his face and the firmly set jaw spoke volumes. He'd come out of OCS with the attitude that he deserved command as a result. But the veterans who had been recruited for the 72nd gave Metzger an expression that only a brother in battle could project.

Captain Peltier nodded. "Within the hour, you will get the details of your mission parameters. I will also inform your adjoining force commanders to meet with you. Plan carefully, Sergeant Metzger. I would hate to fail an entire training class for a bad showing."

The captain smirked with the last quip he made. While it sounded as if he was joking, Metzger wasn't going to take the chance.

The holomap display was impressive and the ground was challenging. Cutting through the middle of the map was a creek that opened to a large pond to the north and a swamp to the south. Flanking the bodies of water were hills on both sides, most covered with scrub trees and brush, though the candidates' side had more hills, and the opposing side had more densely forested areas. At the far ends of each map were the objectives, marked in pulsating crimson on the display.

"Sergeant Metzger," Captain Peltier said. "What are your thoughts?"

Metzger knew that his analysis was part of the evaluation. This was one of the most important parts of any battle: the planning. Being able to adapt to a changing situation was critical as well, but preparing for a fight often determined who would win and who would lose. As he stood at his team's side of the battlefield, he studied the map before responding. He could feel the eyes of the training squadron boring in on him as he squinted at the layout, evaluating every angle.

"Will either side have active intel at the start of the fight?" he asked.

"Negative. We will be able to launch drones once the exercise starts."

Good. That means we can deploy unseen at the beginning.

Reaching one hand over the holodisplay, Metzger clenched his fist and twisted his wrist, rotating the map so that he could look at it from the opposing perspective.

"If I were the enemy commander, I would presume our mechs would come in over the creek between the pond and the swamp. That is the best possible ground for HK-PPs. I would further assume that the armor will come in over the pond... possibly through the swamp."

"Go on," Peltier said.

With a twist of his wrist again, Metzger rotated the display back to its starting position. He reached out again and pulled the intel that was made available on the pond and the swamp—checking depths. Mechs could operate in vacuums or underwater, for at least short periods of time, but the pond was problematic given its depth.

This is a test of risks. If I do what's expected, the enemy will be prepared for that.

"I propose we deploy most of the squadron in those trees along the edge of the swamp," he said. Pinching two fingers, he grabbed the holoimages for the relevant sections and placed them in the trees. The tiny glowing yellow mechs were out of the line of sight for the enemy. "All but our tank platoon, which will deploy in the hills overlooking the creek—right where the enemy thinks we'll come. Sensor suites and counter-drones should jam well enough that they can't get an exact fix on our position, but we'll need to create the illusion that we're all there, moving behind the hills, stirring up dust and such. If I were the enemy, I would assume we're holding the mechs for a highly mobile reserve."

"You intend to take a mech force into the swamp?" Peltier asked.

Metzger nodded. "I do."

"You'll be sacrificing speed and running the risk of getting bogged down there. If you get caught in the middle of that, your force will be easy targets."

"Yes. It's also the last thing the enemy will anticipate us doing, for those very reasons. We won't win by being predictable. Not against this group. The swamp has some unknowns, and it will slow us down, but once we emerge, we can move along the flank of the exercise area while the tankers and infantry reveal themselves as the advance element that goes up the middle. They will assume our mechs are in the rear and will have to react accordingly—they can't ignore what will appear to be a full attack force coming over the creek—which leaves us able to execute a wide arc on the objective and hit their flank before they can do anything about it." Metzger traced the route on the holodisplay, leaving a glowing amber dotted line with his finger.

"This depends on us taking down their observation bots before they can see what we're doing," Peltier commented.

Metzger nodded. "Our drones are going to need to be defensive-minded. We can't let them get eyes on the battlespace. If they do, they'll catch us with our pants down."

"Using our observation bots in that manner means we won't have a view of their deployment," the captain said.

"True. We'll both be operating blind. It will provide intelligence parity."

Tramel spoke up from the far end of the display. "Are you sure about this? Getting bogged down in that swamp means we're sitting poraks." He was still chafing over not being chosen. Tramel was a talker, often boasting about what he would do in battle. Metzger had learned a long time ago that the troops who talked the most, the braggarts, were the first to crumble or fall.

Words are cheap—all that matters in the real world is what you can do, not what you brag about.

"No," Metzger said bluntly. "I'm not sure. I've been in a lot of battles over the years. You can never be sure of anything. Fate deals the cards, and in my experience, she cheats. Once the shooting starts, we need to be prepared to adapt to the changing situation. If we do get across that swamp though, it should upset their plans."

Peltier crossed his arms and looked squarely into Metzger's eyes. "You're not taking any support with you? It all stays with the tankers in Third Platoon?"

"Some. The infantry who can use the handholds on the mechs will come with us. Not more than a squad. We need enough of them on the ground for a convincing thrust in the center. Keeping the opposing force focused on that is important."

Peltier nodded. "It's a dangerous choice."

"They all are, sir," Metzger replied.

The swamp was deep, sinking Metzger's HK-PP down to where the ugly, brackish water splashed up against his cockpit canopy as he waded in. The mech's legs struggled with the mud, the nano-hydraulics whining in protest as they fought to lift the big limbs for each step forward. Light rain only added to the misery of the effort—but he tuned that out. He'd learned a long time ago that complaining about the weather did nothing to change it.

The graduation test was only fifteen minutes underway, and already the swamp was slowing his mech platoons far more than he had expected.

His HK-PP stepped forward, and the footpad must have come down on a submerged tree; his mech rocked hard, teetering close to the point where it might fall over. While the auto-standing routine worked well on dry land, Metzger had zero insight as to how it might work in muck and mire. Something told him he didn't want to find out.

There were several handholds on the rear torso of the HK-PP, where infantry could get a ride. In the rain, wading through the murky mud-churned waters, he almost felt sorry for the squad of soldiers that had come along with his force. But they could get to areas that the HK-PPs couldn't. It was best to have at least some infantry with any mech platoon.

"I'm stuck," Vickerson called out to the right.

Glancing over his shoulder, Metzger saw Vickerson's HK-PP listing heavily to one side.

"Keep moving forward," he coached as his own mech managed to find its footing after the rickety log.

"If I do, I'll fall over."

"Do it. If you fall, we'll help you up."

It was clear that Vickerson had stopped in place and had tried to backstep, which was probably what had gotten her stuck in the first place. But at Metzger's prodding, she started to advance. The HK-PP churned in the muddy water for a minute, looking almost like there were Madden gators swarming around it in some feeding frenzy. It lurched forward hard, sinking deep for a moment, then rose again, coated with mud and dead leaves. Now the rain would be a blessing; it would at least clean off the debris.

"Got it," Vickerson muttered over the squadron's tactical channel.

Captain Peltier's voice came on. "Be advised, the enemy is making a primary thrust down the middle."

"Copy," Metzger said. Their opponents were making the first move before his tank platoon had the chance to show themselves and begin the ruse. He switched channels to that force. "Third Platoon, you have company coming. Hit them from a distance and then execute a series of retrograde actions until we're out. Then counter up the middle and we'll hit 'em on the side."

"Roger that," came the voice of Staff Sergeant Stupp, one of the tank commanders.

Stupp's voice sounded constrained, and was followed by the boom of his heavy blaster cannon. "We have better terrain at our disposal for now, but they're closing. We won't be able to hold them forever."

"Copy that—you won't have to. Good luck."

Before he could even get his head wrapped around the developing battle, another voice came over the comm. "I'm down!" shouted Lieutenant Krock. His tone was annoyed.

"Who's got eyes on Krock?" Metzger asked, checking his tactical display.

Tramel spoke up. "He's right next to me."

"Cesar, can you stand?" Metzger asked, angling his own mech toward Krock's position.

"Negative," he said. "I have zero visual. Scopes say I'm on my side."

"Tramel, I'll move to your position, and you and I will get him up. The rest of you, proceed to waypoint Berlin."

Trudging through the swamp, Metzger knocked over a tree with his right-side blaster as he passed it. He reached Tramel, his mech waist-deep. The waters beside him stirred violently. Krock's supporting infantry had jumped off and were clinging to a semi-toppled tree that jutted out of the murk nearby.

Metzger signaled Krock to check his status. "Still can't stand?"

"I can't get my legs under me."

"Are you at stable zero?"

"Negative."

"Go manual and get to stable one."

The muddy waters churned as he struggled just beneath the surface. "All right, I'm at stable one."

"Good. Hit your external lights so we can see exactly where you are."

The lights went on under the swirling waters, lighting up a small area of the swamp with a greenish-brown haze.

"Tramel, get on his side. We're going to bend, slide our blasters under his, and rise up at once. Krock, you're going to hit your auto-stand once we get you high enough that your legs can reposition. Then the three of us are going to walk forward."

"Lifting him could bog us down too," Tramel cautioned.

He needs to accept my decision. "We're not going to leave him here. We'll be fine—we just need to move forward as soon as he's up." It was a calculus on his part, an educated guess.

Bending at his knees, Metzger sidestepped, dipping his right blaster down under Krock's mech. He heard the metallic scraping sound of contact as he did so. Glancing out the starboard cockpit window, he saw Tramel semi-squatted down like he was.

"All set," Tramel signaled.

"On three, we stand and move. One, two, *three!*"

His HK-PP struggled with the lift; no doubt the muck was doing what it could to suck Krock down. He heard the high-pitched whine of strain and more metallic scraping. It felt as if Krock's mech wasn't moving at all, but then suddenly it broke free and began to rise.

He felt the change the moment the mech's feet were under it. Krock's infantry support clambered back aboard, and Metzger ordered the trio of mechs forward once more.

They continued side by side to the far edge of the swamp, where they joined the rest of their force, all of them wet, with streaks of muck pooling at their feet.

"All right, Second Squad, this is where you get off," Metzger said. "Take a position in the copse of trees at the top of the ridge, give us a clear image of what we're up against, and provide cover fire. Your mission is to ensure containment—prevent the enemy from re-crossing the creek and reinforcing their rear. I want plunging fire from you on any viable targets. If you are engaged, deploy your chaff, and redeploy."

The chaff was a powerful aerosol that not only obscured line of sight, but was treated with a special airborne prismatic element that diffused incoming blaster bolts and confounded targeting AIs. It wouldn't be much against the big blasters that the mechs carried, but it could reduce the punch of the smaller arms.

The infantry squad leader, Staff Sergeant Walton, acknowledged the orders, and his people scampered down from the backs of the mechs.

The voice of Captain Peltier came over the comm. "Sergeant Metzger, be advised the enemy is hitting us in the center hard. We have suppressed their drones, but there are still five of their mechs unaccounted for."

"Copy. We are free and moving to flank," Metzger replied, charging his HK-PP forward. "Extended wings formation," he commanded over the tactical channel, and his team's mechs spread out in an inverted arc, with Metzger in the center.

He could hear the sounds of battle as they moved around the hillside. The explosions of missiles and the whine-bark of the heavy blasters were distinct.

"Be advised," came the cool voice of Walton, "we are in position and providing an updated tactical feed." Metzger's tactical display refreshed with an added level of clarity; the infantry were already identifying not only the objective, but the enemy positions.

He targeted where the enemy base was to be located, rushing along the far flank of the designated battle zone. Running up a low rise, he saw it—along with five enemy mechs broken into two groups: a rapid response force. The rise had masked his mech's sensors, but now his tactical display lit up with possible targets. A sweep formation—one he knew well from his training.

His jaw set as he gave the command. "Engage the enemy. Target the HK-PPs, then the RTCM."

The Roaring Thunder Crater Maker could engage directly, but it was designated mostly as an indirect-fire highly mobile artillery piece. The enemy RTCM was currently fulfilling that role by firing down toward the creek, at least three kilometers away. Its simulated MB (Mummy-Bee) rounds arced high in the air before landing and bursting into a cloud of microdrone explosives that individually targeted or hovered to deny the ground to anyone daring to rush through it.

Metzger sprinted, shifting right and left to make target lock trickier for the enemy. Moving his mech was starting to feel more natural, but there was still the feeling he was fighting against the machine around him. It was reminiscent of his initial struggles with his bionic leg.

The opposing mechs wheeled about and ran off to his right, not realizing they would collide with the part of his force that was still hidden below the low ridge.

Metzger's hand guided the targeting reticle on the second-closest mech and unleashed a full rack of his missiles. The guided munitions roared from the left shoulder box the moment his ring finger hit the trigger, and their launch made the mech tug from the exhaust. It was tempting to follow their flight with his eyes, but he was already aligning his blasters for another shot. He could hear the reloader assembly clicking as a new set of munitions loaded. He could fire once more, then that would be it for his left side.

The dummy rounds exploded with loud cracking booms, though one overshot and tore into the forest in the distance. The enemy HK-PP reeled from the explosions, but managed to unleash a low-power blast from its Mark 14 heavy blasters. A damage indicator flashed amber on Metzger's left leg, and the computer system rocked the mech to simulate at least one of the blasts hitting him. His eyes darted to the display, and he saw that the blast hadn't touched anything vital.

Let's dance...

The enemy moved rapidly, perpendicular to his advance. Rushing straight at your enemy made you an easier target to hit, and the opposition understood that probably better than he did. Leveling his run for a few meters, Metzger locked on and fired his blasters in response, then juked hard to the right. The bolts of energy stabbed higher than his foe's had, hitting the upper body of the HK-PP, near the cockpit. The pilot turned hard and changed its run, trying to put some distance between Metzger and himself.

A blast went off, louder than normal fire. It had to be that RTCM. A moment later, an enormous explosion of white powder smeared all over Krock's mech.

"Damn!" cursed Krock. "I've lost a leg."

"Tramel, move to cover Krock. Vickerson, pursue my target tagged Bravo. I am shifting target to Gamma."

Using the targeting joystick, Metzger changed his angle and shifted to a new target. With his left hand, he reassigned the missile trigger to unleash both of his racks. The enemy pilot seemed to sense what was coming. He changed direction and made a tight loop away, his blasters firing a burst of amber energy toward Captain Stan, tearing into his flank with simulated damage.

To the untrained eye, the tactical display looked like chaos, but what Metzger saw at a glance was that both sides were moving like combat sleds.

"Buck," he sent over comm, "I need you on my left side as my wing."

All that Metzger needed to know about Buck was that he could rely on the former marine to do what he was told. Buck's HK-PP was configured as a B-model, with no shoulder-mounted missile launchers. Instead he mounted heavy Mark 16 blasters for arms. Buck assumed position as his wingman and together they rushed along the western edge of the combat zone.

One enemy, tagged as Epsilon, altered its path to make a counter sweep, heading right into Metzger's path. The olive-green HK-PP discharged a wave of micro-missiles from both racks—five at Metzger, five at Buck. Metzger's incoming missile alert beeped, and he braced himself. Four of the warheads exploded on the upper body of his mech, and the white powder used to mark damage splattered all over the right side of his cockpit canopy.

"He's coming right at us," Buck remarked in his deep voice. Buck's mech had been struck by all five of the missiles that had targeted him. Metzger had to admit he was impressed with Epsilon's pilot; a split shot was no small feat at a full run. Had he done the same with the full-size variety, Metzger and Buck would both be dead.

"On my signal, you juke right, I juke left," Metzger said. "We blast him as we pass." The maneuver would have them crisscross each other behind the enemy, lining up another devastating shot.

"You mean weave him into the shot?" Buck asked.

"That's the plan."

"Copy that."

Three long seconds passed, and Metzger barked out, "Now!"

There was no jabbing at the foot pedals; he applied controlled pressure. Buck crossed in front of him, no more than eight meters away. Metzger turned sharply, feeling himself tossed hard to the right side of the command seat, the safety harness digging into his shoulder. He charged his blasters, their capacitors humming on both sides of him.

The infantry called out over the comms channel as he fought to make the turn. "Be advised, the enemy RTCM has slung his tube and is bugging out. Chances are he thinks you're heading for him. We're painting him now and sending an AP missile his way to keep him moving."

That was some good news. At least for a few moments, he wouldn't have to worry about an artillery strike. Metzger allowed his entire universe to become Epsilon, his sole focus. It would all be over once Epsilon crossed into Buck's field of fire.

Then the enemy HK-PP surprised him, wheeling sharply right before he was about to pass. It was the kind of maneuver that could have toppled the mech, but Epsilon somehow kept control.

The sudden turn made Buck's shot impossible. "Lost the angle," Buck spat. "Giving myself some distance to reacquire."

Damn it all! Metzger swung hard, twisting his waist to keep the enemy locked on with his targeting reticle. But he knew he was going to lose his target lock any second, and he took the shot.

One blaster missed by less than a meter. The second flashed bright amber, right into the side of the cockpit.

"Buck, on me. Stan, you make a break for the objective."

Metzger swung about in the tightest turn he dared make in a running mech. His warning system beeped, but with not nearly enough time for him to react. A pair of missiles slammed into his left leg, making his damage indicator flicker amber, then crimson. His HK-PP shuddered and the leg became much less responsive. He could still move, but his speed dropped significantly, and he had to make adjustments to deal with the damage.

As he wheeled about, Epsilon swung around for another head-on pass. Metzger moved laterally, crossing in front of the opposing mech as it fired at him. One shot hit his good leg, searing simulated armor; the other missed. His own blasters were already charging, his fingers working just a millisecond before his mind. Checking his tactical display, he saw Stan was closing on the objective. *Move faster...*

The tactical display gave him the story. Buck was far out, arcing around to join back up with him, but he was out of effective range—not of the weapons, but of their current ability to use them amid the terrain. Krock was down, as was Vickerson. An equal number of the opposing forces were down, but this was a game where the odds were against him. The enemy not only had more experience in mechs, they'd worked together far more than his team had.

Metzger's mind went to the objective. To win, he had to protect Captain Stan. And if Epsilon got past Metzger's mech, he'd have a straight shot, with nothing between him and Stan.

Epsilon bore down on Metzger despite the cross-cutting move. Metzger's feet adjusted his path as he fired his blasters. One shot savaged Epsilon's left missile rack, the other missed. Adjusting his course, Metzger rushed forward as if he were going to make a fast pass beyond Epsilon. Twisting his waist, he struggled to keep steady aim at the charging mech.

Timing... it's all about timing.

His brain calculated the speed of both mechs, factoring in the slowing effects of his simulated damage. Epsilon was now rushing past, the stomping of its footpads on the ground thunderous even in the safety of the HK-PP's cockpit.

At the last moment, Metzger juked directly into the path of the enemy mech.

The collision was violent, crunching, with metal moaning in protest as both mechs collided, twisted, and fell. Metzger's HK-PP landed across the back of Epsilon's legs. His body ached from the jarring impact, his neck throbbed, and he felt the safety harness cut into him as he was tossed in the fall. His damage indicator screamed at him in yellows and bright scarlet warnings—not simulated, but for real. Epsilon tried to stand, but with Metzger lying on his legs, it was impossible.

A referee came over the comms. "An objective has been secured. All units, stand down."

Looking past the crimson damage indicators that flickered and demanded his attention, Metzger saw on the tactical display that Captain Stan had reached the enemy base.

We won!

He switched to the open broad channel on the comms system. "Epsilon, are you all right?"

The angry voice of Major Meece came back in a growl. "Metzger, your ass is mine for that stunt!"

15

O'Keefe stared at the holographic display. There were a lot of desolate worlds in the Republic, but few were like Vargas. It had essentially been segregated into two distinct parts by the locals: the craters, which were mined by humans, and the surface, or what the humans called the "uplands," which was the domain of the K'llik—a species O'Keefe had never encountered before.

Most of the planet's plant life survived deep inside the massive craters that pockmarked the planet. In fact some of the larger craters had smaller craters inside them, furrowing deep into Vargas's crust. But the uplands were barren, the air thin, the flora sparse. A number of volcanos, some still active, had left ugly flows, rivers of blackness, stretching for dozens of kilometers from their sources. It was these areas that the K'llik mined, to recover what Vargas sought to discharge.

According to O'Keefe's research, the K'llik cities were mostly deep under the surface. They had a strong dislike for off-worlders, and they only grudgingly tolerated the presence of humans on Vargas, and the existence of the Republic altogether for that matter. They had sided with the enemy during the Savage Wars, though perhaps they had been forced to do so. In short, they were best avoided if possible.

Which was fine by O'Keefe; her interest was in the craters. If the lost legion had been on Vargas, the evidence would be hidden here. She was determined to look at the data in each one of them with her own eyes, not fully trusting any algorithm to check for her.

Unfortunately, there were thousands of craters, and just getting the data had taken weeks; some was still trickling in even now. The planet had been surveyed when it was first settled, but after that, there had been no need to do more; the initial sensor sweeps had identified the heavy metal deposits, and from there the mining operations had begun. No one cared about empty craters filled with worthless tailings or long-abandoned equipment. So Dranes had had to engage their colonel in the matter of using some of the few satellites in the system for a new mapping effort.

Colonel Adrian Hughes was a grandfatherly-looking man, complete with the slight paunch and the white mustache necessary to play that role. He had listened intently, taken notes, asked decent questions, and from what O'Keefe had seen, taken action. Most importantly, he hadn't interfered with her research.

The local mining guild had been up in arms about the entire affair. Local news reports from Vargas claimed that the Republic was using the satellites to spy on the miners, that this was "prelude" to a larger Republic interference on the planet. O'Keefe was glad that Dranes and Hughes were the ones who had to deal with the planet's guildmaster on the subject. Politics had never been her forte.

Not that her job at the moment was much easier. *Tedious* was the word she would have used. She had gained an appreciation for how large a planet could be—and how many potential hiding places it contained. Every now and then she had been excited by some observation, but each time a closer look indicated that what she was looking at was just garbage left by miners. It seemed the populated craters often used the spent ones as their dumping grounds for waste, both personal and industrial. She'd seen convoys of waste haulers trundling across the uplands like a snake, moving to unload their worthless contents.

Leaning back in her seat, she closed her eyes and sighed. It still bothered her that the information from the buoy might have been planted, manufactured for her to find. But what really bothered her was her inability to understand why. Was someone toying with them? What could anyone stand to gain by leading them to Vargas? Surely it hadn't been the man who discovered the satellite —Weaver was adamant in his belief that such work was beyond him. Not to mention that it would cost more in slicers to manufacture the info than was paid for the relic buoy.

"O'Keefe."

The voice was in her mind, yet loud and clear. It was Corporal Vex again.

"You know what your problem is?"

"Stop talking," she muttered, cracking open her eyes. Through the light haze of the holographic image of Vargas, she saw him, outlined in a shimmer as if there were a bright light behind him. He stood in his full infantry body armor.

"Your problem is you push yourself too hard," he said.

"Not now, Vex."

The image didn't respond. She scowled and moved on to the next crater.

"O'Keefe, you know what your problem is? Your problem is that you push yourself too hard," the memory fragment repeated.

She checked the time; it would be another hour before she was scheduled to take her meds. For now, she would simply have to ignore Vex. She noted the timing in her datapad, something the doctor had asked her to do, then went back to work.

Focusing once more on her holodisplay, she studied the next crater in her grid search, crater number 107.9. Immediately she saw something of potential interest—a shadow with a defined edge, straight. This wasn't just some piece of rock. The thin upper atmosphere blurred the image, as usual; the wisps of clouds hung low and made observation difficult. O'Keefe pivoted the image and zoomed in on the object that was casting the shadow. It was oblong, somewhat boxy. To her eyes, it looked like an older-model shuttle.

But what would a dropship be doing out there in the middle of nowhere?

As she zoomed in, she saw other images, smaller shadows, and marks in the soil, like old vehicle tracks. Behind the larger object was what looked like a trench. If it was a ship, it had come in for a rough landing, that much was obvious.

"Enhance image at F-15," she said.

The image flickered, then appeared crisper. Yes, it was a dropship—and an old one at that. Late Savage Wars era.

"Zoom in on F-15, times three."

The image flickered again, and now she could make out the lines of the vessel.

"Open window," she ordered her system, and a new pop-up window appeared. "Access files of Task Force Equii off of my work drive. Project all dropships associated with Task Force Equii. Provide summary data and project images of the class of shuttles and drop pods, please."

The *please* was a force of habit, not a necessity for the system to work.

The images of six different classes of atmospheric entry ships appeared in the window. Three she could ignore right off the bat—they were either spheroid or ovoid in shape—basic combat or resupply drop pods. The other three, Ranger, Stingray, and Warhawk-class shuttles— were similar to the ship she saw in the crater.

She flicked away the drop pods that were of no use to her. "Compare image at F-15 and specifications in bravo window for a possible match."

One image highlighted in blue in the space over her table, and a disembodied female voice said, "Ninety-eight percent match with Warhawk-class drop shuttle."

So it was not only a shuttle, it was of the kind that would have been with the task force. She tried to keep her excitement in check; who knew how many thousands of that class of ship were manufactured during its life cycle? She needed more, much more, if they were going to send in an expedition.

Her eyes drifted over the enhanced image of the ship. A series of black marks on the light-gray hull looked vaguely like lettering, but it was difficult to make anything out from this angle.

"Can the angle be adjusted on the details at F-15?"

The image floating above her desk shifted only slightly. It was presented as a three-dimensional image, but it could only show the details that had been captured by the satellite.

"Pause," she muttered, squinting at the new angle.

"O'Keefe, you know what your problem is? Your problem is that you push yourself too hard," Vex said anew.

Instinctively she closed her eyes, not wanting to see him. *Not now.* She waited, hoping that the ghostly memory fragment would not be there when she looked.

Cracking open her right eye, she thankfully did not see Vex. Opening her other eye, she focused on the lettering. It was faint, but from this angle she could make it out: *CLK-225-A.*

That brought a smile. A *wide* smile.

Heavy cruiser, Subjugator class, two hundred twenty-five.

The *Derfflinger.*

The Ohio-class cruiser that the 552nd had been assigned to.

A mix of enthusiasm and reverence washed over her. For decades, researchers like her had been searching for the lost legions. Thousands of leads, thousands of dead ends. Men and women had sat at her desk for their entire careers and had never gotten this close.

This was history. She almost couldn't believe it.

This might really be them.

Not long ago O'Keefe had been broken, washed out of front-line duties as a result of her head injury and relegated to what many might have seen as a minor role, a meaningless position to be shuffled off to. But she had understood that she was still serving the R-A, and doing so in an honorable capacity.

Now she stood at the precipice of solving one of the Legion's greatest mysteries.

The feeling that hit her now was redemption.

O'Keefe didn't put together a dazzling presentation of what she found. She hated soldiers who spent their time working on the glitz rather than the substance. Some of that was her natural personality, but a lot of it came from her time in the R-A. Her former CO used to say, "All I want is solid intel, sweat, and a charged blaster."

O'Keefe presented only one holo. It showed cropped images of crater 107.9 and the shuttle that it held. Those images alone told the story.

"What are those little shadows near the aft of the ship?" Colonel Hughes asked, pointing to the image that hovered over his desk. "They're laid out at regular intervals."

"We don't know," O'Keefe said. "We couldn't get a crisper image with the satellite available to us."

Hughes nodded, then turned to Dranes. "I'd say this is fairly convincing."

Dranes smiled. "I'd say it's the best lead we've ever had to find one of the lost legions."

Hughes smiled too, but held up a hand as if to say, *Slow down*. "Do we still have questions about the source?" he asked O'Keefe.

She nodded. "No change on that front, sir. We had another expert take a look at what Mr. Weaver found. That expert concurs with his conclusion that the data is peculiar."

"Yet it got us here."

"It did, sir," O'Keefe confirmed.

"So, *if* someone is playing us, why get us to Vargas? This isn't an MCR world, despite the locals' apparent desire to act like one. They have a local militia, mostly some cobbled-together mechs and tanks, but they're not exactly lining up to take on the Republic in a fight. Why lure us here?"

His questions were solid and showed his logic. Dranes answered before O'Keefe could. "We have no idea, sir."

Colonel Hughes leaned back in his seat; it squeaked in protest. "These Vargasians are a pain in the ass. It took me almost a week of arguing with their Guildmaster Rune to simply redirect a few satellites. I had to remind him on every call that they're part of the Republic. I can only imagine how this kelhorn is going to react when I tell him I want to bring in an archeological team and a Legion honor guard."

"Sir," O'Keefe said, shuffling her feet slightly as she spoke. "Recovery of military dead is protected by Republic law. They can protest all they want, but we have a right to go there."

Hughes chuckled. "You're talking laws and rights—this is about politics and emotions. It's about people's hurt egos and feelings. Quoting the legal statutes has no meaning when people equate feelings for facts. The guildmaster won't see this as a simple recovery mission; he'll make this about the sovereignty of Vargas."

Dranes nodded. "So what are our next steps, sir?"

The colonel sighed. "I will contact Guildmaster Rune and attempt to convince him that it's in the best interests of his people to let us land there unmolested and do what we need to do. He will, of course, say no. I will then engage the diplomatic and domestic affairs corps to treat with him. They will weave words, make promises, and extend concessions. The guildmaster *may* agree to those terms— but I wouldn't bet on that being successful either."

"Then what?" O'Keefe asked.

"We have a few aces up our sleeve. First, if push comes to shove, you're right, Corporal, we do have the legal authority to go to Vargas and declare the site protected under the Repatriation and War Site Act. Technically, we don't need permission from the local government to come and do our job. It's heavy-handed, but it is our legal right.

Second, once I inform Legion command that we have a viable lead on a lost legion, they'll insist on being involved. And once the Legion learns of this, they're not going to sit back idly to wait for a diplomatic solution."

"That sounds like exactly what the locals are worried about," O'Keefe said.

"This is a Repub world," Hughes countered. "Any troops will be there solely for the protection of the forces we bring down to conduct our investigation and recovery. Though I have a hard time picturing the locals coming at us militarily once we have legionnaires with us." He frowned. "Still, it doesn't hurt to be prepared. Once I inform the Legion, they may or may not want to coordinate affairs with us. Who knows with them? If they do, I want you both to serve as liaisons."

O'Keefe nodded. She had already prepared a detailed list of what a recovery team would need if they found signs of the 552nd on Vargas, but those plans had called for only light security. What Colonel Hughes was suggesting was bigger. This was no longer just planning an archeological dig; this was potentially planning a military operation.

"Sir," she said, "I suggest we'll want to have enough force to deter them from even *considering* striking us."

"That's not a bad thought. What do you have in mind?"

"During Vargas's last little uprising, they relied on mechs and homemade tanks. In addition to the Legion, if we had a HARD unit with us, it might make them think twice. Not to mention, HARD units are R-A... we will have at least *some* say over what they do. The Legion does what it wants."

"That's a good thought," Dranes said.

Hughes considered this for a moment.

O'Keefe briefly mused on just how different rank was treated in the archives as opposed to other Repub Army units. She, a corporal, was speaking freely with a colonel. Dranes, a warrant officer, was in the mix as well, and though he was technically the lead researcher and could have shut O'Keefe out of the briefing, he hadn't done so.

They were all on a team in a way that O'Keefe had never quite experienced before.

"Any unit in particular in mind?" the colonel finally asked.

The question was to Dranes, who shrugged his shoulders. "I wouldn't know, sir. Corporal, since you introduced the idea, I presume you have something in mind?"

O'Keefe masked her grin with determination. "Yes, Chief. I can think of one unit that might fit the bill."

16

"What in the Nine Hells were you thinking with that little stunt of yours?"

Metzger stood at attention under Major Meece's burning glare. He had been on the receiving end of an ass-chewing many times in his career. Sometimes for a thing he had done, sometimes for something he hadn't done, and in a handful of instances for things he hadn't even known about. But this one was deserved.

"Sir, I saw you making a move on Stan. He was almost on the objective. My intent was to force you to break off your charge." There was some truth in this. He'd just conveniently omitted the part about how he'd intended the collision to be the core part of that intent.

"Is it possible that you were unclear on the rules of the engagement, Sergeant?"

"I knew the rules, sir."

"Then why did you violate them?"

"Sir, your instruction on physical contact of mechs was, as I understood it, 'Avoid physical contact between mechs and the opposition, where practical.'"

"Then explain to me why you violated the ROE."

"All due respect, sir. I did not violate them. I merely determined that it was not practical to avoid the impact.

The impact was the only way to stop you. It was the only way to win."

"Those rules were not subject to your interpretation. They were put in place to protect the lives of personnel and the integrity of valuable equipment."

"Yes, sir. I made a decision necessary for our side to achieve victory."

"In the process, you did a hell of a lot of damage to two mechs, not to mention I cracked two ribs in the fall."

"For that, I am sorry, sir."

That comment had no note of snarkiness. He sincerely did feel bad that Major Meece had been injured.

"Sorry my ass, soldier," Meece growled. "Sorry doesn't make up for the damage you did. I have half a mind to dock your pay to compensate for the damage you caused."

"I understand, sir." Given what Metzger made, it would take him several centuries to pay that debt off.

"I had a discussion with the chief technician. He tells me that thanks to your little stunt, it's going to be a solid week before those two HK-PPs are fully operational again. He wants your head or ass on a platter, and I am half-tempted to serve them both up to him. You seem, Sergeant, not to realize that high-speed, full-on collisions are just as dangerous as using fully powered weapons."

Metzger kept silent. Perhaps he was in deeper sket than he'd first realized.

"You seemed to have quieted down a bit, Sergeant," Meece continued. "Odd for a man who seemed to know it all just a few minutes ago. We were discussing the feelings of our chief technician."

Metzger didn't doubt that the major had gotten an earful. "I will apologize to him personally, sir."

"If I were you, I'd wear armor when you do."

"Duly noted."

"And that's only the *start* of my headaches from your little sidestep into my path. I had presumed that you understood that this was a *graduation exercise*—and that you, Sergeant, were honored to be elected by your fellow students to command them. That honor now appears to have been misplaced. What kind of example did you set for them? What do you think they learned from what you did? You realize you've put all of them into the same steaming pile of sket that you're in."

There were a lot of things Metzger wanted to say just then. He wanted to tell the major that he had shown his fellow students how a lone individual can make sacrifices for the benefit of the team. He wanted to tell the major that he had demonstrated for them the value of being creative, of taking actions on an impulse that can secure victory. But while he *wanted* to say those things, he also knew a thing or two about being dressed down by a superior.

In particular, he knew the less he said, the sooner this would be over.

"My apologies, sir. I was focused on us securing a victory. I put that above the safety of others. I see now that was a mistake."

Meece leaned back in his chair, giving Metzger a long, icy stare. For a few moments, he said nothing. Then...

"It has been suggested that I recycle you, leaving you behind so that you understand the gravity of what you did. I'm tempted to go farther than that—fail this entire class and make them go through the entire training again. Considering they selected *you,* which shows an egregious lack of judgment an HK pilot cannot afford."

Metzger had suffered demotion before. He could handle that. But he hated for the others to pay the price for his snap decision. He needed to tread carefully here.

"If you think that is best, sir."

Meece held his stare, then shook his head and cracked a thin, albeit rueful smile. With one hand, he pulled his jumpsuit sleeve back. There was a tattoo there, three crossed swords on a sunburst—the symbol for the Third Division's sixth company, the Radiant Death. Metzger had a tattoo in the same place on his arm, from the 444th. Seeing that gave him a mental center, a realization that they were indeed the same. Here was an officer who had the same connections to the R-A that he did.

"I think we both know what isn't going to happen," the major said. "*They* shouldn't suffer for *your* mistake. Are we agreed, soldier?"

So the punishment will fall on me alone. Fine.

"Yes, sir."

"I'm putting you on report. The other graduates will get a three-day pass after the final ceremony. You will remain here, confined to barracks. You will also spend twenty hours a week in the tech bays working for Chief Technician Ross. You will assist his people in repairing the damage that you caused—and in trying to earn back some of his goodwill. Oba knows you're going to need it as a pilot in this unit."

Metzger wanted to ask for clarification... to validate that he was indeed graduating. But he decided he was better off simply *assuming* that he was graduating rather than risk relighting the fuse on the major's anger.

"Yes, sir."

"In the future, you will adhere not just to the letter of any ROEs, but to their intent. We want your expertise and experience, but within parameters. Piloting a mech puts a lot of firepower in the hands of a single warrior. That makes you infinitely more dangerous... more deadly. With that comes the need for safety and security, especially during training missions."

"Understood, sir."

"Good. The mark of a good pilot is to understand their mistakes and learn from them. People like to say that about featherheads, but you know by now that we expect that from our mech pilots as well. This is your learning moment. Don't let it slip by."

"I won't, sir."

"And one more thing," Meece said, rising, and wincing just a bit as he did, no doubt from his broken ribs.

"Sir?"

"When we go into action, and we will, stack 'em high..."

Metzger gave him a nod. "... and stack 'em deep. Sir, that's one thing I excel at."

The next evening, Metzger was on his way to the repair bays for his assignment when he was approached by a number of his fellow pilots. Tramel was clearly the leader of the cadre, and he was joined by Vickerson, Krock, and Buck.

Tramel moved to block his path, the others forming up behind him. "We all got our asses chewed out by Meece for your little stunt," the young lieutenant declared.

"I was unaware of that," Metzger said.

"Why did you do that ramming attack?" Krock asked. "You had to know it was going to violate the ROE."

"I did what was necessary to win. If that bothers your delicate sensibilities, I'm sorry you're so soft." The moment Metzger said the words, he regretted it.

"You're lucky we aren't the same rank, Sergeant," Tramel replied with a sneer. He balled his fists.

Not that it was necessary. Metzger knew that tone, knew that Tramel wanted a fight. It was tempting to give him the shot, too; he was certain he could take the younger man. He'd spilled blood on a half dozen worlds while this kid was still fresh off his momma's tit. Youth and speed were no match for experience.

"Look, I made a call," Metzger said instead. "In retrospect, it may have been wrong."

Tramel shook his head. "Meece came down on all of us, hard. He said he even considered making us recycle because of what you did."

Metzger nodded once. "He told me that. That's why I'm taking on punishment duty, so that all of you don't have to do that. I have to put in twenty hours a week in the mech bays doing repairs. I sacrificed my three-day pass after graduation too. Now, if you still want to try and take a shot at me," he shifted his stance, balling his own fists, bending his knees, and bracing for an attack, "I will forgo the difference in our ranks. But know this: you throw a punch at me, sir, I will *take you down.*"

His last three words were spoken slowly, deeply.

Tramel was ready for it, but Buck Nelson stepped forward, putting his hand on the lieutenant's shoulder from behind. "You don't want to do that, boy." The former marine understood all too well how the fight was going to go. "He's stepped up and is taking punishment that was never meant for us to begin with. This outfit needs pilots; they aren't recycling him, let alone all of us. Let it go."

"I would have thought a marine would *want* a fight," Tramel said with a sneer.

"Hullbusters love to fight, but we're at least smart about it. The man you're facing has lost a limb fighting for the Republic. If he's letting you take a shot at him, it's only because he knows he'll beat you. If I were you, I'd stand down and let this one pass."

Tramel relaxed, twisting his shoulders to shake loose Buck's hand. With a final glare at Metzger, he walked away.

The others followed, except for Buck, who remained behind.

"Thanks, Buck."

"You don't owe me thanks. I was just saving Tramel from being introduced to the sidewalk."

Before Metzger could answer, Buck took off after the others.

Preceding the graduation ceremony was a far less formal ritual that Metzger found himself looking forward to: the awarding of call signs. The students, and the members of the 72nd who had trained them, assembled in the officers' club for the rite of passage. Drinks flowed freely, as everyone knew that the next day they would be formally joining the 72nd as mech pilots.

Metzger went with an alcohol-free neg-beer. He wasn't about to slide now. If he did, he'd have to deal with O'Keefe.

He'd been made a warrant officer early that morning. It felt odd to no longer wear the sergeant's chevrons on his uniform.

Looking around the dingy club, he wondered why places like this had enticed him so much after he lost his leg. They were all the same: the air tinged with stale beer, the images of warriors and equipment hanging on every spare spot of open wall. The only difference with this bar was that one table had been replaced by the footpad of an HK-PP and its upright foreleg, which barely fit under the ceiling. The leg was pitted from battle—and probably a few bar fights over the years.

After a few rounds, Colonel Inglima read off the name of one of the pilots, and the man was ushered to a back room where he was unable to hear everyone else. Then the debate began as to what call sign to assign him. Call signs were usually some sort of gibe at the pilot, a subtle dig, or had a funny story associated with them. It took long minutes and cold beer to arrive at a call sign that made sense. They were deeply personal, and they would be how the pilots would be known in the unit from that point forward.

Each new pilot took his turn being ushered into the back room, and the debates were intense at times. Stamper got the call sign Hard Stop, thanks to a training run where he miscalculated his speed and slammed into a building. Wanda Vickerson got the moniker Ice Tea, indicating that she was both cool and sweet—which was almost the opposite of her personality. Second Lieutenant Cesar Krock got the call sign Salad, a play on his first name. Buck Nelson was awarded the tag Hullbuster—not every call sign had to be all that creative. Lieutenant Tramel was awarded Broadsword as his call sign, a tribute to the girth of his manhood as seen in the shower. It suited both him *and* his ego.

There was one call sign everyone saw coming well in advance. There was a trio of guys who had become a close-knit group from the very start of training: Tom Snapp, Richard Bartle, and Oscar Gillot-Cain. It was rare to see any of the three without the other two in tow. Which meant it took all of about three days before everyone started referring to them as Tom, Dick, and Harry. A lot catchier than Tom, Dick, and Oscar. There was never any doubt in anyone's mind that if Oscar survived selection, he was getting the call sign "Harry."

When Metzger's name was called, he almost cringed. It was one thing to be picking a nickname for a fellow warrior; it was another to be on the receiving end. There were jeers as he left the bar and was ushered to the back room. He could hear muffled voices in the main bar, along with laughter, which he didn't consider a good sign.

Alone in the back room, he looked at the images on the wall of pilots that had gone before him. The 72nd had been decommissioned at one point after the Savage Wars, only to be reconstituted after the Psydon War. Some of the images were practically antiquated, as evidenced by the uniforms and gear they wore. Some even had cooling suits—the old-model mechs were said to have generated a lot of heat.

He heard another laugh from the bar, and for a moment he worried they'd come up with a call sign that highlighted his bionic replacement leg. Peg Leg. Gimpy. Or worse, Grampa.

He hoped the intake of alcohol would dull his colleagues' ability to get more creative than that.

The door opened back up and WO Rothchild, call sign Thumper, stood there. "All right, Metzger, you're on deck."

He walked to the center of the bar and was surrounded by the other pilots. There were snickers and the refilling of beer mugs as he stood among his peers. Then Colonel Inglima spoke loudly, as he had for each pilot before him.

"Listen up, kelhorns. By unanimous vote, it has been decided that from this point forward, Warrant Officer Carson Metzger shall be known to his fellow pilots by the call sign *Pileup*."

A cheer rang out, and Metzger felt a blush come to his face. Unlike some others in the room, he didn't have to ask where the name had come from.

"To Pileup!" shouted Thumper. And all of them took a toast, including Tramel, who had been cold to him most of the evening.

Metzger spotted Major Meece smiling and hoisting his glass in the air, which Metzger took as an admission of responsibility. He'd been called worse things in his military career, he decided. This would do just fine.

The drinks flowed for another hour, then the group disbanded. No doubt several of the pilots would be nursing hangovers at the formal graduation ceremony in the morning. Metzger was thankful that he would not be among them.

The real ceremony, unlike the call sign ceremony, was remarkably simple. Each graduate was called up, and their wings were pinned on them. That was it.

Colonel Inglima explained the wings at the start of the ceremony. "We made these out of melted armor from mechs that fell in battle. This way, you carry with you the spirits of your brothers and sisters before you. The wings are battle-tested, as you will be. And they are placed over your heart to be your armor there—proof of your connection to the brotherhood of pilots."

Despite its simplicity, to Metzger the ritual was a moving gesture. The R-A had plenty of similar traditions too, and taking part in them was important. It imparted an esprit de corps, it passed on history, and it gave the participants something unique to themselves that they all had in common. When the wings were pinned on him, he couldn't help but glance down at them. They had weight, thanks to their composition. The wings weren't just jewelry or regalia; they were forged in the fires of battle. It was hard to not be proud wearing them.

Afterwards they returned to the bar, and a single drink was provided to each pilot: scotch, the 72nd's official drink of choice. It came with a drop of oil in each glass, a reminder of the mechanized nature of their force.

Metzger set his aside, asking instead for a ginger ale. Complete with a drop of oil, of course.

Colonel Inglima led the toast, holding his glass high in the air. "To the new pilots of the 72nd. Your class completes our re-staffing. We are operational. Tomorrow, you will all be given your squadron assignments in the unit. Then the actual work begins: getting to know your team members, their strengths, and how to coordinate with them in battle.

"Today, we take this drink as comrades in arms. Out there, on whatever planet the Republic sends us to, we will not have time to celebrate our feats of arms. HARD is not just an acronym for us, it is our way of fighting. We will be pushing our mechs, tanks, and support troops to their limits. We will drive hard, shoot fast, and strike fear in the hearts of those foolish enough to rise against us."

Pausing, he raised his glass a little higher. "Speed is our armor!" Then he slammed his drink back.

In unison, the gathered graduates repeated the unit's motto, and followed suit.

Metzger set his glass down and looked around him. His longing for the 444th was still there, but there was a sense of comradeship here that he could not deny—nor did he try to. He took a moment to sweep his gaze across every face in the room.

I will fight with these men and women to the end, and I expect them to do the same for me. May none of us fail.

17

Rexnar Koff watched as the last shuttle lifted off the landing pad. He felt a certain sense of pride in watching it build speed, rising skyward into the night. Major Hunter Sarn stood next to him, arms crossed, appropriately keeping his mouth shut until he was spoken to. It was one of Sarn's best features, knowing when to keep his mouth shut.

He either respects me or fears me. I'm comfortable with either one.

"That should be the last shipment," Koff said, turning from the office window.

"Yes, sir. All five ships were fully loaded for the trip to Vargas."

"I take it the K'llik located the site in question?"

"It took some work—but yes. It's mostly buried because of volcanic activity since the 552nd was there."

"Are we sure the K'llik will respond as we desire?" Koff asked.

"Sir, 'sure' is tricky. My limited exposure to the K'llik indicates that nothing can be assured. Their brains are not wired the way ours are. I think it's safe to say that they will act in their best interests. And at present, having a Republic military presence on their world is not in their interest—not at all. They're fiercely territorial and want nothing to do with Republic interference on their planet. Nothing is certain, but I feel confident they will respond with force."

"I don't want force. I want *overwhelming* force," Koff said in a crisp, firm tone. "I don't want *any* Repub military force surviving this, especially the Legion. Wiping out all of them ensures that only one version of events is told—the one that I approve of."

"The K'llik are a proud race. They will view any troops landing on their holdings on Vargas as a direct threat to their sovereignty. To be honest, they were a little offended that *I* showed up, even after I explained our desire to ensure they were properly armed."

The K'llik worlds were few in number but highly segregated. The insect-like species was xenophobic and unabashed about their feelings. Despite having a representative in the House of Reason, they abstained from all votes, took part in no debates. According to the Diplomatic Corps, they viewed their membership in the Republic as a formality, a title or a license, something necessary for them to do more profitable business.

The K'llik settled on planets that many would consider inhospitable—like the uplands of Vargas, with their desolate dead black lava flows, steaming geysers, and slow, steaming, gurgling volcanos. The K'llik lived underneath the surface, their cities burrowing deep. They were industrious and thrived on interstellar trade, their computer components being some of the best-made in the Republic. Some people even claimed they used stolen Savage Wars tech, though that had never been confirmed.

It was hard for any human to be entirely comfortable around an alien as unique as the K'llik. They were large insectoids in the shape of the common walking stick, with bulbous reddish eyes and sharp maws. Their bodies and limbs were narrow, slender, covered in chitin-like material that made them tough, with tiny finger-like appendages at the end of each spindly leg. They towered over their humanoid counterparts and allegedly, when pressed into a fight, were quick and vicious.

Nevertheless, where most humans cringed, Koff felt the most comfortable.

"What of the Republic?" Sarn asked. "Are you convinced that the government will respond as you expect?"

Koff nodded. "They have the bait. The reaction from the guildmaster indicates they're punching all the wrong buttons with the good people of Vargas. They will come in with good intentions, and set things in motion. If they survive the mining guild, they'll find their way to the K'llik—and there the Legion will bleed."

"Were you able to get the 14th Legion assigned?"

At this, Koff cracked a smile. "More than one member on the House committee owes me, but it took remarkably little effort. Yes, my son's former unit will be present when this little matter is resolved."

"Then everything is proceeding exactly as you planned."

"Of course it is. Some of that, I owe to you. I will not forget your service, Major."

"Thank you, sir. I was merely an instrument. It appears you have this well in hand."

"I do, Sarn. I do. It's easy when you understand the frailties of people's egos and how malleable their pride can be when pressure is applied. The R-A and the Legion will dance to the song that I'm playing, right up until the moment when they're wiped out. They cannot resist. It is in their nature."

"Sir... if they learn of your involvement—don't you fear repercussions?"

It was a pointed question, one that might have dug deep if Koff had not already given it thought. "I am a powerful member of the House of Reason... for a reason. I will simply deny involvement and chalk it up to coincidence. The benefit of the doubt is mine, and my fellows will protect me for their own sake if not for my own. After that... the removal of a few loose ends will make it impossible for anyone to pin this on me personally."

He let those words sink in. Sarn was one of those loose ends. He needed to know the importance of avoiding mistakes.

Sarn bowed his head and departed, and Koff gazed up at the night sky. He could now barely make out the orange glow of the plume under the last shuttle.

When other planetary leaders saw that the R-A and the Legion could be bled, it would make them reconsider the MCR. Those worlds would need arms and munitions—and Rexnar Koff's companies would be there to make sure they got them. Then, when the fighting was over, his companies would oversee the reconstruction.

He smiled. Revenge and profit—two edges to a most deadly sword.

PART TWO:

Echoes of the Past

18

Colonel Tyler Hackett of Cobra Company, 14th Legion, was an imposing man. It wasn't the many colorful ribbons that he wore on his dress uniform jacket, nor was it the muscles he possessed—all straining in some way to get free of that same uniform. It was his presence. His face had three scars, one each on the forehead, the chin, and the left cheek. His gray eyes were piercing, and O'Keefe felt them lock on to her for a moment as he surveyed the briefing room. He wore his hair short, with spots on his upper temples shaved so that his bucket would have better contact. The colonel was a fighting officer—everyone in the Legion was—and just by looking at him O'Keefe knew that he preferred life under fire, leading his troops into battle.

Colonel Inglima, commander of the 72nd Heavy Assault Regimental Detachment, was a little less rigid in appearance than Hackett, but he bore the look of a seasoned officer. Inglima rose and shook hands with Hackett, a sign that the two men knew each other.

Inglima's presence was something O'Keefe had advocated for—though really it was Metzger's presence she was interested in. She hadn't seen or communicated with him apart from a few short messages the two had shared since his assignment. O'Keefe knew he had completed his pilot training and was now a mech-jockey. And if all went well, she'd see him on Vargas.

Guildmaster Rune of Vargas and the K'llik leadership had formally denied the request for O'Keefe and her team to come to their world, just as Colonel Hughes had predicted. The diplomats then got involved, which had only made matters muddier. They came back with some preposterous plan that the locals would do their own archeological investigation into the wreckage seen in crater 107.9. Dranes had asked if there even were any archeologists on Vargas—which had brought back a rather weak response of "no."

It only confirmed O'Keefe's view that diplomats, like most politicians, were worthless. In the history of humankind, they had caused more wars than they'd prevented. Most were the embodiment of ignorance— highly polished, smooth talking, and utterly devoid of value.

Colonel Hughes was a rear-echelon officer, whereas the other two men holding that rank were combat officers. Professionally, they were courteous, but there was a ranking of colonels in the room, and O'Keefe could see that Hughes was clearly at the bottom. Which meant she was even lower on their totem pole than she already was.

"So," Hackett asked as they settled into their seats. "Is it true? Have you really found our 552nd?" His gravelly voice seemed to chew the air in the room.

Hughes looked over at O'Keefe and gave a nod. "This is Corporal O'Keefe. One of our research assistants. She is best suited to respond to that question."

O'Keefe shifted in her seat. She knew to keep it short and sweet. Officers like Hackett weren't prone to listening to speculation; they wanted facts. She laid the information out clearly, complete with the reservations they had. It took less than four minutes to speak her piece.

"So, you have a lead, that could be some sort of ruse, but it has led you to wreckage that may be from the task force the 552nd was part of," Hackett summarized.

"Yes, sir."

He took a deep breath. "We've never had a clue this tangible as to where any of the missing legions are."

"Understood, sir."

"No offense, Corporal, but no, you don't. Not if you aren't Legion."

"We won't forget nothin'," she said, quoting the Legion's unofficial motto.

His eyes widened as he looked at her, then he smiled. "Damn straight."

"As a historian, I take my work seriously, sir. We get a lot of crappy tips about the lost legions."

"And this one is good?"

"It's the best of the crappy tips we've ever gotten."

Hackett smiled again. "You've clearly put good people on this, Colonel Hughes. If she says this is what you have, I accept it."

"O'Keefe has proven herself to be one of our top researchers," Hughes said. "We're lucky to have her. If it weren't for the pressing nature of this discovery, I imagine she'd be finishing up her educational training en route to OCS. But she wants to see this through to completion, as do the rest of us. The only question now is, who goes in to investigate."

"The Legion," Hackett said without hesitation. "We have a commitment to bringing these dead legionnaires home. This goes beyond tradition. We don't leave our dead behind, no matter how long it takes. They will be carried home by their brothers."

O'Keefe flushed. She understood what Colonel Hackett felt. That sense of history had already fueled her obsession with finding the 552nd. She felt it in her chest, like a hunger that could only be filled by learning the truth. As a child, she'd never understood why people studied history for a profession, but now that she had been forced into that field, she appreciated the insatiable desire they felt for unseen knowledge.

Another realization washed over her in that moment: she wouldn't have had a chance to discover this passion if she hadn't been wounded.

"This is where it gets tricky," Colonel Hughes said. "The human Vargasians are kicking up quite a fit over this. They're denying us permission to land and conduct our analysis. They've cut off our access to their satellites as well."

"What's their problem?" Inglima asked.

"They have a list of issues," Hughes replied. "To them, this is an incursion on their sovereignty. Our arriving with a military honor guard is 'an invasion.' We are disrespecting the guild's stewardship of the 'where' in which we will be operating. They've even said that if we were to go there, we would be polluting their environment."

Inglima chuckled. "They're a mining and industrial planet. I've read the survey and seen your images. They pollute far more than we ever could. These are just stall tactics and excuses."

"Agreed," Hughes replied. "The good news is, we have every legal right to go there. There's at least three legal precedents for us to secure that site and conduct our investigation."

Inglima shook his head. "They won't care about laws and rights. If they're making these kinds of arguments, they're already entrenched, dug in mentally. Perhaps physically as well."

Hackett shifted in his seat. "That's a concern. Since they already know which crater is our objective, they'll move on it, if they haven't already. It sounds like they *want* a conflict —and they'll prepare accordingly. That's what I would do if I were them." He drew a deep breath. "Talk to me about the K'llik."

"I'll tell you what I know," Hughes said, "but keep in mind that there's always some translation challenges with insectoid races. That said, the one word that came through from them clearly, time and time again, was 'Denied.' The good news on that front is, the crater is in the humans' territory, not theirs. If we're fortunate, we won't have to deal with them at all."

"Good. So let's focus for the time being on the guild. Do we have a choice other than to press the issue with them?" Inglima asked. "I would hope that we could avoid a shooting match."

"These are miners—local militia," said Hackett. "Are they really a threat?"

"Their recent insurrection shows that they have mechs and a willingness to fight," Hughes replied. "Their resolve is solid when it comes to dealing with the Republic. This is an MCR world waiting to happen in my estimation."

"Those mechs are just enhanced mining mechs though, correct?" Hackett pressed, seemingly uninterested in the R-A colonel's estimations.

"Correct," Hughes said. "But there are also rumors of them securing tanks and heavy weapons, and outfitting a formidable force. Still, this remains a Republic world, with no declaration of loyalty to the causes of the MCR—so I think we need to try again to engage them in a dialogue when we arrive in-system. If there's even a chance of avoiding conflict, we must pursue it."

O'Keefe knew his caution was correct, but it felt detached from reality. From what Dranes had told her, the humans on Vargas were on the cusp of rebellion. Just showing up in orbit with troops was going to be more than enough provocation to ignite a war.

Inglima weighed in again. "Let's assume that they opt to fight. It's the worst-case scenario, but it's the one I most expect. Orbital bombardment or even air support on Republic worlds is a non-starter unless you're lucky enough to space with an exceptional destroyer captain—and we have neither a destroyer nor a captain willing to employ those tactics. A devastating bombardment on the indigs is the kind of stuff the worlds in rebellion *want* to hear about—the oppressive Republic attacking the poor weak locals. I'd rather not find ourselves in the middle of a humanitarian and public relations crisis if it can be avoided."

"I concur," Hackett said, backing his fellow combat commander and surprising O'Keefe. Since when did the Legion care about optics? "And if they're already on the objective by the time we get there, bombardment is not an option. We'll have to go in with force. There's no other way."

Punching the controls for the desk, Inglima pulled up a holographic topographical map of the area, then zoomed out and looked around before zooming back in. "I'd prefer to land right in the target crater, but we can expect them to have defenses ringing it to prevent that kind of assault. That means we land away from the objective—then move in on it. This crater here, number 108.2, is close enough for us to land our troops in safety and set up our necessary logistics and your research team. The edges of the crater aren't too steep, so we can deploy on the crater floor and still have the ability to move out and secure our ultimate objective of 107.9."

Colonel Hackett nodded. "That'll work for your mech forces; you have the speed to get to the objective crater quickly. I'd like to drop my company off closer... in this direction." He took control of the holomap and adjusted it. "Crater 113. We do a hot drop there, in and out, right when the fighting starts. With you moving to engage them, they'll turn their focus on you. That will give us some time to move out."

"No combat sleds?" Inglima asked.

Hackett gave a single shake of his head.

"With that decided..." Colonel Hughes then took his turn at the controls. "Let's take a look at 107.9." He zoomed in on it, then expanded the image so that it filled the space of the holotable. "It's just over fifty kilometers in diameter, and the drop down from the rim is over a kilometer and a half. We've identified three potential paths where ingress can be made. They're man-made, blasted out of the rim of the crater so that vehicles could get to the bottom. Our guess is that these steep curving roadways were part of mining expeditions back when Vargas was first settled.

"There are also some sub-craters in there that have filled with water, forming what amounts to small lakes." He pointed to them. "The ground is uneven. There are boulders the size of buildings out there. The lower you go, the denser the atmosphere. From the planetary survey data, the temperatures during the daytime are around eighteen degrees Celsius. At night, however, it gets down to just above freezing."

"My men have fought on less hospitable rocks," Hackett said proudly.

"Well this one is a real treat," Hughes replied. "The nickel and iron content at the bottom of the crater is through the roof. It generates its own little magnetic field. We can adjust most of the gear for its effects, but it'll play havoc with anything other than short-range scans."

"So we won't know what we're jumping into until we see it?"

"Pretty much."

Inglima spoke up. "I need whatever data you have on the magnetics. I want to make sure my techs adjust our mechs and tanks to compensate."

Hughes nodded. "I'll get you that data before we wrap up."

If the description of the cratered hell on Vargas disturbed Hackett, he didn't show it. O'Keefe expected nothing less from a Legion commander.

"What can you tell me about the plant life?" he asked.

"As you can see on the map, there's ample vegetation once you're down inside the crater. The trees are short, no more than a dozen meters in height, but they grow in thickets that are almost impassable because of exposed root systems and supporting ground brush. The 'grass' you see is actually just thick moss, which seems to grow on everything, including the walls of the crater. The ship is on a flat area here near the center of the area, with limited plant growth."

Hackett pointed to the map. "Those cracks in the crater's wall. They look like narrow valleys, what little we can see of them. What can you tell us about them?"

O'Keefe got the nod from Hughes and spoke up. "Most likely they're the results of the asteroid strike that formed the crater. We don't have good views of what they look like inside, but I did take a look at similar formations in other craters. Assuming they're along the same lines, they're narrow passages, with steep slopes downward. They appear impassable to vehicles or mechs."

Hackett eyed the map silently, as did Inglima.

"What are you thinking, Tyler?" Inglima finally asked Hackett.

So they do *know each other,* O'Keefe thought.

Hackett frowned. "They'll probably place the bulk of their forces down low, making the trip from the crater rim to the floor even more treacherous than the terrain suggests; those 'paths' are little more than rocky outcroppings. But see this crack off to the north? I think that might be the best way to get my legionnaires down quickly without exposing them to fire from below."

O'Keefe spoke up again. "I don't think so, sir."

All eyes went to the outspoken corporal. O'Keefe blushed. This was a regular, joint-force operation. Her place was to speak to the research, not to give battlefield opinions. Her comfort with Warrant Officer Dranes and Colonel Hughes had just caused her to stick her boot in her mouth.

"I'm sorry." She spoke the words quickly.

Hackett stared at her for a beat. "No, please, Corporal. What was it?"

Now invited, O'Keefe said what she'd meant to say a moment earlier. "Our readings suggest that 'crack' is effectively a jumble of boulders. I served in the infantry, and I can tell you that's not a trek that you want to have your legionnaires undertake. It will be very slow, treacherous, and if they get pinned in there, a death trap. And, sir, I understand legionnaires are several cuts above Republic Army... but even so."

Hackett eyed her carefully. "That bad, eh?"

"Yes, sir. I can pull up the imagery if you want."

"That won't be necessary." He turned to the other officers. "We'll take the roadway down from the north then."

"That leaves me with two paths down for my forces," Inglima said. "The MBTs will have a go at it first; they're less dependent on a smooth path down. We'll deploy our infantry to make sure there are no IEDs along the way. We will demonstrate at the path to the southwest, just to make them wonder how we plan to deploy, then take the path down from the west. Once we get onto flat ground, our priority will be to negate any resistance we might encounter. Securing the wreck site can be done easily once the enemies are negated."

For the next two hours, the officers studied the maps, coming up with plans and backup plans—fallback positions, extraction points. Another hour was spent going over communications protocols, reviewing force compositions, and ironing out details of logistics between the two military units. It all sounded clean and precise to O'Keefe; she expected nothing less. Professionals were all about planning, and Hackett and Inglima were professional soldiers. She even found herself enjoying the conversion. It conjured up memories of serving in the 444th.

"Preparation saves lives and ensures that the lives that are lost are the right ones," her former sergeant, Fazzoli, had told her time and time again.

Still, Fazzoli never walked out of Tykaree Valley.

Memories of the planning session for that attack were among the fragmented memories in her mind—she could remember only bits and pieces of the session—but she realized how eerily similar it was to the meeting that she was now in. That realization caused her to shift uncomfortably in her seat. Beads of perspiration broke out on her forehead and in her armpits. Her breath quickened, despite her mentally telling herself to slow her breathing.

"Are you okay, Corporal?" Hackett asked.

His words gave O'Keefe just enough focus to get a grip. "Yes, sir. Just remembering my last combat operation." She was thankful he had spoken to her. She had feared that one of her jumbled memories was about to appear. Nervously she took a long sip from the glass of water near her on the table.

Lunch arrived, and as the others rose to shuffle out for a quick break while the food was brought in, Colonel Hughes sidled up next to her, leaning in so that no one could hear. "Are you all right, Sheryl?"

O'Keefe nodded nervously. "Just fighting some memories, sir."

"I was informed your condition was under control," he said. "I trust it won't compromise the work we have to get done."

"No, sir," she replied. "I take my meds. I have it under control."

That was mostly true. Now and then the memories forced themselves upon her regardless of the drugs. But she'd gotten good at managing her reaction to them.

There was no point in explaining that nuance to Hughes. She wasn't going to risk being pulled from the team going to Vargas.

"Good," he said, offering a smile. "Don't let all this preparation get to you, Corporal. Vargas is a backwater planet. Chances are when they see us arrive in orbit, they won't do a thing. No one wants to tangle with the Legion *and* a HARD regiment."

She gave him a slow nod in response. "Let's hope you're right, sir."

But she had a nagging suspicion that Vargas was going to be a tough nut to crack.

19

Metzger was in the open rear assembly that provided an HK-PP with access to the power assembly. The power plant on the mech was simple, generating energy for weapons and movement at a steady high level. It had all the looks of being heavily reinforced, a magbottle with thick metal bands... some of which had clearly failed, as a chunk had exploded outward, ripping holes in the engine housing and even the armor. The power assembly was a distribution system that controlled the flow of energy to the rest of the mech. This one would never do that again, and Metzger had been tasked with replacing it.

He reluctantly accepted his punishment duty, working on mech repair. When he finished his normal duty assignments, he reported to the mech bays, despite his lack of expertise and training. By the time he finally returned to his bed each night, covered in lubricants and sweat, he often just collapsed; there was no downtime. But he didn't complain. It was better than being left behind.

He became the brunt of a lot of jibes from the other pilots. Tramel referred to him as a "mech monkey." Krock told him he'd found "his true look" in his greasy coveralls. Vickerson reminded him, "They've got bots for that—you do know that, right?" Perhaps the only pilot to not have a laugh at his expense was Buck. The former marine opted out of good-humored abuse. In fact it was so obvious that one night, Metzger asked him why he didn't have anything to add.

"Who knows?" Buck said. "Maybe what you're learning will be of use someday." If nothing else, Buck was pragmatic.

Chief Technician Ross made sure Metzger didn't forget why he was assigned to the mech bays. He complained to him constantly about the staggering amount of work it took to repair the damage from his collision. The more Metzger worked in the bay though, and interacted with the other techs, the more he realized that Ross was exaggerating. It was a trait that most of the techs had adopted, a mix of complaining about their workload and exaggerating how difficult, if not nearly impossible, every minor repair was to complete.

At first they gave him mindless grunt work to do—retrieving tools and parts—and at one point he found himself the brunt of a practical joke, when he was sent to the tool crib to retrieve a quart of "fusion juice." He suspected this was a joke from the start, and so easily absorbed the snickers and jeers when the crib manager told him there was no such thing. After that initiation, the techs more or less treated him as one of their own, mentoring and teaching him, explaining to him what they were doing and why. He suspected it was a rarity for a pilot to be turned over to their whims, but within two weeks, he felt almost like a peer.

There were also some perks associated with being assigned part-time to the maintenance team. Notably, he had been able to get the best painters in the bays to do some artwork on his HK-PP. Whereas most of the crews had only their name and call sign under their cockpit canopies, he now had some art: a stylized mech with an over-large R-A infantryman in body armor riding it as if it were a beast of burden. The almost cartoonish trooper had a giant medieval lance tucked under one arm, and at the tip of the lance, a small red banner hung down with white lettering: *SH-SD*. Stack 'em high, stack 'em deep—the unofficial motto of the Repub Army.

While the art wasn't quite regulation, once his peers saw it, they commissioned their own nose art, and the artists managed to get themselves a highly profitable side gig. Even the tankers got into the act. So far none of the senior command had put an end to the practice, for which Metzger was thankful.

Another perk of the assignment was that he learned to repair most minor damage and replace almost everything on the mechs. Diagnosing problems was easy, and most repairs were simple replacements. He doubted he'd ever have to use these skills, but it was nice to know he had them if the need ever arose.

As he wrestled with his mech's power assembly, turning it with all his might as it hung off the winch, just to align the couplers, he heard his name being called.

"Just a minute!" he called back, finally lining up the assembly and using the winch controls to lower it into place. As he rose and looked down from the gantry where he worked, he saw Chief Technician Ross.

"Metzger, you are out of here."

"Is there a problem?" Metzger asked.

"No problem," Ross said, running his hand back through his jet-black hair. "Word's come down that they need you in two hours for a briefing."

Metzger checked his chronometer: 1848 hours. Something was up for them to call a late-night briefing like this. "I've got the assembly in place," he said as he started down the gantry. "Someone's going to have to do the connections though."

"I'll put a bot on it," Ross replied.

"Any idea what this is about?" Metzger asked as he came down onto the concrete floor.

"You think they tell us techs what's going on? I thought you were smarter than that. I've got word to pack up our gear for forward deployment, though. It looks like the 72nd is about to deliver an ass-kicking."

Metzger stopped in front of the chief technician and held out a grease-stained hand. "Thank you for everything you've taught me."

Ross shook the proffered hand and gave him a smile. "If you ever wash out as a pilot, you're welcome in my gang anytime."

For Metzger, that came as high praise.

He headed back to the barracks, thinking he'd have enough time for a shower and to change into a clean jumpsuit. What he found when he got there was a bustle of activity, with rucks and other gear being packed. He asked around, and it seemed that no one had actually been told they were deploying, but rumors abounded, courtesy of the lower ranks. Metzger took his shower and then joined in on the activities.

Metzger was assigned to the third squadron, given the designation of 510. The other two squadrons had nicknames and logos. The first squadron, the 499th, bore a logo of a heap of dead Savage marines with an HK-PP standing atop them, blasters firing skyward. Their nickname was Greased Lightning. The second squadron, the 208th, was called the Infernos. Their patch was a black silhouette of a repulsor tank and mech against a wall of brilliant flames. Their tanks all had cartoonish flames painted on them. Metzger hadn't heard what their obsession with fire was, but he was sure it was well-earned.

The 510th didn't have a nickname or a logo. Its predecessor had been utterly destroyed on Tralon, making it a new squadron, with no history, no tales to tell. Its tank operators had combat experience in other HARD units, but the mechs were staffed entirely with new pilots. The only exception was their commander, Captain Peltier, who'd moved over from the 499th. He was a capable commander and the best HK-PP pilot in the group.

Metzger didn't see Captain Peltier in the barracks, so he moved over to his section mate/wingman, Buck Nelson. The stocky former hullbuster was all muscle with a thick neck that made buttoning any shirt a challenge. Metzger still remembered their first time talking after they became wingmen. He'd asked Buck, "So, why'd you leave the Marines and join this regiment?" It was a question that many had speculated about, but prior to Metzger, none had asked the man; Buck had hinted he didn't want to talk about it, and had demonstrated he was someone who couldn't be forced into doing a thing he didn't want to.

"I made a mistake," he'd replied with a heavy sigh.

"What kind of mistake?"

Buck wouldn't look him in the eye. "A man in my platoon got himself in a bad situation in a bar. All that kid did was flirt with one of the locals, and the townies there were going to beat the sket out of him. I stepped in—tried to defuse the situation. The locals weren't interested in apologies or a round of drinks. They just wanted to try to kick some marine ass."

"We've all been there."

"Yes, we have," Buck replied.

"So it was a bar fight?"

"More than that. They threw the first punches, and I responded as I had been trained to do. I dropped two of them quick. Then one pulled a gun, a slug-thrower. Old-school, low-tech piece of sket. I didn't have the position to disarm him, so I struck with what I thought was an appropriate force. I didn't intend to kill him, but I did."

Metzger grunted. "You get a court-martial?"

"Yes," he replied with a grim frown. "The townies lied, of course—claimed I started the fight, even claimed I'd produced the weapon in the mix. We had enough evidence to call their claims pure twarg dung, but the local government had a dead body and wanted someone held accountable. I thought I'd end up in military prison, but instead my naval counselor got creative with the sentencing, suggested I get booted from the Repub Marines. They agreed to that, but they wouldn't release me from my commitment to military service. Way I see it, hullbusters turned on me for doing what was right. If I hadn't acted, that townie would have shot that private."

"That's horrible."

"It is what it is."

"And how'd you end up here?"

This time it was Buck who grunted. "I settled on the HARD regiment because they're tough as nails. After my time serving aboard ships, I didn't want to be anywhere but on the ground, applying my skills."

"I can understand that."

"And how did *you* end up here?" Buck asked. "I know you were R-A, but you've always been a bit evasive on the details."

Metzger patted his bionic leg. "I lost my leg—more than once. They couldn't regen me. Inglima and the others, they were looking for veterans to rebuild the 72nd, and they recruited me. You can't keep a warrior down."

Buck smiled oddly, as though trying to decide whether to speak, or stay silent. "No," he finally decided, "I gotta ask. What is with you Repub soldiers calling yourselves warriors all the time? No other branch does that. The Legion don't even do it. And why the hell do you folks talk like university professors in between trying to sound like you're being recorded for a holo-doc?"

Metzger laughed. "What? We don't do that."

"The hell you don't. 'Retrograde.' What the hell does that even mean?"

Metzger just stared at the hullbuster. The R-A was not without its own prejudice. They viewed the Marines and Legions as more animal that human. The spacers of the Navy were more acceptable, but had no stomach for fighting. Now Buck was giving him some insight into how the Marines viewed the Repub Army.

There was less scorn than what was typical from the Legion, at least.

And Buck was now a part of that army. He was quick to apologize. "I don't mean nothing by it. I'm R-A, too, now. You're a good guy, Metzger. I guess we're just two busted-ass warriors," Buck said, forcing a smile.

"Guess so. Our job now is to prove to everyone that they were wrong to send us away."

And ever since then, they'd done just that. Metzger liked Buck. The man was aggressive in all the right ways. He didn't possess a drop of hotdog blood in his barrel-chested body. And when they practiced, as they did almost every day, Buck always positioned himself to provide support for Metzger. Metzger reciprocated. After weeks of training together, they could anticipate each other's moves and act accordingly. Metzger was glad that he had drawn Buck as a wingman. He didn't act like the younger pilots—like he had something to prove. Years of being a marine does that to a man.

"What's the word?" he now asked his friend, keeping his voice low.

"Scuttlebutt, more than anything else," Buck said. "The entire base is prepping to deploy, but so far they've chosen to keep us in the dark."

"Chief Tech Ross sent me back because something was going down."

"Well, at least your time playing tinkerer is over."

"I have to tell you, Buck, I kind of liked it. Most of my career has been blowing stuff up and stacking dead bodies. It was sort of rewarding repairing things, making them whole. That kind of work had a beginning and end, with a physical result that you could see. For all the fighting I did in the infantry, I never got to see the results of anything other than the battle in front of me—and those results were beyond the dead."

Being a ground-pounder had meant using force, fighting wars, but he'd never seen what happened after the shooting stopped. He'd always just packed up, got some rest, and went on to the next fight.

"You're a better man than me," Buck replied as he finished packing his ruck. "I don't have the patience for that job. Wrench-monkeys can have all that fun when it comes to repair and refit. Just make sure my mech is in prime condition and point me at the enemy."

Before Metzger could respond, Captain Peltier entered the barracks. "All right, stow your gear and get moving. There's a mission briefing at the HQ in five."

The briefing room was set up classroom-style. Colonel Inglima entered, and everyone rose to attention.

"As you were," he said as he moved to the flat metallic podium at the front of the room. There were no holoimages to be projected—Metzger could tell by the position of the podium—and he was thankful for that. Too many senior officers relied on audio-visual aids to make their point. Not so with Inglima. Another reason to like the man.

"I'm going to keep this short and on target. The 72nd is deploying to the planet Vargas in support of an archeological and historical team. We will be joined by Cobra Company of the 14th Legion. Our mission is simple: protect the researchers so they can conduct their work. Because this is a Joint Force operation, you'll have legionnaires as support elements—infantry gets leave. Pilots and tankers get to work. I'll give you five seconds to bitch and moan."

Dutifully, the HK pilots and tank crews all gave way to good-natured grumbling, which dried up with Major Meece announcing, "That's good enough," a mere three seconds in.

The colonel continued. "On paper, Vargas is not a hostile world. However, they have shown a high degree of resistance to this operation. Moreover, we believe the factions on-world have been arming themselves as of late, which may be an indicator that they are willing to put up some sort of fight. That said, the presence of the 14th is not intended to be military in nature. They are to be an honor guard of a sort, tied to the historians' mission. There is potential evidence on Vargas of one of their lost legions."

Inglima paused to let his words sink in. And those words hit Metzger deeply. Not only were the lost legions practically mythic in nature, but O'Keefe had been working on finding them. He wondered if she was involved in this operation, and then decided she most definitely was. If anyone could crack the mystery of one of the lost legions, it was Sheryl O'Keefe.

Colonel Inglima continued.

"There are two factions on-planet. The mining guild is human; they operate mostly in the craters. The surface, or uplands, is controlled by a species known as the K'llik. Neither faction is thrilled that we are dropping in. If either one of them decides to put up a fight, they're known to field modified mechs and tanks. This is a planet without a friendly environment. Briefing packets have been prepared for each of your squadron commanders. Suffice it to say, if they decide to fight, everyone is counting on the 72nd to do its part and more, if necessary."

A few murmurs ran around the room. Inglima stifled them by speaking again. "I advise you all to familiarize yourself with the terrain and atmospherics of this mission. We will dust off in six hours. There's no living off the land, so to speak, so full logistical loads and supplies are going as well. Anticipate that the drop shuttles will be packed a little more than usual."

The colonel's words landed on Metzger like incoming artillery rounds. They had been training with each other, running mock battles, getting to know each other's strengths and weaknesses. This was the *real thing*. How would the newbies handle it? It would've been nice to have had a few more weeks of training, to smooth out the rough edges.

Inglima echoed his thoughts. "This will be our first time going out as a unit since Tralon and our refitting. Most of us here have never fought together, never shed blood on the same world. Let's hope it stays that way for the extent of this mission—that the Vargasians see the folly in putting up a fight. They are fellow Republic citizens, after all. But if they fail to see wisdom, I know that each and every one of you will do your duty to the best of your ability. We will be victorious. Always remember, speed is our armor."

"Speed is our armor," the troops replied in unison.

"Dismissed."

20

O'Keefe stood on the firing line and unleashed the fury of the blaster rifle, sending brilliant bolts of deadly energy downrange. She could smell the hint of ozone in the air as vapor drifted from the barrel. Sweat ran down her brow, stinging in the corners of her eyes as she finished pulling the charge pack and self-cleaning the bolt intake.

She'd needed a break from prepping for departure, and keeping up her marksmanship usually relaxed her. She still had the nagging suspicion that someone was luring them to Vargas with false information in the buoy. There was a tenseness from the native Vargasians that felt... wrong. There was no reason for them to be quite this resistant. Someone had convinced the mining guild the Legion was there for nefarious reasons, and as for the K'llik, she had no idea why they were bristling. Yet trying to convince either faction of the Legion's peaceful intentions was a waste of time. They took every denial as further affirmation that they were right.

O'Keefe checked her range score. She had hit ninety-three percent—off from her best, but she was pretty sure she was still outshooting everyone in the historical research branch. Most didn't take the time to keep up working out or shooting. Which made sense: they were, after all, fighting a paperwork war, waging pseudo-battles digitally at their desks. In addition to her range work, O'Keefe also did three sessions a week in physical combat training. One of the base instructors had agreed to spar with her, and while his techniques weren't quite up to her peak in the R-A, it gave her a chance to make sure she didn't lose her muscle memory. Some of her colleagues whispered about all this training behind her back—just loud enough for her to hear—but O'Keefe didn't care what they thought. She had been a front-line soldier and didn't want to lose those skills. She'd learned long ago it was best to be ready for anything in life. If you weren't, you'd just be another victim.

Double-checking the safety on her rifle, she shouldered the weapon, grabbed her sweaty bottle of water, and took the liberty of lowering herself into a folding chair that was behind the firing line. She was alone on the range, which gave her time to rethink what she still had to pack and question if there was more they should be taking. The portable DNA test center was bulky. Should she leave it? No, they would need it if they found human remains. From the Legion archives, she had obtained the DNA profiles of all the members of the 552nd. As cumbersome as the equipment was, It was necessary.

The cool water felt good as she drank. Her shoulder muscles were still tense from holding the blaster against them. She closed her eyes and drew a long, deep breath of the warm air.

"O'Keefe, you know what your problem is? Your problem is that you push yourself too hard," came the voice of Corporal Vex.

He was standing there, directly in front of her.

Most of the time, O'Keefe tried to silence the memories when they came, push them back into the recesses of her mind. She was tired though, and her brain was already a jumble of pre-departure thoughts and checklists. So rather than try to silence the memory, she faced it.

"What do you want, Vex?"

"O'Keefe, you know what your problem is? Your problem is that you push yourself too hard," the voice repeated.

"Yeah, I know. You said that."

"You need to get some focus. It's more than picking your targets. You need to purge all that other sket and keep your eyes on the prize."

O'Keefe was shocked. The Vex memory had actually... *responded* to her. And when she'd spoken those words —"Yeah, I know"—she'd felt a sense of déjà vu. Maybe that was what she'd actually said to him back in real-time?

She was both excited and a little bit afraid. It had occurred to her before that she might be able to pry more from her memory fragments, but she'd always attempted to do so by pushing them, interrogating them... not by simply going with the flow. Had she been taking the wrong approach all this time?

Her weariness evaporated as she sat up, staring at Vex outlined in shimmering white light. He looked as real as the firing bench he stood in front of. What should she say? Her mind darted in different directions as she tried to think of how she might have responded at the time.

"I'm focused, Vex."

Vex didn't move, didn't respond.

Guess that wasn't the right response.

"Vex, what's going on?"

White light washed over Vex, and he disappeared.

Usually O'Keefe wanted nothing more than for her memories to go away, but this time, she felt loss, regret. But the moment was gone, driven into the jumbled bits of her gray matter.

Astin, she thought. She had to tell the doctor. Maybe it could offer some advice, something useful. *But what if it determines I'm unfit for the mission?* O'Keefe quickly dismissed that line of thinking. This wasn't at all like the bar relapse. She was taking her meds, all the proper dosages at all the proper times. This was simply her reporting on an interaction with one of her memories. A harmless one.

She rose to her feet, her knees and thighs protesting at the motion, and pulled on her fatigue shirt over her sweaty tank top. It stuck like glue when it hit her skin. The crater and the dropship would have to wait. First, O'Keefe had another mystery to solve.

Dr. Astin listened intently as O'Keefe relayed the entire incident. When she finished, the bot said nothing, simply looking at her intensely. The silence was maddening, so O'Keefe shattered it.

"What does it mean?"

The bot offered a very slight shrug with a slight hum of its shoulder actuator. "I would say... it means there's more to the memories than you have encountered before. Everything in your case file indicates that your erratic memory encounters are physiological in nature, as a result of your head wound. But the fact that this apparition reacted to your words may indicate something else."

"Like what?"

"That a part of your memory suppression could be psychological."

O'Keefe hated that assessment. "Are you saying I'm *deliberately* blocking my memories?"

"This isn't a blame game, Corporal. I'm merely making an observation."

"But why would I hold back my own memories? I *want* to know what happened back in that valley. I lost *everyone* there, and none of the official reports tells me squat. I've been trying to figure that out for a long time now."

Again, that slight shrug. "What happened when your unit was wiped out was most likely gruesome and traumatic. It's no small thing that you were the only survivor. So if those memories *are* still in your brain, there may be a part of you that doesn't want to dredge them up. Maybe your head is trying to protect you from sights and images that, deep down, you might not be able to handle."

O'Keefe felt hot, not like she had been at the firing range, but with a torrent of embarrassment, rage, defiance, denial, and anger. Astin was challenging her toughness, her intentions, and it was a hard pill to swallow.

The doctor had to be wrong. It was just a machine, after all. What did it know?

"I don't think that—what I mean to say is, I'm certain I *want* to know what happened to the rest of my unit. I've seen things—bad things—before. I'm not *protecting* myself."

"Consciously, I'm sure that's true. Subconsciously, there may be different interests at work. It isn't uncommon. I should also point out, it's still possible that this incident was merely a fluke. Maybe it wasn't a continuation of your memory with Corporal Vex at all. Perhaps you simply imagined the extension of the memory based on what you were seeing."

That didn't make O'Keefe feel any better. The doc thought she was imagining things?

Frustration took hold. "All right, Doc, you're saying I'm a steaming hot mess between my ears. Is that about right?"

"No. You're not a 'hot mess,' Corporal. The truth is, your brain injury should have put you in a forever box. But somehow you have survived and are not only functional, you're brilliantly productive. That's a *far* cry what I would call a hot mess. It shows you're in control, whether you want to believe that or not."

"So what do I do?"

Astin's eyes glowed for a moment, which O'Keefe had come to understand the bot was running its algos. "First, stay on your meds. I see no reason to change your prescription. Second, the next time you get one of these 'visitations,' go ahead and interact with it. You've demonstrated that you can often drive them away. Perhaps it's time to try something new."

"But what do I say? I tried talking to Vex, and he just vanished."

"That, I can't answer; we're in uncharted territory here. But based on what you just told me, I think your immediate idea was a good one: try talking to Vex as if you're actually back there, with him, in that memory. See if you can feel what you felt at the time, so that you can react as you did at the time."

"Is that safe?" O'Keefe asked. The real question she was struggling with was, *Will this make my mental problems worse?*

"It depends on how you define 'safe.' But Corporal, I think this is a good thing. If you really do have a psychological block, then today's incident may be a sign that your subconscious feels that it's time to start chipping away at that block. Time to face what remains."

"Time," O'Keefe muttered. "The timing is awful. I'm about to go on the most important mission of my life."

She surprised herself describing Vargas in that way. But it was true. The research work had finally outmuscled the soldier's work, it seemed.

"There's nothing in what you've told me that suggests you don't have this under control. As long as you continue to manage your meds, this should have no effect on your mission."

O'Keefe got up, catching a whiff of her own body odor. "That's easy for you to say. This is like having ghosts living in my head."

"All biologics have things bouncing around in their heads, Corporal. Yours are just a little more persistent. You're a tough person. You'll be able to govern this."

"I hope you're right," O'Keefe said.

But as she headed back to her quarters, she wondered which of the broken images in her mind might appear next... and when.

21

Through the viewport of a dropship, Metzger saw Vargas for the first time. It was gray, pockmarked with craters—some so massive that they had their own blue atmosphere, complete with clouds. Below the clouds were glimmers from bodies of water, even lush green growth. He estimated these craters were a hundred kilometers across, perhaps more.

He had been briefed on the thin atmosphere of the uplands, and it, too, was visible. A few mountains poked up above the low stratosphere, and black lava flows spilled like tar. There were some forested areas and a few grasslands, but it was clear that most of the hospitable areas were at the bottoms of craters.

Metzger tried to search for words to describe the planet, but came up with only "ugly" and "weird."

Their journey had been without incident. They had gone over the deployment plans so many times that Metzger felt he could give the presentation himself if he had to. But experience had taught him long ago that there was no such thing as knowing too much about the situation you were about to face in battle.

They had been in orbit for several days, giving the forces a solid picture of the objective crater. It was a big one, some parts rocky, others thick with growth. There was no sign of the local militia. Which, to Metzger, was a worrying sign. He'd seen something like that before… and it hadn't turned out well.

When his company had deployed to Xelos, the locals were quiet, meek, downright docile as the 444th secured their DZ outside of the capital city. But that was all a ruse. The insurgency started three days after landing—ambushes, improvised explosives, the usual fare. The division didn't respond passively to the attacks, and that led to three weeks of hard fighting to secure the city. By the time they were done, half the buildings lay in ruin and the locals were harping about "war atrocities." The 444th had prevailed, but at a hell of a cost.

Gordon always joked about Xelos, "I've never been called a war criminal before. You think the Legion will have me?" At the time, it was merely dark humor. Thanks to the Frix, it was now a painful memory.

Between the briefings, there was downtime. Metzger didn't know quite what to do with it once his time playing HK mechanic was over. For most on the dropship, downtime meant games of chance, talking smack, and a few of the more experienced pilots checking their mechs and tanks. And, of course, plenty of speculation as to what was taking so long. Rumors were distilled out of the purified air of the orbiting dropship, flights of fantasy spun up by soldiers before battle.

Metzger entered the rec area and was greeted by the all-too-familiar aroma of people living in cramped quarters. Showers were regular but quick, and when troops lived in close quarters, their individual odors blended into a scent that he had smelled on over a dozen different worlds during his career. The entire 510th was here, minus Captain Peltier, and he was glad to see that bonds were already being strengthened.

Captain Stan had been made leader of First Platoon, along with Vickerson, Tramel, and Krock. Metzger was in Second, with Buck, Rothchild, and Stamper. The scout platoon consisted of Dobbs and the three MBTs. Finally, the captain was obviously in charge of Command Platoon, which he had rounded out with Tom, Dick, and Harry. There had never been any question about splitting up those three.

"I hear they wussed out," Krock muttered between hands of Tailspin, a card game Metzger was certain had been designed by the crafty to liberate the chits of the naïve. He was talking about the miners on Vargas, of course.

Stan shook his head. "It's happening. I was Legion long enough to know that much for sure. Stop wasting your breath wondering. Instead, why can't one of you guys find out just what the hell happened on Tralon, because *that's* what I want to know."

"Squad was wiped out," said Tramel as he showed his hand—a full windshear. He smiled as he gleefully scooped up the credit chits. "Simple as that."

Buck Nelson weighed in. "No, there's more to it than that. Some kind of real, get-thrown-in-the-brig-for-life sket took place from what I hear."

"The marine way, then?" Tramel chuckled after saying it, which only made the wrinkles on Buck's brow become deeper—angrier.

Buck stepped closer to the younger pilot. "Watch where you go with that marine sket. I don't have to take crap from a kid when I've got scars older than he is. You're a hotshot pilot ain't killed nothing yet. Down there, it's the real thing. I'll lay down chits you'll be shitting yourself after the first exchange of fire."

Metzger interceded, though a part of him wanted to see Tramel get knocked down a peg or two. "Hey, you two, take a deep breath. Save it for the bugs and the guild."

Stupp, one of the tankers, frowned. "All I need to know is where the enemy is and if I'm clear to fire on 'em. Everything else is window dressing."

The man had a bluntness about him; he was, after all, enlisted. Like Metzger was before he'd been promoted to warrant. All the joys of being an officer without the paperwork.

Tramel looked over at Metzger. "What do you think? You think the rumors are true?"

Metzger shrugged. "Something happened." That was as much as he was willing to say. Something *had* happened, and depending on who you got your gossip from, it involved anything from a major blue-on-blue cluster, with HK-PP pilots killing one another instead of their targets, to an equipment malfunction that left several commanding officers dead. There were precious few people who knew first-hand. Captain Peltier was one of them, but he wasn't going to talk.

But the rest of the 510th sure were. Some of it was simply people killing time, waging a war of words against boredom. On many ops it had been him sitting at the table, making up stories, losing money at cards. But with all his experience, he no longer took part in the guessing game.

"I'll tell you this, though," Metzger continued. "I think speculation is a waste of time."

At precisely that moment Captain Peltier entered the room, and everyone fell silent.

"Should I step back out?" he asked, a playful smirk on his face.

"No, sir," Buck said, and then to Metzger's surprise, got right down to it. "Captain, we were just wondering what went down on Tralon."

Every head looked expectantly at Peltier. They all wanted to know. It was a secret that seemed to be the only thing keeping them from being fully cohesive, though Metzger knew it wasn't something they *needed* to know in order to do their jobs.

The squadron had been together through training, learning to work together. Learning each other's strengths and weaknesses. For example, they all knew that Captain Stan, "Razorwire," the leader of First Platoon, was a hot-tempered commander. He fought and maneuvered balls to the wall, pushing his HK-PP to its limits and beyond, making him the scorn of the technicians who had to fix the damage he caused. And Wanda Vickerson, his wingman, was the kind of person who tried to keep her aggression in check but usually failed. Together they were a vicious combination.

The lanky captain stood at the front of the room, his long arms crossed in front of him. Completely ignoring Buck's implicit question, he instead went over a summary of the mission. Choosing something they already knew backwards and forwards over what they actually wanted to know.

"Just got back from a briefing. Not much new. The mining guild had a little uprising a while back. They armored up some of their industrial mechs, threw together some tanks out of grav sleds and tunneling vics, and managed to inflict a lot of damage before they were suppressed. I've sent the details to your personal folders for review. Don't get too overconfident that this will be easy—the industrial-grade stuff is actually on par with our military-grade gear. It's built to take a beating. We have every reason to believe they will have rebuilt their forces. Add to that, some of their personnel now have combat experience. Overconfidence can be deadly, so don't exhibit it.

"The K'llik are an entirely different matter. No one seems to be able to get much of a read on them other than a sense of general hostility. Their involvement in the Savage Wars points to them being forced to work for our opposition, but how much of that is theory and how much is reality is up to conjecture."

"Do the bugs have tanks?" asked Sergeant Grunon, a tanker in the scout platoon. Grunon had been with the 72nd before Tralon, but swore he knew nothing about what went down. Usually he looked half awake. It took three cups of kaff to get him this talkative. His buddy, Sergeant Carrow Ivers, was a tough-as-nails fellow tanker who had the misfortune of once being cooked inside a tank that caught fire. She'd survived, but was badly burned. Her regens were sketchy at best, leaving her with several patches of deformed skin, pink with tiny ridges. Like Grunon, she rarely spoke. Maybe she was self-conscious about her looks; maybe she just didn't like small talk. But now she leaned forward to hear the captain's response to Grunon's question.

"Just got confirmation on that," Peltier replied. "Yes they do. And mechs."

Warrant Officer Jeffrey Dobbs, call sign Back Door, manned the scout platoon's sole HK-SW. The scout pilots had spent most of selection being trained separately from the HK-PP group, so the others were still feeling Dobbs out. Now he spoke up. "We've got speed on our side." He made a pistol gesture with his hand and pulled the trigger, grinning broadly, the smile of a man who had little combat experience. Cockiness was a dangerous thing in a firefight.

He had been in the R-A for many years, but working in an administrative position in Supply. For reasons he never spoke about, he'd wanted to get into battle, and rumor was it had taken three attempts to get Colonel Inglima to finally agree to transfer him.

To go from piloting a desk to an HK-SW was a big damn jump. One that meant sitting in an exposed seat on top of a fast-moving pair of mech legs. That took guts, and a bit of crazy. But they all had their own reasons for being there.

"Bold talk for a baby mech pilot," muttered Razorwire. "What are you going to do, use harsh language on them?"

The smaller, less armored HK-SWs really did look like they could be the children of the fully grown HK-PP's. Hence the nickname, Baby Mech.

"Hey," Dobbs countered. "I'll do my job out there. If you do yours, then I've got nothing to worry about."

Metzger understood the unspoken tension in the room. It was the same before every battle. He knew it was going to get worse. Thinking about an approaching fight was almost as bad as fighting one.

Buck joined in. "Any chance the locals are going to wise up and decide to let us do our job in peace? Because that's the one piece of new intel I'd appreciate hearing."

Hullbuster was asking the right question, the question of a true vet: *Can we avoid being shot at?* That was one of the many reasons Metzger liked Buck Nelson as his wingman. He might be a crayon-muncher, but he was much smarter than he looked.

Captain Peltier shook his head. "It doesn't look like it. They see us as violating their sovereignty, or some sket like that. I don't think they'll back down."

"So the fight is a go," Razorwire said.

"I didn't say that. They may just protest, throw rotten food, cuss us out. We'll see. We won't know until they fire on us."

Vickerson stirred. "Just once I wish the R-A would let us fire first. It feels like we're always letting the bastards get the first salvo on us."

"It doesn't matter," Grunon replied. "We have armor. I don't care who fires the first shot. Only the killing shot matters."

Ivers fist-bumped him.

"I've often found the application of the proper amount of explosive material usually solves most problems," Buck said.

He wasn't joking—Metzger could see it in his eyes. The hullbuster's prestige with Metzger went up a notch.

Peltier let them chatter until there was a pause, then spoke up. "Most of you have been in battle, so this is just a reminder. You've got armor all around you and you're moving fast. That makes you harder to kill, but it also draws the attention of the enemy. And we have no idea what the intention or strategy of the Vargasians are. So we will adapt as we go. Stick with your wingman, coordinate your actions. Ivers, Vickerson, that means communicating your status and ID'ing your targets clearly. Dobbs, you are our ECM and eyes out there. No running in and getting in over your head."

He was referring to observations from their training sessions. Peltier wasn't riding their ass, he was simply reminding them of the areas they need to improve on.

The captain's eyes flashed over to Metzger. "And as for you, Pileup, try and avoid driving into someone."

That comment brought a wave of chuckles, from Metzger too.

"Now, the 510th is a new squadron. We don't have insignia. We don't even have a name yet, just a number. We don't get those honors until we prove ourselves in battle. While I'm not looking forward to a fight, if there is one, it will define all of us. Generations in the future will know the name we earn. Let's make sure we don't screw this up. Go in, be the effective stompy warriors I know you can be, and we will get through this."

His words resonated with everyone in the 510th. They understood that the fight was more than just a battle; they were carving a small place in history. But at the same time... he was still avoiding the topic Buck had raised when Peltier first entered the room.

It was Razorwire who brought things back around—with even less tact than Buck had shown. "Was that the plan on Tralon?"

If looks could kill, Peltier's expression would have put Razorwire in a body bag. The captain rocked on his heels as though about to leave. "That's for those who fought there. Unless there's anything else..."

With that, he walked out of the rec room.

Metzger watched him go, considering whether to follow. The question of Tralon was on his mind. It was on the minds of the others. And it wasn't going away anytime soon.

He followed the captain and caught up with him at the ladder heading up to D Deck. "Sir, if I may?"

Peltier stopped. "Go ahead, Mr. Metzger."

"Sir, this thing on Tralon—it keeps coming up. I know it's not our business, but ducking out of the room like that will only give further life to stories and rumors about it that are probably a lot worse than the reality of what went down."

Peltier put his hands on his hips and sighed. "Those of us that got out of that place, witnessed what happened... we promised not to talk about it."

"I understand. Normally, I wouldn't bring this up, but we're a lot of new guys. Even the tankers who were with the 72nd at the time don't know what went on. We're about to go into battle for the first time as a unit. We need to have confidence in the officers who lead us. Having this thing linger out there, it's one more thing that people are going to be thinking about when they need to be concentrated on more important matters."

Peltier's voice was firm. "I think you're exceeding your authority with this conversation, Mr. Metzger."

Nodding once in agreement, Metzger kept his gaze on the captain. "I'm a warrant. From what I understand, part of the job description is exceeding my authority."

It was a joke based heavily on reality and nearly evoked a chuckle from Peltier. Almost. "There's no walking away from this?"

"I don't think so, sir. Keeping this quiet will only be a potential morale bomb to go off later." Metzger's experience was that secrets were just that, time bombs. They had a tendency to go off when you least desired or expected them to. Peltier had to understand that keeping all of this hush-hush was stupid.

Peltier's stance softened. "Okay, listen up."

"Sir, I am the model of discretion, but this is something the squadron—"

Peltier cut him off. "You listen first. Then tell me what the squadron needs to hear."

Metzger waited.

Peltier took a deep breath. "Inglima was a major at the time. Runnin' Meece's current job. The CO was a Colonel

Rogers, an appointed officer. A man not mentally equipped enough to wipe his own ass."

Metzger grunted. "I take it this Colonel Rogers was a disaster." Unlike the Legion, which was still actively resisting the influx of government-appointed officers, they had become commonplace in the Republic Army, Navy, and Marines. A simple fact of life.

"That is an understatement, Metzger," Peltier said. "Inglima is a mech pilot—he knows the nuts and bolts of armored combat. Wasn't so with Rogers. He was better suited to command a desk at HQ than troops in the field. But his family had the right connections in the House of Reason and got him seated in command of the 72nd. Our first combat op with him in command went well, but mostly because his junior officers and NCOs did the heavy lifting. Tralon... was a whole different situation."

Peltier's jaw set and his teeth ground together. Then he continued.

"The part of the planet we came down on was dense jungle. The colonel had picked the LZ despite our protests. Inglima was all over Rogers, telling him it wasn't good ground for our tanks or our mechs. In fact, Inglima tore into him to an extent that he seriously risked a court-martial for insubordination—to his credit. But Rogers insisted that landing in that jungle would surprise the enemy. And it did at first. I think they were shocked that a HARD regiment would be that dumb."

"And then, sir?"

Peltier's head shook, and he lowered his voice. "We deployed, but it was dense growth. Even the mechs struggled, and our tanks had it even worse. We're a unit where speed is our armor, and we had no speed. Our supporting infantry were all riders, simply because walking was out of the question in that growth.

"The zhee, on the other hand, felt right at home in the jungle. They hit us from almost every angle. One of their units even damaged one of the dropships. So Rogers had the ships take off, cutting us off from both our techs and our way off-world. The zhee played him like a cheap fiddle. For days they whittled away at us, chipping away at our strength. He should have had us form a defensive perimeter, but he felt sure he could chase them down. So he kept us pushing out, giving them ample opportunity to make our lives miserable."

"Sounds terrible."

"It gets worse. The zhee put on a show of retreating, luring us into a nearby desert zone, and you know how they love the desert. We were all thankful at the time—at least we could move again. The dunes were good for our mechs and our tanks—or so we thought. But the zhee had bunkers out there, well concealed. We had followed them into a perfectly staged trap, and they came at us from point-blank range.

"The 72nd was down to fifty percent combat strength when Rogers called in the dropships to get us out. It was bad, but not a bloodbath. Not yet. We could have patched up the damaged mechs and been good to go again after a cycle and a better insertion plan. The problem was, the zhee saw them coming down and tried to cut us off from our rides. It got ugly... real ugly. Of the men in my platoon, only two of us made it through their blocking effort and reached the ships. Everyone got hammered, but the squadron the 510th replaced got it worst of all. Its losses were in the ninetieth percentile."

Metzger whistled low. Usually a combat unit that suffered thirty percent or more losses was considered combat ineffective. *Ninety* percent... that was a massacre. No wonder this wasn't talked about. Still, an appointed officer making a mess of things was hardly something to keep secret. There had to be more.

"What happened to Rogers?" he asked.

"Son of a bitch survived," Peltier spat. "His command rig was blown to bits, but somehow that bastard managed to get out alive... unconscious, but alive. Meece lost his mech in the fighting and dragged Rogers back to the dropship right before we dusted off. He still claims it was the biggest mistake of his career, but you know the routine —we try to not leave men behind, even men like Rogers."

"There had to have been an investigation, though, right? A court-martial? You can't screw up the way Rogers did and not have the higher-ups take a look at it."

Peltier lowered his gaze to the floor for a long second. "There was. Rogers's defense was that we were all derelict in our duty. He went so far as to say that it was his junior officers who had suggested dropping in the jungle. One officer, Captain Schwartz, backed Rogers's version of events. Fellow point, albeit one with fewer connections. That man had been kissing the colonel's ass for so long, he couldn't help himself. He stabbed the rest of us in the back. And the worst part was, he seemed to enjoy it, going so far as smirking at us during his testimony. That traitor threw a lot of mud in our direction. Some of it was bound to stick."

"So Rogers got off?"

"Almost. Being a point has privileges, and Rogers pulled all the strings. The inquiry ended up with an inconclusive vote. There was enough evidence for them to bust Rogers back to the rank of captain and get his ass reassigned to some rear area where he couldn't do much damage."

"What about the other point?"

That question made Peltier shift on his feet, clearly uncomfortable. "Schwartz remained in the unit. There was some talk of disbanding the 72nd after all that. When the inquiry didn't put the blame on Rogers's shoulders where it belonged, it broke most of us. You would have had to dig a hole for ten hours to reach the top of where our morale was at that point."

Metzger pressed. "You didn't answer my question, sir. What happened to Schwartz?"

Again Peltier shifted, his gaze averted. "The official report is that he was up late, doing a walk-through of the repair bays. He must have fiddled with one of the gantry cranes... and it dropped a damn missile pod on him."

Metzger wasn't sure what he heard in the captain's voice, but he thought it sounded a lot like guilt.

"That's not what happened, is it, sir?"

Peltier shrugged. "Don't believe it, take it up with the report, Mr. Metzger."

Metzger understood clearly what Peltier was saying. Schwartz's death wasn't an accident. It was barracks justice. Such things happening in military units were very rare. With the Republic military, the few he had caught wind of had all involved points.

It was no wonder no one liked talking about this.

But there was nothing to be gained in pushing the matter forward. "Well," Metzger said, "the 72nd has risen out of that mess and rebuilt."

Peltier straightened once more. "Yes, we have. And I'll tell you something, Warrant. In some respects, I hope the locals here on Vargas do want to make a fight of it. If nothing else, it will help those of us who survived Tralon to put it behind us and move on."

"I appreciate you telling me about it, sir."

The captain pointed a finger at Metzger. "I didn't tell you a thing. If you feel like spreadin' another rumor, that's your prerogative, Mr. Metzger."

Metzger looked down, glancing at his replacement leg. "Understood, sir."

Peltier gave a curt nod. "Make sure everyone is rested, prepped, and ready to drop. See to your section—make sure there are no mistakes."

"Yes, sir."

Metzger turned around, now knowing the truth and yet agreeing with his captain that it wasn't a truth to be rebroadcast. Not until the team had spent more time together.

Maybe not even then.

An hour later, as he finished his fifth check of his HK-PP, Metzger's comms unit chirped indicating a task force personal transmission. Raising his wrist, he saw a friendly face, one that made him smile.

"O'Keefe. I figured you might be in the middle of this."

"What can I say? It turns out I'm fairly decent at this historian gig."

Metzger smile broadened. "I bet you had a hand in making sure I was here too."

O'Keefe shrugged. "I may have tossed out the 72nd for support on this op."

"Should I thank you?"

"That remains to be seen."

"You may be on the inside track. Is this going to be a hot drop?"

O'Keefe gathered her thoughts before responding. "Unknown. The mining guild isn't exactly rolling out the red carpet. The K'llik—well, you can't tell if they're pissed off or just quiet. But you don't have much to worry about, piloting that big-ass mech of yours."

"More like a big-ass target. Still, I'm hoping we can intimidate these locals enough to get down there and do our job."

"Your job is intimidation. Mine is determination. As in, determine if the lost legion was here, and if so, what happened to them."

"We'll clear the way for you. Assuming the Legion lets us have any of the glory."

"I'm counting on it."

"It's good to see you again. Any other... troubles?"

She shook her head. "Nothing I can't handle."

The pre-drop klaxon sounded around him. "Gotta go. See you downstairs, O'Keefe."

"Watch your back, Metzger."

Metzger shut off the comms channel and climbed down the ship's gantry. Things might go wrong when they dropped, but at least he knew he had a good friend there on landing.

22

The descent toward Vargas was remarkably smooth. O'Keefe chalked that up to the thin upper atmosphere. The historical team's dropship wasn't a combat ship, but a simple transport shuttle—reliable, more than capable of delivering cargo or personnel, but lacking in weapons. The ship's name was a bit of a mystery: the *Onondaga*. No one seemed to know the origin of the name, and the ship's database didn't offer anything as to her lineage.

It wasn't until the ship descended into crater 108.2 that O'Keefe felt the abrupt shaking she normally associated with landings. The crater's denser atmosphere buffeted the dropship hard as it maneuvered for landing. They touched down with a thud amid whining repulsors, and the green landing light went on in the ship's passenger section where the research crew was buckled in.

As the ship's artificial gravity switched off, O'Keefe felt the heaviness of Vargas's additional gravitational pull. After unhooking the safety harness, she rose to her feet, feeling even more of gravity's merciless tug. It wasn't horrible, but it would certainly be uncomfortable for the day or two it would take to get used to it. Still, that was nothing compared to her drops in the 444th, when they almost always had to worry about incoming fire.

She had sat through the intel briefings. It looked like the Vargas planetary militia was having second thoughts about attempting to defend crater 107.9; at least, that was the consensus interpretation of the data. The research team was overjoyed, but O'Keefe didn't share in their gleeful optimism. Just because the locals had made themselves scarce didn't mean they weren't planning something.

Three tones sounded over the ship's speakers, followed by a message from the cockpit. "All personnel aboard the *Onondaga*, this is Captain Dodge. We have landed. The HARD regiment is deploying from its landing craft as we speak. Until they give us the go-ahead, all passengers are to remain aboard."

The researchers had been given these orders in advance as well. For most of her team, this was perfectly fine, but O'Keefe chafed at them. She hated being protected by other troops. She had been a combat soldier; she could handle herself. Besides, they were kilometers away from the target crater; chances that they'd be facing hostile locals in this random hole were pretty slim.

As she waited, O'Keefe half-expected the appearance of one of her disjointed and fragmented memories. They sometimes came at times of stress, and oddly at times of high relaxation too. This landing came with a bit of tension, which could have triggered some memory, but none emerged. O'Keefe knew her ghosts were still haunting her gray matter, but for some reason they had kept quiet since her last conversation with Vex.

It had been well over two weeks since that encounter, and the truth was, she was looking forward to another visit. She wanted to try again and see whether she could extract more from these memory fragments than she had thus far.

Dranes rose from his seat and walked over to O'Keefe, taking slow steps as he got used to local gravity. "So far, so good."

Experience gnawed at her. "We only just dropped, and we aren't in 107.9 yet."

The warrant officer gave her a look. "Have you always been so grim?"

Do I really come across as grim?

"I'm not grim—I'm pragmatic. Until we've secured the objective and can start our work, I'm not counting any victories, even the small ones."

Dull thumps sounded from outside the ship, steady and numerous. Dranes smiled. "The 72nd is landing. It won't take them long to secure this hole."

He moved to the viewing ports, and O'Keefe followed.

Her attention was drawn instantly to the mechs. A Hunter-Killer Planet-Pounder and a variant she didn't know by sight thudded past the *Onondaga*, their footpads hitting the ground hard, kicking up gray dust clouds as they moved. Where the HK-PP was symmetrical in its weapons configuration, the other mech had a single large right-shoulder-mounted blaster—easily twice as large as the ones mounted on the HK-PP. Perhaps some type of mechanized sniper unit. You could wage some serious carnage at long range with a weapon like that.

The mechs were fantastic to watch. O'Keefe had been on a combat mission with direct mech support once, and it was one of the few things on a battlefield that intimidated her. If one of those things misstepped, it would turn you into paste—body armor or not.

Another big dropship moved into her field of vision in the distance. It had an aerodyne design, swooping low on large wings, flaps fully flared out. The rear door was open, coming down around four meters off the floor of the crater, and it ejected a pair of repulsor tanks, Anaconda-class, one after the other. As they roared off, coming close to bottoming out, the ship rose sharply and angled skyward. The tanks took off, gliding in their peculiar way as though traveling across glass, spreading out toward the perimeter of the crater floor.

Seeing the armored force eased a bit of O'Keefe's tension.

Turning from the portal, she looked at Dranes. "We should get down and check the equipment and transport."

"You must have heard an okay from the captain of this bird that I missed." Dranes smiled. "Relax for a few minutes, O'Keefe. They aren't going to let us open the bay doors and get the gear out until the 72nd declares this LZ secure. Besides, you need to give yourself some time to acclimate to the gravity."

"No one's shooting here," she countered. "And no one's going to either. The locals know that 107.9 is the prize. They aren't going to waste time with all the surrounding craters."

"That doesn't sound pragmatic to me," Dranes said. "Sounds like eager optimism. But like it or not, we still have a lot of time before they let us debark."

She knew he was right, but felt a flare of resentment. She'd put chits down that she'd been on more combat ops than he ever had.

She left Dranes behind and headed for the shuttle's transport bay. Each step got easier as her body adjusted to the increase in gravity. Dinner was going to be interesting that night. Digestive systems could struggle with heavier gravity, so it was common to make sure the first meal in the environment was "processing-friendly," which could plug up a lot of folks. She wasn't looking forward to it, but there was no way around it outside of a fast.

She went through the airlock, and the door hissed open, releasing a hint of oil and coolant from the big bay. In front of her were two enclosed transport sleds, secured to the deck with straps, and between them was a small, tracked excavator. She walked around all three vehicles, making sure the straps had done their job on landing.

Satisfied, she hefted herself up the rear steps of a repulsor sled to check its precious cargo. Her first attempt faltered, and she had to quickly lower herself back down to the deck—her muscles hadn't yet compensated enough for the gravity. On her second attempt she got in, but she was breathing heavily as a result. Dranes was right. She needed time to get her legs on this rock. She paused, caught her breath, then opened the rear hatch and turned on the interior light.

Her gaze went immediately to the mobile DNA analysis gear, and she was relieved to see it tightly strapped down, just as she'd left it. Everything else was in its place, too, despite the shaking during entry. She knew she needn't have worried, but it made her feel better to confirm.

Shutting off the light, she stepped cautiously back down the ladder, pausing to sit down on the last rung and close her eyes. Her arms felt like they had been dipped in lead, and her knees were protesting. She was pushing herself too hard. Again, Dranes was right. There was plenty of time. Take it slow.

But despite her best efforts, she couldn't suppress her excitement. She was on Vargas, and in a few days she would be at the site of the wreckage, possibly finding evidence of a lost legion.

Then she sensed it coming on—a memory. Slowly she opened her eyes, and she saw a shimmer of white light.

Lying on the deck of the dropship, just a few meters from where she sat, was Sergeant Fazzoli, firing away into nothingness with his Miif-7. His armor was scored with ugly black scars, blaster burn, but it didn't seem to shake him.

This was a new memory, one she'd never seen before. And there was no context, just him firing.

"Damn it, O'Keefe, I need you to crawl up on that position to the left. Get on that little rise—you should be able to bring the rain down on their position. Stack those bastards high and deep!"

"Damn right I'll stack 'em," O'Keefe said in response. In that moment, she realized that the voice she heard came through to her as if she were wearing her helmet and earbuds. She wondered if she'd actually said it before. It felt like she had.

"Less talk, more ass-hauling, O'Keefe," Fazzoli snapped. "We can't hold this position forever!"

What do I do now?

She wanted to extend the memory, find out more, but she had no way of knowing the right way to react to it. To advance the memory, she had to know what to say next; and to know what to say next, she needed to remember it. It was an impossibly frustrating situation.

She started to rise from the rung she'd been sitting on, and she felt a hint of dizziness, just for a moment, a twist of vertigo.

And that was all it took. The image of the prone R-A sergeant firing away disappeared.

O'Keefe reached out to Fazzoli as if she could touch him. "Don't go! Tell me what happened back there. Did I take out that position?"

But it was too late. He was gone, and she was once more alone in the bay.

23

The Kestrel-class dropship *Omaha* came in low over the bottom of crater 108.2. Metzger had done six such drops in training, but this one felt very different. This wasn't a training run, but a possible combat mission, and his heightened senses told him that battle could come at any moment. He shifted in the command seat of his HK-PP, his eyes darting to his displays.

Still in the green. Good.

His mech was suspended on a drop rail, essentially strapped with its back to the rail. Three other mechs were similarly mounted, back to back, ready to deploy. He heard a metallic clunking sound, and light came up from below. Leaning forward, he could see the doors under his footpads retracting. The four squat legs of the *Omaha* that supported the ovoid ship kicked up dust as it maneuvered for a drop. He pushed himself back into his seat. *Better brace for it.*

"Ten seconds to drop," came the voice of Captain Peltier in his earpiece. "I want a quick egress and dispersal. Weapons are to be at the ready—no shooting until I call it."

"Copy that," Metzger replied, along with Buck, Vickerson, and Stan, who shared the same drop rail. Peltier, Dobbs, Tramel, and Krock were on the rail above them and would drop after they'd hit the ground and deployed.

A klaxon sounded in the drop bay, loud and crisp enough to be heard in their cockpits. A green drop indicator flashed on Metzger's displays, projected on his canopy. Pilots didn't control their drops, that was done by the ship's master, but they had an emergency override in case the ship became damaged by incoming fire or some other critical situation happened.

After a slight jolt, he felt himself rise in his seat as the mech dropped beneath the belly of the dropship. The HK-PP slid down the drop rail and fell to the ground below. All around him were the roaring engine plumes, brilliant, searing hot blue-white.

Then the mech landed, its knees bending to absorb the impact, and Metzger felt himself push down hard in his seat, harder than when he had done the test drops. Vargas's gravity was holding him tight, and he could even feel his cheeks sag on the landing.

His feet immediately kicked the mech into motion as he and Buck headed between two of the azure drive plumes from the ship hovering over them, the flying dust and dirt obscuring their vision. The buffeting from the plumes was like walking into a hurricane-strength wind shear, but Metzger leaned into it as he moved.

Once away from the dropship, he twisted the mech's torso, surveying the crater. The light-blue sky ended at the crater's rim, making it look like they were surrounded by a ring of mountains. The *Omaha* was already moving off to its predesignated landing zone, and his tactical display showed only friendlies all around him.

Captain Peltier's voice came on the tactical channel. "All right, Five-Ten, head to the east and the low rise. We're forming a Class S perimeter around the LZ."

Metzger adjusted the map on his display, orienting it for easier reading, then slowly sped up toward the east.

Crater 108.2 was unsettled. There were bright greens, some sort of growth. Pools of water looked clear except for the orange rust color along their banks. There was a complete miniature ecosystem in each crater, making the planet appear less desolate than it did from orbit.

Buck moved on his left and slightly behind. "I'm not picking up anything here."

"There's nothing in this hole to pick up other than us," Metzger replied. He hoped it stayed that way.

"You'd think someone would have settled here. It seems nice enough."

"You spent too much time in orbit," Metzger muttered.

"The mindset of a good hullbuster never dies."

"I suppose that's a good thing. But I served on the ground. And one thing I learned a long time ago: planets are big places. I bet even on a planet as densely populated as Utopion, there's areas like this, unsettled. Besides, the people that came to this rock did so for mining. Chances are the reason you don't see anyone here is that there's nothing of value here. Miners only settle in where the mining companies tell them to."

"I'm getting some fluctuations on my tactical display," Buck said. "You getting the same?"

Metzger checked his tactical display, which flickered like it was being targeted by heavy ECM. They had known the iron concentration and magnetic field variations were going to limit the range of the mechs' sensors.

"Zoom in and trim range to one kilometer," he said. He used his left-hand controls to adjust his own sensors.

"Copy that."

In the distance, Metzger saw the ground sloping up toward the rim of the crater. The other two squadrons were going to be heading to similar egress points off the crater floor. He was feeling heavy and sluggish, no doubt from the gravity's toll, and as he started up the slope, he saw the atmosphere warning indicator come on, alerting him to the thinning oxygen. The mechs were airtight, but that could change if they were damaged.

He plodded on. With each footstep up the slope, the faint blue of the low-hanging sky seemed to dissolve into the blackness of night. By the time he reached the surface of Vargas, the sky above was a brilliant and desolate black. Turning slightly, he looked at the edge of the crater behind him. The shimmer of white along the top of the rim was all that indicated the heavier atmosphere below.

The noise of his footfalls softened in this thin atmosphere. All he could hear now were the sounds within the mech, the hum of the power plant, the light purr of the circulation fan above and behind him, the almost undetectable hum of the knee and leg actuators. Some pilots claimed that the noises all blended together into a dull drone, but Metzger could distinguish each sound individually.

"Push out on your designated paths," Captain Peltier transmitted. "We need to extend the perimeter from the crater and confirm no locals poking around."

So much for enjoying the view.

"All right, Buck, move to 116-dot-14-dot-10," Metzger said. Buck acknowledged, and they started away from the crater.

The members of the squadron got more and more separated as they spread out, forming a wide perimeter. Metzger watched his target coordinates and slowed his HK-PP to a stop at the appropriate location. He tried to adjust his tactical sensors to pick up additional range, but the more he extended his sweeps, the more the signals broke up.

"I'm not getting squat," Buck sent.

"Me either," Metzger replied.

He heard a sound from his mech, a slight moan. He knew it wasn't anything serious, simply the metal protesting either the cold or the thin atmosphere. Either way, it served as a reminder of how deadly the environment was.

"I don't like it much out here," he said. "One little hole and you suffer decompression."

There were emergency patch guns in each HK-PP, holstered next to the pilot's normal sidearm. They fired rounds of self-sealing, quick-setting foam. On paper, they could plug a good-sized cockpit breach, but that assumed the pilot could find the hole, grab the weapon, and hit it. All while, presumably, gasping for oxygen. In the safety briefing they'd been given, the 72nd's pilots and drivers had been told that humans *could* breathe the thinner air here, but it took several days to adjust, and until then... it wasn't safe. If they got breached, they would likely pass out and suffer symptoms of decompression.

Buck chuckled on their private channel. "Worries you, eh? You wouldn't have lasted long as a hullbuster. One of the perks of being a good marine is that you eventually purge your fear of suffocating in space."

"Being comfortable with the concept of suffocation isn't a *perk*. It's a mental disorder," Metzger shot back.

"You're just jealous."

"Of what?"

"The bravery of marines." Pride rang in each word that Buck Nelson spoke.

"There's a fine line between bravery and lunacy."

"Spoken like a man who's still afraid of the vacuum of space. You must be one of those R-A 'warriors' unwilling to admit that marines outclass the Repub Army."

Metzger decided to change subjects. "I feel for pilots like Dobbs in this environment."

Warrant Officer Dobbs piloted the sole Hunter-Killer Scout Walker in the 510th's Scout Platoon. And whereas Buck and Metzger had an armored cockpit around them, HK-SW pilots sat on a perch in the open air. In the thin atmosphere of Vargas's surface, they wore combat environment suits—comvacs—but they still had to feel awfully exposed.

Thinking of Dobbs made Metzger remember Frixon and the dead HK-SW pilot he had pulled the data core from. That memory made him reach down and touch his artificial leg.

"The HK-SWs are going to be fine," Buck said. "It's hard to hit the pilot when those machines are on a full sprint."

"Speed is our armor," Metzger replied with a hint of sarcasm.

"Easier to say when you aren't sitting in the saddle. That was the best part of being a hullbuster, though. You could often kill people without them firing a shot. Sometimes without you firing a shot either. Best battle I never had to fight was the time I put a breaching charge on the airlock of a blockade runner. You expose humans to no atmosphere, you don't have to shoot them. Good times."

"That doesn't seem very fair."

"Screw fair! Nothing about warfare is fair. It's about winning or dying."

"You miss it, don't you?" Metzger said.

He got a moment of silence back before Nelson responded. "Let's talk about something else."

They didn't have time to come up with another topic, as the orders came for the squadron to fan out, extending their perimeter further. The surface was barren and uneven. Millennia of meteor strikes had formed countless tiny craters. As Metzger moved out, he kicked up the metal-rich dust behind him. He had to wonder about the kind of people who would voluntarily come to a planet like this to settle.

No signs of life showed as they extended their perimeter to ten kilometers. Metzger was about to signal in when Captain Peltier's voice came in over the tactical channel once more. "I'm monitoring all your sensor feeds, and this crater perimeter appears secure. That confirms what our data told us on the burn in. Time to move on to the primary objective. Our squadron has drawn point. We are heading to planetary south, echelon formation."

Metzger's tactical display showed a single waypoint on the journey to crater 107.9. It was nothing more than a digital dot on the map. Angling his HK-PP, he trotted straight toward it, with Buck taking another straight-line route that would converge with his own. Ahead Metzger could see a shimmering light-blue-and-white line on the horizon, marking the upper atmosphere of the target crater.

It took seventeen minutes to reach the lip. He stopped a few meters short and dipped his mech's waist to get a good view. Through the thin wispy white clouds, he saw the greens, blues, and oranges of the ground below. Crater 107.9 was much larger than the one they'd landed in, and deeper too. The greens were lusher, and he could make out several lakes and ponds, some with blue water, others tinged orange around the shores. A few boulders were large enough to be seen from above.

Up until this moment, Metzger hadn't put much thought into the lost legion that might or might not have come here to this crater on Vargas. But now he wondered if they were really down there. Those men had lived and died long before he was even born—but they were brothers of battle. If they were there, he would see that they got home. No one deserved to be left behind on some obscure world like this.

His mind shifted to O'Keefe. She was the one who had gotten him here—gotten them all here. She was probably excited as all hell about it... as she should be. This was a big coup.

All right, O'Keefe. Let's get you down there and recover those boys.

24

They had been on Vargas for two days, establishing a base camp before their foray to their target crater to begin their investigation. Most of O'Keefe's time had been spent checking their equipment, making sure nothing had been broken during the trip. Everything was in working order, which was a pleasant surprise—the equipment was notoriously touchy. But impatience was chewing at the back of her brain. She wanted to get to the crashed dropship and start work.

Then word came that the locals were approaching.

After the initial landing, messages had been sent out to the mining guild and to the K'llik, with the hope that hostilities might be avoided. Everyone was surprised when the Vargasians—both human and K'llik—replied to say they were sending a party for further parlay. O'Keefe came out with the rest of the research team to watch the meeting.

The Vargasians arrived at crater 108.2 with little fanfare, kicking up black and gray dust from the uplands as they approached. They continued on down the roadway along the side of the crater, toward the shuttles and dropships deployed at the bottom, traveling in only two vehicles, one for each delegation. The guild vehicle was a heavy mining transport, but with armor plates added to it, along with a blaster cannon in a makeshift turret. It looked both crude and deadly.

O'Keefe's discriminating eyes could see that the blaster was brand-new. Hell, it still had the primer on it. *Someone has been selling weapons to the guild.*

The K'llik delegation's vehicle looked and moved like a centipede, with a dozen or so independent but attached modules, each with four spindly legs. It stood some four meters tall and undulated across the hot black sands as it descended toward the human delegation. When it at last stopped and the hatches opened, four creatures emerged, and O'Keefe saw the aliens up close and personal for the first time.

The K'llik's bodies were a splotched mix of browns and bright oranges. They had six limbs, all slightly skinnier than the ten-centimeter diameters of their tube-like bodies. Those bodies were about four meters in length, and the limbs roughly two meters each. At the end of each limb were four bone-like projections, like fingers on a human hand. Their faces, if they could be called that, looked much like another limb on top of their long bodies— the only difference being it was shorter, perhaps a half meter, and was topped by two bulbous eyes, glossy black and unyielding. As O'Keefe adjusted her face mask and looked closer, she saw tiny slits that must be mouths.

Each K'llik wore only a necklace that clung to the bony joints in their articulated bodies. The fine silver chains and seals swung gracefully as they moved.

O'Keefe was impressed by them, and slightly intimidated. With all their joints and their size, she expected them to be slow—but they were not. Their leader stepped forward, followed by guild representatives, stopping in front of Colonels Inglima and Hackett.

The humans were much less impressive. Guildmaster Rune looked more like a mid-level manager than a miner. He wore a green jumpsuit that looked freshly purchased. It made him look military, though he clearly wasn't. While he was muscular and thick, he wasn't military fit. O'Keefe noticed that he kept his distance from the K'llik leaders, perhaps out of respect, perhaps out of fear. Rune's face bore an expression of frustration tinged with anger. As for the K'llik, it was impossible to interpret their emotions—which would give them an edge in any discussions.

O'Keefe had been a little surprised to learn that the meeting wouldn't be taking place in the privacy of a command trailer—though now that she had seen the size of the K'llik, she supposed she understood why. Instead it had been hastily arranged in a flat open spot of the crater floor, flanked by boulders and low, yellow-leafed trees. A security detail—including several mechs—formed a horseshoe around the meeting site. That sent a clear message of strength, one she hoped the locals would heed. O'Keefe assumed that Metzger was piloting one of those mechs, and that gave her a greater sense of safety.

The two leaders came forward from their transports, the K'llik looming large in front of the colonels. The colonels didn't look intimidated, and O'Keefe did her best to duplicate their expressions—though it was difficult. Two of the K'llik had a weapon strapped to one of their limbs, something similar to a blaster carbine in a holster that looked almost ceramic. Their gun handles were oddly shaped, clearly designed for their sharp, pointed bone hands.

For a long few moments, the two sides faced each other, saying nothing. The K'lliks' black orb eyes rotated slightly, taking in the details of the delegation. Then Colonel Hackett spoke.

"Greetings. I am Colonel Hackett of Cobra Company, 14th Legion." His eyes shifted to Inglima. "This is Colonel Inglima of the 72nd HARD regiment. We are here as honor guard while our archeological team recovers our dead."

The guildmaster responded. "I am Guildmaster Rune of the Mining Guild of Vargas. I would welcome you to our world in other circumstances, but your presence is not desired here given the open hostility of the Republic toward this guild. You have come uninvited, a military invasion force, clearly to impress the will of the Republic on our humble planet."

A dusty translator bot brought by the miners made a series of snaps, cracks, and hisses, to which the leader of the K'llik responded in kind. O'Keefe imagined that some mischief could be done by relying on the miners' bot, but a significantly cleaner Republic translator bot stood by, doing its best to verify that the translation was accurate. The K'llik language wasn't widely known, and a bot was only as good as its learning algos.

The miners' translator bot then spoke with a female voice. "I am T'chal'taka'vis, High Regent of the K'llik. Your presence here is not welcome. You must leave immediately."

O'Keefe was surprised that a small number of noises produced so many words. She was equally surprised that this additional parlay being held on the ground seemed to be proceeding along the exact same lines as the ones done while they were in orbit. No one was willing to budge.

"We mean no harm or disrespect," Hackett said, looking from one leader to the other. "We respect your planet as a member of the Republic. It is our intent to recover our dead, if we find them here, nothing more."

More hisses and pops from the K'llik, then the translation: "You were told to not come."

Rune added to the high regent's argument. "Your pretext for coming here is ridiculous. There is nothing here."

"Then allowing us to look unhindered will result in our hasty departure," Colonel Hackett replied firmly. "Something you have made clear you would like to see."

"I would like to see our sovereignty respected *now*," Rune countered.

"This is not about sovereignty. You are a member of the Republic and enjoy the protection of the Legion and the Republic's own military units. And my legionnaires are honor bound to see about the possibility of our dead being on this world." Hackett looked back at the research team. "Everyone else is here by legal right. Laws you agreed to upon joining the Republic."

The high regent spoke through the translator bot. "Your laws are not ours. We live on a Republic world, but not by choice. You trespass. Your presence is a violation. We do not accept it. You would be wise to pay heed."

"We will not be long," Hackett tried anew. "Once we are done, we will leave."

Inglima added, "Our work would be quicker if you helped us by sharing any information you have about what we might find in the crater."

For a moment, the K'llik leader did not respond. Then came a longer string of hisses, snaps, and pops. "Your predecessors trespassed as well. They came for the others that were acquaintances. War was here. They moved north to the Defilers Pass and the last of them died there fighting."

O'Keefe was thrilled at what sounded like confirmation that legionnaires *were* once here, but she didn't like the sound of these "acquaintances." What did that even mean? Acquaintances of whom? And who killed the legionnaires? Was it the Savages or the K'llik? Her distrust of the massive insects was growing.

"So it's true?" Hackett asked. "There are dead legionnaires on this world."

"The K'llik do not range this far and would not know," Rune answered. "But speaking for the guild, Colonel, I can assure you that there is nothing in that crater. And your presence here remains something we cannot, and will not, allow. We will not be pushed around. We will not be bullied. Your presence is likely to evoke a violent response from the Vargas Liberation Army."

"The who?" Hackett asked, shifting his muscular frame —which somehow looked even more mammoth when confined by Legion armor—to square up with the guildmaster.

"They are a group of independent agitators that led the last revolt against the Republic, and I am doing my best to prevent similar unpleasantness from happening again. While you seem interested only in provoking it."

"Where is their representative?" the Legion commander pressed.

"I do not know. They are most secretive. What I do know is their stance on such matters. They will not allow Republic armed forces to mount another incursion on Vargas."

O'Keefe doubted there was any real distinction between the guild and the so-called "Vargas Liberation Army." It was a thin veil of deniability that Rune was trying to wrap himself in. The man was a coward, and worried that he might be held accountable if his side lost.

Inglima spoke up once more. "We're not coming here for a confrontation. We're coming to find our dead and take them home. Nothing more, nothing less. Your people have nothing to be upset or worried about."

The high regent's hissing and snapping was louder. "It is *not* permitted. Depart immediately before there is conflict."

"We do not desire a conflict," Hackett emphasized. "Surely we can arrive at a compromise? Something mutually beneficial."

"We are past compromise. You have already landed your troops."

Hackett clearly was not a diplomat; O'Keefe could see that he was getting frustrated, and she sympathized with him. Neither the guild nor the K'llik were giving any good ground to negotiate from.

"Guildmaster," he said, "we could have landed right in your capital, but did not. We landed way out here, where none of your people are working. If we were really here to impose ourselves on you, we would be moving to take strategic targets. Instead we are standing here, in a worthless hole in the ground, talking. Consider that, if you would."

Rune remained intractable. "Worthless? Are you a miner, Colonel? Is this *your* world? For all we know, you are merely using this crater as a base to launch a war of suppression on Vargas. Ever since our uprising, the Republic has imposed new regulations and tariffs on our people as punishment. Your presence here is merely an extension of that."

The high regent issued a long litany of sounds before the translator bot processed it. "Stay and further disturb our lands, and you will suffer the fate of those that came before."

That was clearly a threat. And it had been made to Colonel Hackett, a man who had only one response to threats: elimination. Worse, the high regent had to be aware of that. The K'llik *wanted* a war.

Before either colonel could respond, the K'llik swiftly spun in place and climbed back into the modules of their mecha-centipede. The bulbous doors hummed shut and the great machine departed, the last module kicking up some sand that washed over the humans. While O'Keefe doubted that was deliberate, she had to wonder.

Rune spoke a moment later. "It is rare that I find myself in agreement with my counterpart. Today I am. You have come down here looking for a fight. If you don't leave, you will get one." Then he turned and boarded his own transport. It too took off for the long ramp up and out of the crater.

Hackett dusted the grit from his armor. "Well, that could have gone better."

"We got some interesting intel, at least," Inglima said. "The K'llik seem to believe that our 'predecessors' were here."

"But not the human Vargasians," Hackett replied, wiping the sweat from his brow. "I think they're going to push this. We need to be vigilant."

O'Keefe felt a chill run down her spine. Both factions seemed not only willing, but even eager, to start fighting. Why?

She felt a hand on her shoulder and turned.

"Carson!" she said, moving to him and embracing him in a hug, one he returned. "I was hoping you were here."

Metzger's eyes twinkled. "It's damn good to see you again. Then last time we were together—"

O'Keefe cut him off, speaking quietly. "Was when you caught me at a bad time. A *real* bad time. I owe you a round for the way you helped me."

To her surprise, he looked embarrassed, an expression she rarely saw on her friend's face.

"Save the credits, because I stopped drinking. Anyway, I was just coming by to say hello while I could. It sounds like they intend to make this an unpleasant assignment for both of us."

She smiled. "Knowing you're here helps."

25

It took the HARD and Legion troops another two days to survey the floor of crater 107.9 and declare it safe enough for the researchers. And though O'Keefe appreciated their work, she only grew more impatient. The wreckage was there, and the link to the lost legion was undeniable. But it would be up to the research team to prove what now seemed increasingly likely: that the men of that legion, the Howling Banshees, called this planet their final resting place.

By the time the survey was done, and the transport carrying her and the archeological team hissed to a stop in the crater, she was a bundle of suppressed energy, and she rose quickly to make sure she would be the first person to step down onto the site.

The door to the transport opened with a purring sound, and sunlight hit her. Clearly visible just a short distance away was the wreckage. The ship was sixty meters long—or had been. Its landing hadn't been soft. The forward portion of the ship was driven into the ground, the front landing struts sheared off and turned into a trail of scrap metal, the rear ones bent back from the force of the impact. The fuselage was badly crumpled, almost like an accordion, and the entire wreckage yawed to the starboard side. It looked like the sort of crash landing that no one could walk away from.

On the side of the hull, in black lettering that was slightly scored with burn marks from descent, were the letters they had seen from the satellite imagery: *CLK-225-A.* The *Derfflinger.* Under it was smaller lettering, barely legible: *DS-01 Cú Chulainn.* This had not been visible from orbit.

O'Keefe stepped onto the gangway, and the cool air struck her skin. It had a strange aroma to it, a hint of alien pollen—fruity and gritty at the same time. She paused as she surveyed the area around her. It had taken a lot of work to get here. She could only hope it wouldn't all prove to be a colossal waste of time.

"O'Keefe," came Dranes's voice from behind her. "You mind stepping off the gangway so the rest of us can join you?" She wasn't sure, but she thought he might actually have chuckled, a rarity for the warrant officer.

She took a few more steps forward, feeling embarrassed for having blocked the others, but she was in awe of what she saw. This wasn't a mission, it was an experience.

She saw now, in the distance, an HK-PP standing guard over the site, surely only one of many. There had been no sign of the mining guild or the K'llik, but that didn't mean their threats were empty.

Dranes gave orders to debark their equipment from the transport. She started to go and assist the rest of the team, but his hand came to rest on her shoulder. "Not you, Corporal," he said.

"Sir?"

"Let's walk the perimeter of this ship first."

She didn't even try to suppress her smile. "Yes, sir."

Dranes let her walk a pace in front of him as they approached the rear of the crashed vessel. The drive section was somewhat intact, despite its age and the violence of the landing. O'Keefe reached out to one of the thruster bells, feeling the film of dust on it. In one thruster, a vine was growing out, snaking around the bell and slithering around the seams of the ship's hull. They came around the aft of the dropship, and she saw no sign of what had caused it to land so violently. Where was the damage that had brought her down? Perhaps it had been a mechanical failure.

But her questions were answered, at least in part, on the starboard side. An ugly black scar crossed the ship near the engineering section, under what was left of the tail wing. That explained why they hadn't seen the damage from the satellite images. It didn't take an engineer to recognize a massive blaster cannon hit. In the center of the scar, the metal had melted, the blast penetrating into the interior of the dropship. Perhaps it was a miracle that they'd landed at all.

As they continued around the ship, her gaze shifted to a grassy, moss-covered area. The security team had already reported on what they had found here, but for O'Keefe, it was something else entirely to witness it with her own eyes.

The several rows of shadows spotted from orbit... were grave markers. Crude, apparently made with bits of wreckage from the ship.

O'Keefe walked slowly toward them as if drawn by some unseen force. Two of the graves had dessicated weapons marking the dead, metal components rusted away, with only the faded polymer still intact, stabbed into the ground ages before. There were also three battered helmets, all worn down to their carbon-fiber ballistic weave, but they looked like marine helmets, not Legion.

The visor of one was missing, and another was caved in on its side.

It opened the worrying possibility that no legionnaires —no members of the lost legion—had been on planet, just a detachment of marines. Which sounded callous to O'Keefe even as she thought the words.

Hullbusters deserve a homecoming, too.

Scanning further, she saw two more helmets side by side atop a twisted piece of metal, covered in some sort of moss. It was difficult to tell their shape, but her heart fluttered as she stepped closer.

She recognized the style immediately.

These were old MK III Legion buckets.

She stopped before the grave markers, staring at them in silence.

"Oba," muttered Dranes. "Mark Three helmets, late Savage Wars era."

O'Keefe was suddenly aware that her breathing was rapid, and she concentrated in order to slow it down. She had no doubt now: here, in these graves, were lost legionnaires. At least some... though not enough. Not enough to account for the entire lost legion.

Yet.

Dranes spoke into his communications unit. "This is Chief Dranes to Colonel Hackett."

"This is Hackett, go."

"Sir, we've found a grave site and what looks to be Legion Mark Three helmets."

"I will detach a squad to your location." There was a pause, then his voice came back. "You're sure they're Legion?"

"Yes, sir."

"I'll send a squad over."

As O'Keefe stared at the antiquated buckets, she tried to temper her excitement. This *might* not be all of the lost 552nd. It could just be a few legionnaires who had gone down to the planet and were left. The rest of the Howling Banshees could be at whatever stop came next. But then again, did it matter? These were legionnaires. They would be recovered. And that, after all, was the goal.

No matter what, they had found the trail. Found more than anyone before them had even come close to.

"Someone else had to have survived the crash," she said.

"Say again?"

"Someone else survived. The dead didn't bury themselves." She turned to face Dranes.

"You're right," he said. "And that gives some credence to what the K'llik said. Also makes me wonder why the miners were so insistent that what's clearly here—wasn't here."

The two looked around, as though anticipating the arrival of those two hostile groups to come bounding down the crater walls.

Then O'Keefe spoke again. "Let's get our internal perimeter set up before the legionnaires arrive." Now that confirmed Legion dead were in play, an honor guard would be posted. "Everything around this site is historical evidence. I don't want it trampled."

"I'll have the teams give us some room."

Together, they looked once more at the grave markers.

"You did it," Dranes said proudly.

"*We* did it. And we still have a lot of work to do."

While the archeologists used ground penetration equipment to mark the graves and survey the site, Chief Weaver and a naval engineer concentrated on the wreck of the dropship. Their conclusion was that the wreck was relatively stable, was free of radiation, and could be entered carefully. The best means of entry came in the form of a blast door that had long ago jammed shut. It took a heavy, portable plasma torch to burn it open.

O'Keefe joined Weaver when the door was removed, just to get a glimpse inside the dead ship. It was dank, the air moist and reeking of mold. With their masks on, it was tolerable. The insides were a jumbled mess of rusted and broken equipment, shattered wall sections, and long-decayed gear. Plastic wrappings, perhaps from field rations, littered the angled floor. But most notably, a cot had been set up and positioned level in the room, and on it, barely hidden by a rotting green thermal blanket, were skeletal remains. The figure's jaw hung wide, as if uttering a scream no one could hear.

O'Keefe wondered if this was the person who had buried the dead. Had they been alone... the sole survivor of the crash?

A lonely way to die.

She pushed away the dark thought and let her clinical thinking take over. "We'll need to check the body for identi-chits—and run a DNA test to be sure."

Weaver nodded. "While you're working on that, I'll see about accessing the ship's data. I've brought the right interface gear for this era of hardware; I just need to find a terminal. But, fair warning, there may well be nothing here to recover."

"If there is, I know you'll find it. But let's not just go diving in. We need to proceed cautiously. Everything in this room needs to be carefully removed, cataloged, and checked."

"That's going to take a while, Corporal."

"I know, Mr. Weaver. This isn't a rush job. We need to do this right."

"I'm on it."

O'Keefe stepped out of the bay and squinted against the bright sun creeping across the sky. Another HK-PP stood guard in that direction, some distance away. There was still no sign of the locals, but a squad of legionnaires would be stood over the grave sites at all times, on rotational duty, while a rotating selection of the 72nd watched the perimeter. The bulk of both forces was topside, patrolling the vast emptiness surrounding crater 107.9. O'Keefe felt secure.

Removing her breathing mask, she drew some cool air. As she did, she felt that slight mental tug, a hint that a memory was returning. She braced herself for it, closing her eyes, wondering which of her former comrades might appear. But when she opened her eyes, she saw nothing. Instead a voice came to her, as if riding the wind that hit her face.

"You can do it, O'Keefe. I know you can. All you have to do is hit the damn target..."

She knew the voice: Private Faulkner. They'd called him Slither because he'd had a pet lizard at some point—some sort of half-snake, half-chameleon.

But once again, this was an entirely new memory. She'd never gotten just a voice before, and she'd never heard from Slither. She wanted to know more, to ask about the target, to find out if she hit it, but she could tell the memory was already gone.

Redonning her mask and drawing another deep breath, she started down the steps. Slither was right about one thing: she could do this. She would get to the bottom of what had happened here.

Their first few days on Vargas were productive, but not fruitful. While Chief Weaver meticulously cleared the ship, O'Keefe oversaw the disinterment of the graves. They started with one marked with an old Legion bucket. The helmet had a serial number, but the Republic records from the Savage Wars era were spotty, and there was no record now of who this headgear had been assigned to. That, however, *did* serve as additional confirmation that the bucket was in fact from the expected era, and based on its style and estimated age it could very well have been with the troops in Taskforce Equii. Bit by bit, they were putting together tiny pieces of evidence.

It's a lot like my memory fragments in that regard.

The team didn't have to dig deep to find the skeletal remains in the first grave. Whoever the unfortunate person was, they had faced severe trauma—two broken legs. The uniform had mostly decayed, and the parts that remained didn't help with identification. There were some coins in the grave, most likely buried in the pockets of the victim—all were late Savage Wars era. Yet another tiny piece of confirmation.

O'Keefe now stood in the boxy repulsor trailer where the archaeological team had set up a base of operations— effectively a self-enclosed laboratory and storage facility. She was monitoring the DNA test unit, currently processing the sample from the disinterred body. In O'Keefe's mind, this was the only result that would truly, without a doubt, prove that they had found the 552nd. Unfortunately, this had been yet another test of her patience. Getting a good DNA sample was a slow and tedious process—steps had to be taken to avoid cross-contamination, and factors had to be analyzed for the soil and native insects and other vermin that might have touched the long-decomposed bodies. It didn't take long to run the test itself, but getting a good sample had taken longer than she'd expected.

Her eyes were now fixed on the readout, which showed the percent of the test completed. When it crossed the ninety percent mark, O'Keefe felt her heartbeat pick up. In moments she would know. Not just believe, not just suspect, not just hope... but *know*.

At ninety-two percent, a rumble sounded from outside, like distant thunder echoing around the crater. So far on Vargas, there had never been thunder. Rain, sure, but even that was little more than a misting. She had been outside just a short while before, with no sign of bad weather—the clouds were mere thin white streaks in the sky.

When a second rumble sounded, she knew something was wrong—and possibly dangerous.

She was just turning toward the vehicle's door when it flew open and a hulking human appeared. Her hands moved up into a defensive posture, but a blow from his rifle butt came faster than she could deflect it. The strike to her chest knocked her backward onto the padded floor, struggling to pull in air.

Two other humans came in after the first. All three were filthy, covered in light gray dust that clung to the sweat and the beard stubble on their faces, and all were armed with older-model N-3 blaster rifles, a version retired at least a decade before, prone to overheat its charge packs and therefore quickly discontinued.

From outside the mobile lab came the sounds of blaster fire.

The man who'd hit her leveled his blaster at her, and she could see the fury in his eyes as he looked over the rest of the researchers. "Nobody move."

"Who the hell are you?" Dranes asked, stepping forward.

"Hold it right there, fella," said a second man as he stepped inside. He aimed his weapon at the warrant officer and grinned.

"We are the Vargas Liberation Army," said the first man proudly. "And you can be corpses or our prisoners, depending on how well you listen."

How? wondered O'Keefe. *How are they here?* The crater had been thoroughly cleared. There were guards, Legion and Repub Army.

From outside came another distant rumble, which she now thought must be some sort of explosive detonating.

"Get up," the leader said, still pointing at her with his blaster.

Another rebel crowded into the lab.

O'Keefe calculated mounting an attack, but the math was horrible. Three armed men, weapons at the ready, in a tight space. Against her, Dranes, and a few other historians and scientists who had been at work in the lab. If she had a pistol, the equation would have worked out much better. As it was, if she sprang at them, she'd be dead before she could take even one of them down. So she merely rose slowly, feeling where the butt of the weapon had slammed into her chest.

Suddenly, a chime sounded. The DNA test was complete.

For a moment, everyone looked at the testing unit. One shooter raised his weapon, aiming at it.

"No! Don't. It's just a DNA test," O'Keefe blurted out. "Let me attend it."

A blaster bolt crashed into the machine, sending up sparks and smoke. Destroying it, along with its results. O'Keefe felt as though she had been gut-shot herself.

"Do what we say or you're all in for much worse than that," the leader said with a growl. "You're hostages, for now. Try anything stupid... you'll be dead."

Outside, blaster fire erupted. Some of it Legion N-4s, but most of it something else.

There was a lot more of the something else.

26

The Legion forces were mostly welcoming to the members of the 72nd. But though the conversations were warm and respectful, they were also distant. It wasn't Legion arrogance, just pecking order. The Legion knew where they stood—outside of the Republic military structure, with their own Constitutional rights, protections, and obligations. And even if that weren't so, the Legion was decidedly on the elite end of the spectrum. The HARD unit was there as support, despite what Colonel Inglima thought. Metzger found it hard to blame the legionnaires for their attitude. They operated in a universe of their own.

He himself had wanted to join the Legion—dreamed of it, really—but now, with his bionic leg, even the dream was gone. It would never be possible. And that was the hardest part of spending time with the legionnaires. They were a reminder of his life that might have been. And now never would be.

And yet he had come to accept the 72nd as his new home. It wasn't perfect, but what home was? From Buck's stories of icing naval ships to Tramel constantly calling him a mech monkey... he felt a sense of familiarity. Even... comfort. What more could a man ask?

The other two squadrons were posted topside of the crater, a menacing blockade meant to make the miners and their alien allies think twice about coming and disrupting the planned research excavation. The legionnaires of Cobra Company were posted with the main force as well, all except for a small honor guard who had left their comrades topside in order to ceremonially guard the gravesite that had been discovered. Lieutenant Mandal led that honor guard—stout men who never budged from their duty, not even to assist with morning patrols of the crater floor.

So much for having legionnaires as replacement for infantry. Only the HARD squadrons up top were so lucky.

But then, so far infantry support hadn't been needed. Despite the locals' blustering, there were no signs of hostility or military presence. In fact, Metzger found the patrols to be stunningly routine and boring. At the same time, they gave him an appreciation for Peltier. The man wasn't playing it safe. Every patrol went on a different route, and set out at a different time. Vickerson said Peltier was being paranoid, that the locals were too afraid to attack, but Metzger appreciated the thinking behind it.

Besides, he wasn't going to complain about the patrols being dull. The other option was fighting, and while he felt invigorated in battle, as a seasoned veteran he knew that conflict wasn't something one hoped for. After all, he only had the one real leg left.

As he and Buck skirted the north end of the crater floor, he heard a rumble, deep and throbbing, from up above. Leaning his mech back, he saw an avalanche of rock pouring down from the lip, slamming down onto the ramp-like road that led in and out of the crater. The road disappeared in the landslide, and when the rockfall slowed, it became clear that that road would never be used again. Parts of it had crumbled away, utterly destroyed, while other parts were now buried under tons of boulders and debris.

Metzger got on the comm with Buck. "Hullbuster, go weapons hot, now!" he barked. Then he sent a transmission topside. "We have a situation down here. Explosion on the road off to the east. Are you seeing this?"

Even as he spoke, another pair of blasts went off, and he looked toward the sounds. Two more landslides occurred, each positioned directly above the two remaining roadways in and out of the crater.

This isn't good... not at all. They had checked for explosives along the roadway, but not on the wall all the way to the crater lip. There was simply too much ground to cover. Even for the patrols, the 510th had been forced to split up into sections in order to cover the vast interior of the crater, each HK-PP moving with its wingman, with the scout platoon and its tanks splitting up similarly. They were distributed all across the crater.

Buck came on the comm. "I'm picking up a faint signal, something fast-moving, but I can't get the battle book to ID it."

"Bearing?"

"Sixty-three degrees from my mark, grid A5."

Metzger moved swiftly in the direction of Buck, and as he did, he detected the signal at the extreme range of his sensors. "Buck, I'm not getting a response from topside. Try and signal the base—let them know we have hostiles in the hole with us and that they've cut off the ramps." His feet worked the pedals of the HK-PP as he came up over a small rise, where he finally made eye contact with Buck's mech.

"No response," Buck fired back.

That was both of them, then. Was it the natural interference of the crater, or the locals jamming prior to an attack?

Using his left hand, he pulled up the comms and switched to the special channel set up to communication with the legionnaires and their cryptic L-comm. "To any Legion command—we have hostile forces here in the crater."

He transmitted as he moved alongside Buck.

"Copy that," came a static-hissed, garbled voice. Metzger wasn't entirely sure it was a reply from the Legion L-comm, or a delayed response from one of the 72nd. As it was, the message was barely received at all. Metzger tried to reach them again, but no further response came.

"How the hell did they get down here?" Buck responded.

It was a damn good question.

They moved to higher ground in the hopes of getting a better comms situation.

"Pileup—how copy?" It was Captain Peltier on the tactical channel.

"Solid copy," Metzger said excitedly, relieved to have some communication back. "We have enemy forces of unknown size and composition moving from the north toward the base camp. How copy?"

Judging by the dots on his tactical display, whatever the enemy units were, they were moving fast.

"Solid copy," came the voice of Captain Peltier, who was on the opposite end of the crater. "Topside has signals of their own incoming. With the roads blocked, we're on our own. I'm sending Waypoint Alpha to your displays. I want the squadron to converge there. I'm trying to connect with the legionnaires at the crash site but nothing yet. You and

Buck are authorized to fire on any target that doesn't have a valid IFF signal, at your discretion."

The waypoint appeared on Metzger's display. Eight klicks out. All the various patrols would converge there.

"Copy that, Slick. Section Two responding," he transmitted. "Come on, Hullbuster, it's time for us to hoof it."

"What about those signals?"

"Relay them to the captain as we go. We gotta earn our pay!"

"Demons on deck... hell to repel!" he replied.

Despite the tension, Metzger cracked a grin at Buck's response. Once a marine, always a marine.

About halfway to Waypoint Alpha, Metzger picked up a trio of signals running parallel to them. "Hullbuster, you seeing this at two-seventy?"

"Yes, I am. I paint three targets—matching our course."

"They may be hoping we see them as sensor shadows."

"They aren't closing. We could ignore them." Metzger knew Buck didn't mean that; the man was just tossing out the option.

"We don't have much choice," Metzger replied. "They're using us to lead them right to Waypoint Alpha. If we don't engage them, we could compromise the rest of the squadron." He switched to Peltier's channel. "Slick, this is Pileup. We have three bogeys at the edge of our sensor range, apparently tracking us."

"Can you take them?"

"Unknown," was all Metzger could honestly reply. He wanted to say "Of course!" but knew that would have been his testicles answering, not his brains.

"It's your call. But you can't lead them to us."

"Copy that," Metzger replied. That meant he had two choices: either lead them on a wild goose chase, possibly stumbling into more enemies in the process, or take them on and wipe them out.

"Hullbuster," he said. "We're going to mess these guys up."

"Understood," Buck replied. "How do you want to do this?"

Metzger went over the options. The traditional doctrine was to engage at distance while in motion, get on their flanks, and catch them in the crossfire. But that was also a tactic that could backfire. Two of the enemy could tie down him and Hullbuster, allowing the third to whittle away at them.

He considered what he knew. The enemy units were mirroring his and Buck's movements, which meant they had the same mobility and would be difficult to encircle. But the pilots... they would be local militia. They might have some training, but odds were they lacked any actual experience.

That was something he could take advantage of. Rattle their nerves.

He tagged the enemy on their displays so he and Buck could keep them straight. "I'm tagging these targets as Alpha, Bravo, and Charlie. We head right at them—you break right, I break left—and move up on them at point-blank range. My guess is they'll scatter. After our pass, follow me and we'll concentrate our fire."

"Full speed, I presume."

"Speed is our armor." Metzger couldn't see Buck's face, but he knew the man was smiling in his cockpit. "We go on my mark." Metzger paused, doing another quick check of his tactical display. "Let's ride!"

He pushed his right pedal down and lightened up on the left to make the tight turn. The moment he was aligned with the enemy, both pedals went down all the way. The HK-PP's power plant kicked up a notch, throbbing at a higher pitch. He leaned forward, and his movement translated to the mech, which mirrored his stance. His blaster capacitors were humming in the arms of the HK-PP on either side of him as he routed power to them.

He had to swerve sharply around the boulders that appeared in his path. His eyes darted to the tactical display and saw that the trio of targets slowed, apparently realizing they were about to be engaged. As Buck pulled up thirty meters to Metzger's right, plowing through the low limbs of a tree and snapping timber, Metzger saw the enemy targets make a slow arc toward them. In that moment, he wondered if he was indeed facing unskilled militia.

Wanna play chicken, boys?

"We are in range," Hullbuster said, his voice terse and crisp.

"Start a low weave pattern behind me by about ten meters, in case they're trying to line us up for a shot," Metzger said. He angled his path slightly to the right, then back to the left.

A warning indicator flared: *Incoming Fire.* There was a whooshing sound off to the right of his cockpit as a projectile cut the thin air next to him, close enough to buffet his mech. Behind him he heard the *crack-boom* of an explosion as the shell hit something other than him.

"They've got projectile weapons."

"Copy," Hullbuster said.

A pair of explosions went off at his wingman's position. Metzger's sensors showed no appreciable damage to Hullbuster's mech—the shots had come in low, showering him with tiny bits of shrapnel. But even antiquated weapons could cripple a mech through attrition.

Metzger banked slightly and saw the enemy. In the center of the formation was a tank, but it didn't look at all like those that the 72nd used. This one had two large pontoons on the side, and the armor plating didn't look like military-grade composite, but rather crude metal plates with ugly welds and burn marks. It also lacked a turret, but the big cannon was forward mounted—and as soon as Metzger saw it, it fired at him. The shell went off in front of his HK-PP, shrapnel stabbing at his mech, rattling off his cockpit canopy and peppering his frontal armor.

Near the aft end of the tank were several infantry, their uniforms a variation on thick miners' jumpsuits and jackets, behind rudimentary blast shields, firing blasters at him wildly. Brilliant yellow bursts of fire hit his HK-PP, but did little more than mar the paint. The damage indicator showed just as it did for Hullbuster—lots of minor hits from the shrapnel, nothing deep and penetrating... yet.

The tank was joined by two "mechs," far off on his and Hullbuster's flanks. They were clearly industrial machines —commercial lift haulers with massive legs—that had been converted for mining and then military use. The arms, once used to hoist heavy materials or drill into rock, were now rigged with blasters, and he had to assume the racks of tubes were armed with something nasty.

"Up the middle, tear that tank apart."

Metzger angled his HK-PP in a tight jerk to throw off any attempts to lock on to him, then rushed along the tank's right side. Craning his mech's waist around, he brought his targeting reticle onto the tank for both his missiles and his blasters. On a side pass, only one of his blaster cannons would get a shot, but he hoped that would be enough when combined with Hullbuster's fire.

The missile lock tone rang in his cockpit, and he unleashed a single aero-precision missile as he closed to within twenty-five meters of the tank. The vehicle made a turn away from him, angling more for Hullbuster, and the missile slammed into the tank's side. The concussion from the explosion rocked his mech, and his subsequent blaster shot tore through the smoke at the target, searing a glowing scar in the thick metal armor as the tank whipped past, already slowing.

The shrapnel had cut one of the riding infantry in half. His bloody torso hung over the blast plate he had been using for cover.

Another explosion tore into the smoking tank as it fired its big gun again, this time at Hullbuster. The round slammed into the hip of Buck's mech, sending bits of armor flying and leaving a sickly black smoke trail as he wobbled. Metzger's sensors told him that his wingman was still operational, but was going to be slowed by the damage.

The Vargasian tank was saved from total destruction by the extra armor, which was blown off by the missile. The front dipped low enough to hit the ground as they passed each other, causing it to violently pivot, tossing most of the riding infantry and leaving only two men desperately attempting to hold on.

Before Metzger could enjoy the view, his sensors again flashed *Incoming Fire* on his canopy. Six rockets fired from one of the mechs, coming at him in a wide spread. The weapons were unguided, and most roared around him—but two managed to find their mark, slamming into the side of his mech's left leg and torso.

The concussion was far worse than the shrapnel. The explosions violently tossed him about and almost caused him to topple over mid-stride in his run. His damage display flickered with amber warnings that his armor was compromised.

"Wheel to the left and follow me," he transmitted.

Hullbuster did so, but not before firing a blast at the enemy tank as it tried to maneuver. The blasters from Buck's HK-PP tore into the rear of the tank. While Metzger couldn't see the resulting damage, he saw one of the infantrymen caught in the wake of the blast explode into a crimson mist, his body superheated by the huge blaster. In that instant Metzger remembered what it was like being infantry on the battlefield with tanks in motion.

The last time, it cost me my leg.

The tank billowed a gray-white smoke and sat still as Metzger moved in an arc to come in behind the enemy mech. Hullbuster moved in behind him, matching his running arc. The enemy mech pilot must have sensed that he was next; the mech had already turned hard to Metzger's left, angling in front of the ruined tank, heading off toward his own wingman.

The enemy fired one rocket at a time from the next rack down, no doubt using the tracking of each to adjust his aim. Two missed, but the third and fourth slammed into the thighs of Metzger's mech. From the lower window on his right he could see where one of the rockets had hit. The armor there had peeled back slightly from the impact. It wasn't bad, but he didn't want to suffer any more such shots.

You want to play with rockets... game on.

Metzger brought his missile reticle onto the converted mech, unleashing two aero-precision warheads downrange. Unlike the enemy rockets, *his* weapons were guided. They twisted and turned in the air, their contrails undulating like white snakes. Both hit the enemy mech in the same leg. There was a hot splash of superheated hydraulic fluid that vaporized in a greenish-yellow cloud, then bits of metal rained down on the gray crater floor. The enemy mech was immobilized.

Metzger locked on with his blaster's targeting reticle. Hullbuster unleashed a missile of his own at the mech. The brilliant orange explosions devoured the upper body in a fireball of carnage and blasted metal, and the enemy mech was out of the fight.

A moment later the mech's power plant exploded with a flash so brilliant that it made Metzger's eyes ache. A piece of armor the size of a human head slammed into his cockpit canopy, right in front of him, and he flinched—purely instinctual. A brilliant crimson ball of flame rolled skyward, twisting in on itself as it climbed higher. It burst open like a balloon, going from red to black smoke, rising like a pillar of death.

Metzger continued his arc, looking for the remaining mech, but his tactical display showed that it was fleeing. "Good shooting," he transmitted to his wingman, his voice strained by the rush of adrenaline and his muscles tensing.

"Same to you. Request permission to go after the remaining mech and unalive him."

Metzger released some of the pressure from his footpads, slowing his HK-PP. "Negative. Our goal was to stop them from following us. I think we've achieved that. We need to get to Waypoint Alpha and get a better idea of what's happening here."

Waypoint Alpha was a tall rock formation, taller than Metzger's HK-PP. Around it were the members of the 510th, as well as the honor guard of the Legion. But a quick count indicated not everyone was here. That was a gut punch.

We've already bled on this rock. How the hell did that happen?

Captain Peltier came on the comm. He gave a rundown of the losses so far.

Tom and Harry hadn't arrived at the waypoint and weren't responding to comm transmissions after an initial report of contact. They were officially missing in action.

Scout Platoon was down one of its fast MBTs. Staff Sergeant Stupp was KIA.

The Legion honor guard had withdrawn under fire, losing a third of their numbers, though they had only been nine to begin with.

Razorwire's platoon was intact, as was Metzger's, but Rothchild and Stamper were in even worse condition than Metzger and Buck, and Metzger wasn't sure how much longer they could stay combat effective.

"We're dealing with a new situation," the captain continued. "The research base is in the hands of the local miners. Roads to the surface are karked, and the forces topside are dealing with an enemy force that's moving in on Crater 113."

"Where did their troops come from?" came the voice of Lieutenant "Ice Tea" Vickerson. "All that armor doesn't just appear out of thin air."

Chief Dobbs answered. "From what I saw of them, they were filthy—even for miners. I think the kelhorns had dug tunnels into the crater walls and obscured the entrances. They've been down here the whole time, hiding, watching us, studying our positions."

Either that, or those tunnels led to someplace where they staged, Metzger thought. He should have seen that coming. They all should have. Of *course* miners would have dug hiding holes.

What else hadn't they considered?

"I estimate their strength here to be at least two to one over us in terms of hardware," said Sergeant Callison of the legionnaires. His lieutenant was among the dead. "Probably twenty to one matching man for man."

Peltier considered this for a moment. "The smart move may be for us to wait for the topside to settle matters up there and then bring down the dropships with reinforcements."

"That's no good," said Callison. "Before we fell back, I saw them bringing in a mobile battery of anti-ship missiles. I've already passed the word to Colonel Hackett topside. Bringing a dropship into this crater would compound disaster."

Tramel sounded agitated when he spoke. "With the kind of numbers we're talking about, plus topside being out of the picture, we need to stay mobile."

Krock agreed at once. "They'll come looking to take us while we're isolated, for sure."

"We should hit them, take back the base and that missile battery," said Razorwire.

Peltier shook his head. "Chances are that's exactly what they expect. If we go in there guns blazing, they have numbers on their side. In addition, we have the archaeological team to consider. If they're being held prisoner, that complicates things. I'm going to try and raise them again."

Thus far the comm transmissions had been going through, but no one had answered. This time was the exception. But it wasn't an archaeologist or historian on the other end of the line.

"This is Major Kinch of the Vargas Liberation Army. Identify yourself."

Peltier spoke through gritted teeth. "This is Captain Peltier, 72nd HARD."

"Captain. Good. Captain Peltier, I am offering you a single opportunity to save the lives of your fellow bootlickers. *If* you listen to what I tell you. We are holding your research team as hostages. Any attempts to attack our position will result in their immediate termination. All Republic forces are to stand down and surrender immediately. You will be treated fairly, and no harm will come to you. If, however, you decide to attack—your people will die."

While the conversation continued—Peltier wasted no time getting on with negotiations—Metzger barely heard it. His attention was fixed on one word.

Hostages.

Hostages meant alive. O'Keefe might not be dead.

But for how long would that remain the case?

He would find a way to get her out of there. He would find a way to save her life.

After all, she saved mine.

27

The Vargasians dragged Weaver in unconscious and tossed him on the floor of the mobile lab where the researchers were being held. He had been in the tech trailer, working on a helmet that had been left conspicuously on a workstation within the *Cú Chulainn*, as if just waiting to be found. It was a leej helmet, one of those used during the late Savage Wars era, pitted, battered, its paint faded in some spots to nothing—but Weaver had claimed it was in good enough shape that he might be able to get it operating, and had immediately set to work trying to figure out what it had to say.

The warrant officer was in no condition to be working on *anything* right now. It was clear that he had put up a fight. His face was already purple from bruises, his right eye badly swollen. His cheekbone looked like it might be broken.

O'Keefe raised her eyes from Weaver's limp form to the table in the middle of the enclosed truck, where the DNA test unit still smoked. Maybe the damage to both of them wasn't as bad as it looked. She wanted to check on Weaver, but she knew that any movement was likely to elicit a violent response from their captors.

Dranes sat nearby, his expression a mix of humiliation and frustration. O'Keefe felt exactly the same.

She shifted her focus to her captors. They didn't wear traditional military uniforms, no patches or regalia, just filthy, dull gray jumpsuits—the clothing of a miner. They reeked of body odor, as if they hadn't washed for at least a week. Their weapons and gear were military-grade, but older models. Surplus, probably.

The tension in the mobile lab was thick with the suppressed fear of the hostages and the fury of the hostage-takers. There had been a battle fought outside for several minutes; no doubt the Legion honor guard had engaged the attackers. That meant the enemy had suffered losses, because the Legion wouldn't withdraw without inflicting damage along the way.

But those legionnaires *had* left. The researchers wouldn't be captive if they hadn't. Which meant there were likely more rebels outside, not just the three guarding them now. O'Keefe had to assume that they were severely outnumbered and outgunned.

She felt her forehead throb. Mostly a pressure headache, but part of it felt like a shadow, the presence of one of her memory fragments. Slowly, she pulled her sleeve back and looked down at her chronometer. She was coming up on the time to take her medication.

She looked up at the hulking man who seemed to be the leader of their captors. She knew that asking for permission to get her pills wasn't going to be warmly received. Still, she had to try.

"What are you looking at?" the gruff man asked in a low, rumbling tone.

"I have some medicine I need to take," she said. "It's in my kit."

The man glared at her. "What's it for?"

O'Keefe could feel the eyes of everyone boring into her. Dranes knew of her condition, but no one else did—and she didn't want them to know. It would change how many of them interacted with her.

"It's for headaches," she replied, semi-truthfully.

The man chuckled. "You'll survive without it."

Dranes cut in, though she wished he hadn't. "Her headaches are serious. It's from a combat injury."

The man turned toward Dranes, holding his blaster at his hip and aiming it in the warrant officer's general direction. "I don't care."

"You can pull them out if you don't trust me," O'Keefe suggested.

He turned back to her. "What part of *no* don't you understand? You'll just have to deal with your little headache until we get what we want."

"What is that, exactly?" Dranes asked.

"You leaving, and taking your Legion lapdogs with you," the man said firmly. "You came here uninvited. The Republic has no business coming here, digging up old bodies. Not without our permission." There was pride in his words. He was offended, just like the guildmaster.

"We meant no harm," Dranes said. "All we want to do is —"

The man jabbed the barrel of his blaster into Dranes's mouth, cutting him off. It chipped one of his teeth in the process, and he winced in pain, his face turning red.

"No one wants your talk." The leader turned to one of his men. "Time to tie them up. If they don't shut up, gag them."

The other man produced a handful of flex cuffs, each comprising two rings of plastic with a small box in the middle. Ener-chains were far superior, but more expensive; maybe these miners had blown their entire rebellion budget on weapons. Whatever the case, O'Keefe was happy to see the cuffs, because she had gotten training on them when she was in boot camp. Training on how to get out of them.

The man ordered them to lie on their stomachs and put their hands behind their backs. When he leaned over O'Keefe to apply the cuffs, he was so close that his body aroma assaulted her nostrils; she could practically taste his sweat on her tongue. She had smelled a lot of body order in the R-A, but this was the stink of a working man, not a warrior. It was different, earthier, more metallic on the back of her throat.

She ignored it; she had to act fast.

The man slid the first loop over her right wrist. As he moved to put the loop over her left, she quickly put her fingers along her right wrist, under the loose loop of plastic. A light tug on her part ensured he didn't immediately hit the tighten button. He jerked her arm at her slight resistance, then hit the button.

The loops tightened snug, but on her right wrist, they wrapped around her fingers as well.

The man stood and moved away, but she could still taste his sweat. Once everyone was tied, the rebel leader told them they could get comfortable. He actually managed to sound magnanimous about it, like he hadn't just assaulted and bound them all.

O'Keefe rolled onto her butt and wriggled back into a sitting position against the wall of the trailer. Then she methodically pulled her fingers, one at a time, out of the loop. Her fingers had provided a gap, not a big one, but hopefully enough. Leaning forward slightly, she tried to slide the loop off her wrist. It snugged up tight against her thumb. She paused; she didn't want to look as if she was straining.

She shifted, pulling her legs tight under her so that she could rise quickly if she had to. Watching her captors' every move, she carefully tested the loop against her thumb. It was going to hurt, but she was fairly sure she could pull her hand free.

The shadow of a memory surged forward.

No—not now!

Her brow throbbed as the fragment grabbed control of her conscious mind and inserted itself. Instinctively, she closed her eyes; she didn't want to see a memory, especially under these circumstances. She couldn't control it, couldn't make it go away.

She opened her eyes slowly. Before her was Corporal Eli Geroux, outlined in a white glow, right where her captors stood. He was crawling, but he didn't seem to move. His body armor was scored in several spots, blaster hits that hadn't penetrated. When he spoke, it was muffled, as if it were being played through her helmet's comm.

"We can do this, O'Keefe. Just another few meters and you can plaster these bastards!"

Just beyond the ghostly image, she saw an explosion that rained down dirt on Geroux's armored back.

The ache in her temple surged. She had seen this memory before, but not for months. Now it was back, and at the worst possible time.

"Not now," she muttered.

The leader of the captors turned to her, and in doing so, the visage of Geroux disappeared. "What did you say?"

"It—it's just my headache," she said. "It's starting."

"Feh." Disgusted by what he clearly saw as weakness, the leader stomped off to check on something else.

The experience was humiliating. Only her doctor had ever seen her coping with her random memories. Now others were going to witness it. She saw Dranes look at her, saw the chip in his tooth and the thin rivulet of blood drizzling down his chin. *He* knew she was struggling—and yet he could do nothing to help. But he gave her a silent nod, and from that gesture, she was able to draw a little strength. A little control. The ache in her head faded. It wasn't gone, but it was muted, driven deeper into whatever broken part of her brain it had emerged from.

Still, she knew this was only a momentary reprieve. The longer she went without her medication, the worse she would get. She would reach a point where she wouldn't be able to dispel the bits of memory that emerged.

Her only hope was to hang on as long as she could... and seize an opportunity to overpower her abductors before she reached that point.

O'Keefe had been a combat trooper once—she could be so again.

28

"We need a plan," said Captain Peltier to the small gathering of troops in the shadows of the mechs that surrounded them. "Their initial surprise attack took advantage of the fact we were spread out; they won't be so lucky now that we're back together. But now they have another advantage: the hostages. Anything we do needs to be done with their safety in mind."

Metzger was glad to hear Slick talking about engaging the enemy. Sometimes officers got it in their heads to start rambling on about winning the hearts and minds of the enemy—or in this case pointing out that these were Republic citizens, not part of the MCR, *blah, blah, blah.* All that mattered here was that the enemy—Republic citizens or not—had attacked first. The politics was something for the diplomats to work out later. This was combat, plain and simple.

The decision of how to proceed, once Peltier had passed it up the chain of command, had been left to Captain Peltier and Sergeant Callison. Apparently the fighting topside was brutal, a full-scale war that was keeping the legionnaires and the rest of the 72nd completely occupied. Casualties were already high. Anyone who had underestimated these miners and their K'llik allies was having second thoughts now. The enemy had fielded a lot of mechs and tanks, everything from converted and armed mining equipment to military-grade gear.

Thin atmosphere. Nasty, brutal fighting.

Who would have thought we were the lucky ones down here?

They had put First Platoon on patrol and formed a tight perimeter, if only to give them time to plan. Metzger had volunteered to take his platoon out, but was told by Peltier that he was wanted in the planning session.

"The clock is running," Legion Sergeant Callison said coldly, standing in front of Slick, holding his bucket under one arm. He had a chiseled face, hard, almost harsh. His blond hair was trimmed so short that he looked bald. There was a sense that he was tolerating the HK-PP pilots as a courtesy, but only for so long. "We need to get mobile. They'll send out patrols to try to pin us down."

"Where do you suggest we get mobile to?" Peltier asked. "We're in a big hole in the ground. There's no way out."

Like most legionnaires, Callison had an answer ready. "Toward the enemy. If we stay concentrated and close for support, we'll encounter their patrols out looking for us. Comms are already weak down here, should be easy to jam. Hit them hard and then disengage before they can concentrate their full numbers. Then do it again. Hit and fade."

"That's tricky stuff," Slick said.

He was right. Engaging the enemy was hard; breaking off an engagement was harder. Done improperly, it could result in a rout, or worse, a slaughter.

"We don't have a choice," Metzger said, speaking up for the first time in the session. "We're a HARD unit, so let's act like it. Speed is our armor. We move, and move fast. The key is to take out their individual patrols or bleed them bad enough that we can disengage and redeploy."

Sergeant Callison gave him a nod of agreement.

"What about the hostages?" Peltier asked.

Callison responded crisply. "When the time comes, we'll rescue them. Chances are pretty good the miners won't execute them except as a last resort—or an act of defiance, if they're the type—because the minute they do, they'll no longer have leverage over us. These miners aren't dumb enough to want an unchained Legion after them."

Metzger wasn't so sure about that, but his thoughts went once again to O'Keefe.

Hang in there, Sheryl. The cavalry will be coming soon enough.

Peltier nodded at the Legion officer. "You'll be riding on us, I assume?"

"Never run when you can ride."

"If this proves to be a running fight, it's going to be hard as hell to hold on," Slick cautioned. "And the enemy is going to be shooting at *us*, first and foremost."

"We aren't infantry," Callison said. "We're Cobra Company. My leejes sweat kaff and piss blood. We'll be just fine."

"We'll rack 'em if you stack 'em," Metzger replied, forcing another nod from the Legion sergeant.

Peltier nodded. "We will need to deploy in a spread wing formation, a wide arc, spread out but able to overlap our fields of fire. When you make contact with the enemy, it's critical that you destroy or disrupt them quickly; they'll be looking to find us and call in the rest of their buddies. Back Door, you've got an ECM pod on your HK-SW. Your job will be both to scout ahead and jam their transmissions as a precautionary measure. I don't want to rely on the crater to do that for us, not with everything on the line. Now, we aren't looking for a general engagement, we just need to level the playing field at this point. Every kill reduces the enemy's combat effectiveness, but our margin of error is thin. We've already lost one tank and a pair of mechs, and we can't lose too much more. Got it?"

The gathering nodded.

"Once we grind them down, then we can talk about an assault on the base. Hopefully our ammo depot is still there as well. For now, the name of the game is dumping an overwhelming amount of firepower on every mech and vehicle we encounter. Cripple or destroy them, then move on. Resist the urge to pursue or exploit. You go chasing after them, chances are they're going to lead you to the rest of their buddies."

As the group broke up, Callison walked briskly over to Metzger. "Your captain seems pretty level-headed."

Metzger was cautious in his reply. "I've got no complaints."

"The 72nd has a reputation," he said in a low tone so his voice didn't carry.

Metzger understood. The legionnaire had heard about Tralon and was wondering if he had anything to worry about. He wanted to know if the mechs would walk his men into another strategic disaster.

"Don't believe everything you hear," Metzger replied, his own voice just above a whisper.

"So we're solid?"

"We are."

"Good." Callison slid on his bucket. "Let's give this Vargas Liberation Army a flaming enema."

Metzger grinned. That was a new one. "You can count on that, Sergeant."

He walked over to his HK-PP and surveyed the damage once more. It was covered with pits and burns from shrapnel, and some melting damage from blaster fire. He hated to see it banged up like this, but in truth, none of it was serious.

Which was a very good thing. He couldn't afford to take serious damage—none of them could. Their maintenance platoon was topside. A mech that took critical damage would be out of commission, and that could mean the end of the long game here.

He climbed up into the cockpit, hit the canopy seal control, then put on his helmet and started the power-up sequence.

"What's the word, Pileup?" Hullbuster asked. Buck had remained in his mech during the planning session, just in case the enemy made an appearance.

"We're going to keep moving. When we engage, we jam them, pour on the firepower, and leave 'em hurting. We're trying to avoid a general engagement."

"Sounds delightful," Hullbuster replied, sarcasm ringing in his voice.

Metzger's HK-PP hummed to life. Displays appeared in front of him, projected on the inside of his canopy, and his trained eyes swept over them. "Let's get going."

"Copy that, Pileup. I'm ready to teach these rock diggers not to mess with us."

Metzger was on the extreme left flank of the formation. Clinging to the back of his HK-PP were two leejes, and every few strides, he thought he could hear their armor bump against his mech. The entire formation could move only as fast as the slowest member, in this case the repulsor tanks that hung in the center. At Peltier's suggestion, they moved in a series of circles, each loop advancing farther, overlapping the previous run.

After an hour or so, Razorwire signaled on the tactical channel. "Contact, two-eighty, three bogies, two moving like mechs." There was an iciness in his voice, a coolness that came only from experience in controlling one's emotions.

"Roger that," came Peltier's voice. "Now we invert the arc. Pileup and Hullbuster, swing forward and around, try to get in behind them, cut them off. Back Door, jam their comms now."

Metzger confirmed and picked up the pace, using his foot pedals to swing the mech in a high arc. "Time to get off, fellas," he transmitted to the legionnaires hanging on his HK-PP's back. He could feel the shove in his cockpit seat, pushing him to the left as he accelerated.

His eyes swept his tactical display constantly, looking for the enemy and making sure that Buck was alongside him. Coming through some dense brush, he almost lost his footing when he came down on some exposed uneven rocks—a risk of running so fast. Feathering his pedals slightly gave him back his footing as he continued forward.

Suddenly a crimson dot appeared at the top of his screen: a target with no IFF transponder. Then another. His battle book tagged the first target as a Kris repulsor tank, then changed it to a Falchion... then back to a Kris. It couldn't decide what to make of their cobbled-together tank.

"You seein' this, Hullbuster?"

"I have two on the screen, closing fast. Tagging targets now," Buck replied. A moment later he added, "They must have picked us up. They're turning to run."

"Not today, they're not. I'm angling to block their retreat. They'll be in weapons range in fifteen seconds."

"Copy—coming in on your four o'clock. Weapons hot."

Blaster capacitors hummed on either side of Metzger's cockpit, and he enabled the targeting reticles for both missiles and blasters. "We hit Alpha first, missiles, two each. We pass him in front, then do a tight turn to the right, and if he's not dead yet, we finish him off. If not, we'll be coming up the ass of the other one."

"Running in front of his gun?" Hullbuster said.

"He'll get off a shot or two, but we're cutting right in front of him, which will make us a harder target."

"Copy. This should be fun," Buck said, the sarcasm heavy.

Metzger drifted his targeting reticles with his right-hand joystick, moving them onto the distant dots that were closing. As he hovered over his target, he waited for the missile lock tone, which seemed to take forever.

"Come on," he muttered through gritted teeth. The long tone filled his ears as the reticle flickered to green for a lock. "Missiles away."

From above him he heard the metallic click and whoosh of the missiles racing out of the boxy shoulder mounts—one each. They stabbed through the air, their thin contrails the only thing visible other than the plumes from their engines.

Hullbuster's missiles tore through the air right after them.

A quick series of flashes marked the warheads doing their deadly work. A millisecond later came the explosions, and then came the concussion, buffeting the pair of HK-PPs as they continued on, racing in front of the path of the tank.

The tank was dead, but its cannon roared, a string of loud bangs in rapid succession, before meeting its fate. The rounds tore through the air, two slamming into the side of Metzger's mech and exploding on impact. Damage indicators flared crimson on one of his legs, and he staggered but didn't slow. The mech felt as if it was fighting him, but he fought right back.

"I got hit," Hullbuster called as he ran through the stream of fire.

"Same here. I'm still good." That was an exaggeration. Metzger's damage display showed that his knee joint had been compromised. But it was still working—for now. Just to be on the safe side, he slowed his speed by ten kilometers per hour, continuing his ever-shortening arc.

The two other approaching signals skidded to a stop at the sight of their comrade's funeral pyre. Both were still unidentified mechs according to the battle book.

"Tighten up on my flank," Metzger said to Hullbuster. "Let's go after the closest one."

"Copy that," Buck replied, bringing his HK-PP in line with Metzger's.

They ran, their footfalls pounding in unison, thudding the floor of the immense crater so hard that it was like someone was banging a bass drum. As Metzger zoomed in on his display, he saw the enemy mech clearly.

It lacked the crudeness of the first mech he had faced, but not the deadliness. It was squat, with an oblong spheroid shape. One of the narrow ends jutted out front and served as a cockpit. Its arms mounted two blasters that hugged the sides of the fuselage closely, and beyond them, two circular pods mounted either missiles or rockets. This wasn't some cobbled-together war machine; this was a mech built for combat.

The people of Vargas had gotten illicit help, that much was for sure.

The mech fired, a half dozen rockets, three from each pod. Metzger ignored the *Incoming Fire* warning on his canopy HUD as they came at him, unguided but deadly. He jabbed his right foot pedal down and reversed on the left for a millisecond, then jabbed it down too. His HK-PP jerked hard to the left, then went perpendicular to the enemy mech.

Two of the unguided rockets found him, exploding against his HK-PP's upper torso. One hit the canopy with a fiery explosion that caused a spiderweb of cracks to form in one panel of his viewing ports. Metzger half expected the reinforced canopy to break under the blast—with shrapnel that would fill the cockpit and slice him to shreds —but it held.

Hullbuster fired an aero missile at the smooth-sided mech, the blast hitting the upper left thigh of the enemy's bird-like legs, wreathing them in flames and blowing one off at the knee actuator. Metzger followed suit, firing his blasters. One shot missed, but the second dug under the enemy's torso near where the legs came together at the hips. The flash of amber seared into the composite armor there, leaving a black scar framed by glowing hot melted metal, marking the penetration.

The enemy mech stumbled about to the left, then turned toward Hullbuster's mech, unleashing a wave of eight rockets. Hullbuster's HK-PP had been caught mid-turn toward the enemy and was devoured in a rapid series of explosions. For a moment, Metzger couldn't even see his wingman due to the flames and smoke—and when he did finally see Hullbuster emerge from the carnage, his mech was wobbling. Armor plating on the HK-PP's legs was twisted and blackened, as was the upper torso. One of his wingman's shoulder-mounted missile racks was now little more than scrap metal, belching white smoke. The rear hatches on that missile rack were open, showing that the auto-ejection system had dumped the missiles rather than letting them blow up.

Hullbuster staggered, then dropped with a metallic crunch.

Metzger clenched his jaw. This had to end quickly or they weren't going to survive. The miners were proving to be better pilots than HARD troopers, a reality that stung deeply.

His tactical display indicated that Sergeant Grunon was coming into range with his MBT, moving along the enemy mech's far right flank. It was good to know he wasn't alone.

"Hold tight, Hullbuster," Metzger said as he turned his mech hard to the right, just in time to dodge a yellow-white blaster bolt from the opposing mech. He twisted his torso and turned slightly so that he could place both targeting reticles on his target. He fired his blasters in succession, first the right, then the left.

The blaster cannon bolts sliced the thin air and slammed into the smaller mech, one of them hitting the already damaged hip. The armor there superheated and blew off under the charged energy fury that sliced into the already compromised metal, and the left leg bent severely. Then with a metallic moan, it gave way entirely, severing at the hip.

The mech fell forward, sans the severed leg, as Metzger got missile lock, the tone singing in his ears like a siren's song. He let loose with a single aero missile, despite the mech being downed. Part of it was vengeance for what it had done to Hullbuster's mech, part of it was from his experience as a soldier. *Always make sure your dead are dead.*

The missile didn't waver as it streaked in at the stationary target. It hit the cockpit dead square, and Metzger saw it punch through the canopy just before it detonated. The blast engulfed the pilot, and the internal guts of the mech, in blistering flames.

Grunon's tank must have fired its long-barreled rail gun too, because another blur stabbed into the carnage that Metzger had unleashed, this time setting off a massive explosion. The concussion came like a lightning-fast ripple that cut through the thin air and rocked Metzger's HK-PP hard.

He slowed to a near stop, taking a second to savor the enemy's destruction. The only piece of the mech left intact was the leg that it had lost, which lay on the ground behind it, barely visible through the ripples of heat.

"Hullbuster—you okay?" he barked as he angled back to where his comrade had gone down.

"I'm okay, Pileup," said Buck, panting. "How are these guys so good?"

Metzger had been thinking about that too. "They're experienced operators," he said. "They may not know combat, but they've been living in these machines, all day, every day, for years. It gives them an advantage we don't yet have." That still didn't explain the strength of their firepower. Clearly they were being supported by some outside benefactor—a wealthy one—but to what ends, he couldn't begin to fathom.

"Yeah, well, my mech is going to need some serious work." Hullbuster staggered to a standing position. His mech looked charred, mangled, but still operational.

"Don't sweat it," Metzger said. "We'll get you patched up. Eventually."

Before Hullbuster could respond, Captain Peltier's voice came over the channel. "One got away, but we have him jammed still. We need to redeploy immediately. I want all forces to fall back to phase line Lima." The line appeared on Metzger's tactical display.

For a moment, he brought his mech to a standstill. Releasing his joysticks, he saw his hands were trembling from the rush of the battle and the surge of adrenaline. He had seen that before, on other battlefields—including on Frixon, where he had lost his leg. Drawing a long inhale through his nose, he regained control of his breathing.

"Copy that, Slick," he transmitted to Peltier. "Falling back to Lima."

Switching to the local channel, he signaled the legionnaires that he'd left prior to moving to engage. "You two still there?"

"Affirmative," came back a ragged voice. "But seeing that up close... we might just walk."

"Gonna have to be a full sprint if you're gonna keep up," Metzger said. "Comin' your way to pick you back up. Best hold on tight... I don't think we're out of the bumpy stuff just yet."

29

O'Keefe wore a sheen of sweat as she sat on the floor. It was hard for her to determine how much time had passed since they had been taken hostage. People were complaining about thirst, and some had been forced to endure the indignity of reliving themselves with their pants on; these captors were not humanitarian-minded. The mobile lab was balmy and humid, and the body odor of her captors hung thickly in the air. There was also an ambient hissing sound, faint but sure, that didn't seem to have a source.

She'd picked up some chatter a while back when the rebels spoke into their shoulder communicators. Not much detail, but she'd heard panicked voices at several points, indicating battles. And the more news that came in, the angrier the rebel leader looked.

He huddled with the other miners several times, whispering. They spoke quickly, nervously. O'Keefe studied their faces and saw the wrinkles of tension. Now and then they would gesture to her and the other hostages on the floor.

Clearly things weren't going their way, and they weren't sure what to do about it.

Through it all, her memory fragments had been visiting her with increasing frequency. It reminded her of the early days after her injury, before they were able to diagnose her problem and medicate it. They would come in short bursts, not always coherent, just mental blurs of sounds and images all jumbled and out of order. Voices of former comrades, sometimes laughing, sometimes screaming, filled her head as if they were in the room with her, and bursts of blaster fire were so real that at one point she thought her captors were actually shooting.

She wanted to plead again with the miners to let her take her meds, but she knew it would be a waste of time. They didn't care about the unleashed madness that was consuming her. They didn't even know about it, and there was no way she could explain. Without her meds, she lived in two worlds at once. One was here, in the mobile lab, as a hostage; the other was back in Tykaree Valley on Frixon. Neither was a place she wanted to be.

For now, her brain seemed to want to live in the present. She watched as the burly leader took out a scrambler communicator and squeezed the orange transmit button, sending a request for an update from topside. All he got back were incomplete messages, garbled by electronic interference. Twice he demanded they retransmit, and both times he got the same communications garbage. Sweat beaded on his forehead, trapped in the growing wrinkles there.

And then another memory flared like a mental geyser, forming between O'Keefe and her captors: Lieutenant Ringer, elbow-crawling in the mud in his R-A body armor. Blaster bolts surrounded him, closing on him as he moved.

His face turned to her, where she sat on the floor of the mobile lab. "Keep low. The Frix are tearing us up."

Another new memory, and yet... it felt familiar. That was different. The rest of her jumbled memories were completely detached from any conscious recognition, but this one tugged at her brain as if it were trying to somehow connect.

"The incoming fire is hot," she said softly, as if in a dream. "I can't get up there. They'll kill us before we make cover."

Her captors, standing just beyond Ringer, turned and glared at her. "You—shut up!"

She ignored the miner—barely heard him. Her focus was on the memory fragment.

"My leg is hit," Ringer said. "You can do it. Get into that gully over on the left. You can enfilade them from there without being exposed. Use your smokers!"

O'Keefe shifted where she sat. "I'm on it," she said as the memory came back to her.

The hostage-takers were not pleased. The short one stepped right through the white-outlined memory of Ringer and loomed over her. Balling his fist, he swung at her, hitting her hard on the left side of her face, toppling her over. She struck the floor, feeling its coolness on her cheek.

The impact made Ringer disappear, shattering the memory that had been unfolding.

What gully? she wondered. *Where is the enemy? What did I do there?*

Tears formed in her eyes, not from the pain of the blow, but from being violently ripped away from the memory. She had been participating in it… moving it forward. She had been close to finding answers.

She lay there, her eyes rolling in her head slightly before settling on the feet of the man who had just hit her, She fought back a sob, but refused to let her colleagues see her break. She curled enough to get back to a sitting position and better hide her wrists. The field of view in her left eye was starting to narrow, indicating her cheek was swelling from her captor's blow. She was tempted to pull her hands free from the cuffs and lash out—she knew she could do it—but the moment had not yet arrived. She would only have one shot at this, and she had to wait for the right opportunity, or all her efforts would be wasted.

Equally destructive, for that matter, was pursuing her memories. She hadn't meant to, hadn't tried to… but it was like sleepwalking. She needed to stay awake if she was going to stay alive.

The captors went back to their quiet mutterings. As time passed, they only seemed to get more agitated. Whatever they were hearing—or not hearing—about events outside had them on edge. Though the men did their best to keep their voices low, she caught them saying something about losing a tank, then a mech, then another mech. O'Keefe wanted to smile at their angst, but she knew better. If they saw her grinning, it would only earn her another blow. A broken cheekbone and two eyes swollen shut would do her no good.

Finally the leader grabbed the big communicator and depressed the orange transmit button again. He spoke loudly this time, as if he wanted to ensure that the hostages would hear.

"Republic forces in crater 107.9: surrender immediately, or we will start killing the prisoners one by one."

He smiled at O'Keefe as he released the button and held the communicator close to his ear, waiting for an answer.

None came.

The smile on his face faded, replaced by a scowl of anger. He tossed the communicator down and waved his blaster at the hostages. "Apparently your Repub forces don't believe we have the resolve to kill you. Well, they're full of mill tailings. We will kill one of you to demonstrate we mean business."

"You don't want to do that," Dranes said. The dry blood on his cheek was cracked on his beard stubble. "I know these officers. Let me talk to them. I can broker some sort of agreement."

O'Keefe admired Dranes a little more in that moment. He was trying to buy time, keep them alive a little longer.

"Tricks!" the leader barked, angling the barrel of his blaster in Dranes's direction. "*Words*—that's all the Republic cares about. You come here, despite our stated desires, despite our warnings to not come. You ignore our sovereignty and our right to rule ourselves. You don't come in peace, you come with armed troops—your vaunted legionnaires—yet claim you are here in *friendship*. Well, we don't want *your* kind of friendship. The natives of Vargas, the members of the Guild, we are proud people who will *not* be intimidated. Look at what we have done! We have already killed some of your Legion troops, and here you sit as our prisoners. We are stronger than you thought."

Dranes remained calm. "I know the officers," he said again. "I can help you get what you want."

"We don't *need* your help," the leader growled. "You think we're bluffing, don't you? Just like your friends out there. You think we're just deep-diggers. Miners too dumb, too afraid to take action."

"You're misinterpreting the situation and my intent," Dranes said calmly. "The Legion is only here as an honor guard. And the only reason the HARD regiment is here is to provide security because it was clear you didn't want us to come. You're wrong about—"

"I am *not wrong*!" the leader bellowed. "And I am going to be true to my word."

For a moment, O'Keefe thought the man would shoot Dranes. Instead, he turned and stared directly at her. She met his gaze, unflinching.

"If we don't get a response soon, she dies." He pointed the barrel of his weapon at her forehead. Then, as if remembering that it wasn't Dranes who needed to know that information, he depressed the orange button on the handheld comm. "Leave, or hostages die today."

O'Keefe felt no fear. That was the only benefit of the memory-war raging between her ears. She was being tortured enough already by what was going on in her head. Nothing these men could do would hurt her worse than what she was already going through.

All his threat meant was that she had less than a day now to overpower the men without getting everyone killed in the process.

30

Metzger brought his HK-PP in a straight line to intercept the mech that was slugging it out with Razorwire and Ice Tea. While they had hit it several times, the hulking four-legged unit was larger and better armored than any of the other ones that the Vargas Liberation Army had put into the field so far. Rothchild couldn't say the same. His canopy had just been blown out from a direct hit, leaving no doubt that the man inside was dead. The sight of it in real time made Metzger want to retch. He'd seen dead men in combat before, but this was the first time as an HK-PP pilot.

You knew that you weren't invincible inside the machines. But somehow all that talk about being a blaster magnet felt like just that: talk. Metzger himself had absorbed a pounding since landing in the crater.

If there was any good in seeing Rothchild go out the way he did, it was to remind the rest of them that they had to stay sharp. There were few second chances inside a mech once the missiles started flying.

Hullbuster was coming in behind him by half a kilometer, still slowed by his earlier damage. Metzger's mech wasn't moving at full speed either. Without tech and logistics support, the mechs were having their combat-effectiveness slowly whittled away. It didn't help that the two pilots had taken direct hits in every engagement so far.

"Pileup!" came the call from one of the two legionnaires clutching the back of his mech. "We'll jump off here and paint that target."

Metzger slowed his gait. "You're good to go."

The leejes jumped off. "We're clear. Good luck and good hunting."

As he rounded a rock formation, Metzger got a visual on the enemy mech. It was boxy, with a crude hexagonal turret mounted on top and curved bulldozer blade acting as a blast plate on its front. At some point it had been an instrument of mining; now it was pressed into battle. Its four legs were thick and moved with dull methodical precision, thudding the crater floor hard as it moved.

It didn't seem to notice that he was coming into range... it was concentrating on Ice Tea. Vickerson weaved and bobbed her HK-PP from side to side in an ever-widening series of turns as it tried to lock on to her. Razorwire dodged too, making himself a harder target to hit, then unleashed a pair of missiles. One slammed into a front dozer blade with a brilliant orange plume of fire, furrowing through to the next layer of armor beyond. The other hit the left front leg, throwing off chunks of armor. White smoke hissed into the air from some sort of hydraulic leak, but the mech didn't slow its fire. One of its big blaster shots hit Ice Tea just below the cockpit, and her HK-PP twisted and fell to the ground.

The two legionnaires Metzger had dropped off were using their blasters to paint the target, or so Metzger's tac sensors told him. That would increase the odds that electronic jamming wouldn't hinder his missiles from flying true, though with such a large mech, the thing would be pretty hard to miss anyway.

For a moment the canopy felt like it was right in Metzger's face, just like the dropdown tactical display on his infantry helmet. Was this the experience the other pilots talked about—becoming one with their mech? He sidelined that thought, focusing on the battle. With every bit of precision he could muster, he brought the targeting reticle onto the damaged front leg and fired both blasters, the hum and throbbing of the release of deadly energy wrapping around him. One shot bored into the knee of the fat leg, leaving a smoking black hole, while the other shot missed by mere centimeters, curling the paint on the mech as it passed.

Razorwire unleashed his own blasters, one hitting the turret and one the front armor. Metzger couldn't see the hit on the front as he adjusted his own angle toward the enemy mech's rear, but the turret splattered yellow and crimson globs of molten metal across the top of the mech, some bits hitting the ground and leaving white spots of smoke where they fell.

From the side of the turret, a secondary blaster opened up in Metzger's direction. At first he was pleased to see that the shots were far too wide; then he realized they were aimed at the rock formation where the legionnaires were covering while they painted the tank. The enemy's primary weapon flashed as well, striking the ground in front of Razorwire's mech. Much too close for comfort.

"Oba, that thing is big," Hullbuster said, firing his one working blaster, hitting side armor and cutting a glowing hot scar up the mech's side.

"Aim for the damaged front leg," Metzger said.

"Copy that."

The mech fired another shot, though Metzger couldn't see what it was targeting—he only saw the brilliant burst of deadly energy stab off into the distance. Then the turret started to swivel around, and he knew it would be on him and Hullbuster in a matter of moments.

Not if I can get my shots off first.

Metzger waited a few milliseconds for his blaster capacitors to charge, then fired as he broke left, toward the rear of the mech. Both shots hit in the same spot as Hullbuster's, digging deeper into the mech's mechanical guts. Then his wingman's blaster sent a bolt into the damaged knee of the four-legged miscreation. The knee joint exploded, turning the metal into red-hot shrapnel, and the leg seized entirely, suffering a massive failure.

The big quad-mech tried to continue forward. Three of the legs responded, but the damaged one remained rigid, dragging into the crater floor like like an anchor before it broke off, left behind, still standing. The hulking mech was now hopelessly imbalanced, and it tumbled forward, slamming into the ground with enough force to rattle Metzger's HK-PP.

"Nice shooting, Hullbuster."

"I aim to please," Buck quipped. "You get it, right? *Aim to please.*"

There was no way Metzger was going to respond to that; he'd only encourage the former marine.

Instead, he focused on the enemy. With the mech's front left side sunken hopelessly to the ground, the turret couldn't elevate enough to fire. Worse yet for its pilot and gunner, its top was exposed to Razorwire—and to Ice Tea, who had managed to right herself. They fired their blasters at once. The armor on top of the mech was thin, evidently just the standard protection the mining vehicle had initially been equipped with. Their shots blasted deep.

The vehicle looked as if it had lost all power. Smoke billowed out of the holes from the blaster hits, followed by roaring flames, some soaring nearly five meters high.

Metzger slowed, checking his tactical display to make sure the dying mech didn't have any nearby support. When he was satisfied that wasn't the case, he allowed himself a moment to look at the plumes of bright red tinged blue that marked something burning off from the inside of the colossal mech.

An instant later, the vehicle exploded. The blast was white and triggered the polarization filter on the cockpit canopy, suggesting it was the power plant that had been devoured. As the filter recalibrated, he couldn't make out the mech, so he halted, with Hullbuster moving up alongside him.

When the canopy reverted back to its normal view, he saw very little to distinguish the flaming and blasted debris as a mech at all. There was no point in looking for survivors—nothing could have survived that explosion.

Hullbuster moved up to the standing leg and kicked it with his HK-PP, knocking it over. Then he stepped on the stump, hopping his mech up and down several times.

"I think we got him, Hullbuster."

"I know," he said, stopping. "But they deserve this."

"I've got nothing on my sensors," said the cool voice of Razorwire.

"Same here," Metzger replied. "How are you, Ice Tea?"

"Battered and bruised. I lost a missile rack, and my left blaster is bent skyward. But I've had worse Saturday nights at the officers' club after closing time."

Her sense of humor was almost as bad as Buck's. Worse, her combat effectiveness was shot.

Metzger was about to respond, but Captain Peltier's voice cut him off. "Grunon's tank is down. Ivers was knocked out too. Tramel and Krock led the attackers away, so I need someone to get over to see if they're still alive before the miners return."

One of the legionnaires responded that they were on their way.

That must have been what this big bastard was shooting at, Metzger thought. He hoped that Grunon and Ivers survived, but he knew that when a tank went down under fire, the odds of the crew surviving were slim.

Peltier continued. "All forces, I'm setting a waypoint, designation Delta. Our commanders will reach out to us in two hours. Update and likely a new FRAGO waiting for us there."

To Metzger, this was a good sign. They had been playing hit-and-run with the Vargas Liberation Army since the morning of the day before. Sleep had been a short, in-the-cockpit affair. Meals were onboard rations, which he didn't mind; he had eaten less and worse-tasting during his military career. But what he longed for more than anything was to get out of his cockpit, stretch his legs, and be in some other position than strapped in his command seat.

And to know the status of O'Keefe.

"You heard the Captain, Buck," he transmitted to Hullbuster. "We have a rendezvous. This time, don't forget to pick up those leejes."

Buck had left his leejes waiting and had to circle back a few hours before. They had given him hell for it, rightfully so.

"Yeah, yeah," Hullbuster muttered as he formed up slightly back of him in a welded wing formation. "For the record, I'm getting tired of all this sket. I know I don't get paid by the kill, but I'd rather a straight-up fight than this hit-and-fade crap. That's the beauty of fighting on a ship: nowhere to run and hide... except out an airlock."

"I hear you," Metzger said. "But we have a job to do. And the way these guys fight, I'm not sure we should want a straight-up fight. We're outnumbered and outgunned."

"Are we still though? We've taken down a lot of these guys."

It was a question that Metzger had been thinking about as well. They had destroyed the enemy at every engagement. At the same time, they'd taking a beating and were dropping in combat effectiveness with every encounter.

"Guess we'll find out," he said.

"Ask me," Buck said, "all we need to do is keep shooting 'til we outnumber them."

Waypoint Delta was at the edge of a large, shallow, orange-shored pond. The rocks along the shoreline were marked with high water lines of varying shades of brown, signs of previous flooding. They had an almost artistic look to them.

Metzger opened his canopy and began to climb down from his battered HK-PP. He could smell the burned armor and seared paint, and as he came down the hand rungs, his eyes traced the outline of each bit of damage. She was doing well, considering, but she only had another fight or two left in her before she'd need some serious repairs.

His joints protested as he dropped to the ground. Old aches, like the one in his back, came to him. His bionic limb was the only part of his body that didn't complain.

Looking around, he saw Sergeant Grunon's MBT sputtering into the waypoint, belching smoke. It was good to see the man still alive. There was no sign of Ivers though, nor would there be—that tank and its crew were gone.

Metzger made his way over to Captain Peltier. The man's jumpsuit was soaked with sweat, and his usually well-kept hair was wet, oily, and looking as if he didn't own a comb. Bags hung under his eyes as he nodded to Metzger. The haunted look on his face told Metzger right away that the captain had lost another mech from his platoon. Peltier was now all that remained of Command.

The legionnaires removed their buckets. Like everyone else, they looked exhausted. Metzger didn't know who had it rougher, the pilots in the cockpits or the leejes having to hang on. Hullbuster joined him, standing at his side, and Vickerson was on his other side.

For a few moments, Captain Peltier didn't say anything. He seemed to be a lot like Metzger—just savoring a few minutes of standing upright. When at last he spoke, it was as if he had to summon a reserve of energy just to do so.

"Fighting is still going on topside. We're driving them away from HQ, but the enemy is making an orderly withdrawal. "

That HQ was the whole reason the main joint force element was up top to begin with. The expectation had been that any miner or K'llik movement toward the crash site would be via the surface, coming down the same access ramps that the 510th had used. With the majority of legionnaires and HARD squadrons up there, one would have to be crazy to try and sneak in and plant mines or other insurgent-type tactics.

Because that's what they had expected if there was going to be trouble—sniping, roadside bombs, things of that nature.

Instead they got a bloody nose and a full-on fight against a force that was far larger, far better equipped, and far more aggressive than anyone could have anticipated.

Peltier continued. "Our forces have the upper hand—for now. Which means the miners in this crater have to be aware by now that they're cut off and surrounded. That's going to make them increasingly desperate, and their recent communications to us reflect that. They're now threatening to kill a hostage every hour on the hour if we don't stand down. My belief is they're just stalling for time, rethinking their position, but we have to be aware of the potential that they follow through on their threat."

Just hearing those words—*kill a hostage*—gave Metzger a surge of anxiety.

"Meantime, we have new orders that will force the issue either way," Peltier went on. "We're to make a forceful demonstration on the research base, retaking it if possible. We're also tasked with taking out any missile batteries we find that might prevent dropship support."

Razorwire raised a question. "They don't think the miners will kill 'em all? The hostages, I mean."

Peltier shrugged. "I couldn't tell you what the brass thinks in that regard. We are to take actions that ensure the safety of the hostages. One possibility is that these holdouts might just throw their hands in the air when they see us coming. We're not counting on that, but we've been given pretty wide discretion in the execution of our orders."

Metzger agreed with the captain's assessment. While it was nice to entertain the idea that the Vargas Liberation Army would just fold, his gut told him otherwise. They had fought hard thus far. When pressed, they might feel forced to take drastic action.

And if they started wasting hostages, things would get messy real fast.

Sergeant Callison of the Legion spoke next. "My men have all undertaken our share of snatch-and-grabs. If you can get us into that camp, we're your best chance to get in there and neutralize whoever's holding our hostages."

Peltier didn't reply. His eyes panned the circle of warriors until his gaze fell on Metzger. Then he turned back to Callison.

"I want our hostages secured, Sergeant. But I can't risk getting them killed in the crossfire."

Callison nodded. "Understood, Captain. No one wants that. With that clear, the offer stands."

Metzger noted that the legionnaires mostly kept to themselves. What few comments he did hear from them tended to be critical about R-A tactics and decision making. He also noted that the sergeant didn't say, "sir."

Unless you were Legion, they never did.

31

O'Keefe's nerves were raw, and the tension of the situation was doing nothing for her condition. Her brain was now under assault once every few minutes. Voices and faces of the dead came in like a barrage, all of them vying for her attention. Sometimes the memories came as still frames, hitting her fast like a strobe light, blurred and chaotic. At other times she watched multiple scenes, or fragments of scenes, play out in front of her, superimposed. Yet despite the whirlwind unfolding in her brain, she managed to maintain a mask of composure and calm.

The leader of their captors had made it clear that when it did come time to kill a hostage, it would be her. She assumed she'd be taken outside for the deed, if only so as not to bloody up the holding area, and she had decided that when that time came, it would represent her best opportunity to make a move. She was fairly certain that not all three of the men would go outside just to shoot a single handcuffed prisoner; one or more would remain behind to keep an eye on the rest. In moments of calm between the furies in her head, she carefully thought through every scenario. The situation wasn't good, and neither were the odds. But they weren't going to get any better.

One thing giving her solace was the anxiety her captors displayed. It continued to be clear that the battle was not going well for the Vargas Liberation Army. That could mean that at some point the base camp would be recaptured and she and the other hostages would be freed. But it felt equally likely that any threat to the base camp would make her captors so desperate that they would simply slaughter all of their prisoners. At that point, what more would they have to lose?

She watched the men holding her hostage. They didn't seem prepared for a long standoff. They had brought no food or water. There was some in the research facility, and they had already greedily consumed it all. It was apparent that things were getting worse for them... worse for everyone.

Suddenly the leader of the trio spun on her. "What is it with you?" he demanded. She must have been too obvious, staring at them too openly.

"Nothing," she said, averting her gaze. "I'm just... not feeling well, that's all."

"She's ill," Dranes cut in. "That's why she needs her medication."

The leader gave Dranes a contemptuous look. "She won't be ill for much longer. Our patience wears thin. All I'm waiting for is an order."

The way he said it was far from comforting. Perhaps O'Keefe would soon be presented with the opportunity she sought.

"None of you will be spared, you know," the leader continued, clearly wanting to instill fear in the hearts of those trapped in the lab. "The legionnaires and techs we captured outside have already been executed. All you had to do was stay clear of our world, and they would still be alive. The same will be said of you if your commanders don't respect our sovereignty. All of this blood is on *your* hands."

No one argued the point; this wasn't a discussion. They were hostages. *Just keep your head down,* O'Keefe thought to herself. *You'll get your chance.*

It came sooner than she wanted. The next comm that came in brought the order their captors had been waiting for. The order to kill. O'Keefe couldn't hear the words as the leader spoke into his comm, but she knew what was going on by the way he looked at her.

But first, the rebel leader made a transmission of his own. He depressed the orange transmit button on his communicator and said, "Republic forces, you seem to think we're joking. You are wrong. I will now execute a member of your science team."

Setting the communicator down, he looked O'Keefe in the eye. "Where's that brave face now?"

O'Keefe wanted to glower at the man, but instead she looked down, once more reminding herself to be patient. The last thing she wanted was to agitate her captors into a messy, indoors execution. Let them bring her to her feet, take her outside... then the odds would be slightly more in her favor.

A voice crackled over the communicator. "Vargas commander, this is Captain Peltier. We should meet and talk, discuss how to get out of this without further loss of life."

"No meetings, no talk," said the leader. "Only surrender. That is the only solution we will accept. Terms can be discussed in between executions, but the woman now before me... her time is over. Do not fail the next one as you did her."

"We need time—"

The man shut off the communicator, bent down, grabbed O'Keefe's forearm, and yanked her roughly to her feet. Her legs ached from being bent on the floor for so long, hurting almost as much as the throbbing in her forehead.

But it was the memories that worried her most. If she got caught up in them, she was doomed.

She glanced over her shoulder at Dranes. He had stood up with her, but was looking down a blaster barrel as a result. O'Keefe shook her head; he didn't need to die attempting to be brave. He gave a slight nod and then lowered himself amid the shrieks from the captors to get back down. Dranes looked as though he wanted to tell her goodbye, but couldn't bring himself to say the words. Instead he gave her a single nod, which she responded to in kind.

Her captor guided her to the door of the repulsor trailer. When he opened it, the fading daylight washed across her, making her squint. With one huge paw holding her forearm, he led her down the steps to the ground.

She twisted slightly, enough to break his grip on her. "I can walk on my own," she said firmly.

The movement allowed her to turn and start to slide her wrist free of the plastic strap. She felt the plastic digging into her flesh. It was tight, but her skin was now wet with sweat, which would help.

If she couldn't get it off, it was all over. She was about sixty seconds from being dead.

As they moved, she saw other rebels—lots of them. But none were close by, and all had their backs turned to the research trailer, watching for signs of the evasive HARD mechs and Cobra Company legionnaires still in this crater. Their focus was on an expected counterattack.

O'Keefe was willing to bet they had good reason to be concerned. But she was no longer waiting for the cavalry. If she was going to survive the next few minutes, it would be entirely up to her.

Her captor tried to take her elbow and guide her again, but she shook him off.

"You're a fierce one," he said.

"I'm not afraid of dying, if that's what you mean. With my condition, I'd rather die than live without my medication." The words spilled out of her mouth, but they were chillingly accurate. "You're doing me a favor."

The leader didn't seem to know what to say about that. He seemed almost sheepish as he changed the subject. "I have no blindfold for you."

This man was no hardened killer. But he'd crossed a line, and there was no way back that didn't involve violence.

"I don't want one." With all of her effort, O'Keefe managed to pull her wrist free without making a show of it.

"Move over there." He pointed away from the trailer toward the burial mound. "Gaines," he said, then looked around. "Gaines!"

The skinny man came running. "Was just telling Kex that we finally got the order."

"I want a holo of the execution," the leader said. "Otherwise they might think we're bluffing."

Gaines nodded and pulled a datapad from his pocket. It was a miner's device, dirty and encased in a comically thick protective case.

It was still two on one, but at least Gaines's weapon was slung, his hands busy with his pad.

Still, even if O'Keefe managed to overpower them both, how would she deal with the rest of the guards around the site?

Maybe it didn't matter. Perhaps this was it, and at the grave of the lost legion O'Keefe would die a warrior's death, taking as many with her as she could.

That's how she'd always imagined the lost legion had gone out—a fitting, final blaze of glory.

She pushed such thoughts aside and assessed the situation. Everything she had ever learned about hand-to-hand combat surged to the forefront of her mind.

Gaines is slower, his weapon is back-slung, and his hands are holding his datapad to record me. He's not the immediate threat. The big guy needs to go down first.

She had a laundry list of options, from punching his liver to going for a knockout, unlikely given the size differential unless she landed a perfect kick or knee strike. It was tempting to try to disarm him, but doing so would leave him able to fight, and he was larger and more muscular than her.

Better to disable first, *then* disarm.

"Move," the leader said, nodding toward the crashed dropship.

As O'Keefe took a step, walking backward to keep her free hands out of his view, she saw where he intended her to go. A stack of corpses—dead legionnaires and a few of her colleagues there—had been piled up against the dropship, left to rot.

She swallowed her rage and her grief, and mentally walked herself through the exact form of her attack. She felt sure she would get in at least one or two hits before her captor could respond. And back here, she was out of sight of the other miners around the encampment. If she could manage this without too much noise, too many blaster bolts...

"Turn around," her captor ordered.

At that moment, she felt the mental shadow wash over her... and Lieutenant Ringer materialized between her and the big man.

No! Not now!

His shimmering, war-weary countenance turned to her. "We have to take out those tanks or the team will get slaughtered."

For an instant, she froze. In that moment, she was in two realities. One in Tykaree Valley, the other on Vargas. She could see Ringer lying prone before her captor on Vargas, and she could see the leader standing over Ringer in Tykaree Valley. Both at once. Both equally real.

Through gritted teeth, she responded to the dead man.

"Stack 'em high..."

She controlled her breathing, slightly winded by the thin air. Ringer seemed to fast-forward slightly, if only for an instant.

"... and..."

She could barely see it, but it was almost as if a smile was starting to form in the corners of Ringer's mouth.

The rebel miner was confused, but he didn't shoot. "What—"

"Stack 'em deep!" she finished.

"Damn right!" Ringer responded. "Go get 'em!"

O'Keefe embraced the words of the memory and sprang at her captor, moving with a speed that only a trained and experienced warrior could muster. Her first blow was a solid jab to his thick neck, right in the windpipe. His eyes went wide in shock. The hand that wasn't holding a blaster reached up to his throat, a survival instinct, and O'Keefe seized the opportunity. She grabbed his blaster rifle with both hands, leveraging her grip to turn the weapon upward and back toward him. No matter how strong the man was, there was no way for him to maintain his grip with the weapon craned back, and she ripped it free as he staggered back, still gasping, both hands now fumbling at his throat.

She didn't hesitate, the rumbling from battle memories filling her mind. In a fluid motion, she raised the blaster and fired, sending a bolt of energy right into her tormentor's face. His head exploded in a spray of superheated blood and brains, and his big body fell backward onto the ground. With a quick sidestep and turn, she leveled the weapon at Gaines. He was frozen with his datapad in his hand, and a part of her wondered for an instant if he'd just recorded his own friend's death.

His eyes went wide. "No, no, no—"

O'Keefe squeezed the trigger. A blast of brilliant yellow energy slammed into his lower torso, and he fell backward, moaning as he dropped. O'Keefe's nose caught a hint of burned uniform and the aroma of seared flesh. He was still alive, but he wouldn't be for long.

She undid the strap of the blaster he had slung behind him. A hint of excrement told her that he had either soiled himself or the blaster bolt had torn open his colon.

Her eyes swept the area to make sure no one was in view, no one was coming to investigate. But no one showed. Her two shots had been close together; just the execution of a hostage. Nothing to see here.

In her mind, she heard Ringer's voice. "Blow them to hell!"

I am!

She'd already planned her next steps. Back to the trailer, release the hostages, hold off anyone who tried to force their way in. Try to alert Metzger and the legionnaires.

She ran back to the trailer, climbing the two steps, and threw open the door.

Her remaining captor was caught flat-footed. His jaw dropped open at the sight of her with the blaster aimed at him. His weapon was limp in his hands.

"Drop it," she commanded, her eyes flitting to the side, ears straining for more guards to come in after her. He obeyed without hesitation. Stepping forward, she kicked the weapon behind her. "Now release them. Starting with him."

She motioned toward Dranes.

The man nervously complied as she continued to keep the blaster trained on him. When Dranes was free, he picked up the man's discarded blaster rifle and took over for O'Keefe in training his weapon on their former guard while she closed the door and readied herself to kill anyone who attempted to come inside.

"Where are my friends?" the guard asked as he freed the last hostage.

"You already know," she said coldly.

The sound of the blaster bolts outside would have been unmistakable. And seeing as *she* wasn't dead…

The miner's face went pale, then hardened into a look of disgust. "We'll kill you for that."

She wanted to kill *him*, but she held herself in check—barely. "Someone go to my pack and get me my meds."

A fellow researcher brought her pack over. Still watching the door, O'Keefe plunged her hand inside and came back with the medicine. She dialed up a double dose and slammed the pills back in her throat without the benefit of water. One felt like it wasn't going down right, so she swallowed hard. The memories would soon be under control.

But then, from outside the trailer, came shouting voices, as if men were staging.

O'Keefe tightened her grip on her weapon, covering the door. "Everyone get down and hug the floor."

All obeyed, leaving Dranes and O'Keefe to provide defense.

From a kneeling position, using the counter below her DNA testing machine as cover, O'Keefe watched the door to the trailer gently swing open. She caught the glimpse of a rifle barrel. There was no target in view, but the walls to these mobile research trailers were thin—so she opened fire and stitched blaster bolts along the doorframe. Shafts of light punched through into the darkened interior of the research trailer. The body of a dead miner fell forward, rifle clattering in front of him.

The door remained open, letting out some of the smoke from the blaster fire.

No return fire came.

They still need us alive, O'Keefe told herself.

But she knew that need might only be a temporary one.

32

Metzger approached the camp at a trot, his HK-PP's footpads thudding the ground hard. His mech had shed a few hundred pounds in the form of blasted composite armor, but it was still heavy. Three of the leejes that had once served as part of the honor guard were now using the back of his mech as their ride, and the other three rode with Hullbuster.

"Tally ho," called out Chief Dobbs, who was slightly ahead in his HK-SW. "I'm picking up enemy mechs and a tank at my outer marker. Designating the four mechs as Tango, Uniform, Victor, and Whisky. Enemy repulsor tank is marked as X-ray." There was a pause; no doubt he was checking his sensors. Riding on an HK-SW, scanning, and trying to relay the information in an open cockpit called for a specialized skill set. "Zulu is our SAM battery."

The tactical display on Metzger's mech showed the targets that Dobbs had called out, flickering little crimson dots.

"This is Pileup, I copy," he said as a chorus of voices from the squadron confirmed the same.

"Good work, Back Door," Captain Peltier signaled.

Their primary objectives were destroying the missile battery and extracting the hostages. The bulk of the force was to go right at the enemy, exchange shots, then break off in the hopes of drawing pursuit. Pileup and Hullbuster were to drift back, out of sensor range, with the legionnaires, who would seek to secure the research site while the two HK-PPs handled the SAM battery.

The plan was dicey, Metzger knew. His father used to say that cornered rats bit hardest. Not only that, but a lot was riding on the assumption that the rebels in this crater wouldn't consolidate forces at the research base in an attempted last stand. The belief was that the miners would feel such a consolidation was unnecessary; the miners still had superior numbers, enough so that they could spare units to roam the crater in hopes of destroying the cut-off HARD squadron when those chances presented themselves.

It was that aggression that Peltier's ruse would take advantage of.

"Roger, Slick," Metzger transmitted. "We're going to drift back out of range and wait for your signal."

He slowed his HK-PP, then pushed his heels in, moving the mech in reverse. The thundering of the other mechs drifted away with his actions. When he was satisfied with his distance, he came to a stop.

"Hold up here," he said to Hullbuster, who formed up on his side. "Sergeant, your guys can dismount if you want to stretch your legs."

"Copy that," Callison replied.

Metzger had learned long ago how to cope with waiting. Sitting and doing nothing was where he guessed he'd spent fifty percent of his time in the military. Sure, there was combat training, calisthenics and exercise, time on the range. There were hours of battle too, however rare. But surrounding all of those activities was doing what he and the small cadre of troops were doing now: nothing.

The end of the long wait was marked by explosions echoing off the crater walls in the distance, followed by Peltier's voice over comms. "Enemy engaged," he said. "We're falling back. Section two, you're up."

"Mount up," Metzger said. It was a formality. The moment he'd heard the explosions, he'd felt the tug of weight on his HK-PP as the leejes boarded.

"Echelon formation," he transmitted to Hullbuster.

"Copy that."

Metzger snugged his safety harness and throttled up his power plant. The mech surged to life all around him, enveloping him in a sense of comfort. His trained eyes swept the displays projected on the inside of the canopy, and he took in a deep breath.

"Stay close," he told Hullbuster.

"Don't I always?"

Grinning, Metzger accelerated, slowly depressing the foot pedals and plotting a path forward. His left hand worked the tactical display, zooming out and showing the identifiers as they came onto the screen. After a half minute, he was up to full speed. He could see the tags for the base, the crashed dropship, and the enemies. One mech had remained behind, the one ID'd as Tango.

He and Hullbuster began a slow arcing turn, dodging several small mounds of rock debris. Another hundred meters of charging brought Zulu into view, on the far side of the crashed dropship, beyond the camp.

"Zulu is on the board," he said.

"Got it."

Metzger used his left hand to project a course for them, using the crashed dropship to provide cover from the defending mech, at least until it started moving. "Sergeant, course up on plot. We will debark you at the dropship inside the camp perimeter."

"Confirmed."

"All right," he said. "I've got three missiles left. How are you set, Hullbuster?"

"I have one."

"We're at extreme range now. When we're in nominal, lock on to Zulu and fire."

"That leaves only blasters for the mech."

"Yeah."

Metzger understood the implications. The missiles could be devastating. Blasters alone against an unknown enemy mech would take longer and, with the damage they had already endured, could be a fatal choice.

But Zulu would be destroyed.

They tore through low brush, shredding the foliage as they ran. Coming up over a rise, Metzger saw the base camp of trailers and tents, and the crashed dropship they had come to inspect. Beyond it, barely visible, was a mech. While he couldn't make out the details, it looked very much like a modified loader frame, ugly and brutish. A crude mockery of what a mech should look like.

Metzger charged his blasters and searched for the SAM battery. His sensors said it was out there, but he didn't see it. While his aero-precision missiles didn't require LOS on target, it increased their accuracy—and gave him peace of mind that he was firing at what he wanted to be firing at.

As he came through a low clump of scraggly trees, he finally spotted it: a squat, tracked launcher vehicle armed with four ship-killing missiles. It was already kicking up dust as it tried to crawl away.

It wasn't going to outrun an HK-PP.

Metzger's sensors picked up a painting shot from the leejes, who must be doing it one-handed while holding on for dear life. That qualified as crazy in his book. But as it fed into his targeting system, it allowed for a tighter zoom on the target.

Bringing his targeting reticle on the SAM, he got tone quickly.

"Firing," he said as the last of his missiles cleared the rack, their whoosh and the slight buffet of their exhaust washing his HK-PP. Hullbuster called out the same single word, his missile following.

Metzger didn't watch to see if they hit; they would. Instead he banked hard for the base camp. The explosion came a moment later, a deep vibration cutting the air and shaking dust off of leaves. Through the mech, he felt the shock wave roll past, then saw a ball of crimson fire blossoming skyward.

The enemy mech was moving to his right, apparently looking for a good angle. Metzger slowed to half-speed. "Debark," he called, and waited for the legionnaires to drop off. Even at that speed, it was going to be a hard bounce for the troopers, but any slower would make him a target.

Once his passengers had signaled clear, Metzger juked hard to the left to skirt the antiquated dropship. Rockets from the enemy mech soared through the air over the camp vehicles and tents, raining down on Hullbuster. The wingman's angle had cost him dearly. Damage indicators for Hullbuster's mech flashed horrific crimson; his legs had been fully compromised, and his upper torso wasn't doing much better.

"Hullbuster!"

"I'm down for the count," came an exasperated voice, one that was clearly attempting to hide pain and failing miserably. "Sorry, Pileup."

Damn!

As Metzger rounded the dropship, he danced his targeting reticle on the enemy mech and fired. His blasts slammed into its boxy torso, burning ugly hot glowing scars on the ad hoc armor. The enemy pilot broke to his left, exposing his rear, but Metzger's blaster cannons needed a moment to energize the particle—the bolt—so the split-second opportunity was lost. In no time the converted mining mech was coming around, probably to release another rocket salvo.

He darted hard to the right, twisting the waist of his HK-PP to keep his target lock. The enemy mech was much slower, and by matching its turn, he was making it very hard for his foe to line up the shot. As his reticle remained on target, he fired again. The energy bolts tore into the upper body of the mech just as it unleashed a wave of rockets.

Thanks to the superior speed of the HK-PP, the rockets lagged behind him, and he heard them exploding with a shriek of metal. Some had probably hit the derelict dropship he'd just run past. The archaeologists and historians wouldn't like that, but on the other hand, they'd like to be rescued. And all that mattered to Metzger at the moment was taking down the mech. If he couldn't do that, the legionnaires moving into the base would be at risk, and there was no way he would let that happen.

As his mech channeled another surge of power to the blasters, he tightened his turn and increased his speed. He almost slipped in doing so—the gray sand covering a flat rock formation acted like a sheet of ice—but he fluttered his feet on the footpads and somehow maintained his balance.

The converted mining mech fired again, not rockets this time, but some sort of military-grade laser—an antique from a bygone era. The prolonged scarlet beam cut down trees as it followed Metzger, then caught the side of his mech and burned a deep scar right below his cockpit. Through the lower cockpit window near his feet, he saw the glowing melted metal that had been his armor. A hydraulic warning indicator flashed the same color of crimson on his damage display. He shunted the flow through a backup line as his HK-PP staggered a few uneasy steps.

Another wave of missiles would be roaring in at any second, and his mech's sudden slowness meant that he was going to catch it this time—and the wave might very well take him down as it had Hullbuster. This might be his last chance.

He zoomed in to the maximum and brought the targeting reticle squarely on the enemy cockpit. The Vargas mech had slowed too, lining up his shot, which helped. It was going to be a matter of who fired first.

Metzger's entire body tensed and his breathing stopped as he concentrated on the shot.

He fired his blaster cannons.

The bolts of charged particles filled the space between the two opponents, hitting the cockpit of the enemy almost dead-on. Because Metzger was zoomed in, he saw the energy hitting the armored glass and superheating it, furrowing deep and punching through—right at where the pilot should be sitting.

The enemy mech listed backward just as it unleashed its rockets. As a result, they were aimed skyward in a wild spray; they went up and came raining down, detonating harmlessly. The rebel mech toppled over and hit the ground with a thud. Metzger halted his HK-PP in place, watching to see if the converted mining mech tried to stand.

It didn't.

Metzger sucked in a breath of air. "Pileup to Slick. Zulu is down, as is Tango. Hullbuster is down but alive."

For the first time since the skirmish had started, he felt the sting of sweat at the edges of his eyeballs and the dryness of his throat as he spoke. He became aware of his crushing grip on the joysticks in his hands, and forced himself to relax his grasp.

Major Meece had been right about piloting a mech being equally grueling as infantry fighting.

"Copy," came Peltier's voice. "Is the base secure, Sergeant Callison?"

"Base is secure," the Legion sergeant answered. "Looks like they *did* kill some of the hostages, though. Kelhorns."

O'Keefe!

Metzger whipped his HK-PP around and raced toward the base.

33

O'Keefe could feel the drugs working. The voices in her mind, the sounds, the fragmentary staccato of battle, they were all fading. She didn't delude herself into believing things were back to any sort of normality, only that she was, for now, on top of her internal situation.

Their lone surviving captor had been bound and gagged. She could see on Dranes's face that he was suppressing the urge to inflict some harm on the man. It was a sentiment she shared. Beating or shooting him, defenseless, was tempting, but she refused to respond to that compulsion. Like one of her misfiring memories, she forced herself to ignore it.

She wanted to believe this was a noble decision, a purely moral one, but it wasn't. The truth was, they weren't out of this yet—and a living hostage was more useful than a dead body. Especially with who knew how many more rebels somewhere outside. They hadn't tried to push on her position again, probably figuring—accurately—that the historians and scientists were still their prisoners, so long as they couldn't leave the trailer.

But now there was a change in their circumstances: the distinctive sound of fighting in the distance. Heavy fighting —tanks, mechs, and other furious machines.

She heard a low rumble, steady... mech footfalls. Then came an explosion, not too far away, perhaps just beyond the dropship crash site.

Weaver, now once again conscious, asked the question prompted by the sounds of battle outside. "Should we try to head out?"

"We stay here," O'Keefe said firmly, then looked, from her vigil covering the door, over to Dranes for a nod of support—which he gave. "This lab is defensible. There's only one door, and we can cover it."

But they could do more than *just* that. As her mind returned again to what she considered normal, she realized how much time she'd spent just watching the door instead of fortifying their position. She pointed to one of the rolling lab tables. "We should make a firing stoop on the other side of the bench. Then let's get some equipment blocking the entrance and make it difficult for anyone who tries to come inside."

As injured as Dranes and Weaver were, they didn't hesitate in getting to work. Even the other techs and historians, some of whom had never served outside an office or a lab, pitched in to help.

O'Keefe knelt beside their prisoner. He was in obvious distress. Clearly he'd realized that his body was part of the protective concealment she was creating.

"You're worried you're going to get shot?" she said.

He couldn't speak through his gag, but he nodded, fast and furious.

"You should have thought of that before you came into this crater looking for a fight." It was impossible for her to muster any pity for the man. An hour ago, he'd held *them* prisoner, and had been perfectly willing to execute O'Keefe just to make a point. POWs were always that way in her experience—one minute trying to shoot you, the next begging to not be shot. "I won't shoot you to prove any point to your leaders," she said. "The Republic are the good guys. But... if your buddies break down that door, blasters blazing... well, it sucks to be you."

With the improvements finished, she rested her blaster —one of the two they had taken from their captors—on the edge of the overturned table and aimed at the door. A wave of strobe-like memories washed over her, but they weren't nearly as intense now, and lasted for only a few moments; her medicine was taking effect. The resulting feelings of control and suppression were intoxicating to her, warm and tingly.

Dranes reached across the central workbench and handed her a water flask. She popped the top and took several long gulps.

A blast rocked the trailer, making everything vibrate. Glassware bumped and added to the melody from the explosion. Muffled sounds came from somewhere very close by, and everyone inside went quiet.

She hoped no one would decide to just kill them all. It would be pitifully easy to do so. A simple incendiary device tossed inside would burn them out, and then they could be shot at leisure while attempting to escape through the sole door or any windows they blasted out. Which, she had to admit, was better than burning to death.

Or, as she had already demonstrated, they could just shoot indiscriminately through the walls of the trailer. Take out enough resistance, then surge in and regain control of whoever had been fortunate enough to dodge the blaster bolts... if that's what they wanted. Maybe they were too occupied with whatever was happening in the crater with the HARD squadron and legionnaires.

O'Keefe hoped that her fighting here was done. She didn't want to die. She didn't want any more of her colleagues dead. And for that matter, she didn't want to see any of the sensitive equipment be further damaged—especially the DNA tester.

It was already broken, of course. There was a big hole where the samples were loaded, and the holoscreen was cracked, and she wasn't sure if either one was something that could be fixed. But she knew the test she'd been running had finished prior to the machine being shot, which meant those test results were still in there—she just had to access them. If she could get the time to rig up something to send the output to a datapad... she'd have her answers.

A final confirmation.

The moment she'd been dreading finally came. Heavy footsteps outside the entryway.

O'Keefe braced herself, aiming her blaster.

"Republic legionnaires!" came a menacing voice through what sounded like external helmet speakers. "We have this building surrounded. Release your prisoners or we *will* come in and take them by force."

That was actually a remarkable show of restraint by the Legion. Usually they would just toss in bangers and clear the place. That they didn't might indicate a lack of equipment or sufficient manpower. The Legion weren't negotiators.

But she hadn't heard any up-close blaster fire, either. This could be a ruse. Perhaps the rebels had somehow managed to make one of the dead legionnaires' helmets operate? That wasn't supposed to be possible, but she wasn't willing to risk her life on possibilities.

O'Keefe held her weapon steady. "What do you think, Chief? Might be the rebels..."

"Hold your fire!" Dranes called back. "This is Chief Dranes. We have overpowered our guards and have retaken the lab."

"Come on out with your hands out, weapons slung," the voice called from outside the door.

Dranes exchanged a look with O'Keefe. "How do we know you're Legion and not just luring us out now that we took back the lab?"

It was a good question.

"Anyone can put on the armor, but only a leej can use the L-comm," the voice responded. "You got a comm on that lab, right? Talk to me through our JF channel."

Dranes again looked to O'Keefe, who gave him a shrug. That sounded right—the L-comm was one of the Legion's most protected pieces of technology.

More sounds of battle drifted in from outside, shaking the grav trailer. There was still a fight going on.

O'Keefe went to the lab's comm panel and activated the joint forces channel that allowed her to speak on an open net to the Legion. "KTF," she said. "This is Corporal Sheryl O'Keefe."

"KTF, O'Keefe," came the response. "This is Sergeant Callison. We're right outside the door."

"It's Sergeant Callison," O'Keefe said to the trailer a grin. "The Legion is here."

Applause erupted from the research team, which O'Keefe found amusing. Among her colleagues, who had never fired a weapon in anger, the Legion was typically viewed as backward and primitive—a chauvinistic, exclusive, species-ist group of war addicts who, yes, were once needed to defeat the Savages, but who were now an embarrassment to the new galaxy. The Republic Army was different. It was often said within its leadership that the R-A was a force for good, not a force for fighting.

It was a funny thing how quickly those political opinions vanished once the heavily armed soldiers were seeking to get them all to safety. Dranes slung his weapon, and O'Keefe followed suit. He went out the door first, slowly, hands up so they could see he wasn't a threat. She followed, leading their prisoner, along with the other members of the lab team who had been captured. As she stepped outside, the light made her eyes throb, and she smelled expended explosives in the air.

Two leejes stood right outside and hurried them into a clump of low brush. Their former captor was treated roughly, but fairly, given the circumstances. They double-checked him for weapons and made sure that he was secure, removing the rag that had been pressed into service as his gag. Other leejes were providing security, spread out, weapons at the ready.

"Are any of your people needing medical attention?" Callison asked.

"Some," Dranes said. "Nothing too serious."

"Speak for yourself, Chief," muttered Weaver, whose bruises appeared much worse in the light of day.

O'Keefe felt the approach of the mech before she saw it. The crater floor seemed to quiver with each footfall. When it emerged from behind the wrecked dropship, she was stunned by its condition. Black scars tore through its armor, and there were so many pits and seared spots that the green camouflage paint scheme was almost impossible to make out. One knee joint oozed a sickly green goo, and the thigh armor above it was peeled back from what had to have been some sort of projectile hit. Several holes were still wisping light trails of gray smoke.

This bad boy had seen some serious action.

Despite the damage, she could still make out the nose art painted near the cockpit—a cartoonish image featuring an armored infantry trooper with a medieval lance tucked under one arm. At the tip of the lance hung a small red banner with white lettering: *SH-SD.*

Stack 'em high, stack 'em deep.

Sergeant Callison paused, dipping his head slightly, probably receiving a message. Then he turned to Dranes and O'Keefe. "We're not showing any more hostiles in this vicinity. The 510th is in pursuit of what we believe is the last of them down here."

As he finished speaking, a stocky man entered the base perimeter on foot. His jumpsuit was stained with sweat, both fresh and crusty old. His helmet identified him as a mech pilot—it had a distinctive rounded shape very different from leej helmets—and his jumpsuit bore the name *Nelson* and the call sign *Hullbuster.*

"It looks like I missed the end of the show," he said.

It was then that the canopy of the nearby HK-PP hissed and opened, and its pilot rose in his seat. "Buck, you okay?" he called down.

Hullbuster gave a thumbs-up.

It was only then that the sweaty pilot in the HK-PP removed his helmet, and O'Keefe's face broke into a broad smile. It was Metzger.

She hurried over as he climbed down from his mech. "Glad you finally decided to show your sorry ass," she said.

He matched her grin. "I'm just glad you came through this alive."

"Too bad we can't say the same thing about your mech." She nodded to the HK-PP behind him.

He grimaced. "Yeah. The locals proved rather annoying. Those miners have a lot more hours in a mech than most of us. More than me, anyway."

"Well, at least it's over now." She saw the look on his face. "It's not over, is it?"

"Afraid not. Which is why I need to get moving, see what we can do about getting our equipment repaired. I'll catch up with you when I can." He paused. "It really is good to see you alive and well, Sheryl."

"You too, Carson."

A few minutes later, a leej worked over the researchers —wounds were treated, skinpacks applied, broken ribs were wrapped. Every legionnaire had some medical training, and their buckets could help them through anything they didn't know. An odd sense of normalcy came as another pair of mechs arrived.

"Dranes," O'Keefe said, "I'm going to go back in the lab to see if I can get our DNA tester working again."

He nodded. "Let me know what you find out."

She went over to the trailer steps and climbed inside. The interior was much more of a mess than she remembered it. She picked up the tables before turning her attention to the DNA tester.

She wasn't really going to bother trying to fix the thing— that was beyond her—but she was hoping she could manage to extract the latest test results. She grabbed a datapad and set to work making the connection with the tester. The unit wasn't designed to be accessed this way, and for a moment she thought she'd need to wait until she could get Weaver's help, but with a little more effort she stumbled on the right command.

She was in.

Now she just needed to bring up the test results. Yet something made her hesitate.

What if this was all a waste of time? What if our people died for nothing?

She took in a deep breath and pulled up the DNA tester's output.

Her mouth fell open.

Sergeant Joachim Andersen, LS-209-552-6. Last Posting 552nd Legion, Teal Company.

O'Keefe stopped breathing; it was as if her entire body had locked up. Years of historians and researchers who had gone before her, looking for the lost legions, had never been blessed with such a moment as this.

The 552nd was here, on Vargas. This was where Sergeant Andersen died.

And now you will finally go home. With honor.

34

Captain Peltier assembled what was left of the 510th Squadron in a huddle in front of his HK-PP. They had been at the base for an hour, getting the humans patched up and trying to piece together their situation as best they could. Metzger had seen the dead bodies of two squadron techs, thrown in a pile by the Vargas Liberation Army along with some researchers and legionnaires. It sickened, then angered him. He knew some of these techs from his punishment detail.

They were slaughtered, and for what?

Peltier planted his fists on his hips as he spoke. "Reports from topside are that both of the enemy factions are falling back to some lava plains about sixty kilometers west of our position. It's a running battle. As for the action down here, Scout Platoon has found no sign of further hostiles in this crater. We know we knocked out a lot of them, but certainly not all. They either have an alternate route out of here, or they're in hiding. And perhaps it's best they stay that way—we're in no condition for extended action."

He both looked and sounded exhausted. Then again, they all were. He was right: the 510th was no longer ready for combat. Every mech had been damaged, some badly, and with the fighting topside still raging, it would be days before help arrived.

Metzger felt the same way, but instead of looking at obstacles, he looked for possibilities. "Sir," he said. "We have tools here, and some emergency armor patch kits."

"Which don't do us a lot of good without techs, Pileup."

"Can't we just get a dropship down here with repair bots?" Tramel asked. "The bots do most of the work anyway."

Peltier shook his head. "Even with the SAM battery out, not any time soon. Navy says that topside has SAMs still in operation, and they don't have a drop path to reach this crater that won't run afoul of them. But here's the reality: they would extract us if they needed us, and they don't need us in the state we're in. We're beat to hell and of no use to the fight up above. We've secured the recovery site and freed our people. That looks to be our final role in this— beyond staying vigilant."

Several of the legionnaires scoffed at this. There was still fighting to be done, and until that wasn't the case, they weren't going to rest. That was fine and well for them— Sergeant Callison and the Legion boys were plenty capable of climbing out of this hole if they wanted to. The mechs and tanks though, it would seem, were grounded.

That needed to change. There was no guarantee the miners wouldn't hit them again.

"Sir..." said Metzger. "I spent weeks in the repair bays. I'm not a full-blown tech, but I know how to do a few things. I can teach the others, sir—enough to get started, anyway."

"I appreciate the initiative," said Peltier, "but it's not just a matter of know-how. We need parts, too."

Metzger was prepared for that. "We brought the basic stuff down and we can salvage parts from the enemy mechs and tanks. We'll make do with what we have. The goal isn't to be in perfect condition, just combat-worthy. We can do this, Captain."

Peltier said nothing for a long moment. Then he nodded. "It's better than sitting on our hands. At least we'll be ready for another dust-up if the miners want it."

"I think we can be ready for more than that, Captain," said Sergeant Callison. "The rebels' disappearance has me hopeful that we can get back in the main fight."

Peltier looked at the man. "What are you thinking?"

"That they didn't just hide in some caves and wait for us. That they tunneled their way down here, and now they've left the same way they came. And unless they blew those tunnels behind them—and I didn't hear no charges go off—we can follow them."

No surprise that a legionnaire would have already turned his attention to finding the next fight.

Callison continued. "Call your scout platoon back and have them take us to the last known position of those miners. We'll sniff out any tunnels, sure as sket, and then find out if they're dead ends or if they lead somewhere."

All eyes went to Peltier.

He sighed. "It's a plan. And I'm not particularly keen on letting others fight while we wait for rescue. Metzger, you're in charge of repairs. Callison, we'll get your forces in position to check out the tunnels. We're still in this. Let's get to work."

Most of the pilots handled the welding unit as if it were some exotic new weapon they had never seen before, so Metzger leveraged that, making his "class" more like a weapons orientation. He did the same with the torch cutter, and within two hours he had teams salvaging armor off of the downed enemy mechs and welding the plates, albeit crudely, onto their own mechs. Even Peltier was helping out, organizing a team with a tractor to drag back what was left of Ivers's blasted tank.

Replacing damaged weapons was the next priority. Metzger set Hullbuster—who was *extremely* comfortable with a cutting torch from his days in the marines—and Razorwire to that task, showing them where to remove assemblies and how to winch them down.

He chose Grunon to work with him on extracting other spare parts. This wasn't something he could delegate, so the best he could do was borrow the extra pair of hands. The subsequent repairs, such as replacing the actuator on Hullbuster's HK-PP, were ugly kludges—the stolen parts rarely fit properly—but they functioned, which was all that mattered. On some of the tougher repairs, Metzger opened comms with Chief Technician Ross topside, who walked him through the steps he needed to take.

"Anything to save me some work once we finish this Oba-forsaken op."

Armaments came next, with Metzger organizing teams to reallocate missiles from their small ammo depot. The pilots formed a fire brigade line to carefully move the missiles so that every mech was armed.

They slept in shifts, keeping watch and keeping the repairs going non-stop. When Metzger's time to rest came, he tossed and turned. The hiss of the plasma cutter, the banging of hammers on armor plates, and the chatter of the pilots made it difficult to sleep in anything except fits. Eventually he just got up and rejoined the work.

There were no complaints from the pilots, though, even when Vickerson hammered her thumb hard enough to turn it purple, or when Dobbs tried to weld overhead and burned himself with a splatter of molten metal. There was a job to do, and a battle to be fought. There was no time for complaining. Or energy, either. The work was exhausting. Metzger's arms ached from winching up the armor plates, and his shoulder throbbed from leaning hard into some of them while he tack-welded them in place. The grime from the coating on the armor stuck to his sweaty skin, forming a grayish oil.

Yet he also found the work rewarding, and he could tell he wasn't alone. Repairing the mechs gave the 510th purpose—and brought them closer together. If he hadn't gotten his ass busted and sent to the mech bays, they'd all be sitting here doing nothing. At least now they'd have a chance to get back in the fight.

Finally, he had the pilots line up the squadron for inspection. The exhausted pilots stood together and reviewed their handiwork. The replacement armor looked like a quilt of steel in most places, strange metals melted together with no hint of camouflage. Replacement parts jutted out from housings that didn't fit them. All in all, the mechs, and the one functional tank, looked hideous.

And beautiful.

Tramel spoke up first. "We're all mech monkeys now!" he shouted, slapping Metzger on the back.

They were congratulating themselves on their work when Sergeant Callison returned to the camp, his bucket cradled in his arm. His leej armor was covered with a light gray powdery dust, and streams of sweat ran down from his face and into the depths of his armor. As he and Captain Peltier huddled together, everyone else quieted, listening for any clue as to what the leejes may have found.

Then Peltier looked at his personnel... and cracked a smile.

Meltzger grinned.
We're back in the damn battle!

35

While the HARD unit repaired their rides, O'Keefe led the researchers in getting back to work. Some had been badly shaken by their time as hostages. They were historians and scientists; they hadn't seen battle before, and had never expected to. They'd never experienced the terror of having their lives in danger. But O'Keefe, by contrast, felt like she'd come through the ordeal stronger than before. Ever since her injury, she had felt… less than. She had questioned who she was. Whether, despite her constant training, she was still truly a soldier.

And now she had proven that she was. When the time had come for her to act, she had.

Weaver and Dranes both looked like hell. Weaver's face, especially his cheek, was deep purple and swollen, as was Dranes's lower lip. Weaver also had a small oblong disk—a cerebral pulser—attached to his forehead to treat a concussion. But it was Weaver who provided everyone with the spark of energy to keep going—or at least, it was his repair work that did so. He somehow managed to fix the broken DNA tester, and they had used it to test samples from five more of the graves. All were identified as members of the lost legion.

As Dranes said, "It's already a victory."

But O'Keefe's mind was already working the next problem. There were only enough graves here to account for a fraction of the 552nd. The question now was: *Where are the rest of them?*

For that, she again relied on Weaver. After fixing the tester, he had crawled into the bowels of the crashed dropship and had emerged with a number of old-school memory slats, storage plates for data. He had also recovered a legionnaire helmet, which he had been tinkering with ever since. O'Keefe thought the headgear was a waste of time, but Weaver assured her it wasn't, especially with legionnaires on-hand to help him. He alternated between the two projects, muttering to himself as he worked.

And he found something.

He summoned both O'Keefe and Dranes to the tech trailer. "The slats for the dropship's main systems were DOA," he began. "Not surprising, given how long this stuff has been down here. But the ones from their comms system gave up a few secrets."

His fingers flew over his control pad, and a holographic image flickered to life in front of them. Text, some of it garbled. A map. Bits and pieces of OPORDs. It scrolled upward as O'Keefe looked on.

"It was called Operation Dynamo," Weaver said. "From what I've been able to gather, the Savages got here to Vargas and found the K'llik. They enslaved them, or maybe allied with them—that part is a little fuzzy. Regardless, the K'llik were producing weapons for the Savages. The Legion was attempting a covert landing with the intent of destroying a weapons depot. Their ships got plastered— long-range anti-ship missiles, a lot of them. What survived from Task Force Equii crashed here. Dynamo was devised after they hit the ground."

Weaver scrolled to the Dynamo orders. "The details of Dynamo are mostly intact, thankfully. Basic context, a force of legionnaires along with some Repub marines who were also on the ship, identified a force of K'llik and Savages at a location in some pass. See this snippet here: 'These forces will then proceed to rally point Bravo and join with the rest of the assault force at target Charlie.' I was able to plug in the old-style map coordinates for Charlie and overlay it on the current map. The location is in what the K'llik now call Defilers Pass."

"Let me guess," O'Keefe said. "The Legion were the defilers."

"I don't know that for sure," Weaver replied, "but it makes sense. From the scraps I was able to salvage from the comms network, as soon as they got into that pass they were ambushed."

"How?" Dranes asked.

"The ship's net didn't have details. But that's where this bucket comes into play." He looked proud as he patted the old legionnaire helmet that was sitting on the bench in front of him, hardwired into a nearby processing unit. "This belonged to Sergeant Major Klaus Teuber, who died during the crash. And... well, I'll just show you what our Legion friends helped me uncover."

With a flick of the controls, the holographic image disappeared and was replaced by a map. It looked like a series of rivers. *No,* O'Keefe realized. *Tunnels.*

"A subterranean network," she said.

Weaver smiled. "Yup. Volcanic vents of some sort, and they're all over that pass."

O'Keefe reached out and adjusted the view, drinking in every twist and turn, dip, and egress point. "How did the bucket capture this?"

"When the legionnaires discovered these tunnels, they released mapping drones, with the resulting intel being transmitted back to their buckets. It seems that a Sergeant Joachim Andersen—his was the first body we positively identified, as it turns out—used Teuber's helmet as a dedicated hub to compile all that data, and then he set it up in a long-term hibernation for the sake of whoever might come next. It took a while, but... that 'whoever came next'... that's us."

"So this pass..." said Dranes. "That's where the lost legion met their fate."

Weaver nodded. "That's what it looks like to me."

O'Keefe continued to zoom in and out, examining the network from every angle. Then suddenly, the image vanished.

"That wasn't me!" she said.

A faint whiff of ozone rose from the old bucket and a tiny thread of white smoke curled upward.

"Sket!" Weaver sat down and worked furiously at the controls. Cursing again, he checked the bucket, grumbling.

"Problems, Mr. Weaver?" Dranes said.

"The old helmet couldn't handle the power. Even in hibernation mode, it was barely clinging to life."

"But you have a copy, don't you?" O'Keefe asked.

The look of desperation on Weaver's face gave her the answer even before he spoke. "Ah... you know how closed Legion tech is. This was an open broadcast that started almost as soon as I began the inspection. I came to get you guys as soon as I read the file. I was worried this would happen before I could show you, let alone back it up."

Dranes's face didn't show his disappointment, but it was there, hanging in the confined space like a static electric charge. "Well, then it's lost."

"No," O'Keefe said with a smile. "It isn't."

"What do you mean?"

Turning to face her CO, she tapped her temple. "Eidetic memory, remember? I got a pretty good look at the map. It's still in my head. Every last detail."

Dranes matched her smile. "I'll go find you a datapad."

PART THREE:

The Haunted Ground

36

Major Sarn stood in front of Rexnar Koff. "The operation on Vargas isn't unfolding quite as we expected."

"Details, please," Koff said, leaning back in his chair.

"The miners who took the hostages were overrun. We've lost the crater. And our forces on the surface aren't doing well either. The K'llik and what's left of the Vargas Liberation Army are falling back."

"What of our friend, the guildmaster?"

Sarn shifted slightly. "He is claiming no knowledge of the entire affair. He's telling the Republic forces that the Vargas Liberation Army is not sponsored by the government, and has been a domestic terror threat since long before the Legion landed."

"That's what we would want him to say. He made no mention of our visit, I trust?"

"None that I am aware of, sir."

Koff nodded. Plausible deniability was always a shield for nefarious political activities. Koff knew that the guildmaster's excuse wouldn't hold up to thorough investigation, but Rune could be dealt with before that happened. There were multiple means of making a man disappear—permanently.

"It seems we must now count on the K'llik to do their part," Koff said.

Sarn shifted on his feet again.

Koff didn't like the look of that. "Will the K'llik do what we need them to?" he pressed.

Sarn nodded, but not firmly. "The K'llik have no love of humanoids, and they're legitimately upset that the Republic brought a military force to their world. They have been fighting alongside guild forces thus far. But... they are complicated, and it's hard to get a straight answer from them. Being insectoid, attempting to read them is damned impossible. Plus their language is unconventional, and the translator bots struggle with it."

"I was always led to believe they were quite cunning."

"They are, sir. Extremely. From what I have gleaned from our meetings, they keep their cards close to their chests, so to speak. But more importantly, they're also cruel. They have no regrets, no conscience—at least none that I've seen evidence of. If the Legion shows up and tries to intimidate or strong-arm them, the K'llik will respond ruthlessly. It is their nature."

"Good. Because I need them to wipe out all of Cobra Company and the other Republic armed forces on Vargas. Post-battle investigations are best when there is no one there to interview."

"Their plan involves leading the 14th Legion and their HARD support into a place called Defilers Pass. They say they destroyed a legion force there once before, and they will do it again."

They had better, Koff thought. *Tamar, you will be avenged.*

37

O'Keefe was present when Dranes presented the information to the military commanders from the communications trailer. The holographic images of the commanders hovered in the space above the table, as if they stood in the room with those present. The information was broken down simply, with no detail. Their research, combined with the admission of the K'llik themselves, suggested that Defilers Pass had been the site of an ambush during the Savage Wars. The tunnel system would allow the K'llik to surround and overwhelm any forces there, just as they had done to the lost legion.

Colonel Hackett was the most expressive when he got the news. "This stinks like an open latrine in a tropical sun," he spat. "We've got these people on the run, and now you're telling me it's on purpose."

"They're leading you right to where the K'llik wiped out the rest of the 552nd," Dranes replied. "This species seems to have a long memory, and they're counting on what worked before against the Legion to work again."

"We'll need to slow our advance," Colonel Inglima said. "Stopping would indicate we know what they're up to. Right now, we have a vague idea of what their plan is. That's an advantage I don't want to squander. It's best if they think they still have the upper hand."

"Agreed," Hackett said. "I understand these maps are drawn from memory. That doesn't give me a great deal of confidence."

Dranes nodded. "Understood, sir, but Corporal O'Keefe has a holographic memory. Whatever she has down, you can trust that it's accurate."

Dranes turned his head to O'Keefe, who felt his eyes stabbing at her. She knew what he was thinking.

"Sirs," O'Keefe said, "I can re-draw that exact map right now if it would help you believe what Chief Dranes is telling you. I didn't see all of it, but I know what I *did* see well enough that I'm confident I could orient your forces based on their own mapping of any tunnels they enter. You can send them to me here, and I will send back my analysis. You might even be able to flip the table with this. Ambush those who are looking to ambush you."

She resisted the urge to bite her lip. Presumption and acting above her rank was what had gotten her busted down to corporal to begin with.

Colonel Hackett brushed his smooth-shaved chin in consideration. "That assumes we maintain clean comms once in the pass. I won't make that assumption."

"Captain Peltier," Colonel Inglima said.

The HARD captain stepped forward. "Sir."

"When your squadron moves through those tunnels the legionnaires discovered, I want Corporal O'Keefe with you."

Colonel Hackett nodded at this.

"Yes, sir," Peltier said. "She can guide us along the way."

His enthusiasm bothered her. *He has no idea what he's asking me to risk.* O'Keefe wasn't afraid of combat; she was worried that the jumbled memory fragments in her head would emerge and compromise not only herself, but everyone else in the squadron. If she had another big flareup, if those memories overpowered her, a lot of people would die. And the pressure of thinking about that possibility might be enough to trigger them all on its own.

Looking over at her, Dranes frowned. Once again, he seemed to know her thoughts as well as she did. "There may be a complication. The corporal here has suffered a traumatic brain injury. While her memory of current events is just fine, she has crippling flashbacks from time to time. She's on medication for it, but that is no guarantee that she won't have an episode if she goes."

The stares from some of the officers shifted from hope to pity, perhaps even annoyance from the legionnaires among them. O'Keefe's stomach knotted and ice water ran down her spine. A mix of shame, embarrassment, and frustration tore at her. She understood that Dranes had no choice but to share this information; it could affect the mission, and the officers needed to know about it in advance. But she hated it all the same.

Colonel Inglima was the first to speak up. He locked eyes with O'Keefe. "Corporal, if we can use those tunnels against the K'llik, it might well turn the tables in this conflict. But I need complete honesty here. Will your medical condition compromise your ability to do this?"

"Sir, I can assure you, as long as I'm on my medication, I can keep my mind under control." Saying those words seemed to release the pressure, if only slightly.

Inglima didn't break his stare. "And you understand you'll be dangerously exposed. You'll likely find yourself on the back of a mech while it's in active combat. There won't be a place to debark you."

"I understand that, sir."

"Then the decision is yours, Corporal. I could order you to do this, but I'm not nearly the sonofabitch that most noncoms think. You've apparently already been through hell."

For a moment, she closed her eyes, gathering her strength against the pressure that was being placed on her shoulders. "The 552nd went into that pass and never came out," she said, her voice getting louder and firmer. "We came here to find them and bring them home. That is why I'm here. People have already died because of the lead I chose to follow to this world. I intend to see this through—to the end."

"Excellent," Colonel Inglima replied. "Now then, let's craft a plan that puts this uprising down once and for all. Peltier, we'll see about sending down some parts and repair techs."

It was a moment the 510th had been waiting for, though Peltier betrayed no gloating satisfaction in his reply. "No need, sir. We handled that on our own."

Two hours later, O'Keefe gazed up at Metzger's HK-PP with a renewed sense of respect and awe. It was an ugly kind of majestic. Replacement armor plates were attached everywhere. Streaks of lubricant ran from actuators and from battle damage that had been covered up. The one she stood before had a spiderweb of cracks on the cockpit canopy, evidence of a shot that was only barely stopped.

"She's a bit bandjacked," a familiar voice said from behind her, "but she'll do fine."

O'Keefe turned to see Metzger. He had changed into a clean jumpsuit since the last time she had seen him. Gone was the stubble of days of not shaving. Clearly he'd gotten a shower.

"I had a feeling you'd be my ride out of here," she said.

"Initially you were going to ride with the captain, but I insisted I get the honor. When Captain Peltier heard I wouldn't have even been a mech jockey without you... he was fine with the idea."

"I just hope I'm not a liability," she replied.

"You'll do fine."

She frowned. "You don't know that, Carson. This stuff in my head, it goes off randomly."

"Sheryl, you won't let us down, even if you have a relapse."

"You don't know that for sure. No one can."

"Actually, I do. You've always been strong. This injury of yours, it's an obstacle, that's all. You'll either go around it or plow through it. And I'm not saying this because you're a hell of an infantryman, though you are. I'm saying it because you don't know how to fail. You've always been the best of us. Gordon, Tang, and I all talked about it."

Conjuring up the memories of their dead comrades made her eyes sting. She fought back the tears. "This is hard, Carson. Harder than anything else I've ever tried."

"And I'll be here for you—the same way you were there for me."

"Thank you. So... where exactly do I ride?"

"We have rungs on the backs of the legs to ferry infantry. Not exactly a luxury sled, but we do get you where you're going. Your drop-down will give you my camera feed from the cockpit. It'll be just like you're sitting beside me."

"Except for the part where I'm hanging on for dear life, exposed."

"I won't let anything happen to you."

It was reassuring to know that her oldest friend was going in with her. "All right then. For Gordon and Tang."

Metzger shook his head. "No. Not for them."

O'Keefe gave him a confused look.

Metzger explained. "You know what drove me to drink, O'Keefe? I got caught up in self-pity, thinking I had lost where I belonged in the universe—the 444th. Drinking numbed that for me. It didn't make the self-pity go away, but it dampened it." He sighed. "Then you had your relapse, and that... that was a wake-up call. I never told you, but when I was carrying you to the hospital, there were a few times I fell. Not because I was excited, but because I had been drinking. I've been in a lot of battles, but I was never as afraid as I was that night. I was worried not only that you might die, but that me and my stupid pity-driven drunkenness might be the *cause* of you dying."

"Carson—"

"No, let me finish. While I was waiting for you to wake up, I came to a few conclusions. Home isn't a place—it's a people. Whoever we surround ourselves with, that's our family. New people are always coming into that circle, and others are always leaving—and we often have zero control over that. So although I *thought* I had lost home, what I had really lost was my definition of what home *is*. It was thanks to you that I found it again. When I'm in that cockpit, piloting my HK-PP, that's my new home—that, and the guys in my squadron. And you, Sheryl."

Tears sprang to her eyes again, but they were of a different sort this time.

"So, here's the thing," Metzger continued. "We can't go backwards. We can't make this be about Gordon or Tang. I love them, but they're gone. If we want to honor them, we have to do it by moving forward, with our new families."

O'Keefe understood. "All right. If not for Gordon and Tang, how about we do it... for us?"

Metzger gave her a solemn nod of agreement.

38

The plan was simple. Topside, the bulk of the 14th Legion and the 72nd were going to continue to pursue the enemy into Defilers Pass. They would concentrate mostly on the higher ground, but otherwise they would allow the K'llik to believe their ambush was coming together. Yet in reality, it was the K'llik who would be stumbling into a trap. The 510th would hit the enemy in the tunnels, either destroying them outright or causing confusion and forcing them out of the tunnels prematurely, where the Legion and the rest of the 72nd would be waiting. After that, the 510th was going to come at the bugs from underground wherever they deemed most suitable to do to the enemy what it had intended to do to the Republic.

The tunnel O'Keefe directed them along was wide enough for mechs in single file, but it never felt that wide to Metzger. Several times he slowed his gait out of fear of grinding into the walls on either side. He was relieved when they reached the openness of another crater. This was where the miners had staged from, but it wasn't the 510th's ultimate destination. Another entrance would take them from this crater into the maze of passages inside O'Keefe's head, and from there, into Defilers Pass.

As they moved along in the open, Metzger did a quick comms check with his rider.

"You still hanging on back there, O'Keefe?" he asked on the private channel.

"What choice do I have?" Her breath was muffled by her face mask. "Angle five degrees to your right. We're about three kilometers from the access point."

"Hold on tight."

"Like I'd hold on loosely."

Metzger grinned. He stepped up the pace of his HK-PP, knowing that the rest of the squadron was right behind him.

The battle in the crater had required a restructuring. Metzger and Buck were effectively folded into Peltier's command platoon, with Metzger on point, given he had O'Keefe. Stamper's mech had taken too much damage to be repaired, so he was now riding in a tank in case one of the HK-PP pilots should be disabled but their mech could still function. Dobbs and the scout platoon had taken losses, but the captain determined they didn't require a restructure. Only First Platoon—Razorwire, Vickerson, Tramel, and Krock—were unchanged since their arrival on Vargas, as they hadn't yet lost a man or a mech.

Several minutes later, O'Keefe signaled. "It should be coming up, fifty meters ahead."

All Metzger saw was gray and black sand, swirling in a breeze. Slowing to a walk, he moved ahead and stopped. The mountain ridges along the flanks rose up from the sandy and rock-pitted area where he stood. "I don't see anything, O'Keefe."

"It should be right in front of you, just a little to the left."

With delicate control, he barely pressed the foot pedals to move the mech forward. On the third step, he felt the sand under him shift dramatically—more than enough to get his attention. "I think I have something here. The ground is soft."

"That's got to be it," she replied.

"So how do we get down there?" Hullbuster asked as the rest of the squadron moved in behind them.

The tunnel rumbled from the combination of mechs and tanks, and Metzger wondered how far the sound could be heard by any careful listeners.

He stared at the ground, but it was just sand there—no sign of a trap door or anything like that. "Stand by." He powered up his blasters and aimed down at the sand, taking a careful step backward so he could get a good angle.

"What are you—" O'Keefe started to ask as he unleashed a barrage from his blasters.

The bolts of searing energy hit the sand and exploded it outward and down. He recharged and fired again for good measure. That was all it took. The explosion of the superheated energy had opened a shallow ramp into an underground passage. O'Keefe had said this tunnel would be large enough for mechs, but as Metzger looked down into the hole, he wasn't so sure.

Moving forward slowly, he adjusted his stance with his left-hand joystick and shuffled down the ramp. The ceiling was low, and he had to duck his mech down, but at least he didn't scrape the sides.

The darkness devoured him, and he activated his external lights. After several dozen meters, the space opened up dramatically, with not only a high ceiling, but enough width for two or three mechs to walk side by side. The floor here was gray stone, and the walls were made of some kind of glossy rock that glistened in the glow of his headlamps.

He walked his HK-PP forward as the rest of the squadron followed.

"You could have warned me you were going to fire," O'Keefe said.

"I'm a mech pilot. You should always assume I'm going to be shooting something."

He could almost feel her rolling her eyes. "This tunnel runs north about two kilometers, then splits off," she said. "There's a few side tunnels to the left along the way, but you can ignore them. We want to bear to the right."

"Copy that," he said. "You're amazing, by the way."

It was tempting to run, but the ground was uneven, rising and dropping sometimes a meter at a time. There were also subtle turns, each of which could provide cover for an enemy, and he wasn't going to rush into an encounter and make matters worse.

Hullbuster formed up on his right side. "I wonder, if we start shooting down here, if all of this is going to collapse."

"That's not funny, Buck."

"Who said I was joking?"

Metzger looked around the cavern, and it was hard to disagree.

Best to focus on the mission. If this all collapses, there's nothing anyone can do about it.

They came to the split, and he followed the tunnel to the right. After a few more turns at O'Keefe's direction—Metzger had to admit he was thoroughly lost at this point—she said, "We're coming up on the center of the pass in a half a klick."

"In other words, we should be seeing some enemy targets soon," Metzger replied.

"I wouldn't be surprised."

Metzger passed the word to the rest of the 510th.

"This is also where the map starts to get complicated," O'Keefe said.

"*Starts* to?" Metzger said.

"Fine. *More* complicated. There's a three-way split up ahead. All of them head into the pass, but I wouldn't classify any of them as the main highway."

"Which means?"

"Which means you can pick any of them. The two on the right reconnect a ways up. The other one snakes off toward the west and goes along the rock formations there. All three routes should be passable."

In other words it required a guess, and sometimes it was best to let the officer in charge make that call. In this case, there was no right or wrong. "Captain, we have a choice here," Metzger transmitted, outlining what O'Keefe had told him as he arrived at the intersection and stopped his stride.

Peltier took a moment to consider before responding. "We're going to split up," he said. "Our purpose here is to clear these tunnels and deny the enemy an ability to use them in the battle above us. Command will take the middle tunnel. First Platoon down the far right tunnel. Scout Platoon, hold back here to serve as a QRF. We'll converge where the tunnels come together. We'll ping each other every so often, just to make sure we aren't wandering down the wrong path. If you get lost, O'Keefe will relay any changes you need to make. Take it slow and watch your corners down here. We don't know how safe these tunnels are, so stick to your blasters. If you find the enemy, kill the enemy."

"Stack 'em high and stack 'em deep," Vickerson said.

"Hey, boss," Metzger said. "Why don't you stick with Scout Platoon while me and Hullbuster move ahead. There's not room for three mechs to maneuver this stretch, so we may as well keep a good interval."

"Copy that. Good hunting."

Metzger and Hullbuster began to advance. There was a steep dip, and Metzger's mech slid slightly on the black rock. If he fell over backwards, O'Keefe was going to be nothing but an ugly smear on his rear. At the bottom he paused, angling his light upward as the ground rose again.

He saw it at the same moment his targeting sensors blared a warning of a target. At the crest of the next rise was a monster of a mech. It reminded him of the transport vehicle he had seen with the K'llik delegation, but this one was on steroids. It was twice the size of an HK-PP, with ten narrow metallic legs, each with two sets of articulating joints. The main body was shaped like a large lozenge, with a smaller bulbous bulge on the front that seemed to serve as a head. Jutting out of the forward part of the body were two weapons pods, both seamless tubes, already sweeping toward him and Hullbuster. There was no cockpit canopy visible; everything was just smooth silvery metal.

As the mech turned toward him, four K'llik, clinging to its bottom, dropped to the tunnel floor. Hullbuster called in the contact to Peltier.

Logic called for blasters in the tunnels—Slick had told them to stick to blasters. But upon seeing the size of the massive mech, Metzger made the decision to defy those orders. With icy precision, he linked his targeting reticles for both missiles and blasters together. The hum of the blaster capacitors filled his ears, punctuated only by the high-pitched whine of the missile lock. He unleashed carnage with a single tug on the joystick trigger.

His HK-PP rocked back as a single missile and both blasters roared. Taking out the mech's legs made little sense since it had so many of them, so he'd aimed at the body. Hullbuster fired his blasters as well, just a millisecond later, joining in the barrage.

The blasters hit first, scarring the side of the round torso black and glowing yellow. The missile struck high, near the forward bulbous "head" of the mech, with a blast that sent an abnormally large concussive blast back down the tunnel at Metzger. Bits of rock and fine dust from the ceiling rained down all around both him and the enemy.

The alien reeled from the impact, twisting hard as a wave of black sand hit it from above, and the spindly K'lliks scrambled clear, climbing halfway up the walls. Two started firing weapons that sent bright red bolts stabbing Metzger's way. They were hitting, but he didn't see any indication on his damage display that showed they were effective.

The enemy mech's weapons pods would be another story, he was sure; they hummed for an agonizingly long moment, then fired. Brilliant blasts of crimson energy lit the tunnel as they stabbed at him and Hullbuster. The shot that came at him was a glancing hit on his left hip, spraying hot metal everywhere as it went farther back and nicked Captain Peltier's mech as it arrived behind him. The damage indicator flashed amber. Instinctively Metzger angled his mech to the right.

"Carson!" O'Keefe yelled—he had just exposed her to fire, not to mention the bits of rock falling from above. This was too dangerous. He quickly swiveled his leg to give her that column of protection.

Hullbuster caught a shot square on his lower torso, just above the mech's waist pivot. Metzger glanced out his side window and saw the ugly glowing red hit that seemed to melt the armor where it splattered some kind of superheated plasma. He wanted to move, wanted the speed that was so crucial to the use of mechs, but there was no room, no space other than the eighty meters between him and the enemy.

Peltier's blasters sent bright yellow bolts past him, striking the K'llik mech's lower body; holes glowed wherever they were hit. Metzger didn't think it was possible, but the alien mech looked angry. It crouched as if to pounce.

He smothered the fear that tried to grab him, pushing it deep down, using his training and experience as his guide. Angling his targeting reticle lower, he heard the tone of missile lock and unleashed another salvo. He hit a leg joint that the mech was swinging around as it squatted. The bolt tore through the actuator and out the other side, spattering hot metal as it went. The leg was severed, and the lower portion clanged to the floor.

Then the missile hit its mark. This explosion was even louder than the first one, the blast wave filling the tunnel with dust and smoke and rocking Metzger's HK-PP back a quarter step as he fought to keep it upright. The wave of sand grated across his canopy like a sandblaster, and he could only hope he was sufficiently shielding O'Keefe from the impact. Then a burst of light appeared up ahead. The explosion had collapsed the roof of the tunnel right on to of the enemy mech, burying it under rocks and debris, revealing a tall shaft that apparently opened onto the surface.

Metzger felt like smiling, but he was suddenly confronted by a new threat. The K'llik warriors sprang at him and Hullbuster. One jumped up to his cockpit, grabbing onto the side of his mech and clinging to it. A gangly limb thrust a weapon right up against the armored canopy glass and fired. Bright crimson plasma hit, and the armored glass started to smoke inside the cockpit.

There was no way to shoot the K'llik there. Instead, Metzger twisted the waist of his HK-PP to the right, lowering his blaster vertical so that it wouldn't hit the tunnel wall. Leaning hard in the same direction, he crushed the alien with the bulk of his mech into the wall. The K'llik made a grinding sound as its thick limbs crunched, then it popped with a hiss that he assumed came from its mouth. As he straightened up, he saw an ugly oily brown smear on the canopy, the goo from whatever the K'llik called blood.

"Sket!" came the voice of O'Keefe on his leg. "There's another one back here!"

A millisecond of panic set in. She was defenseless except for a blaster rifle, which wouldn't be easy to aim while holding on to an HK-PP.

"Pileup—don't move," Back Door called from behind him in his HK-SW. The rest of the QRF raced into action.

Metzger had never been so happy to see repulsor tanks.

There was a flash of yellow behind him, and he felt a jerk of weight shifting on the rear of his mech. The scout walkers had very minimal firepower, and he hoped that Back Door had gotten a clean kill before O'Keefe could be injured.

"Splash one," Back Door called.

Off to Metzger's left, Hullbuster stomped the foot of his HK-PP down hard, catching the last of the K'lliks under his mech's weight. Its lower half pulverized, the alien made a hissing and popping sound, twitched twice, and died.

"You okay back there, O'Keefe?" Metzger called.

"Yeah," came the winded, tinny sound of her voice over the comm system.

"Pileup," the captain snapped. "I thought I specified no missiles in the tunnels."

"A calculated risk, sir."

He half expected to get chewed out, but Peltier simply said, "Let's get moving."

After all, it *had* worked.

39

O'Keefe's arms ached as the mech started forward again. There were straps to hold her in place, but to avoid being battered against the leg, you had to hold on tight. She glanced down at the K'llik that the scout walker behind her had shot, illuminated by the external lights of the trailing HK-PPs. It had spotted her as it was crawling up the leg of the mech, and for a moment she'd considered letting go and taking her chances on the ground. At least on the ground she would be able to move, to evade, to respond.

She might also get stepped on. Colonel Inglima was right: debarking was not a good option.

With her right arm wrapped through a rung at the elbow, she adjusted the view of the map on the pad on her left forearm. Her body armor hugged her tightly, digging into her skin at a few points. It didn't matter. If anything, putting on R-A armor felt good, strangely reassuring.

They passed beneath a hole that had been blasted to the surface, and for a few moments, sunlight stabbed down into the blackness of the tunnels. It was reassuring to think that she could potentially climb that chimney and get out if the mech went down. But after that last battle, the bigger threat in her mind was burial by cave-in. The others were at least encased in mechs—they had a chance they'd stay alive in their cockpits long enough for rescue. She'd suffocate within minutes, if she wasn't crushed instantly. Neither death sounded particularly appealing.

The mechs moved steadily down the contortions of the tunnel. There were two sharp turns right, and a gradual arc left. The other task force pinged her twice, and she looked at their dot on her map and had Metzger signal that they were on the right path. She shook her head. The decision by Metzger's CO to split the team up had seemed like a mistake to her, but she would do what she could to make it work.

"Hold it," she called after a few minutes, and Metzger's mech stopped. "There are two tributaries jutting off of this tunnel up ahead—one right and one left. They're about twenty meters up and right across from each other."

Metzger's voice came over the channel to his wingman. "Hullbuster, we move up together—you go left, I go right. Slick, I recommend you come up the middle."

Gripping the rungs, O'Keefe braced for the inevitable turn. It came just as she knew it would. The HK-PP pivoted hard, and as it did, the blasters hummed to life, then fired. She could feel a blast of heat as they discharged, roaring on both sides of her—and the mech tugged backward. Hullbuster's HK-PP had shifted behind her and moved past, leaving Captain Peltier to hold the rear. Scout Platoon had been forced to backtrack and provide support to First, who had run into some heavy fighting of their own.

O'Keefe glanced behind her to the opposite passage, the one Hullbuster had gone down. Even as she turned her head, she saw a furious burst of crimson light blasting from somewhere deeper in that direction, coming right at Metzger's friend. One shot missed his HK-PP, hitting the rock floor behind him. The superheated plasma made the rocks explode, filling the air with jagged bits of stone, some of which hit her, glancing off her chest plate. One bit hit her leg, and she felt a hot sensation rise from it.

Raising her leg, she saw a bit of stone sticking into her thigh, blood soaking into her fatigues. Seeing it triggered the inevitable pain. She bent the leg up and used her left hand to reach down and pull the shrapnel out. It throbbed up her thigh and into her lower back, but she ignored it.

It didn't hit an artery—I'll live.

Heat from mech blasters going off on both sides of her filled the cramped space. Metzger's mech sidestepped twice, still blazing away. His movements were fast and abrupt, and she lost her footing and her grip—only to find herself hanging by the harness, her legs flailing.

A crimson flare engulfed Metzger's mech, and this time she felt the scalding heat danger-close. Whatever was going on, the situation was untenable; she needed to get clear. But she couldn't undo her harness while dangling like this.

"Cut me loose!" she shouted over to the comm to Metzger.

He didn't respond, but he must have hit the quick release on the harness, because an instant later she fell free, landing hard and rolling to spread out the impact energy. A hot glob of plasma splatter landed right next to her, sizzling on the rock. She scrambled toward the side wall, feeling insignificant and overwhelmed. O'Keefe wasn't entirely convinced she was any safer here than she had been on the leg of the mech. She was the most defenseless thing in the battlespace, and hated the feeling.

Then it came—the shadow in her mind. Tykaree Valley was attempting to assert its power over her once more.

"Not now!" she muttered angrily as the flanking enemies unleashed their plasma weapons again. The air filled with a cherry glow, and the metal of the impacted mechs hissed. More superheated splatter rained down around her, much too close for comfort.

In her brain, she heard a voice. "Run, O'Keefe!" She couldn't place who it was.

"No!" she replied sternly, and the voice faded away to whatever dark corner of her brain it was stored in. A small victory.

A roar sounded from Metzger's mech as a pair of missiles launched, their hot backblasts pushing the air around her. The explosions came a moment later, so close in timing it sounded like a single blast. A hand-sized chunk of stone fell from the ceiling directly onto her head, but bounced harmlessly off her helmet.

More blaster bursts echoed from the other direction. The captain had joined his fire with Hullbuster's. Someone fired a missile, and the air was filled with a haze of smoke and fine particles. She no longer had any idea what was happening: all was light and sound.

And then everything went still, and she was swallowed by a comforting darkness.

Metzger's voice pierced the calm. "You okay, O'Keefe?"

"I'm fine," she replied, coughing in her face mask.

"It's too dangerous for a passenger in here. We should never have agreed to bring you along."

"Like you could have stopped me. Now get over here and pick me back up. We've still got a job to do."

40

The tunnel felt smaller with each passing meter. Metzger knew it was a mental illusion, a latent feeling of claustrophobia, but it still affected him.

"There's a small side shaft coming up on the right. It runs deep, but it's a dead end," O'Keefe said as they moved forward.

Metzger's trust in O'Keefe was total. He didn't question her memories of the map. "Tunnel is clear," he transmitted, and they moved forward again.

They took a gradual slope downward, but just ahead the passage took a sharp angle up, meaning his line of sight was blocked. But he could see yellowish light reflecting on the stone ahead, meaning there was a hole to the surface somewhere up there.

Metzger moved slowly, cautiously; so far they had taken no losses, but they were in sorry condition. The K'llik plasma weapons had melted away precious armor, penetrating deep in some areas. Amber and crimson damage warnings showed up all over his display.

"O'Keefe," he said. "How far to our connection with the rest of the squadron?"

"Not far at all," she answered. "This shaft angles up a hundred and twenty meters. At the top is where the two tunnels connect. The exit to the surface is just beyond."

He appreciated the precision of her response given these directions and distances were all based on her memory.

"Oba, I *feel* it," Hullbuster said suddenly. His tone was crisp, excited.

"What are you talking about?" Metzger asked.

"I feel it, Pileup, just like the vets say. I'm one with the mech. Like the armor's my skin. There are baddies up there, I know it. I can practically smell them. It's like the sensors are a part of me." He spoke as if it was almost a religious experience, one that made Metzger a little bewildered.

Other pilots had spoken of this experience, of their mechs becoming an extension of their bodies, some sort of mythical merging between pilot and war machine. Metzger wondered how much of that was just social contagion—they felt it because they wanted to *believe* they felt it.

"You might be right," he said. "About the bugs, I mean. Now let's step out together—weapons hot."

"Copy that," Buck said. "Lead the way."

"O'Keefe?"

"I'm here, Carson."

"We're going to pop out and engage. The ride is likely to be bumpy. You drop off when you see fit. Now, if you want."

"The way you guys drive, I'll just get trampled. I'll hang on for a while yet."

He notified the others of his intent, then switched back to a direct channel with Hullbuster. "On three," Metzger said, shifting in his seat to brace for battle. "One, two, *three!*"

He stepped his mech forward, and the moment his sensors got clear line of sight, his tactical display showed two K'llik mechs up ahead, a short distance shy of the side tunnel that First and Scout Platoons would be coming through. Another two quiet steps forward and he could see the mechs himself, their backs to him, silhouetted against the sunlight streaming through a wide ramp to the surface. They seemed to be queued up to exit.

Captain Peltier communicated the situation to Razorwire. There was a chance they could combine forces in time to give these mechs hell. But there also looked to be a chance of missing out on a kill altogether.

"Don't let them get to the surface undamaged," the captain finally ordered.

"Tally ho," Metzger muttered. "I've got the far one. Buck, you take the close one."

He zoomed in and brought his reticle onto the rear of his target. Tone squealed in his ear for missile lock, and he sent a pair of aero precision missiles roaring toward the enemy.

Hullbuster beat him to the shot, using both of his blasters. The brilliant yellow bursts of deadly charged particles hit the round body of the closest of the mechs, furrowing deep. Metzger unleashed his own barrage, his blaster shots precise, striking the farther mech. Only one of his missiles hit his target, but the other slammed into the leg of Hullbuster's target, so it wasn't wasted. The twin explosions rocked the tunnel hard, flames from the blasts roaring up to the ceiling and bringing down bits of rock and sediment.

The K'llik wheeled about in place to face this unexpected threat. Metzger backstepped a bit, then turned slightly to move closer to the tunnel wall. The space felt incredibly cramped, even more than before. His capacitors hummed as they charged his blasters, and he decided to unleash two more missiles as he tried to keep his weapons lock.

The enemies fired first. Crimson plasma blasts stabbed downward, rippling the air, one hitting Hullbuster in the right leg and another in the lower torso. Metal melted instantly, and Hullbuster went sideways, right into the wall, crunching his blaster in the process. Additional shots struck the rock beside him, causing an explosion of shards.

Metzger didn't allow himself to be distracted. He kept his eye on his targeting reticle, concentrating so intensely that it felt as if the cockpit canopy and displays were closing in on him. He didn't need to move his eyes to see the displays: everything was in his field of view.

Only then did he truly understand.

It wasn't social contagion. It was *real*.

Metzger was experiencing what Buck had been talking about, what the older pilots talked about. It was as if his senses had changed, somehow... evolved. He was no longer *fighting* the mech, as he now realized he had been doing all along; the controls were instead an extension of his body and mind. The feeling was invigorating, exciting, and terrifying all at once. He wasn't a pilot anymore; *he was the mech*.

He knew that wasn't possible in the literal sense, but... it was true all the same. His feeling of control had never been so complete as it was in that moment.

The tone of missile lock didn't shake the experience. He fired through the smoke and chaos, and felt as though his eyes were riding the missiles downrange. Both found their marks, one slamming into the bulbous "head" of the K'llik mech, the other striking the body. Orange and yellow flames wrapped around the target, rocking it hard, knocking it back so viciously that the rear legs collapsed and the vehicle seemed to take a seated position.

Its weapons pods were angling down at him, but before they could shoot, he unleashed his blasters. His shots hit the weapons pod on the target's left side, and it exploded with even more force and energy than his missiles had caused. Uncontrolled plasma, yellow and red, splattered on the mech, the floor, the walls. The target careened sideways, then collapsed, sliding downslope and hitting the mech in front of it, crunching into its spindly legs.

Hullbuster seized the distraction. He fired three missiles, all of which plowed into the smooth round hull of the spider mech, right above the top joints of the heavier legs. A massive piece of ceiling dropped onto the mech at the same instant that the legs gave way, dropping the K'llik machine to its knees. Buck's remaining blaster punctured the top of the mech's torso. It rumbled, trembling and quaking, then went still.

What followed was silence and smoke between the squadron and daylight.

"Those thing must've been staged to hit our guys," Buck said.

"Razor reports that he's engaging more," Peltier said. "He's pushing them back toward the intersection ahead. If we link up, together we can force those bugs to the surface, out into the open before they're ready. Let's keep the pressure on."

Metzger charged his HK-PP forward, rushing up the sloping ramp-like floor. He almost lost his footing at one point. When they reached the downed K'llik mechs, he didn't try to skirt them, but instead ran right over them, savoring each delightful, crunching footfall. Perhaps it was immoral to enjoy the sensation, but it reminded him of being a young boy and squashing insects for fun. Of course, as a child, the bugs weren't trying to kill him. He was more justified now than back then.

Just ahead, a blaster bolt flew into view, perpendicular to his running path. He heard the dull thrums of a K'llik plasma weapon discharging, and then an enemy mech emerged from the converging tunnel, moving backward.

It wasn't alone.

There was no shortage of enemy mechs being pushed back by First Platoon. It was instantly clear that Command Platoon had gotten the easy end of the deal—*here* was the bulk of the K'llik ambush. Just before the ramp to the surface, the two tunnels converged into a cavernous space, and yet that space was suddenly filled wall to wall with armor and weaponry, lights and sound.

Had the topside force been flanked by this... it wouldn't have been pretty.

Metzger readied his blaster cannons and unleashed them both at nearly point-blank range. The brilliant charged particle blasts sliced into the armored hide of the nearest enemy mech as a missile blast washed over it from the other platoon.

The alien mech driver panicked from the sudden attack and turned about wildly, looking for an avenue of escape. Hullbuster's blaster destroyed one of its legs in a brilliant blast of fire. A friendly repulsor tank and HK-PP emerged from somewhere in the confusion, and a loud *whomp* came from the tank's rail cannon as it punched a hole in the enemy's torso. Bits and pieces of mech armor rained on the sandy slope that ran up to daylight as the K'llik collapsed, oily black smoke rolling out from a gaping hole in its side.

"Carson," O'Keefe coughed. "It's getting a little hard to breathe back here."

She had a re-breather mask, but under the circumstances, it was no doubt struggling to keep up. He maneuvered her away from the smoke.

"Hang on, O'Keefe, we've almost got 'em."

A brief battle raged in the staging area where the tunnels converged. The K'llik mechanized forces that had been waiting to ambush the 72nd and its Legion element, were now instead being hit, and hit hard, by powerful, precision shooting from what remained of the 510th. The enemy was exposed, attacked from two sides, and despite their numbers, they were in trouble. Metzger didn't know how the bugs' command structure worked, but they didn't dither. A decision was clearly made, as the entire force turned as one and hurried up the ramp into the open, emerging on the battlefield well ahead of the forces it had intended to ambush.

"Slick, are we following?" Tramel asked from his mech.

"Not all the way," Peltier said. "Watch where they went and be ready to light 'em up if they try and come back down."

The sounds of battle were underway above them, long-range missile fire impacting among the K'llik mechs that had just been forced to surface.

"Pileup, Hullbuster," Peltier said. "Watch the tunnels. I don't want the locals sneaking up on us."

Metzger moved with his wingman at once. He asked O'Keefe if she remembered anything he could be looking for, but the vast tunnel system was relatively simple in this region. They only needed to watch their own converging back trails, plus one other passage that led away to the north.

"Razorwire," Peltier said, switching his focus to the other element, "What's your status?"

It was Ice Tea who replied. Her HK-PP was blackened and had several armor plates that were either missing, peeled back, or melted away. "Razor's okay, sir, but his mech is inoperable. Personal comm is out, too, so anything you wanna say is gonna have to be passed word of mouth. He's hitching a ride with Dobbs to make that easier—Razor's gotta be crazy to be the plus one on a Scout Walker."

Metzger chuckled at that. Razorwire had always been crazy.

The captain talked with Dobbs to see how well the scout platoon had withstood the encounter. Sergeant Grunon's MBT showed deep furrows in its replacement armor, but it was all right. The platoon had been blessed with good luck after the earlier losses of Stupp and Ivers.

While Peltier confirmed status, Metzger consulted with O'Keefe on their current location relative to topside. Based on her mental map of the tunnels, matched against the holomaps the 72nd was transmitting of the developing battle topside, she determined that the main force of the K'llik was north-northeast of where the 510th was now. It looked as though the enemy had planned to draw the 72nd into what would essentially have been an L-shaped kill box.

That was no longer going to happen. The 510th had driven the enemy ambush into the open before it could strike. The question now was... what else could the 510th achieve from the current position behind enemy lines?

"Let me ask you this, O'Keefe," Metzger said. "Can we go east from here?"

She nodded toward the unexplored tunnel to the north. "We can go anywhere you want—this place is a warren. Unfortunately, my mental map only extends a few more klicks to the east. The leejes' mapping drones went further, but that's as far as I happened to pan the original map before the bucket shorted out."

"That should be enough. You up for a bit more spelunking?"

"Lead the way."

"Ha. That's your job."

Metzger gave Captain Peltier his plan.

The captain considered for only a moment; Metzger got the impression the man had already been thinking along the same lines. "If we can surface in the right spot behind the enemy, this fight can be done that much quicker. Let's see what we can find. If we run into trouble, we can move back to this location and join the fight as we find it."

"Understood, sir."

Metzger allowed himself a grim smile. The end of this damned mess might finally be in sight.

The tunnel system was empty of mechs, but it was clear that more had been here earlier. Disturbances in the sand told the story, as did sensors picking up synthetics with parts-per-million in the air much too high unless a tank had rumbled through in the last hour or so.

What they did encounter were individual K'llik sentries.

Metzger and Buck, in the lead, killed those quickly. The sentries were no match for a pair of lumbering HK-PPs. The K'llik had to have known that, which meant these sentries were sacrificial pawns, likely serving as an advance warning network to notify those on the surface of where the Republic forces were moving within the tunnel system.

That meant two things as far as Metzger was concerned. First, their presence had spooked the rebels enough that they had abandoned the tunnels and consolidated their forces topside. Second, those forces were watching for the 510th's eventual resurfacing. Their surprise emergence topside might not be as surprising as they wanted it to be—assuming at least some of these K'llik sentries got word out before they were turned into smoking carcasses by the HK-PP's blaster cannons. Still, the 510th represented one more threat the rebels would have to deal with. Setting armor or infantry aside to watch tunnel entrances while the 72nd and a host of angry legionnaires pounded them would amount to fewer blasters in the fight.

As they approached another ramp to the surface, O'Keefe consulted with Metzger and Peltier, and the captain called the squadron to a halt.

"This is our stop," Peltier said. "You only need a working set of ears to know the battle is right above us. The question is, what part of the battle. Holomaps from Command show us coming up right in the midst of the rebels, but keep in mind that this is an armor battle and things change quickly. Right before we surface, I'll transmit our intent to Command, and they'll break off fire nearby—last thing we want to do is get pasted by our own. Metzger, you continue to take point. When we come out, we form a tight perimeter, and we break to the west. The element of surprise is going to fade fast, so make your shots count. Once everyone is on the surface, we move full out. Speed is our armor."

"Speed is our armor," replied the battered members of the 510th in a ragged but unison voice.

Metzger charged his blasters and shifted in his seat, bracing for the winds of war. "Hold on tight," he said to O'Keefe. "If it gets too hot back there, drop off at your discretion. Unless you want us to leave you here."

He'd been trying to convince his friend to stay behind in the tunnels for a while now. She wasn't having it.

"Not on your life, Carson. I refuse to die before I see the sunlight one last time."

There was no sense arguing. No time, either. "Thanks for getting us this far."

"You just worry about driving this walking tank," she said. "I've got your six."

The HK-PP lunged forward as if Metzger's mind willed it rather than his feet throttling the charge. He broke the surface and saw the carnage of the battlefield. Just twenty meters away was the flaming hulk of an HK-PP marked with the logo of Inferno Squadron. Blasted chunks of armor and mech parts littered the ground all around. Smoke rolled from other downed mechs, and a trio of explosions thundered across the black sands.

At first it was difficult to tell if they had emerged behind their own lines or the enemies'. Evidence of both sides lay ruined before them. But Metzger quickly realized they had come up almost in the middle of things, pretty much the worst place they could have picked, except for the fact that they *were* behind the rebel skirmishers' forward-most armor.

As he moved, he saw a larger enemy mech than any of those they had seen thus far. It was shaped like a lobsterrik, with short legs, but instead of large forward claws, it sported rail guns. Its body had articulated armored plates that shifted as it moved away from him in pursuit of some target.

Metzger's targeting reticles moved over the enemy's rear as if they had a mind of their own. He heard the tone and his fingers squeezed, sending a pair of aero-precision missiles filling the air between him and the target. Then his blaster cannons lit up, firing just a millisecond before the missiles found their mark. The ordnance slammed into the extended tail of the enemy mech, ripping apart armored plates and sending them into the air, riding the orange plumes of the explosions. One of the blaster shots caught the back of one of the rail-gun weapons, melting and charring the weapon housing, splattering bits in every direction.

Grunon's MBT floated past him, hovering a meter and a half over the sand, firing at the same target, while the K'llik turned to face the sudden threat to its rear. The tank's rail-gun round was a blur in the air, making a circular ripple over the black sand as it went supersonic. It hit near the lobsterrik mech's tail, penetrated, then came out the front —spewing bits of armor and destroyed internal mechanisms as it tore through. It ended in the sand, throwing up a huge plume as it finally ceased its flight.

Flames burst out of the back of the alien mech, brilliant torches—no doubt from a compromised power plant. The mech spasmed, then its short legs gave way and it dropped to the sand as a funeral pyre roared from its back.

As Metzger angled off to the west, a crimson burst of plasma slammed into his left side, searing deep into the blaster. The energy systems melted away, and an erratic bright azure electrical arc danced along the side of his mech and up to the canopy. Training overrode fear, and he killed the power feed to the weapon. His damage display was a bright red, confirming what he already knew. The weapon was gone.

His breath caught as he checked on O'Keefe. He exhaled as he saw that she had dropped off on her own this time. Hopefully she'd found somewhere safe to cover.

The shooter was another of the spider mechs, some two hundred meters away. Metzger rushed to the west until he saw several entrenched squads of legionnaires from Cobra Company that didn't need any trampling. His targeting system swirled around the enemy mech as he raced in a wide arc, twisting at his waist to keep it aligned with his foe. Another blast from its plasma weapon narrowly missed him as he struggled to get a weapons lock on the enemy. Sweat stung at the corners of his eyes as his body strained to keep the HK-PP aligned.

The lock tone came like sweet music to his ears, and he unleashed a trio of missiles from his racks. The mech tugged from the launch, and the loss of weight came to him in the form of less struggle against the planet's heavy gravity. The missiles twisted and turned, snaking through the air, seeking their target. He saw two of them find their mark, the explosions sending a ripple outward that whipped at the ebony sands. Black rolling smoke obscured the fate of the third.

The enemy pierced through the smoke, heading for him. Its plasma blasters, meant for melting through rock, both fired, their crimson bolts racing straight at him. Metzger twisted at the waist at the last moment, more out of self-preservation than anything else. One blast hit his right missile rack, the other the blaster on his right side.

The rack had two missiles in it. The warheads didn't detonate, but the solid propellant did. The sizzling of the metal above him was joined by the rushing sound of the propellant cooking off. The pair of unguided missiles tore through the mangled rack, wildly shooting skyward, spinning madly over the carnage of the battlefield.

Metzger's damage display screamed at him in color— all crimson. His left missile rack was empty, his right worthless scrap that drizzled melted metal onto the shoulder of his HK-PP. His last remaining blaster was showing as damaged and offline. He didn't trust the display at first and tried to shut power to the weapon, only to hear a crackling noise where the capacitors usually hummed. The blaster was altogether gone.

A grim realization came to Metzger... he was weaponless.

His brain countered quickly. *No, your mech is a weapon.* Memories of his final test on Tibul came back to him. *I earned the call sign Pileup. Now to live up to it.*

"Hullbuster, come up on my right and see if you can get that bastard's attention."

"On it," Buck replied. His blaster shots tore into the enemy mech, sending charged energy dancing across its surface.

Metzger's angle sharpened as he zeroed in on the K'llik mech. He poured it on, pushing both legs and feet as far forward as they could go. The HK-PP ran all out at its maximum speed, even a little faster than that, given the armor and parts it had shed as weight.

"Um, Pileup, what are you doing?" Buck asked as he fired another blaster salvo.

"My job," he muttered as he picked up speed. It felt for a moment as if he were running, his bond to his mech was so complete.

The K'llik pilot clearly didn't comprehend what was about to happen. It stopped, perhaps in amazement, perhaps in fear. Both reactions played to Metzger's advantage.

His mech slammed into the alien mech full-on.

The sound of grinding and protesting metal washed over him, a sickening crunching and twisting noise that consumed him. It felt as if his own body was being battered in the charge. The canopy before him cracked and spiderwebbed from the impact, making it impossible to see. His body was thrown forward; the safety harness dug into his shoulders and crotch like knives. He might have broken his neck if not for the head restraint. Then he was tossed to the right—metal shrieked and tore—and to the left, and something hit his head, hard. Even with his helmet, his ears rang and his vision tunneled. The power went off. The sweet smell of ozone tugged at his nostrils as what was left of his HK-PP fell forward, leaving him hanging in his harness. He tried to breathe, but smoke choked him.

Looking down, he saw a jagged piece of metal sticking out of the thigh of his bionic leg. He felt only a twinge of sensation. *If that had been an organic leg, I'd be bleeding out.* With one hand, he twisted out the piece of canopy frame sticking into him.

Coughing, he felt hot, hotter than when he had been in the thick of battle. Struggling to breathe, he felt nausea grip him. Slapping on his mask, he got air, stopping the tunneling of his vision, rallying his mind. He grabbed his emergency kit and blaster, and focused on getting out of his mech.

He hit the emergency release, popping open the side canopy. As he climbed out, his hand recoiled from the heat of his HK-PP's armor. His bionic leg was moving, but not fully—it was more like a dead weight attached to his hip. All that time getting used to feeling the limb was his own, and now it was a foreign object once more.

He slid down the side of the destroyed mech and saw that he had taken out the K'llik as planned. Its spindly legs lay limp, and sparks flew from a rent where his own mech had penetrated its hull.

The thunder of heavy footsteps came near him, and he turned to see one of the Vargas Liberation Army's cobbled-together mechs move past him some fifteen meters away. The initials *VLA* were crudely painted on it in red. It paused to fire at Hullbuster, an easy target, but missed with its lone remaining military-grade blaster.

The smart move was to put some distance between himself and the mech. But Metzger saw the legs' big hydraulic hoses arcing behind the industrial actuators. On

R-A mechs, these hoses were armored, protected by flexible plates. Not so on the converted mining machine.

Raising his blaster, a simple, rapid-firing PDW, he took careful aim at the hoses and fired.

It took three shots to destroy the hoses. A sickly green fluid bled down the leg from two places. The VLA mech sagged on the side as the pressure fell.

The pilot tried to move, but the leg was now worthless metal, even more so than Metzger's own leg. It dragged a quarter-step, then lost its balance and fell, crunching and grinding into the rocks and sand.

Metzger didn't hesitate—he limped forward, using his bionic limb as the peg leg it now was, moved alongside the fallen enemy, and approached the cockpit. It took a moment to find the external hatch release, and he hit it. The side hatch hissed as it opened, and Metzger aimed his blaster at the pilot, who was still in his seat.

It was an older man, with a white scraggly beard and a bald head. His pot belly told Metzger this was not a warrior, but a miner.

The man held his hands up. "Don't—don't shoot."

"Get on your comms," Metzger barked so loudly that even with his breather mask on, his words were crystal clear. "Tell your people to stand down, now!"

"You think they'll listen to me? I ain't authorized—"

Metzger pointed the blaster. "This is your damned authorization."

The man stabbed his stubby fingers at the communications controls and pulled the wired microphone to his mouth, squeezing the transmit button. "This is Red Rover. Stand down! Everyone, stand down!"

Metzger relaxed slightly. He had no expectation that this would work, but he thought it might at a minimum add some confusion to the battle that his comrades could exploit. "All right, now get out of there."

The portly pilot undid his harness. "I guarantee they won't listen to me. And I can tell you for certain that the K'llik don't give a space rat's ass what any human's got to say."

An explosion roared nearby, raining down sand.

"Don't worry about them," Metzger said. "Anyone stupid enough to keep shooting is going to end up dead before this is over."

41

O'Keefe released her harness and let go of Metzger's HK-PP. Her arms were so weary that she doubted she could hold on any longer even if the fighting hadn't been so intense. That last hit had nearly cooked her. She hit the sand and rolled, her helmet digging into the back of her neck on impact. For a moment, she didn't move. Even if she had told her body to move, it wouldn't have obeyed. Every muscle in her body expressed its hate for her in the form of pain.

Then she got up and began running toward a group of dug-in legionnaires. She stumbled, fell once, and then again. The battle raged above her and for a long moment she just lay still, daring not to move lest a stray bolt claim her.

Strange hands grabbed at her, pulling her at the shoulders where her armor straps were. Her chest armor dug into her abdomen, and she craned her head to see who it was. A man in leej armor.

She was brought into an improvised position in a crater-like hole. She managed to sit up and saw two legionnaires looking at her.

"Good way to get yourself killed, Basic," one said. "What are you even doing here?"

"I'm Corporal O'Keefe, R-A historian. I came up with the 510th."

An explosion went off to their left, showering them with a mist of fine sand. It was close enough that even the two leejes ducked slightly.

"Stay down and out of the way," the other said.

"No, I can help."

The nearest one leaned in toward her. "Help by shutting up. I'm already down three of my people."

O'Keefe struggled to think of a way she could contribute to the fight. She wanted to prove something to these men for reasons she couldn't articulate.

"I have comms with the HARD mechs," she said. "I can see about getting mortar fire down." She knew the RTCM mechs were mobile heavy-caliber mortar platforms. They could deploy, aim, and fire a five-pack of mortar rounds in a matter of seconds, as long as someone gave them coordinates to target.

The legionnaire stared at her, his helmet expressionless. "We've been trying to get you Basics to do that all day. If you can convince them, do it." He dropped against the inside of their hastily dug position and brought his N-4 into play.

O'Keefe considered how much her responsibilities had changed in a short span of time—researcher, hostage, security detail, guide, and now fire support. With hallucinations all along the way. She wondered if she was in a dream, a nightmare, or already dead. Her forehead throbbed, harder and sharper than any pain she had felt from one of her memory surges.

No...not now!

It *always* seemed to come when she least wanted it to. It wasn't fair.

She slumped, still gripping the comm as a hot white light enveloped her.

O'Keefe was no longer on Vargas facing the K'llik. A stiff wind stung at her face as Frixon materialized around her. It was the day that her unit was wiped out.

A blast came from a Frixon tank, hitting the boulder she was covering behind. Shards of granite ricocheted off her plate as she hugged dirt. Looking over, she saw Sergeant Fazzoli doing the same.

I was running... that's how I got here.

"Damn it, O'Keefe, I need you to crawl up on that position to the left. Get on that little rise—you should be able to bring the rain down on their position. Stack those bastards high and deep!"

"Damn right I'll stack 'em," O'Keefe replied.

"Less talk, more ass-hauling, O'Keefe. We can't hold this position forever," the sergeant barked.

Murdaugh spoke up from his cover on the left. "Do you see the Frix a-comin'?"

O'Keefe poked up for a moment and saw an advancing Frix grav tank, smoke billowing from several holes seared into the frontal armor. It was lumbering but seemed to sense her, and turned toward the boulder.

Lieutenant Ringer moved awkwardly, with a terrible limp. A blast of Frix fire almost caught him as he dove in behind her rock. His leg was wet with blood, to the point where the dust blowing in the wind was sticking to it on the outside of his thigh armor plate where he had been hit. "We're going to need to call in fire support." He handed her his battleboard, and just for an instant she thought back to Vargas and the leej that expected the same from her.

"You're going to have to get up topside on this hill and call in the fire. Keep low—the Frix are tearing us up." He elbowed his way forward so that his entire body was behind the rock.

"The incoming fire is hot," she said. "I can't get up there —they'll kill us before we make cover."

"My leg is hit. You can do it. Get into that gully over on the left. You can enfilade them from there without being exposed. Use your smokers!"

"I'm on it," she said, pulling a smoke grenade.

"We have to take out those tanks or the team will get slaughtered," he said through clenched teeth, clearly fighting his agony.

"I've got this. You can count on me."

Before she threw the grenade, she glanced over at Geroux, then back to Fazzoli.

"Damn it, O'Keefe, I need to you to crawl up on that position to the left. Get on that little rise—you should be able to bring the rain down on their position. Stack those bastards high and deep!" Fazzoli was angry as he called out to her.

Had he repeated himself in reality, or was this just a jumbling of the memory?

"Can't," she replied as another blaster from the Frix shattered the boulder near her sergeant, cracking it in half and sending big chunks flying in the air. "LT gave me orders to get topside." She poked up, firing her blaster at the closing tank. The shots hit, but only scored the turret armor. Ducking back down, she slid the FO pad into her belt and prepped the grenade.

"I'll go with you," Geroux said.

She gave him a nod.

"We haul ass on three. One, two, *three!*" She threw the grenade. It went off, but the nasty winds of Frix tore at its output, not giving them nearly the cover they needed.

She sprinted as fast as she could. The Frix tank fired, hitting somewhere behind her—she didn't look. Moving up the ridge, she dove behind another boulder. There was another trooper there, and she almost landed on him as she fell flat, with Geroux coming in behind her. Looking down, she saw that it was Vex—but she knew this only because his name was stenciled on the armor of his chest plate. His head was gone, burned off.

He never had a chance.

"O'Keefe," Fazzoli called out. "Where's that damned fire?"

"I'm on it!" she called back. Time for another sprint. "Follow me, Geroux."

He nodded in agreement as she rose and darted to the left, aiming for the gully that Ringer had pointed out. Blasts went off all around her, throwing sod everywhere. Bits of rock peppered her armor, but she ignored them, moving faster than she ever had in her life. When she reached the gully, she dove flat on her stomach. Her breasts ached from the impact, but she didn't care.

Her head whipped around to look for Geroux. She saw him—crumpled on the ground only a few meters from the boulder they had been hiding behind. His body was bent awkwardly, and he wasn't moving.

Sket!

Turning her head in the other direction, she saw Slither lying behind a low rock.

"You can do it, O'Keefe. I know you can. All you have to do is hit the damn target," he called out.

A huge blaster bolt from the tank hit the rock Slither lay behind. For a moment, O'Keefe could see nothing in the whipping winds. As they cleared, she saw him, with a big piece of the rock lying on his back, his blaster tossed out in front of him. Then she saw him move, rolling the stone off of him, coughing but alive.

Damn it, we're getting slaughtered here.

She summoned her strength for another sprint up the hill. As she did, she saw Fazzoli again, this time in a new position, firing at another tank that was angling toward him, then at her. "Run, O'Keefe! Run, damn it!"

O'Keefe did what she was ordered to do. Everything was a blur as she juked right and left to dodge shots coming at her. One tore the air so close she could feel the heat from it, but it didn't stop her. Her legs were moving so fast, she was worried she might fall. After another minute, she reached the top of the ridge. She angled around a thick tree, ducking behind a rock outcropping.

Pulling her battleboard, she saw the pulses of crimson marking the tanks. *Sket! They're right on our positions!* There were four of them, creeping up the hill. *If they overrun us, the entire division is flanked.* She knew the implications in terms of deaths and destruction. She was bringing the fire in danger close. If there were members of her platoon out there, she would potentially be bringing the artillery fire down on them as well as the Frix.

There was no other way.

She punched in the fire order coordinates, not even calling for a spotting round. The artillery signaled back to the pad. "This is FO," she barked over the symphony of war noise all around her. "Stand by for a fire mission."

"This is Ramrod fire control," came a voice. "Awaiting coordinates."

"Center on my position, fifty meters all directions, danger close."

"Danger close. Please confirm."

It was the hardest thing she had ever done, and a part of her both feared and hoped it would kill her, especially if any of the incoming fire hit her platoon.

Some of us might survive. It's possible.

She had run out of alternatives. "Fire for effect."

The first explosion came down right on the lead Frix tank. It went up in a massive ball of orange flames that coiled skyward with ugly black wind-torn smoke. The next round came down where Sergeant Fazzoli had been. O'Keefe let out a whimper at that realization, one lost to the cacophony of battle. Another explosion went off right in front of her. She knew for an instant that she was airborne, flying back. There was a sensation of hitting the ground, but no pain. Her vision tunneled. The white light of her lost memories erupted like a volcano in front of her, washing over her again, searing her soul, cauterizing her agony.

O'Keefe was back on Vargas, back in the shallow hole. The legionnaires fought on without her; they cared little what she did or didn't do. They probably thought she was cracked. Her headache was lessening with each pounding beat of her heart, and as she caught her breath, she realized something: the memories were there now, in her head—in order and crystal clear. They all made sense even. The chaos had taken shape, or at least that was how she thought about it in that moment.

I did it. I'm responsible for what happened in Tykaree Valley. I'm responsible for my own injury.

In that moment, she was comfortable with her newly recovered decision.

She elbowed her way up to the edge of the sandy berm and was shocked when a white bone, bleached from long exposure, poked out at her from under the sand. She didn't need to analyze it—she knew it was from one of the Howling Banshees. The lost legion. Finding it was a stark reminder that she was on a battlefield that had been fought on before; an entire legion had died here. Or most of one.

She slid past the bone and surveyed the target zone beyond. She saw a vast battlefield of carnage in every direction. If the K'llik believed their ambush would devastate Cobra Company and the 72nd, they were learning the folly of that plan. Damaged spider mechs littered the sand beside damaged and destroyed Republic mechs. K'llik foot soldiers crawled out of several holes used in their ambush, splattering crimson plasma fire up at the Legion forces. Shooting at the K'llik proved difficult, as their incredibly narrow profiles and speed made them hard to hit.

The leej next to her was watching her get up and move. "I'll give you the coordinates from my bucket, you call it in."

For the first time in a long time, O'Keefe felt as if she were in control of something.

I'm a warfighter, and now I'm going to prove it.

She pulled up the comm system. "This is FO, embedded with Legion element," she said. "Stand by for a fire mission."

"This is Blunderbuss," came a voice. "Awaiting coordinates."

She relayed the details. "Grid C—102 and 103."

"Spotting round?"

She didn't hesitate. No time for niceties. "Fire for effect."

"Five rounds coming your way."

From a distance came the high-pitched whine of incoming rounds. The RTCMs squatted to fire, creating a launching platform off of their backs and auto-loading munitions as needed. The cluster of large-caliber mortar rounds zoomed in with a tight pattern, designed to optimize the damage they caused.

She had brought the barrage down on the path of the K'llik, rather than where they had been. The bugs had spread out their formation, if you could call it that. As a result, some survived the barrage—but a squad's worth did not. The explosions threw deadly anti-personnel flechettes in a deadly swarm that devoured everything around. Several of the long limbs, blasted from their owners, rained down from the core of the explosions.

"Dead on, Blunderbuss." She glanced to her left, where a spider mech was crawling up on a squad of leejes that were pouring fire into it. "What's that one?" she asked the legionnaire next to her.

He gave her the solution.

"New mission. Grid E—204. Hard target."

"Grid E—204," the RTCM pilot repeated. "Heavy stuff coming your way."

The rush of incoming rounds screamed in moments later. The explosions this time were more a cracking, like lightning bolts on a summer storm. They were off, though. One leg of the spider mech was hit, twisted into worthless slag, but the machine was still operational.

"FO to Blunderbuss. Adjust right ten, forward five. Bring it again."

"Adjusting and firing."

The mech moved on the dug-in leejes; it was only fifteen meters away. O'Keefe's stomach knotted. If she got it wrong, it might kill them.

The roar overhead came again, this time raining down right on top of the K'llik mech. Roiling white and black smoke obscured the target. Had the shots been effective?

The leejes rose from their position and fired again. As the breeze caught the smoke and cleared it, she saw the leejes' pinpoint fire zip into the holes her barrage had caused.

"Target eliminated," she said.

"Stand by, FO—we're redeploying," came back Blunderbuss's voice.

The leej next to her reached over and gave her a hard pat on the shoulder. "Nice work."

Turning in the hot sand, she saw that the K'llik offensive was waning. To the east, a Republic MBT savaged a spider mech with its heavy blaster cannon, sending bits of metal and legs flying. A gigantic explosion went off to her left, not sounding at all like the artillery fire from the RTCMs. Sand rained down over her, grinding on her helmet, sticking to the moisture in the corners of her eyes.

It had to be the K'llik artillery.

Searching through the haze of the battle, she glimpsed Metzger's mech. It was splayed across the back of a downed spider mech, its legs spread out, its blasters little more than fried stumps, missing one missile rack. It wasn't moving, or even trying to right itself. Smoke rolled from the mech underneath it.

Damn it, Carson, you had better be alive!

A tap on her arm came from the leej next to her. He pointed off in the distance, and she saw a strange mech she hadn't seen before. It reminded her of a praying mantis, with two large legs supporting an articulating upper torso, and two short arms equipped with a rapid-fire plasma weapon. It was currently firing streams of molten plasma at a squad of legionnaires using a downed spider mech for cover.

A set of coordinates quickly followed.

"This is the FO—fire mission—Grid J, 100—05. Target is a big mech—so bring the pain."

"This is Blunderbuss, confirming coordinates—" He quickly rattled through the targeting.

"Confirmed."

"Incoming."

The praying mantis mech started to move. With its height advantage, the leejes were going to be easy targets if it got much closer.

Move slow, bug. Just hold for one more second—

Incoming RTCM rounds roared in with a vengeance. Three rounds slammed into the enemy mech while the rest tore into the sand and exploded. Hot shrapnel flew through the air.

The mantis went down, sliding in the sand. Before it could even consider standing back up, the legionnaires it had been targeting surged out of their cover and swarmed it. They brought improvised det bricks taken from the crash site and initially meant for excavation, and affixed it in all the right places while their blasters concentrated fire on whatever served as the cockpit. Then—as one—they faded and return to cover.

The mech went up in a series of explosions, dead.

Losing that big mech seemed to have an outsized impact on the enemy across the battlespace. It was almost as if the K'llik shared some sort of bond and felt the loss. O'Keefe saw a twitch with the fall of the enemy, a physical jerking reaction that rippled out among the other aliens.

They know the battle is lost; somehow they sense it.

The K'llik that were still operational began to skitter back toward the tunnels, only to be pursued by the 72nd and Cobra Company. The Republic forces clearly didn't want the aliens to get away. It was an emotion that O'Keefe shared. The retrograde turned into a rout, and the aliens that didn't make it to their holes in the ground were chewed apart by small arms and mech fire. But pursuit didn't continue into the tunnels themselves. The K'llik knew the underground better than their adversaries, and following them would only open up troops and mechs to ambush.

O'Keefe's body sagged, released from the tension and the emotional rollercoaster ride she had been on. She sat down in the sand, trembling, then pulled off her helmet. The warm desert breeze felt strangely cooling. She had experienced this feeling before, after a battle—the elation, the grief, and the relief, all swirled together.

Leaning back against the sand berm, she felt the uncomfortable grit stick to the sweat on her skin. It didn't matter—she was alive. And she had proved to herself that she still had the skills to be able to contribute.

She had her eyes closed when a voice came to her. "Good job." Her mind raced—trying to place the voice, but she couldn't.

This must be a new memory.

Cracking her eyes open again, she was surprised to see a leej standing over her, extending his hand. "You okay? I said good job, Basic."

It wasn't a memory—it's the here and now.

She took his hand, and he helped her to her feet. "I try."

"Seriously, though, wish more R-A strap-hangers were like you."

O'Keefe bent down and grabbed her helmet. "Thank you. I have to go—I have a friend down there somewhere."

At least she hoped she did.

"Then you'd better get to him."

Running in the sand was far from easy, but she reached Metzger's mech and the spider-mech it was entangled with. Heat rippled off both damaged mechs, enough to hold her back.

"Repub better not expect me to pay for that," came a voice from behind her.

Wheeling around, she saw Metzger. His face was covered with black smears, and his uniform was soaked with sweat. One of his jumpsuit pant legs was ripped open, and there was an open cut on his bionic leg, exposing some electronics. His steps were labored as he moved toward her, dragging the cybernetic limb through the sand.

A smile spread over her face, and she held out a hand to him. He returned the smile as he grabbed the proffered hand and squeezed hard. She saw then that his arm was cut, as was his shoulder. And—not surprisingly—he looked exhausted.

"Yeah, that'll cost a pretty credit. Don't think they can just buff out those dents," she said, nodding at the destroyed mech oozing trails of white smoke. "Not to mention the damage to your leg. Again? Really? That's three times. Not that I'm counting."

He chuckled. "With my luck, they'll make me be the one to repair it." He pulled out a hydration flask and took a long drink, then handed her what was left. Warm water never tasted as good as it did to her in that moment.

"I'm glad you made it through," Metzger said.

She wanted to tell him what she had experienced, about the Frix, but it wasn't the right time.

"Same with you. Those tunnels were pretty terrifying, I have to admit."

"You got us through them, and that's what matters."

"It wasn't me alone. You can thank Sergeant Major Teuber," she said. "If it wasn't for him and the map in his bucket, none of this would have been possible."

"No. If it wasn't for your damned holographic memory, we would have been drawn into a much bloodier engagement. Might've ended up like that lost legion you found." Metzger searched her face. "Are you okay?"

Her mouth opened, but no words came out.

Was she okay?

"Yes," she said, giving a small smile. "More okay than I've felt in a long time. I got a few moments of... redemption in all this. Something happened there, when I was bringing in the iron rain. Something wondrous."

"What was it?"

Looking into his eyes, she smiled. "I'll tell you later."

He looked at her curiously. "I'll hold you to it."

She looked around the battlefield, savoring the moment of calm. "Somewhere, under all the sand, is the rest of the 552nd. This is where they died."

"It's going to take a lot to get to them," Metzger said. "Especially after this fight."

"We'll do it though," she assured him. "This is one lost legion that's coming home."

42

After the fighting in Defilers Pass, the high regent sent a message to the Republic forces that they were suspending military operations. No apology was offered, nor was one expected. The Vargas Liberation Army had been all but obliterated in the fighting. Most of their survivors surrendered. Colonel Hackett had talked about dragging Guildmaster Rune out on charges of treason, but before that could happen, a sled accident ended Rune's life. While it seemed to tie a nice bow on matters on Vargas, Metzger felt that they had been robbed of their chance to see justice done.

The med techs had worked on Metzger's injured leg, repairing the damage. He no longer thought of the replacement limb as a mechanism. It was a part of him now, just as much as its flesh counterpart. If anything, he appreciated it more. It had, in a way, saved his life.

And yet the damn thing still had a target on it. He chuckled. He'd heard a rumor that Krock was running a pool on when was the next time he'd lose it.

The historian team, including O'Keefe, had been busy for the last three weeks, locating the remains of the dead in Defilers Pass. Two mass graves had been found, along with a number of scattered sites where skeletons of the long-lost 552nd Legion had been recovered. Most of the missing couldn't be accounted for, but O'Keefe told him that was to be expected; the vast majority of them had been destroyed by the Savages in orbit as the initial dropships came down to the surface. It was Weaver who had pulled that info out of the memory slats, with careful coaxing and copious amounts of patience.

During his idle time, he watched the archeologists and historians respectfully exhume the dead and delicately place them in transport coffins. There was something reassuring about the process. It gave him comfort that if he ever died on the field, the people that would handle his body would be just as reverent.

His idle time was limited, though. The surviving technicians of the 72nd were swamped with repairs, and Metzger volunteered to help them. He was surprised to see Vickerson and Hullbuster join in as well, and he was downright shocked when Tramel dropped in to assist.

"What?" the young lieutenant said, waving off the others' stares. "A good pilot ought to know how to care for his mech. Right, Pileup?"

Ross came over and put him to work, and not another word was said on the matter.

After three weeks there was a summons for a ceremony. It took place in Defilers Pass. Metzger stood there in his dress uniform with the rest of the 72nd, lined up behind the Legion troops. Arrayed before them were eighty-eight coffins in four long rows, perfectly positioned equidistant from each other—all they had managed to find of the thousand legionnaires belonging to the Howling Banshees.

A Legion honor guard was poised at the end of one long row. Sergeant Callison's people had taken the time before the ceremony to meticulously fold Legion flags that had been draped over each coffin in a perfectly flat triangle.

That was curious to Metzger. They used their own flags, and not the Republic's.

The Legion remained an enigma.

Colonel Hackett moved out before the rows of coffins and saluted the dead, and the rest of the gathered forces did the same. No verbal order had to be given, and the salutes were in perfect unison. "Today we undertake a most sacred duty. These legionnaires disappeared centuries ago and were thought lost to the dust of time. But the Legion never forgets its own, even those who have disappeared into the mists of the ages. Now, for the first time, we bring these wayward warriors home. Their souls, we know, have fought to their final resting place. Their mortal remains will return to rest in a place of high honor."

The quiet in the pass was stifling yet filled with emotion. Several holo-recording bots covered the brief ceremony, no doubt sending their holos to the rest of the Legion. The white-gloved firing squad aimed their blasters high and unleashed three volleys, twenty-one shots, skyward. As they finished, a drum beat three rapid booms, and the colonel barked, "Dis-missed!"

Metzger saw O'Keefe and cut through the gathering to her. She looked different. Not so much happy as relieved. He had spent time with her after the battle, usually at night. O'Keefe had told him about what had happened, how the firing mission had triggered something in her that brought back her memories. How she had been forced to call in a bombardment that might have killed some of her own unit, and had injured herself in the process.

Metzger wondered whether he would have blocked that out too if that had happened to him.

Seeing her in her dress uniform brought back memories of graduating boot camp... happier days with friends long gone.

"Look at you, all dressed for a ball," she said with a wry grin.

"That was my kind of ceremony," he replied. "Short." He tugged at the collar of his uniform shirt.

"Our work here is just about done." Her eyes swept the pass for a quick moment. "Or rather, our rotation. A Repub dig team tied to one of the big core world universities is going to come out."

"That bother you?"

"Nah. I found it. That's what counts. I'm looking forward to leaving this place."

"I would have thought you'd want to stay. After all, you are responsible for bringing home a lost legion. That's pretty big stuff."

"Yeah. My colonel tells me the media is lined up back at our base, all wanting an interview about this," she said, rolling her eyes.

"See, you're a celebrity!"

"No. I'm a historian."

"Come on, O'Keefe, even you have to admit this is a big deal."

"It is," she assured him. "But I look at it differently."

"How's that?"

"Simple. One down," she said, winking at him. "Four to go."

It was not bravado on O'Keefe's part, it was determination.

Metzger smiled. This wasn't the Sheryl from boot. This was someone new, someone charting a new course in her life. "Do you have any ideas how you're going to find those other lost legions?"

"Not yet. But my CO believes the publicity from all of this will generate some new leads. Of course, most will probably be dead ends—it amazes me that there are people out there who will try to scam credits off of dead soldiers."

"Not me. The House of Reason is filled with people that send me to bleed so they can make money off of my pain. They've been doing it for a long time, since long before we enlisted."

He saw a hint of worry wash across her face.

"What's bothering you?" he asked.

"Nothing... just something I've been thinking about."

"I know that expression. The thought can't be a good one. What is it?"

She met his eye. "We got our lead to Vargas from an old ship's buoy. But there were indications that the data on that buoy had been manipulated... maybe even planted. Our tech is still quite confident that's the case. And yet... it led us here, and we found the Howling Banshees."

"That doesn't make sense," Metzger said. "Why would someone go to all that trouble? Why not just tell you to look here?"

"That's what's bothering me." She shook herself, as if ridding herself of the worry. "I need to let it go. Dranes and Colonel Hughes told Colonel Hackett about it—they have the data and are more than capable of handling it. I'll just have to file that under 'someone else's problem.'" She smiled. "So what's next for you?"

"We're departing back to Fort Archie, get patched up again. We lost some good people on this piece-of-sket planet. Plus just about everyone needs repair and refit at this stage; some of us lost our rides altogether." He pointed at himself. "Major Meece told me these things were blaster-magnets; he wasn't kidding."

"Well, fixing hardware is easy. Fixing people takes a lot more," O'Keefe said.

He knew she was talking about her head, but his hand drifted down to his artificial leg. "Well, when the dust settles, we should coordinate our leaves so we can connect."

"Absolutely."

As she leaned in and gave him a hug, he was thankful that both of them were no longer broken—that they had, each in their own way, reached stable one.

43

Newly promoted, Warrant Officer Sheryl O'Keefe lay on the couch in Dr. Astin's office.

"You look well," said the bot. "In fact, if I might be so bold, you look better than I have ever seen you appear."

O'Keefe smiled—not a forced smile, but a genuine one. "It's been a long four months. A lot has happened."

"So I gathered, from reading the reports of the operations you were on. The finding of the 552nd is nothing short of remarkable. Everyone is talking about it. You moved the Historical Division from obscurity to front-page news."

"We didn't find all their remains, but we did get them all accounted for," she said proudly. The data that now-*Chief* Warrant Officer Weaver had recovered from various buckets had filled out the picture of the Howling Banshees' last stand.

"I understand that they're planning a memorial for the Banshees," Astin commented.

"I've heard that too. We've been asked for input on it. I'm not big on statues and such. I really didn't have much to offer. The best thing we can do to remember them is what we did, bring them home and tell the universe their stories—give their deaths some meaning and context."

Her left hand slid to her pants pocket where she kept a piece of cloth recovered from Vargas. A patch from the 552nd. Several had been recovered and couldn't be connected to any soldier in particular. Just touching it gave her strength, mental focus.

"They promoted you for your efforts."

O'Keefe shrugged. Ranks and promotion were handed out like candy in the R-A. She knew that. But... she was still thankful for the acknowledgement. "I was just doing my job."

"You went into battle. Hardly a researcher's job."

"Yes—I did."

"Did you have any issues?"

"Yes... and no."

"Perhaps you would care to elaborate? And explain that big smile on your face."

O'Keefe laughed. "There's a lot to tell. But the short version is, the memories that were a hot jumbled mess... they're all sorted out now. You were right: I was blocking myself from knowing about the trauma of what had happened. And what... I had done. I wasn't ready to deal with it yet. But now I am. And now I remember it all."

"That's remarkable. How do you feel about that?"

"Guilty—but at peace. What I did... I didn't have a better choice."

"Has this affected your visions? Do you still have them?"

"They still surface from time to time. But... muted. It's like once I got them sorted out, they didn't need to reach out to me as often."

"And how *did* you get them sorted out?"

"That I can't say, exactly. But getting back on a battlefield, under fire, was a part of it. A big part of it."

"That's not the kind of therapy my programming would have recommended."

"Perhaps not. But you've been a big help. Thank you, for all you've done for me."

"I didn't do anything. You did it all. Now you're the most famous military historian in the Republic."

She rolled her eyes. "For whatever that's worth."

The bot's glowing eyes fixed on her. "What's next for you?"

"People keep asking me that. In reality, my work has just begun."

That night, O'Keefe entered the Nuts to Butts. The smell and look of the bar hadn't changed since the last time she had been there, nor had she expected it to. The place was mostly empty, which she preferred. The bartender bot, Wade, gave her a nod as she passed it.

"So, you're back on this ugly rock," it commented.

O'Keefe smiled. "For a while at least."

"Everyone's talking about what you did. I made a drink in your honor, called it the O'Keefe. Two shots Carnorian chocolate vodka, and a splash of Tessrin peppered liqueur, two-hundred proof."

"That sounds horrible," she said with a laugh.

"It's guaranteed to block your memory of drinking it."

O'Keefe chuckled at that and then deadpanned, "How appropriate."

"I'd be happy to pour you one, on the house," Wade offered.

"Not tonight," she replied. "I'd rather remember tonight."

She headed over to the wall of honor. Dozens of bits of armor, patches, and other mementos were hung up there, left by comrades to commemorate their long-lost friends. She reached into her pocket and pulled out a small piece of an old Legion bucket she'd asked Weaver for. It was a piece from the side, featuring the logo of the 552nd and the name of its owner: Sergeant Major Klaus Teuber.

You completed one last mission, Sergeant Major. You belong here, in a place like this, where your fellow warriors congregate.

As she attached it to the memento wall, she heard Wade come up behind her.

"From someone close to you?" the bot asked.

"One of the lost—who's finally come home to his comrades," she replied, turning to leave the bar. "In a strange way, he saved us all."

The return to Camp Archie on Tibul for the 72nd came with pride. It wasn't the band playing for them as they debarked, or the raising of the flag ceremony that showed that they were indeed back at their base—it was the sense that the stigma of Tralon had been healed. They had suffered losses, that was for sure, but the 72nd had shown that it had what it took to hang in on a major battle. Before they had left Vargas, Colonel Hackett of Cobra Company came out and buried the stigma of the Battle of Tralon once and for all with a simple few words. "I've told the 14th Legion that if we ever need heavy armored support, I will demand that it be the 72nd HARD Regiment. You men are willing to fight, at least. That's something."

On a personal level, Metzger felt like he had finally arrived. That moment on the battlefield when he felt as if the mech was a part of him—that had been a moving experience. He knew, intellectually, that he was simply his senses extending outward, heightened by the staccato of battle—but experiencing it was something else entirely. The cockpit was his second skin now; the mech was his armor. He was a whole warrior again, in a massive suit with exceptional firepower at his disposal.

It's funny how things work out. My mother was right; everything in life happens for a reason.

He no longer entertained fantasies of joining the Legion. Piloting a mech was what he did, how he waged war, who he was.

What more could I want?

As he entered the repair bays, he got his first glimpse of his replacement mech. It had been drawn from the unit's maintenance pool, an HK-PP like his previous ride. His now-experienced eyes drank in every armored plate, every seam, every detail with careful scrutiny. Chief Tech Ross had even arranged to have his custom nose art added.

And he spotted an additional detail, something new. The outline of an enemy mech, marked in white paint, with a row of hash marks next to it, tallying his official kills. Seeing it, he realized that he was a mech ace now.

A tech had opened the left blaster access port, performing some maintenance. As the tech worked, his tools clicking on the internal mechanisms, Metzger's hand drifted down to his bionic leg. The sensors registered the presence of his hand, and in his mind, it almost felt like a human touch. When he looked down, the leg looked just like the organic one he used to have.

Everything can be replaced. Everything can be fixed. Even busted-up infantrymen like me.

As he admired his new mech, he heard footsteps come up behind him. Turning, he saw Captain Peltier.

"I trust it meets with your approval?" the captain said.

"Sir, I won't know until I take it out and get some range time with her—but she looks just fine to me."

"Your performance in the recent campaign caught the attention of the colonel," Peltier said.

"Is that a good thing or a bad thing?"

"As with most things in life, it's a matter of perspective." Peltier pulled out a small blue box and opened it. Inside was an insignia for his new rank. He'd jumped up quite a bit. Something unusual for any branch save the Republic Army and Navy. "In this case, he's seen fit to promote you. Congratulations."

Metzger eyed the box with a cocked eyebrow. "I somewhat doubt these Captain's bars come without additional responsibility."

Peltier smiled. "I've been bumped up to the command staff. You heard about Major Meece. HK pilots rarely live to see old age unless it's in a repulsor chair or chock full of cybernetics. Things move quickly. For all of us. I was asked who I wanted to take command of the squadron. I said you. The old man wholeheartedly agreed."

Command of the squadron! A promotion was one thing, but this... this was much more. Metzger wondered if he'd truly performed well enough to deserve it. Peltier, at least, had believed so. As did Colonel Inglima.

"I—I'm not sure what to say."

"You don't have to say anything, and nothing you do say will change it. You earned that job. You've shown yourself to be the kind of person who pushes the metal and the people to the limit. That's exactly what an HK squadron needs."

Peltier's words hit him squarely.

He truly was home.

"Thank you, sir. And congratulations on your new assignment. I won't let you down."

"I know you won't, Chief."

Metzger fondled the box, then looked up at his commander. "So, what's going to be done about the K'llik and the mining guild?"

Peltier shrugged. "That's in the hands of the House of Reason."

Those words soured the air between them. "Politicians. That means they'll never be held accountable."

"Maybe not. Then again, maybe." Peltier quirked a smile. "Word is the Legion has its own intel people looking into things. They lost good men on Vargas. They don't take that lightly."

Metzger matched Peltier's grin. "And they will handle matters with calm, efficient, professional brutality."

"I have no doubt. In the meantime, we have our own work to do. The colonel has authorized us to name our—now *your*—squadron. And create a logo, too. We more than proved ourselves in battle. The time has come."

"Actually... I'm way ahead of you on that—*and* the colonel," Metzger said. "Follow me."

He led Peltier over to a workbench. He'd been working with the techs to come up with a logo he thought appropriate, and had been intending to show it to Peltier anyway. Now he pulled off the cover to reveal a wickedly grinning skull. The crossbones were two large wrenches. Underneath was the proposed name—*Hot Steel*—in flaming gothic letters.

"Hullbuster suggested 'Mech Monkeys,' but this has a bit more edge to it," Metzger said, allowing himself to beam. "What do you think?"

"Nailed it," Peltier replied.

44

Rexnar Koff nursed the glass in his hands, turning it from side to side, watching the ice slowly melt. It was late at night, and in the comfort of his palatial estate's home office, he felt secure. Here, and here alone, he could think through the debacle on Vargas.

It had taken months to clean up the mess. The death of Guildmaster Rune certainly gave the investigators a convenient scapegoat, and Major Sarn had taken care of any others who'd had even a minor role in the affair. Most were eliminated; a few were spared their lives and were paid off handsomely from accounts that even the best forensic AI accounting software would never be able to trace back to him. There was nothing he could do about the K'llik, but he had felt assured from the start that they would never reveal his role in matters. Those insects rarely spoke to anyone, let alone investigators looking to lay blame at their doorstep.

Yes, he was certain that the much-vaunted investigation by the House of Reason into the events on Vargas would come back inconclusive at best, muddled at worst.

There would be no conspiracy found.

And yet Koff had not gotten what he wanted. He was unaccustomed to that, and it didn't sit well with him. He had failed to exact vengeance for the loss of his son, and the fighting on Vargas had done nothing to boost the MCR —and thus nothing to line his pockets.

If it had just been Cobra Company, everything would have gone exactly as he planned. He hadn't expected the Legion to bring a HARD regiment with them. Whose harebrained idea was that?

Someone would feel his wrath, he was sure of that. Perhaps the commander of the 72nd. Perhaps *all* of them.

It would take time to formulate a plan, but Koff felt confident in his mental prowess. He would find a way… he always did. He wouldn't be denied either profit or vengeance.

He was a man who was not used to losing.

He heard a noise outside his office, not quite a footstep, not a shuffle. Rising, he walked to the door and opened it to the hallway. He had a security detail at the estate, but they usually stayed off the third floor where his living quarters were. It was probably nothing. His security staff was the best that money could buy. They were heavily armed, all courtesy of his armament companies. As if anyone could get past his top-of-the-line surveillance systems anyway.

Still, the noise was disturbing.

"Hello?" he said into the dark hallway.

No response.

Turning, he headed back to his desk and his drink.

He had just activated his holodisplay and started to check the market values for his holdings when he heard another noise, this one from outside the building. Rising and going to the window, he looked out at the vast gardens that extended into darkness. He saw nothing out of place.

Normally, he wasn't paranoid. He paid people to be paranoid *for* him. But something felt off. Taking a large gulp of his bourbon, he activated his desk's comm system and hit the button for security. There was a chirp as he signaled for the shift supervisor, but no response came back.

Now genuine concern washed over him. Something was wrong. He hit the virtual button once more. Again, no one answered.

His eyes darted to the desk drawer where he kept a blaster pistol. It was a custom piece, outfitted with an enhanced targeting scope, modified grips, a light suppressor, and an extended power cell. The modifications and add-ons to the weapon had cost more than the gun itself. Pulling the drawer open, he was stunned to see that the blaster wasn't there.

He pulled open two more drawers, but there was no sign of the weapon. His heart pounded in his chest. *Where is it?* He leaned back in his chair—

And saw two men standing on the opposite side of his desk. Both wore black Legion armor.

Koff had a panic room. He hit the secret stud hidden on the desktop and heard the door open just behind him. He sprang for it—only to find a third man emerging from the panic room itself, wearing the same black Legion armor and holding Koff's missing pistol.

The man aimed the gun at him with one hand and pushed him back into his desk with the other. One of the first two operators grabbed his wrists and locked them in ener-chains.

"You can't do this," Koff sputtered. "Don't you know who I am? I'm a member of the House of Reason!"

It was impossible to see their faces; their helmets obscured them. The man holding Koff's pistol shook his head. "Of course we know who you are, Rexnar Koff. We also know what you are responsible for doing." He tossed down the custom pistol and pulled out his own sleek blaster carbine. It lacked all the shine, ornamentation, and enhancements of Koff's weapon, and as such, it appeared far more menacing.

"You can't come in here and take me prisoner!" Koff sputtered. "This can not possibly have been authorized!"

"You're right. Never would be."

Koff's face went ashen. "This is all a mistake—a misunderstanding."

"Gag him," the man told his colleagues in an annoyed tone.

An isolation hood went over Koff's head, cutting off all sight and sound. He could feel a prick against his wrist, and suddenly his arms and legs grew thick and heavy; he'd been drugged.

As Koff fought to remain conscious, the hood was pulled up from his head just slightly—not enough for him to see, but enough that he could hear.

"I'm sure you have a lot of questions, Mr. Koff. I'm not here to answer them. I'm here to tell you that you won't be allowed to jeopardize things like this, ever again."

Koff's eyes widened, and he tried to speak, but only a mumble surfaced through the haze of the drug and the stark raving panic washing over him. "You're... you're not... Legion. Neth... Nether."

The words were a struggle.

"You knew when they brought you into this," the man said. "This was always the price for failure."

Koff felt the cold barrel of his blaster pistol pressed beneath his jaw. He tried to struggle, but his muscles didn't respond. He became aware that he was no longer standing under his own power.

The man spoke again. "The delegate sends his regrets."

Rexnar Koff never saw the blaster bolt.

The following day, the House of Reason would morn the murder of a promising delegate from a scandalous and brazen home invasion.

Then... the galaxy would move on.

EPILOGUE

Utopion

Sheryl O'Keefe was seated to the side of the stage, mixed in with a few dignitaries and politicians. Dranes and Weaver had to sit in the row behind her on account of an usher bot that didn't seem particularly good at its job. Next to her was the new guildmaster of Vargas, a pleasant enough fellow, who was on hand for the ceremony as a show of commitment to the Republic. He'd made a point of apologizing for how his fellow miners had behaved once he'd heard some of her story.

No similar K'llik representative was there. No one had expected there would be.

She'd hoped that Carson would be there, but he, along with the rest of the HARD unit, was busy elsewhere. The entire 72nd had been invited, but only Colonel Inglima and his personal aide were on hand. Men like Carson lacked the scheduling flexibility O'Keefe enjoyed as a researcher, and the fighting with the Mid-Core Rebellion was ticking up everywhere. Both the Repub Army and the Legion had their hands full.

But this was an Order of the Centurion ceremony, and so, busy as it was, it was still well attended by the Legion. There were perhaps more former legionnaires than active, but they made sure every seat was taken. No one who received the award did so alone.

Even the old among them still looked dangerous. Hard, lethal men. That was the impression that came to O'Keefe's mind.

The day served as something of a triumph for Colonel Hackett, who was set to retire following a battlefield injury that had left him with a limp that meds and regens couldn't fix. It wasn't uncommon for senior officers, on their way out, to champion a candidate for the Legion's highest honor. Hackett's choice might have set a record for time elapsed between event and award. O'Keefe made a mental note to look into that.

She was becoming something of a specialist when it came to researching the Legion. She might never find another lost legion, but the organization fascinated her. Continued, careful work at the crash site had uncovered new details, and O'Keefe was proud to hear some of those included in Hackett's brief speech.

"When the 552nd Legion found its transport ship, hounded by the enemy, severely damaged inside of Savage territories, they might have been excused for ignoring the discovery of a Savage-controlled mining and manufacturing operation in favor of a desperate attempt to break out. Instead, they elected to abandon ship, preferring a final, decisive act that would cripple Savage operations on Vargas.

"We know from the fantastic rediscovery of this once-lost legion that their mission was successful, though the cost was high. Not a legionnaire survived."

Colonel Hackett paused—an impromptu moment of silence and respect.

"Those men gave their lives with the hopes that their brothers might live. The destruction of the Savage mining operation and manufacturing depot denied the enemy a continued ability to field the engines of war they had relied on in that sector of the galaxy.

"But one legionnaire in particular embodied this will to save his fellow legionnaires from his own fate, and it is he whom we are gathered here today to honor: Sergeant Joachim Andersen, LS-209-552-6. Last Posting 552nd Legion, Teal Company.

"Sergeant Andersen, despite being mortally wounded from close-in fighting following their landing on Vargas, continued to operate at his final resting place—amid the ruins of the drop shuttle *Cú Chulainn*. Through what was likely an agonizingly painful death, Andersen monitored the mapping of a subterranean tunnel structure. He discovered—too late—what was used to kill his fellow legionnaires to the last man. Rather than die in sorrow, Andersen lived on, among a final few survivors who would care for each other to the end. Though not a technician, he set the buckets of his dead fellow warriors to receive holo-mapping data from bots programmed to scan Vargas's vast subterranean tunnel system until the end of their runtime."

Hackett looked out at the crowd, who remained rigid, their attention fixed. O'Keefe felt goose bumps rise on her arms in anticipation of what came next.

"Republic Army researchers were able to slice their way into Sergeant Andersen's biometric data files. The leej had been gut shot and was battling an infection that would ultimately take his life. He had a painful fracture in his left hip, and evidence suggests he dragged himself across the crash site to attend to his duties. He refused ration packs, preferring to live his final days in a state of starvation rather than take limited calories from those Republic marines and legionnaires in better condition than he.

"And through it all, he continued to oversee the data collection. He worked tirelessly on a solution that would keep the buckets in a state of constantly receiving the transmissions for however long the drones still sent them.

"Sergeant Andersen knew that, someday, the Legion would return. His dying desire was that they would not see the same fate as the 552nd.

"It would be centuries before the Legion came for Sergeant Andersen. I was in command of the legionnaires who brought him home, and I have no deeper career satisfaction. But *our* fate may well have matched that of the lost legion... had it not been for the data that Sergeant Andersen so meticulously saved. Because of his determination, Republic armor from the 72nd were able to use the tunnel system against the same enemy that had once destroyed an entire legion, battered and isolated as they were.

"The Order of the Centurion is the highest award that can be bestowed upon an individual serving in, or with, the Legion. When such an individual displays exceptional valor in action against an enemy force, and uncommon loyalty and devotion to the Legion and its legionnaires, refusing to abandon post, mission, or brothers, even unto death, the Legion dutifully recognizes such courage with this award. Standing on the other side of the centuries that separate us from Sergeant Andersen's actions, having benefited from those actions and having seen my command spared destruction due to those actions, it is with abundant gratitude that I now present to Sergeant Andersen the Order of the Centurion."

Crisp applause came from the legionnaires. There was no hooting or hollering. It was somber, professional. O'Keefe felt another surge of goose flesh.

Andersen had no surviving relatives. He had been a young man when he died. An only child whose parents had died at the hands of the Savages.

It was the Legion commander who accepted the award on behalf of the dead who had no family.

No, O'Keefe thought. *That's wrong.*

She looked around at the legionnaires, who now stood in their applause as the simple medallion was presented.

He does have a family. They're all right here.

THE END

HONOR ROLL

Jason and Nick would like to thank those whose Galaxy's Edge Insider Subscriptions saw the Order of the Centurion stories continue.

Cody Aalberg

A. Isaiah Abney

Artis Aboltins

Guido Abreu

Daniel Adams

Chancellor Adams

Garion Adkins

Ryan Adwers

Elias Aguilar

Neal Albritton

Aleksey Aleshintsev

Jonathan Allain

Byron Allen

Justin Allred

Paul Almond

Joachim Andersen

Galen Anderson

Levi Anderson

Jarad Anderson

Jennifer Andrews

Pat Andrews

Robert Anspach

Melanie Apollo

Benjamin Arguello

Thomas Armona

Jonathan Auerbach

Sean Averill

Nicholas Avila

David Azur

Sam Baccoli

Benjamin Backus

Zachary Badger

Shane Bailey

David Baker

John Baker

Daniel Baker

Sallie Baliunas

Nathan Ball

Kevin Bangert

Brian Bardwell

Brian Barrows-Striker

Richard Bartle

Sean Battista

Robert Battles

Eric Batzdorfer

John Baudoin

Adam Bear

Nahum Beard

Michelle Beaver

Mike Beeker

Randall Beem

John Bell

Mark Bennett

Edward Benson

Mark Berardi

Gardner Berry

John Bertram

Kevin Biasci

John Bingham

Gregory Bingham

Francisco Blankemeyer

David Blount

Liz Bogard

James Bohling

Rodney Bonner

Brandon Boone

Douglas Booth

William Boucher

Aaron Bowen

Darren Bowers

Brandon Bowles

Alex Bowling

Keiger Bowman

Michael Boyle

Derrick Boyter

Chester Brads

Richard Brake

Andrew Branca

Logan Brandon

Ernest Brant

Chet Braud

Dennis Bray

Christopher Brewster

Geoff Brisco

Wayne Brite

Spencer Bromley

Raymond Brooks

Dodson Brown

Matthew Brown

RFC Brumley

Jeff Brussee

Benjamin Bryan

Nicholas Burck

Austin Burgans

John Burleigh

Jay Burritt

David Butler

Karl Butsch

John Byrd

Daniel Cadwell

Brian Callahan

Decker Cammack

Mark Campbell

Chris Capone

Tyler Carlson

Daldos Carr

Rafael Carrol

Robert Cathey

Brian Cave

Shawn Cavitt

Brian Cheney

Brad Chenoweth

Caleb Cheshire

James Christensen

Cooper Clark

Andrew Clary

Ethan Clayton

Sean Clifton

Adam Cobb

Morgan Cobb

Michael Cole

Curtis Colgate

Curtis Colgate

Christian Collins

Jason Colson

Jerry Conard

Robert Conaway

Bronson Conlin

James Connolly

James Conyers

Kevin Cooper

Jacob Coppess

Michael Corbin

Anthony Cotillo

Seth Coussens

Andrew Craig

Zachary Craig

Collin Creel

Ben Crose

Ben Crowley

Christopher Crowley

Jack Culbertson

Phil Culpepper

Scott Cummins

Ben Curcio

Luigi Cusano

Jason D. Martin

Robert Daly

John Dames

David Danz

Matthew Dare

Chad David

David Davis

Ivy Davis

LeRoy Davis

Ben Davis

Brian Davis

Nathan Davis

Andrew Day

Ron Deage

Chris DeBeer

Joel Defauw

Anthony Del Villar

Anerio (Wyatt) Deorma (Dent)

Douglas Deuel

Michael Dickerson

Jack Dickson

Alexander Dickson

Christopher DiNote

Matthew Dippel

Gregory Divis

Jeffrey Dobbs

Graham Doering

Shawn Doherty

Gerald Donovan

Ward Dorrity

Adam Drucker

John Dryden

Garrett Dubois

Marc-André Dufor

Thomas DuLaney II

Brendan Dullaghan

Evan Durrant

Christopher Durrant

Samuel Dutterer

Virgil Dwyer

Justin Eilenberger

Brian Eisel

Jonathan R. Ellis

William Ely

Kelvin Emdy

Michael Emes

Paul Eng

Andrew English

Ethan Estep

Richard Everett

Jaeger Falco

Stephen Farnett

Nicholas Fasanella

Carlos Faustino

Michael Feher

Steven Feily

Julie Fenimore

Meagan Ference

Adolfo Fernandez

Rich Ferrante

Brandon Field

Austin Findley

Albert Fink

Alex Fisher

Lamar Fitzgerald

Rhys Fitzpatrick

Matthew Fiveson

Daniel Flanders

Daniel Flores

Geoffrey Flowers

William Foley

Steve Forrester

Kenneth Foster

Paul Fox

Bryant Fox

Martin Foxley

Dennis Frank

Greg Franz

Luke Frazer	John Giorgis	Michael Hale
Kyle Freitus	Johnny Glazebrooks	Marlon Hall II
Griffin Frendsdorff	Bob Gleason	Leo Hallak
Timothy Fujimoto	Martin Gleaton	Kelly Halma
Bob Fulsang	James Glendenning	Nathan Hamilton
Jonathan Furnery	Seth Glenn	Chris Hammond
Elizabeth Gafford	Jared Glissman	Chris Hanley
David Gaither	William Frank Godbold IV	Greg Hanson
Matthew Gale	Justin Godfrey	Tyler Hardy
Zachary Galicki	John Gooch	Jeffrey Hardy
Kyle Gannon	Jacob Goodin	Ian Harper
Dave Garbowski	Justin Gottwaltz	Revan Harris
Joshua Gardner	Gordon Grant	Adam Hartswick
Michael Gardner	Mitch Greathouse	Matthew Hathorn
Alphonso Garner	Gordon Green	Adam Hazen
John Gasperino	Matt Green	Richard Heard
Jordan Gass	Shawn Greene	Colin Heavens
Marina Gaston	John Greenfield Jr.	Jonathan Heiden
Robert Gates	Anthony Gribbins	Jesse Heidenreich
Craig Gentry	Eric Griffin	Brenton Held
Cody George	Ronald Grisham	Jason Henderson
Gregory Gero	Robert P. Gunter	Jason Henderson
Eli Geroux	Joshua Haataja	Fynn Hendrikse
Dylan Giles	Michael Hagen	John Henkel
Joe Gillis	Kelton Hague	Daniel Heron
Oscar Gillott-Cain	Levi Haines	Bradley Herren
Nathan Gioconda	Joseph Haire	Felipe Herrera

Paul Herron	Aaron Huling	Ryan Kelstrom
Sven Hestrand	Mike Hull	Caleb Kenner
Kyle Hetzer	James Hurtado	Zack Kenny
Korrey Heyder	Wayne Hutton	Daniel Kimm
Matthew Hicks	Gaetano Inglima	Kennith King
Lance Hirayama	Antonio Iozzo	Caleb Kirkwood
Ty Hodges	Michael Jenkins	Joshua Kivett
Jonathan Hoehn	Jacob Jensen	Kyle Klincko
Charles Hoisington	Robert Jensen	Brendan Klinger
Bryan Holden	Eric Jett	Brendan Klingner
Aaron Holden	Caleb Johnson	Albert Klukowski
William Holman	Gary Johnson	Marc Knapp
Clint Holmes	Anthony Johnson	William Knapp
Jason Honeyfield	Cobra Johnson	Robert Knox
Charles Hood	Eric Johnson	Ethan Koska
Tyson Hopkins	Nick Johnson	Evan Kowalski
Nicholas Hornung	Josh Johnson	Bodhi Kruft
Jefferson Hotchkiss	Randolph Johnson	Jacob Krute
Jack House	Micah Jones	Neil Kubitz
Ian House	Jason Jones	Mitchell Kusterer
Ken Houseal	Tyler Jones	Nathan Laidlwe
Joseph Howle	David Jorgenson	Ian Lamb
Nicholas Howser	Robert Kammerzell	Mark Landez
Mark Hoy	Chris Karabats	Megan O'Keefe Landon
Kane Hubbard	Timothy Keane	Kevin Lash
James Huff	Cody Keaton	Jacob Leake
Adrian Hughes	George Kelly	David Leal

Andy Ledford

Isaac Lee

Furman Lee

Nicholas Lee

Joseph Legacy

Brenden Lerch

David Levin

Luke Lindsay

Eron Lindsey

Andre Locker

Drew Long

Richard Long

Oliver Longchamps

Litani Looby

Joseph Lopez

Lucas Lorentz

Joey Lorenzi

Kyle Lorenzi

David Losey

Erin Lounsbury

MDavid Low

Andrew Luong

Jesse Lyon

Taylo Lywood

Collin Macall

David MacAlpine

John Machasek

Patrick Maclary

Derek Magyar

Richard Maier

Chris Malone

Jake Malone

Adam Manlove

Andrew Mann

John Mannion

Brent Manzel

Robert Marchi

Jacob Margheim

John Marinos

Jacob Marquis

Jeffrey Martin

Bertram Martin

Edward Martin

Bill Martin

Logan Martin

Lucas Martin

Trevor Martin

Tim Martindale

Cory Masierowski

Nicholas Mason

Wills Masterson

Mark Mathewman

Michael Matsko

Simon Mayeski

Joseph Mazzara

Will McAleer

Timothy McAleese

Sean McCafferty

Kyle McCarley

William Mcdaniel

Shane McDevitt

Connor McDonald

Jeremy McElroy

Hans McIlveen

Rachel McIntosh

Richard McKercher

Ryan McKracken

Jacob Mclemore

Wayne McMurtrie

Daniel Mears

Kile Mendoza

Brady Meyer

John C. Meyers

Corrigan Miller

Darren Mills

Robert Milsop

Jesse Miner

Sarah Miron

David Mitchell

Reimar Moeller

Jacob Montagne

Ramon Montijo

Douglas Montijo

Eric Moore

Maxwell Moore

Sherry Moore

Nicholas Moran

Matteo Morelli

Todd Moriarty

Matthew Morley

Daniel Morris

William Morris

David Murray

Bob Murray

Jeff Murri

Ben Myhre

Joseph Nahas

Vinesh Narayan

Colby Neal

James Needham

Ray Neel

Joel Negron

Adam Nelson

Timothy Nevin

Michael Newson

Jon Newton

Bennett Nickels

Mason Nicolay

Trevor Nielsen

Andrew Niesent

Sean Noble

Otto (Mario) Noda

Brett Noll-Emmick

Michael Norris

Ryley Nortrup

Douglas Norwood

Greg Nugent

Christina Nymeyer

Brian O'Connor

Patrick O'Leary

Patrick O'Rourke

Quinn Oehler

Kevin Oess

Nolan Oglesby

Gary Oneida

Max Oosten

Anthony Ornellas

James Owens

Will Page

Nic Palacios

John Park

Matthew Parker

Shawn Parrish

Andrew Patterson

Ken Paul

Thomas Pennington

Hector Perez

Kevin Perkins

Trevor Petersen

Nicholas Peterson

Charlie Phillippe

Jeremy Phillips

David Phillips

Jon Phillips

Sam Phinney

Dupres Pina

Michael Pister

Jared Plathe

Matthew Pommerening

Nathan Poplawski

Michael Portanger

Rodney Posey

Brian Potts

Jonathaon Poulter

Thomas Preston

Matthew Print

Darren Pruitt

Max Quezada

Shahik Rakib

Joe Ralston

Dillard Rape

Michael Rausch

Joshua Ray

T.J. Recio

Blake Rehrer

Ryan Reis

Paul Richard

Augustus Richardson

Robert Richenburg

Eric Ritenour

Paul Rivas

David Roark

Scott Robertson

Chris Robertson

Walt Robillard

Daniel Robitaille

John Roche

Paul Roder

Josias Rodriguez

Adam Rogers

Aaron G Rood

Andrew Rose

Elias Rostad

Nick Rusch

Chad Rushing

Tim Russ

Zarren Rutledge

RW

Matthew Ryan

Justin Ryan

Mark Ryan

Greg S

Zachary Sadenwasser

Robert Salmon

Connor Samuelson

Lawrence Sanchez

Dustin Sanders

Giovani Sandoval

David Sanford

Levi Schaefers

Jaysn Schaener

Jason Schapp

Daniel Schmagel

Kurt Schneider

Peter Scholtes

Kevin Schroeder

William Schweisthal

Ethan Scott

Connor Scott

Rylee Scott

Andrew Scroggins

Phillip Seek

Kevin Serpa

Austin Shafer

Mitch Shami

Ryan Shannahan

Kevin Sharp

Steven Shaw

Chris Shay

Charles Sheehan

Wendell Shelton

Ian Short

Glenn Shotton

Kaleb Sigler

Dave Simmons

Chris Sinor

Chris Sizelove

Andrew Skaines

Chris Slater

Steven Smead

Robert Smith

Charles Smith

Caleb Smith

Cory Smith

Ian Smith

Sharroll Smith

David Smyth

Tom Snapp

Andrew Snow

David Snowden

Cody Speak

John Spears

Anthony Spencer

Troy Spencer	Lawrence Tate	Dylan Tuxhorn
Thomas Spencer	Kyler Tatsch	Joshua Twist
Dustin Sprick	Alyssa Tausevich	Jalen Underwood
Super Squirrel	Brandon Taylor	Leo Vaccaro
Travis Standford	Justin Taylor	Joel Vail
Paul Starck	Robert Taylor	Joel Vail
Jolene Starr	Tim Taylor	Erik Van Otten
Maggie Stewart-Grant	Christov Tenn	Thomas Van Winkle
Edmond Stone	Doug Thien	Paden VanBuskirk
Fredy Stout	David P. Thomas	Patrick Varrassi
James Street	Marc Thomas	Daniel Vatamaniuck
Joshua Strickland	Jacob Thomas	Robert Vaughn
Shayla Striffler	Kyle Thompson	Abel Villesca
Brad Stumpp	Chris Thompson	Cole Vineyard
Joshua Sturnfield	Donald Thompson	Leo Voepel
Shaun Sullivan	Jonathan Thompson	Jeff Wadsworth
Ned Sullivan	William Joseph Thorpe	Anthony Wagnon
Randall Surles	Beverly Tierney	Joshua Wallace
Michael Swartwout	Yvonne Timm	Joshua Waltzing
Bryan Swezey	Jonathan Tindal	Dylan Wannamaker
George Switzer	Russ Tinnell	Andrew Ward
Carol Szpara	TJ Trakas	Wedge Warford
Travis TadeWaldt	Jameson Trauger	Scot Washam
Allison Tallon	Oliver Tunnicliffe	Tyler Washburn
Daniel Tanner	Ryan Turner	John Watson
Joshua Tate	Brandon Turton	Bill Webb
Blake Tate	John Tuttle	Ben Wedow

Zachary Weig

Garry Welding

Tanner Wells

Hiram Wells

Jack Weston

William Westphal

Lewis Wheeler

Paul White

Jamie Whitmer

Grant Wiggins

Joel Williams

John Williams

Taylor Williams

Christopher Williams

Jack Williams

Patrick Williford

Justin Wilson

Dominic Winter

Edward Wise

Tripp Wood

Reese Wood

Robert Woodward

Sean Woodworth

Robin Woolen

John Wooten

John Work

Jason Wright

Adam Wroblewski

Kevin Zhang

Pamela Ziemeck

Attila Zimler

Andrew Zink

Jordan Ziroli

Nathan Zoss